A Malamud Reader

A
Malamud
Reader

 FARRAR, STRAUS AND GIROUX · New York

To Chet and Louise

Introduction

That Bernard Malamud is one of the very few writers of stature to emerge on our literary scene since the last war is now scarcely open to question. The author of four novels and two volumes of short stories, he has received several national prizes and his due measure of recognition from critics and reviewers. But he has also been frequently extolled for the wrong reasons, by critics who do not properly sort out or define with precision the imaginative qualities peculiar to him that make up his creative individuality; and sometimes he has been appraised as a special sort of genre-writer, dealing with the "laughter through tears," the habits of life, exotic to outsiders, of immigrant Jews, an ethnic group considered to stand in a marginal relation to American society at large. Generally speaking, he has been assimilated all too readily to the crowd of American-Jewish writers who have lately made their way into print. The homogenization resulting from speaking of them as if they comprised some kind of literary faction or school is bad critical practice in that it is based on simplistic assumptions concerning the literary process as a whole as well as the nature of American Jewry, which, all appearances to the contrary, is very far from constituting a unitary group in its cultural manifestations. In point of fact, the American-Jewish writers do not in the least make up a literary faction or school. And in the case of Malamud, the ignorant and even malicious idea that such a school exists has served as a way of confusing him with other authors with whom (excepting his Jewish ancestry) he has virtually nothing in common.

The truth is that many writers are Jewish in descent without being in any appreciable way "Jewish" in feeling and sensibility;

and I am noting this not in criticism of anyone in particular but simply by way of stating an obvious fact usually overlooked both by those who "celebrate" the arrival of American Jews on the literary scene and by those who deplore it. It is one thing to speak factually of a writer's Jewish extraction and it is something else again to speak of his "Jewishness," which is a very elusive quality and rather difficult to define. In this respect Norman Mailer may well serve as a conspicuous example. Mailer's consciousness of himself as a Jew is, I would say, quite unimportant to him as a writer, if not wholly negative. Among the protagonists of his fiction his favorite alter ego appears to be a character called Sergius O'Shaugnessy—a name not without significance. Other American-Jewish writers either back away from their Jewishness or adopt an attitude towards it which is empty of cultural value; it is only in their bent for comic turns that they call to mind some vestigial qualities of their ethnic background. In any case, what is mostly to be observed among these writers is ambivalence about Jewishness rather than pride or even simple acceptance. Malamud differs, however, from such literary types in that he fills his "Jewishness" with a positive content. I mean that "Jewishness," as he understands and above all feels it, is one of the principal sources of value in his work as it affects both his conception of experience in general and his conception of imaginative writing in particular. One can see this in the very few instances when his characters touch on literature in their extremely articulate but "broken" speech. Thus in the one-act play "Suppose a Wedding" (not included in this volume), the retired Yiddish actor Feuer tangles with a young man who can only speak of tragedy in terms of Aristotle's theory of catharsis. Feuer says:

> Don't quote me your college books. A writer writes tragedy so people don't forget they are human. He shows us the conditions that exist. He organizes us for the meaning of our lives so it is clear to our eyes. That's why he writes it, that's why we play it. My best roles were tragic roles. I enjoyed them the most though I was also marvelous in comedy. "Leid macht auch lachen."

The last sentence is a saying in Yiddish which means that suffering also makes for laughter. If you are looking for Malamud's "poetics," it is in such speeches of his characters that you will locate it, not in any explicit critical pronouncements. Another equally revealing passage is to be found in his novel *The Assistant*, when Helen Bober, the Jewish girl so pathetically aspiring in her dreams of a college education, is on the verge of becoming involved with the unlettered Italian clerk in her father's grocery. They meet in the branch library of their neighborhood:

> He asked her what she was reading.
> "*The Idiot.* Do you know it?"
> "No. What's it about?"
> "It's a novel."
> "I'd rather read the truth."
> "It is the truth."

Malamud's conception of literature, as a mode of truth-saying, undercuts all our old and new debates about the role of the aesthetic motive in our lives. For in his context of profound commitment to the creative word the very term "aesthetic," with the compartmentalization of the human faculties that it suggests, seems almost out of place, if not frivolous; and it strongly reminds us of Kafka's moral earnestness in his approach to the making of literature, of which he conceived as a sacred expenditure of energy, an effort at communion with his fellow men, the reflected splendor of religious perception.

Malamud's "Jewishness" is also connected with a certain stylization of language we find in his fiction, a deliberate linguistic effort at once trenchantly and humorously adapting the cool Wasp idiom of English to the quicker heartbeats and greater openness to emotion of his Jewish characters; and it is particularly in the turns and twists of their dialogue that this effort is most apparent and most successful. These people are emotionally highly charged and desperate in their urgency to make themselves heard. Malamud insists on giving them their head, on letting them speak out of their genuine fervor—and to achieve this authenticity of speech he refuses to censor their bad, even laughable grammar, distorted syntax, and vivid yet comical locutions that sound like apt imitations of Yiddish. In this regard, any one of his narratives —such as "Take Pity," "The Mourners," "The Magic Barrel," "Idiots First," etc.—in which "Old World" Jewish types predominate can serve as a case in point.

Another "Jewish" trait in Malamud, as I read him, is his feeling for human suffering on the one hand and for a life of value, order, and dignity on the other. Thus he is one of the very few. contemporary writers who seems to have escaped the clutch of historical circumstance that has turned nihilism into so powerful a temptation; nihilistic attitudes, whether of the hedonistic or absurdist variety, can never be squared with Malamud's essentially humanistic inspiration. The feeling for human suffering is of course far from being an exclusively "Jewish" quality. It figures even more prominently in Dostoevsky. The Russian novelist, however, understands suffering primarily as a means of purification and of eventual salvation, whereas in Malamud suffering is not idealized: suffering is not what you are looking for but what you are likely to get. Malamud is seldom concerned with the type of *allrightnik* Jews who lend themselves to satirical treatment (as in Philip Roth's *Goodbye, Columbus*); his chief concern is rather with the first-generation, poor hardworking immigrants, whose ethos is not that of prosperity but that of affliction and endurance. Hence he is at times inclined to speak of suffering as the mark of the Jew and as his very fate. Leo Finkle, who is among the major characters of that extraordinary story "The Magic Barrel," draws out of his very discomfiture the consolation "that he was a Jew and a Jew suffered." Frank Alpine in *The Assistant*, thinking of what it means to be a Jew, explains it to himself as follows: "That's what they live for . . . to suffer. And the one who has got the biggest pain in the gut and can hold onto it longest without running to the toilet is the best Jew. No wonder they got on his nerves." This is of course an outsider's point of view, and it remains for Morris Bober, the unlucky and impoverished owner of the grocery store, to correct his Italian clerk's assertion that Jews like to suffer:

> "If you live, you suffer. Some people suffer more, but not because they want. But I think if a Jew don't suffer for the Law, he will suffer for nothing."
> "What do you suffer for, Morris?" Frank said.
> "I suffer for you," Morris said calmly.
> Frank laid his knife down on the table. His mouth ached. "What do you mean?"
> "I mean you suffer for me."
> The clerk let it go at that.

Here Malamud transcends all sectarian understanding of suffering, seeing it as the fate of the whole of mankind, which can only be mitigated when all men assume responsibility for each other. The contrast between Jew and Gentile is thus resolved on the level of feeling and direct intuition, and what this resolution suggests is an affinity with the Dostoevskyan idea of universal brotherhood and mutual responsibility. Yet Dostoevsky's correlative idea that "we're all cruel, we're all monsters" (as Dmitri Karamazov phrases it) is quite alien to Malamud. Frank Alpine is the guilty one when he takes Helen Bober against her will just as she has begun learning to love him. After the violation she cries: "Dog—uncircumcised dog." What restitution can Alpine possibly make for abusing Helen's trust? After much brooding and many incidents Alpine enters a symbolic death and rebirth, and his decision is made without Helen's knowledge or prompting. "One day in April Frank went to the hospital and had himself circumcised. For a couple of days he dragged himself around with a pain between his legs. The pain enraged and inspired him. After Passover he became a Jew." So *The Assistant* ends, with the sentences I have quoted. Frank Alpine's act is not to be understood as a religious conversion. Within the context of the novel, what Frank's singular act stands for is the ultimate recognition by this former hold-up man and thief of the humanity that he had so long suppressed within himself.

Along with the theme of suffering, one finds in Malamud the theme of the meaningful life, which is the antithesis of "the unlived life" against which his leading characters are always contending. The college teacher S. Levin, in *A New Life*, becomes involved in what threatens to become a sordid affair with Pauline, another man's wife. But when she probes him for what he thinks life offers at its best, his reply is: "Order, value, accomplishment, love." Levin, who is at times prone to consider himself "his own pathetic fallacy," struggles to discover an authentic self amidst the circumstances that surround him; nor is he likely either to overestimate or underestimate himself. "Why must Levin's unlived life put him always in peril? He had no wish to be Faust, or Gatsby; or St. Anthony of Somewhere who to conquer his torment nipped off his balls. Levin wanted to be himself, at peace in present time." And again: "He left to Casanova or Clark Gable the gourmandise, the blasts and quakes of passion." Levin comes to a state of the Far West looking for welcome and a chance of organizing his existence anew. He begins as S. Levin, a half-anonymous *schlemiel*, and in the last chapters he has turned into a *mensch* called Seymour Levin, who against all odds had become a husband to Pauline and the father of her children.

But the irony of the *schlemiel* turning *mensch* pervades the book, tempering the exaltation of the last pages. Levin's first lovemaking to Pauline takes place in a forest glade, and "he was throughout conscious of the marvel of it—in the open forest, nothing less, what triumph!" And when he first kisses her, "he was humbly grateful. . . . They were standing under a tree and impulsively kissed. . . . They kissed so hard his hat fell off." The displaced hat is an ironic counterpoint—the signature of reality inscribed in a romantic pastoral. An identical irony is to be encountered in many of Malamud's stories. In "The Last Mohican," Fidelman, "a self-conscious failure as a painter," gets off the train in Rome and soon discovers the remains of the Baths of Diocletian. "Imagine," he muttered. "Imagine all that history." He confronts history as Levin confronts nature in Marathon, Cascadia (Oregon?). Fidelman likes to wander in the old sections of Rome near the Tiber. "He had read that here, under his feet, were the ruins of Ancient Rome. It was an inspiring business, he, Arthur Fidelman, after all born a Bronx boy, walking around in all this history." But Fidelman, for all the thrills that history provides him, is a person lacking in genuineness—cautious, withdrawn, self-centered. It takes Susskind, the starving and demanding refugee, a nuisance to Fidelman, to supply him with the revelation he so badly needs. Susskind steals the briefcase containing the first chapter of Fidelman's scholarly work on Giotto—the only chapter he had managed to write. The last paragraphs of the story are wonderfully conceived and written: a model of economy in expression. After much importunity, Susskind returns the briefcase.

> Fidelman savagely opened it, searching frenziedly in each compartment, but the bag was empty. The refugee was already in flight.
> With a bellow the student started after him.
> "You bastard, you burned my chapter."
> "Have mercy," cried Susskind, "I did you a favor."
> "I'll do you one and cut your throat."
> "The words were there but the spirit was missing."
> In a towering rage Fidelman forced a burst of speed, but the refugee, light as the wind in his marvelous knickerbockers, his green coattails flying, rapidly gained ground.

It is only then that Fidelman, moved by all "he had lately learned, had a triumphant insight." Half sobbing, he shouts: "Susskind, come back . . . All is forgiven." So the spirit missing in his life and studies finally descends upon the hapless Fidelman.

Of all Malamud's stories, surely the most masterful is "The Magic Barrel," perhaps the best story produced by an American writer in recent decades. It belongs among those rare works in which meaning and composition are one and the same. Who can ever forget the matchmaker Salzman, "a commercial Cupid," smelling "frankly of fish which he loved to eat," who looked as if he were about to expire but who somehow managed, by a trick of his facial muscles, "to display a broad smile"? The pictures of prospective brides that the matchmaker shows the rabbinical student Finkle, intent on matrimony, prove very discouraging—all these girls turn out to be either old maids or cripples. But Salzman contrives to leave one picture in Finkle's room by which his imagination is caught as in a trap. The description of the picture is full of mystery, yet admirably concrete; it is as good as, if not better than, the description of the picture of Nastasya Filippovna which makes so much for the vitality of the first part of *The Idiot*.

Caught, Finkle in turn must now pursue Salzman, who has suddenly become elusive. When tracked down, he swears that he had inadvertently left the fatal picture in Finkle's room. "She's not for you. She is a wild one, wild, without shame. . . . Like an animal, like a dog. For her to be poor was a sin. This is why to me she is dead now. . . . This is my baby, my Stella, she should burn in hell." But Finkle will not relent. It is Stella he must see, and Salzman arranges their meeting "on a certain street corner." The last sentences of this tale are like a painting by Chagall come to life.

> He appeared, carrying a small bouquet of violets and rosebuds. Stella stood by the lamp, smoking. She wore white with red shoes, which fitted his expectations, although in a troubled moment he had imagined the dress red, and only the shoes white. She waited uneasily and shyly. From afar he saw that her eyes—clearly her father's—were filled with desperate innocence. He pictured, in her, his own redemption. Violins and lit candles revolved in the sky. Leo ran forward with flowers outthrust.
>
> Around the corner, Salzman, leaning against a wall, chanted prayers for the dead.

Thus the rabbinical student who, as he confesses, had come to God not because he loved Him but precisely because he did not, attempts to find in the girl from whose picture "he had received, somehow, an impression of evil" the redemption his ambiguous nature demands.

It seems to me that "The Magic Barrel," a story rooted in a pathology that dares to seek its cure in a thrust towards life, sums up many of the remarkable gifts of insight and expressive power that Malamud brings to contemporary literature.

PHILIP RAHV

Contents

Part One

Three Journeys

To Chicago

Roy Hobbs pawed at the glass before thinking to prick a match
with his thumbnail and hold the spurting flame in his cupped
palm close to the lower berth window, but by then he had figured
it was a tunnel they were passing through and was no longer
surprised at the bright sight of himself holding a yellow light
over his head, peering back in. As the train yanked its long tail
out of the thundering tunnel, the kneeling reflection dissolved
and he felt a splurge of freedom at the view of the moon-hazed
Western hills bulked against night broken by sprays of summer
lightning, although the season was early spring. Lying back, elbowed up on his long side, sleepless still despite the lulling train,
he watched the land flowing and waited with suppressed ex-
pectancy for a sight of the Mississippi, a thousand miles away.

Having no timepiece he appraised the night and decided it was
moving toward dawn. As he was looking, there flowed along this
bone-white farmhouse with sagging skeletal porch, alone in un-
told miles of moonlight, and before it this white-faced, long-
boned boy whipped with train-whistle yowl a glowing ball to
someone hidden under a dark oak, who shot it back without
thought, and the kid once more wound and returned. Roy shut
his eyes to the sight because if it wasn't real it was a way he sometimes had of observing himself, just as in this dream he could
never shake off—that had hours ago waked him out of sound
sleep—of him standing at night in a strange field with a golden
baseball in his palm that all the time grew heavier as he sweated
to settle whether to hold on or fling it away. But when he had
made his decision it was too heavy to lift or let fall (who wanted

a hole that deep?) so he changed his mind to keep it and the thing grew fluffy light, a white rose breaking out of its hide, and all but soared off by itself, but he had already sworn to hang on forever.

As dawn tilted the night, a gust of windblown rain blinded him —no, there was a window—but the sliding drops made him thirsty and from thirst sprang hunger. He reached into the hammock for his underwear to be first at breakfast in the dining car and make his blunders of ordering and eating more or less in private, since it was doubtful Sam would be up to tell him what to do. Roy peeled his gray sweatshirt and bunched down the white ducks he was wearing for pajamas in case there was a wreck and he didn't have time to dress. He acrobated into a shirt, pulled up the pants of his good suit, arching to draw them high, but he had crammed both feet into one leg and was trapped so tight wriggling got him nowhere. He worried because here he was straitjacketed in the berth without much room to twist around in and might bust his pants or have to buzz the porter, which he dreaded. Grunting, he contorted himself this way and that till he was at last able to grab and pull down the cuff and with a gasp loosened his feet and got the caught one where it belonged. Sitting up, he gartered his socks, tied laces, got on a necktie and even squirmed into a suit coat so that when he parted the curtains to step out he was fully dressed.

Dropping to all fours, he peered under the berth for his bassoon case. Though it was there he thought he had better open it and did but quickly snapped it shut as Eddie, the porter, came walking by.

"Morning, maestro, what's the tune today?"

"It ain't a musical instrument." Roy explained it was something he had made himself.

"Animal, vegetable, or mineral?"

"Just a practical thing."

"A pogo stick?"

"No."

"Foolproof lance?"

"No."

"Lemme guess," Eddie said, covering his eyes with his long-fingered hand and pawing the air with the other. "I have it—combination fishing rod, gun, and shovel."

Roy laughed. "How far to Chicago, Eddie?"

"Chi? Oh, a long, long ways. I wouldn't walk."

"I don't intend to."

"Why Chi?" Eddie asked. "Why not New Orleans? That's a lush and Frenchy city."

"Never been there."

"Or that hot and hilly town, San Francisco?"

Roy shook his head.

"Why not New York, colossus of colossuses?"

"Some day I'll visit there."

"Where have you visited?"

Roy was embarrassed. "Boise."

"That dusty sandstone quarry."

"Portland too when I was small."

"In Maine?"

"No, Oregon—where they hold the Festival of Roses."

"Oregon—where the refugees from Minnesota and the Dakotas go?"

"I wouldn't know," Roy said. "I'm going to Chicago, where the Cubs are."

"Lions and tigers in the zoo?"

"No, the ballplayers."

"Oh, the ball—" Eddie clapped a hand to his mouth. "Are you one of them?"

"I hope to be."

The porter bowed low. "My hero. Let me kiss your hand."

Roy couldn't help but smile yet the porter annoyed and worried him a little. He had forgotten to ask Sam when to tip him, morning or night, and how much? Roy had made it a point, since their funds were so low, not to ask for anything at all but last

night Eddie had insisted on fixing a pillow behind his back, and
once when he was trying to locate the men's room Eddie practically took him by the hand and led him to it. Did you hand him
a dime after that or grunt a foolish thanks as he had done? He'd
personally be glad when the trip was over, though he certainly
hated to be left alone in a place like Chicago. Without Sam he'd
feel shaky-kneed and unable to say or do simple things like ask for
directions or know where to go once you had dropped a nickel
into the subway.

After a troublesome shave in which he twice drew blood he
used one thin towel to dry his hands, face, and neck, clean his
razor and wipe up the wet of his toothbrush so as not to have to
ask for another and this way keep the bill down. From the flaring
sky out the window it looked around half-past five, but he
couldn't be sure because somewhere near they left Mountain
Time and lost—no, picked up—yes, it was lost an hour, what
Sam called the twenty-three hour day. He packed his razor,
toothbrush, and pocket comb into a chamois drawstring bag,
rolled it up small and kept it handy in his coat pocket. Passing
through the long sleeper, he entered the diner and would gladly
have sat down to breakfast, for his stomach had contracted into
a bean at the smell of food, but the shirt-sleeved waiters in stock-
ing caps were joshing around as they gobbled fried kippers and
potatoes. Roy hurried through the large-windowed club car,
empty for once, through several sleepers, coaches, a lounge and
another long line of coaches, till he came to the last one, where
amid the gloom of drawn shades and sleeping people tossed every
which way, Sam Simpson also slept although Roy had last night
begged him to take the berth but the soft-voiced Sam had insisted, "You take the bed, kiddo, you're the one that has to show
what you have got on the ball when we pull into the city. It
don't matter where I sleep."

Sam lay very still on his back, looking as if the breath of life
had departed from him except that it was audible in the ripe snore
that could be chased without waking him, Roy had discovered, if

you hissed scat. His lean head was held up by a folded pillow and his scrawny legs, shoeless, hung limp over the arm of the double seat he had managed to acquire, for he had started out with a seat partner. He was an expert conniver where his comfort was concerned, and since that revolved mostly around the filled flat bottle his ability to raise them up was this side of amazing. He often said he would not die of thirst though he never failed to add, in Roy's presence, that he wished for nobody the drunkard's death. He seemed now to be dreaming, and his sharp nose was pointed in the direction of a scent that led perhaps to the perfumed presence of Dame Fortune, long past due in his bed. With dry lips puckered, he smiled in expectation of a spectacular kiss though he looked less like a lover than an old scarecrow with his comical, seamed face sprouting prickly stubble in the dark glow of the expiring bulb overhead. A trainman passed who, seeing Sam sniff in his sleep, pretended it was at his own reek and humorously held his nose. Roy frowned, but Sam, who had a moment before been getting in good licks against fate, saw in his sleep, and his expression changed. A tear broke from his eye and slowly slid down his cheek. Roy concluded not to wake Sam and left.

He returned to the vacant club car and sat there with a magazine on his knee, worrying whether the trip wasn't a mistake, when a puzzled Eddie came into the car and handed him a pair of red dice.

"Mate them," he said. "I can't believe my eyes."

Roy paired the dice. "They mate."

"Now roll them."

He rolled past his shoe. "Snake eyes."

"Try again," said Eddie, interested.

Roy rattled the red cubes. "Snake eyes once more."

"Amazing. Again, please."

Again he rolled on the rug. Roy whistled. "Holy cow, three in a row."

"Fantastic."

"Did they do the same for you?"

"No, for me they did sevens."

"Are they loaded?"

"Bewitched," Eddie muttered. "I found them in the washroom and I'm gonna get rid of them pronto."

"Why?—if you could win all the time?"

"I don't crave any outside assistance in games of chance."

The train had begun to slow down.

"Oh oh, duty." Eddie hurried out.

Watching through the double-paned glass, Roy saw the porter swing himself off the train and jog along with it a few paces as it pulled to a stop. The morning was high and bright but the desolate station—wherever they were—gave up a single passenger, a girl in a dressy black dress, who despite the morning chill waited with a coat over her arm, and two suitcases and a zippered golf bag at her feet. Hatless, too, her hair a froth of dark curls, she held by a loose cord a shiny black hat box which she wouldn't let Eddie touch when he gathered up her things. Her face was striking, a little drawn and pale, and when she stepped up into the train her nyloned legs made Roy's pulses dance. When he could no longer see her, he watched Eddie set down her bags, take the red dice out of his pocket, spit on them and fling them over the depot roof. He hurriedly grabbed the bags and hopped on the moving train.

The girl entered the club car and directed Eddie to carry her suitcase to her compartment and she would stay and have a cigarette. He mentioned the hat box again but she giggled nervously and said no.

"Never lost a female hat yet," Eddie muttered.

"Thank you but I'll carry it myself."

He shrugged and left.

She had dropped a flower. Roy thought it was a gardenia but it turned out to be a white rose she had worn pinned to her dress.

When he handed it to her, her eyes widened with fascination, as if she had recognized him from somewhere, but when she

found she hadn't, to his horror her expression changed instantly
to one of boredom. Sitting across the aisle from him she fished
out of her purse a pack of cigarettes and a lighter. She lit up, and
crossing her heartbreaking legs, began to flip through a copy of
Life.

He figured she was his own age, maybe a year or so older. She
looked to him like one of those high-class college girls, only with
more zip than most of them, and dressed for 6 A.M. as the girls
back home never would. He was marvelously interested in her,
so much had her first glance into his eyes meant to him, and already felt a great longing in his life. Anxious to get acquainted,
he was flabbergasted how to begin. If she hadn't yet eaten breakfast and he could work up the nerve, he could talk to her in the
diner—only he didn't dare.

People were sitting around now and the steward came out and
said first call for breakfast.

She snubbed out her cigarette with a wriggling motion of the
wrist—her bracelets tinkled—picked up the hat box and went
into the diner. Her crumpled white rose lay in the ashtray. He
took it out and quickly stuck it in his pants pocket. Though his
hunger bit sharp he waited till everyone was maybe served, and
then he entered.

Although he had tried to avoid it, for fear she would see how
unsure he was of these things, he was put at the same table with
her and her black hat box, which now occupied a seat of its own.
She glanced up furtively when he sat down but went wordlessly
back to her coffee. When the waiter handed Roy the pad, he absently printed his name and date of birth but the waiter imperceptibly nudged him (hey, hayseed) and indicated it was for
ordering. He pointed on the menu with his yellow pencil (this is
the buck breakfast) but the blushing ballplayer, squinting through
the blur, could only think he was sitting on the lone four-bit
piece he had in his back pocket. He tried to squelch the impulse
but something forced him to look up at her as he attempted to
pour water into his ice-filled (this'll kill the fever) glass, spilling

some on the tablecloth (whose diapers you wetting, boy?), then all thumbs and butter fingers, the pitcher thumped the pitcher down, fished the fifty cents out of his pants, and after scratching out the vital statistics on the pad, plunked the coin down on the table.

"That's for you," he told the (what did I do to deserve this?) waiter, and though the silver-eyed mermaid was about to speak, he did not stay to listen but beat it fast out of the accursed car.

Tramping highways and byways, wandering everywhere bird dogging the sandlots for months without spotting so much as a fifth-rater he could telegraph about to the head scout of the Cubs, and maybe pick up a hundred bucks in the mail as a token of their appreciation, with also a word of thanks for his good bird dogging and maybe they would sometime again employ him as a scout on the regular payroll—well, after a disheartening long time in which he was not able to roust up a single specimen worthy to be called by the name of ballplayer, Sam had one day lost his way along a dusty country road and when he finally found out where he was, too weary to turn back, he crossed over to an old, dry barn and sat against the haypile in front, to drown his sorrows with a swig. On the verge of dozing he heard these shouts and opened his eyes, shielding them from the hot sun, and as he lived, a game of ball was being played in a pasture by twelve blond-bearded players, six on each side, and even from where Sam sat he could tell they were terrific the way they smacked the pill—one blow banging it so far out the fielder had to run a mile before he could jump high and snag it smack in his bare hand. Sam's mouth popped open, he got up whoozy and watched, finding it hard to believe his eyes, as the teams changed sides and the first hitter that batted the ball did so for a far-reaching distance before it was caught, and the same with the second, a wicked clout, but then the third came up, the one who had made the bare-handed catch, and he really laid on and powdered the pellet a thundering crack so that even the one who ran for it, his beard parted in the wind, before long looked like a pygmy chasing it and quit running, seeing the thing was a speck on the horizon.

Sweating and shivering by turns, Sam muttered if I could ketch the whole twelve of them—and staggered out on the field to cry out the good news but when they saw him they gathered bats and balls and ran in a dozen directions, and though Sam was smart enough to hang on to the fellow who had banged the sphere out to the horizon, frantically shouting to him, "Whoa—whoa," his lungs bursting with the effort to call a giant—he wouldn't stop so Sam never caught him.

He woke with a sob in his throat but swallowed before he could sound it, for by then Roy had come to mind and he mumbled, "Got someone just as good," so that for once waking was better than dreaming.

He yawned. His mouth felt unholy dry and his underclothes were crawling. Reaching down his battered valise from the rack, he pulled out a used bath towel and cake of white soap, and to the surprise of those who saw him go out that way, went through the baggage cars to the car between them and the tender. Once inside there, he peeled to the skin and stepped into the shower stall, where he enjoyed himself for ten minutes, soaping and re-soaping his bony body under warm water. But then a trainman happened to come through and after sniffing around Sam's clothes yelled in to him, "Hey, bud, come outa there."

Sam stopped off the shower and poked out his head.

"What's that?"

"I said come outa there, that's only for the train crew."

"Excuse me," Sam said, and he began quickly to rub himself dry.

"You don't have to hurry. Just wanted you to know you made a mistake."

"Thought it went with the ticket."

"Not in the coaches it don't."

Sam sat on a metal stool and laced up his high brown shoes.

Pointing to the cracked mirror on the wall, he said, "Mind if I use your glass?"

"Go ahead."

He parted his sandy hair, combed behind the ears, and managed to work in a shave and brushing of his yellow teeth before he apologized again to the trainman and left.

Going up a few cars to the lounge, he ordered a cup of hot coffee and a sandwich, ate quickly, and made for the club car. It was semi-officially out of bounds for coach travelers but Sam had told the passenger agent last night that he had a nephew riding on a sleeper, and the passenger agent had mentioned to the conductor not to bother him.

When he entered the club car, after making sure Roy was elsewhere Sam headed for the bar, already in a fluid state for the train was moving through wet territory, but then he changed his mind and sat down to size up the congregation over a newspaper and spot who looked particularly amiable. The headlines caught his eye at the same time as they did this short, somewhat popeyed gent's sitting next to him, who had just been greedily questioning the husky, massive-shouldered man on his right, who was wearing sun glasses. Popeyes nudged the big one and they all three stared at Sam's paper.

WEST COAST OLYMPIC ATHLETE SHOT

FOLLOWS 24 HOURS AFTER SLAYING OF
ALL-AMERICAN FOOTBALL ACE

The article went on to relate that both of these men had been shot under mysterious circumstances with silver bullets from a .22 caliber pistol by an unknown woman that police were on the hunt for.

"That makes the second sucker," the short man said.

"But why with silver bullets, Max?"

"Beats me. Maybe she set out after a ghost but couldn't find him."

The other fingered his tie knot. "Why do you suppose she goes around pickin' on athletes for?"

"Not only athletes but also the cream of the crop. She's knocked off a crack football boy, and now an Olympic runner. Better watch out, Whammer, she may be heading for a baseball player for the third victim," Max chuckled.

Sam looked up and almost hopped out of his seat as he recognized them both.

Hiding his hesitation, he touched the short one on the arm. "Excuse me, mister, but ain't you Max Mercy, the sportswriter? I know your face from your photo in the articles you write."

But the sportswriter, who wore a comical mustache and dressed in stripes that crisscrossed three ways—suit, shirt, and tie—a nervous man with voracious eyes, also had a sharp sense of smell and despite Sam's shower and toothbrushing nosed out an alcoholic fragrance that slowed his usual speedy response in acknowledging the spread of his fame.

"That's right," he finally said.

"Well, I'm happy to have the chance to say a few words to you. You're maybe a little after my time, but I am Sam Simpson—Bub Simpson, that is—who played for the St. Louis Browns in the seasons of 1919 to 1921."

Sam spoke with a grin though his insides were afry at the mention of his professional baseball career.

"Believe I've heard the name," Mercy said nervously. After a minute he nodded toward the man Sam knew all along as the leading hitter of the American League, three times winner of the Most Valuable Player award, and announced, "This is Walter (the Whammer) Wambold." It had been in the papers that he was a holdout for $75,000 and was coming East to squeeze it out of his boss.

"Howdy," Sam said. "You sure look different in street clothes."

The Whammer, whose yellow hair was slicked flat, with tie and socks to match, grunted.

Sam's ears reddened. He laughed embarrassedly and then remarked sideways to Mercy that he was traveling with a slam-bang young pitcher who'd soon be laying them low in the big leagues. "Spoke to you because I thought you might want to know about him."

"What's his name?"

"Roy Hobbs."

"Where'd he play?"

"Well, he's not exactly been in organized baseball."

"Where'd he learn to pitch?"

"His daddy taught him years ago—he was once a semipro—and I have been polishin' him up."

"Where's he been pitching?"

"Well, like I said, he's young, but he certainly mowed them down in the Northwest High School League last year. Thought you might of heard of his eight no-hitters."

"Class D is as far down as I go," Mercy laughed. He lit one of the cigars Sam had been looking at in his breast pocket.

"I'm personally taking him to Clarence Mulligan of the Cubs for a tryout. They will probably pay me a few grand for uncovering the coming pitcher of the century but the condition is—and Roy is backing me on this because he is more devoted to me than a son—that I am to go back as a regular scout, like I was in 1925."

Roy popped his head into the car and searched around for the girl with the black hat box (Miss Harriet Bird, Eddie had gratuitously told him, making a black fluttering of wings), and seeing her seated near the card tables restlessly thumbing through a magazine, popped out.

"That's him," said Sam. "Wait'll I bring him back." He got up and chased after Roy.

"Who's the gabber?" said the Whammer.

"Guy named Simpson who once caught for the Brownies. Funny thing, last night I was doing a Sunday piece on drunks in baseball and I had occasion to look up his record. He was in the game three years, batted .340, .260, and .198, but his catching was terrific—not one error listed."

"Get rid of him, he jaws too much."

"Sh, here he comes."

Sam returned with Roy in tow, gazing uncomfortably ahead.

"Max," said Sam, "this is Roy Hobbs that I mentioned to you. Say hello to Max Mercy, the syndicated sportswriter, kiddo."

"Hello," Roy nodded.

"This is the Whammer," Max said.

Roy extended his hand but the Whammer looked through him with no expression whatsoever. Seeing he had his eye hooked on Harriet, Roy conceived a strong dislike for the guy.

The Whammer got up. "Come on, Max, I wanna play cards."

Max rose. "Well, hang onto the water wagon, Bub," he said to Sam.

Sam turned red.

Roy shot the sportswriter a dirty look.

"Keep up with the no-hitters, kid," Max laughed.

Roy didn't answer. He took the Whammer's chair and Sam sat where he was, brooding.

"What'll it be?" they heard Mercy ask as he shuffled the cards. They had joined two men at one of the card tables.

The Whammer, who looked to Sam like an overgrown side of beef wrapped in gabardine, said, "Hearts." He stared at Harriet until she looked up from her magazine, and after a moment of doubt, smiled.

The Whammer fingered his necktie knot. As he scooped up the cards his diamond ring glinted in the sunlight.

"Goddamned millionaire," Sam thought.

"The hell with her," thought Roy.

"I dealt rummy," Max said, and though no one had called him, Sam promptly looked around.

Toward late afternoon the Whammer, droning on about his deeds on the playing field, got very chummy with Harriet Bird and before long had slipped his fat fingers around the back of her chair so Roy left the club car and sat in the sleeper, looking out of the window, across the aisle from where Eddie slept sitting up. Gosh, the size of the forest. He thought they had left it for good yesterday and here it still was. As he watched, the trees flowed together and so did the hills and clouds. He felt a kind of sadness, because he had lost the feeling of a particular place. Yesterday he had come from somewhere, a place he knew was there, but today it had thinned away in space—how vast he could not have guessed—and he felt like he would never see it again.

The forest stayed with them, climbing hills like an army, shooting down like waterfalls. As the train skirted close in, the trees leveled out and he could see within the woodland the only place he had been truly intimate with in his wanderings, a green world shot through with weird light and strange bird cries, muffled in silence that made the privacy so complete his inmost self had no shame of anything he thought there, and it eased the body-shaking beat of his ambitions. Then he thought of here and now and for the thousandth time wondered why they had come so far and for what. Did Sam really know what he was doing? Sometimes Roy had his doubts. Sometimes he wanted to turn around and go back home, where he could at least predict what tomorrow would be like. Remembering the white rose in his pants pocket, he decided to get rid of it. But then the pine trees flowed away from the train and slowly swerved behind blue hills; all at once there was this beaten gold, snow-capped mountain in the distance, and on the plain several miles from its base lay a small city gleaming in the rays of the declining sun. Approaching it, the long train slowly pulled to a stop.

Eddie woke with a jump and stared out the window.

"Oh oh, trouble, we never stop here."

He looked again and called Roy.

"What do you make out of that?"

About a hundred yards ahead, where two dirt roads crossed, a moth-eaten model-T Ford was parked on the farther side of the road from town, and a fat old man wearing a broad-brimmed black hat and cowboy boots, who they could see was carrying a squat doctor's satchel, climbed down from it. To the conductor, who had impatiently swung off the train with a lit red lamp, he flourished a yellow telegram. They argued a minute, then the conductor, snapping open his watch, beckoned him along and they boarded the train. When they passed through Eddie's car the conductor's face was sizzling with irritation but the doctor was unruffled. Before disappearing through the door, the conductor called to Eddie, "Half hour."

"Half hour," Eddie yodeled and he got out the stool and set it outside the car so that anyone who wanted to stretch, could.

Only about a dozen passengers got off the train, including Harriet Bird, still hanging on to her precious hat box, the Whammer, and Max Mercy, all as thick as thieves. Roy hunted up the bassoon case just if the train should decide to take off without him, and when he had located Sam they both got off.

"Well, I'll be jiggered." Sam pointed down about a block beyond where the locomotive had halted. There, sprawled out at the outskirts of the city, a carnival was on. It was made up of try-your-skill booths, kiddie rides, a freak show and a gigantic Ferris wheel that looked like a stopped clock. Though there was still plenty of daylight, the carnival was lit up by twisted ropes of blinking bulbs, and many banners streamed in the breeze as the calliope played.

"Come on," said Roy, and they went along with the people from the train who were going toward the tents.

Once they had got there and fooled around a while, Sam stopped to have a crushed cocoanut drink which he privately spiked with a shot from a new bottle, while Roy wandered over to a place where you could throw three baseballs for a dime at three wooden pins, shaped like pint-size milk bottles and set in pyramids of one on top of two, on small raised platforms about twenty feet back from the counter. He changed the fifty-cent piece Sam had slipped him on leaving the train, and this pretty girl in yellow, a little hefty but with a sweet face and nice ways, who with her peanut of a father was waiting on trade, handed him three balls. Lobbing one of them, Roy easily knocked off the pyramid and won himself a naked kewpie doll. Enjoying the game, he laid down another dime, again clattering the pins to the floor in a single shot and now collecting an alarm clock. With the other three dimes he won a brand-new boxed baseball, a washboard, and baby potty, which he traded in a for a six-inch harmonica. A few kids came over to watch and Sam, wandering by, indulgently changed another half into dimes for Roy. And Roy won a fine leather cigar case for Sam, a "God Bless America" banner, a flashlight, can of coffee, and a two-pound box of sweets. To the kids' delight, Sam, after a slight hesitation, flipped Roy another half dollar, but this time the little man behind the counter nudged his daughter and she asked Roy if he would now take a kiss for every three pins he tumbled.

Roy glanced at her breasts and she blushed. He got embarrassed too. "What do you say, Sam, it's your four bits?"

Sam bowed low to the girl. "Ma'am," he said, "now you see how dang foolish it is to be a young feller."

The girl laughed and Roy began to throw for kisses, flushing each pyramid in a shot or two while the girl counted aloud the kisses she owed him.

Some of the people from the train passed by and stayed to watch when they learned from the mocking kids what Roy was throwing for.

The girl, pretending to be unconcerned, tolled off the third and fourth kisses.

As Roy fingered the ball for the last throw the Whammer came by holding over his shoulder a Louisville Slugger that he had won for himself in the batting cage down a way. Harriet, her pretty face flushed, had a kewpie doll, and Max Mercy carried a box of cigars. The Whammer had discarded his sun glasses and all but strutted over his performance and the prizes he had won.

Roy raised his arm to throw for the fifth kiss and a clean sweep when the Whammer called out to him in a loud voice, "Pitch it here, busher, and I will knock it into the moon."

Roy shot for the last kiss and missed. He missed with the second and third balls. The crowd oohed its disappointment.

"Only four," said the girl in yellow as if she mourned the fifth.

Angered at what had happened, Sam hoarsely piped, "I got ten dollars that says he can strike you out with three pitched balls, Wambold."

The Whammer looked at Sam with contempt.

"What d'ye say, Max?" he said.

Mercy shrugged.

"Oh, I love contests of skill," Harriet said excitedly. Roy's face went pale.

"What's the matter, hayfoot, you scared?" the Whammer taunted.

"Not of you," Roy said.

"Let's go across the tracks where nobody'll get hurt," Mercy suggested.

"Nobody but the busher and his bazooka. What's in it, busher?"

"None of your business." Roy picked up the bassoon case.

The crowd moved in a body across th etracks, the kids circling around to get a good view, and the engineer and fireman watching from their cab window.

Sam cornered one of the kids who lived nearby and sent him for a fielder's glove and his friend's catcher's mitt. While they were waiting, for protection he buttoned underneath his coat the washboard Roy had won. Max drew a batter's box alongside a piece of slate. He said he would call the throws and they would count as one of the three pitches only if they were over or if the Whammer swung and missed.

When the boy returned with the gloves, the sun was going down, and though the sky was aflame with light all the way to the snowy mountain peak, it was chilly on the ground.

Breaking the seal, Sam squeezed the baseball box and the pill shot up like a greased egg. He tossed it to Mercy, who inspected the hide and stitches, then rubbed the shine off and flipped it to Roy.

"Better throw a couple of warm-ups."

"My arm is loose," said Roy.

"It's your funeral."

Placing his bassoon case out of the way in the grass, Roy shed his coat. One of the boys came forth to hold it.

"Be careful you don't spill the pockets," Roy told him.

Sam came forward with the catcher's glove on. It was too small for his big hand but he said it would do all right.

"Sam, I wish you hadn't bet that money on me," Roy said.

"I won't take it if we win, kiddo, but just let it stand if we lose," Sam said, embarrassed.

"We came by it too hard."

"Just let it stand so."

He cautioned Roy to keep his pitches inside, for the Whammer was known to gobble them on the outside corner.

Sam returned to the plate and crouched behind the batter, his knees spread wide because of the washboard. Roy drew on his glove and palmed the ball behind it. Mercy, rubbing his hands to warm them, edged back about six feet behind Sam.

The onlookers retreated to the other side of the tracks, except Harriet, who stood without fear of fouls up close. Her eyes shone at the sight of the two men facing one another.

Mercy called, "Batter up."

The Whammer crowded the left side of the plate, gripping the heavy bat low on the neck, his hands jammed together and legs plunked evenly apart. He hadn't bothered to take off his coat. His eye on Roy said it spied a left-handed monkey.

"Throw it, Rube, it won't get no lighter."

Though he stood about sixty feet away, he loomed up gigantic to Roy, with the wood held like a caveman's ax on his shoulder. His rocklike frame was motionless, his face impassive, unsmiling, dark.

Roy's heart skipped a beat. He turned to gaze at the mountain.

Sam whacked the leather with his fist. "Come on, kiddo, wham it down his whammy."

The Whammer out of the corner of his mouth told the drunk to keep his mouth shut.

"Burn it across his button."

"Close your trap," Mercy said.

"Cut his throat with it."

"If he tries to dust me, so help me I will smash his skull," the Whammer threatened.

Roy stretched loosely, rocked back on his left leg, twirling the right a little like a dancer, then strode forward and threw with such force his knuckles all but scraped the ground on the follow-through.

At thirty-three the Whammer still enjoyed exceptional eyesight. He saw the ball spin off Roy's fingertips and it reminded him of a white pigeon he had kept as a boy, that he would send into flight by flipping it into the air. The ball flew at him and he was conscious of its bird-form and white flapping wings, until it suddenly disappeared from view. He heard a noise like the bang of a firecracker at his feet and Sam had the ball in his mitt. Unable to believe his ears he heard Mercy intone a reluctant strike.

Sam flung off the glove and was wringing his hand.

"Hurt you, Sam?" Roy called.

"No, it's this dang glove."

Though he did not show it, the pitch had bothered the Whammer no end. Not just the speed of it but the sensation of surprise and strangeness that went with it—him batting here on the railroad tracks, the crazy carnival, the drunk catching and a clown pitching, and that queer dame Harriet, who had five minutes ago been patting him on the back for his skill in the batting cage, now eyeing him coldly for letting one pitch go by.

He noticed Max had moved farther back.

"How the hell you expect to call them out there?"

"He looks wild to me." Max moved in.

"Your knees are knockin'," Sam tittered.

"Mind your business, rednose," Max said.

"You better watch your talk, mister," Roy called to Mercy.

"Pitch it, greenhorn," warned the Whammer.

Sam crouched with his glove on. "Do it again, Roy. Give him something simular."

"Do it again," mimicked the Whammer. To the crowd, maybe to Harriet, he held up a vaunting finger showing there were other pitches to come.

Roy pumped, reared and flung.

The ball appeared to the batter to be a slow spinning planet looming toward the earth. For a long light-year he waited for this globe to whirl into the orbit of his swing so he could bust it to smithereens that would settle with dust and dead leaves into some distant cosmos. At last the unseeing eye, maybe a fortune-teller's lit crystal ball—anyway, a curious combination of circles —drifted within range of his weapon, or so he thought, because he lunged at it ferociously, twisting round like a top. He landed on both knees as the world floated by over his head and hit with a *whup* into the cave of Sam's glove.

"Hey, Max," Sam said, as he chased the ball after it had bounced out of the glove, "how do they pernounce Whammer if you leave out the W?"

"Strike," Mercy called long after a cheer (was it a jeer?) had burst from the crowd.

"What's he throwing," the Whammer howled, "spitters?"

"In the pig's poop." Sam thrust the ball at him. "It's drier than your granddaddy's scalp."

"I'm warning him not to try any dirty business."

Yet the Whammer felt oddly relieved. He liked to have his back crowding the wall, when there was a single pitch to worry about and a single pitch to hit. Then the sweat began to leak out of his pores as he stared at the hard, lanky figure of the pitiless pitcher, moving, despite his years and a few waste motions, like a veteran undertaker of the diamond, and he experienced a moment of depression.

Sam must have sensed it, because he discovered an unexpected pity in his heart and even for a split second hoped the idol would not be tumbled. But only for a second, for the Whammer had regained confidence in his known talent and experience and was taunting the greenhorn to throw.

Someone in the crowd hooted and the Whammer raised aloft two fat fingers and pointed where he would murder the ball, where the gleaming rails converged on the horizon and beyond was invisible.

Roy raised his leg. He smelled the Whammer's blood and wanted it, and through him the worm's he had with him, for the way he had insulted Sam.

The third ball slithered at the batter like a meteor, the flame swallowing itself. He lifted his club to crush it into a universe of sparks but the heavy wood dragged, and though he willed to destroy the sound he heard a gong bong and realized with sadness that the ball he had expected to hit had long since been part of the past; and though Max could not cough the fatal word out of his throat, the Whammer understood he was, in the truest sense of it, out.

The crowd was silent as the violet evening fell on their shoulders.

For a night game, the Whammer harshly shouted, it was customary to turn on lights. Dropping the bat, he trotted off to the train, an old man.

The ball had caught Sam smack in the washboard and lifted him off his feet. He lay on the ground, extended on his back. Roy pushed everybody aside to get him air. Unbuttoning Sam's coat, he removed the dented washboard.

"Never meant to hurt you, Sam."

"Just knocked the wind outa me," Sam gasped. "Feel better now." He was pulled to his feet and stood steady.

The train whistle wailed, the echo banging far out against the black mountain.

Then the doctor in the broadbrimmed black hat appeared, flustered and morose, the conductor trying to pacify him, and Eddie hopping along behind.

The doctor waved the crumpled yellow paper around. "Got a telegram says somebody on this train took sick. Anybody out here?"

Roy tugged at Sam's sleeve.

"Ixnay."

"What's that?"

"Not me," said Roy.

The doctor stomped off. He climbed into his Ford, whipped it up and drove away.

The conductor popped open his watch. "Be a good hour late into the city."

"All aboard," he called.

"Aboard," Eddie echoed, carrying the bassoon case.

The buxom girl in yellow broke through the crowd and threw her arms around Roy's neck. He ducked but she hit him quick with her pucker four times upon the right eye, yet he could see with the other that Harriet Bird (certainly a snappy goddess) had her gaze fastened on him.

They sat, after dinner, in Eddie's dimmed and empty Pullman, Roy floating through drifts of clouds on his triumph as Harriet went on about the recent tourney, she put it, and the unreal forest outside swung forward like a gate shutting. The odd way she saw things interested him, yet he was aware of the tormented trees fronting the snaky lake they were passing, trees bent and clawing, plucked white by icy blasts from the black water, their bony branches twisting in many a broken direction.

Harriet's face was flushed, her eyes gleaming with new insights. Occasionally she stopped and giggled at herself for the breathless volume of words that flowed forth, to his growing astonishment, but after a pause was on her galloping way again—a girl on horse-back—reviewing the inspiring sight (she said it was) of David jawboning the Goliath-Whammer, or was it Sir Percy lancing Sir Maldemer, or the first son(with a rock in his paw) ranged against the primitive papa?

Roy gulped. "My father? Well, maybe I did want to skull him sometimes. After my grandma died, the old man dumped me in one orphan home after the other, wherever he happened to be working—when he did—though he did used to take me out of there summers and teach me how to toss a ball."

No, that wasn't what she meant, Harriet said. Had he ever read Homer?

Try as he would he could only think of four bases and not a book. His head spun at her allusions. He found her lingo strange with all the college stuff and hoped she would stop it because he wanted to talk about baseball.

Then she took a breather. "My friends say I have a fantastic imagination."

He quickly remarked he wouldn't say that. "But the only thing I had on my mind when I was throwing out there was that Sam had bet this ten spot we couldn't afford to lose out on, so I had to make him whiff."

"To whiff—oh, Roy, how droll," and she laughed again.

He grinned, carried away by the memory of how he had done it, the hero, who with three pitched balls had nailed the best the American League had to offer. What didn't that say about the future? He felt himself falling into sentiment in his thoughts and tried to steady himself but couldn't before he had come forth with a pronouncement: "You have to have the right stuff to play good ball and I have it. I bet some day I'll break every record in the book for throwing and hitting."

Harriet appeared startled then gasped, hiding it like a cough behind her tense fist, and vigorously applauded, her bracelets bouncing on her wrists. "Bravo, Roy, how wonderful."

"What I mean," he insisted, "is I feel that I have got it in me—that I am due for something very big. I have to do it. I mean," he said modestly, "that's of course when I get in the game."

Her mouth opened. "You mean you're not—" She seemed, to his surprise, disappointed, almost on the verge of crying.

"No," he said, ashamed. "Sam's taking me for a tryout."

Her eyes grew vacant as she stared out the window. Then she asked, "But Walter—*he* is a successful professional player, isn't he?"

"The Whammer?" Roy nodded.

"And he has won that award three times—what was it?"

"The Most Valuable Player." He had a panicky feeling he was losing her to the Whammer.

She bit her lip. "Yet you defeated him," she murmured.

He admitted it. "He won't last much longer I don't think—the most a year or two. By then he'll be too old for the game. Myself, I've got my whole life ahead of me."

Harriet brightened, saying sympathetically, "What will you hope to accomplish, Roy?"

He had already told her but after a minute remarked, "Sometimes when I walk down the street I bet people will say there goes Roy Hobbs, the best there ever was in the game."

She gazed at him with touched and troubled eyes. "Is that all?"

He tried to penetrate her question. Twice he had answered it and still she was unsatisfied. He couldn't be sure what she expected him to say. "Is that all?" he repeated. "What more is there?"

"Don't you know?" she said kindly.

Then he had an idea. "You mean the bucks? I'll get them too."

She slowly shook her head. "Isn't there something over and above earthly things—some more glorious meaning to one's life and activities?"

"In baseball?"

"Yes."

He racked his brain—

"Maybe I've not made myself clear, but surely you can see (I was saying this to Walter just before the train stopped) that yourself alone—alone in the sense that we are all terribly alone no matter what people say—I mean by that perhaps if you understood that our values must derive from—oh, I really suppose—" She dropped her hand futilely. "Please forgive me. I sometimes confuse myself with the little I know."

Her eyes were sad. He felt a curious tenderness for her, a little as if she might be his mother (That bird.) and tried very hard to come up with the answer she wanted—something you said about LIFE.

"I think I know what you mean," he said. "You mean the fun and satisfaction you get out of playing the best way that you know how?"

She did not respond to that.

Roy worried out some other things he might have said but had no confidence to put them into words. He felt curiously deflated and a little lost, as if he had just flunked a test. The worst of it was he still didn't know what she'd been driving at.

Harriet yawned. Never before had he felt so tongue-tied in front of a girl, a looker too. Now if he had her in bed—

Almost as if she had guessed what he was thinking and her mood had changed to something more practical than asking nutty questions that didn't count, she sighed and edged closer to him, concealing the move behind a query about his bassoon case. "Do you play?"

"Not any music," he answered, glad they were talking about something different. "There's a thing in it that I made for myself."

"What, for instance?"

He hesitated. "A baseball bat."

She was herself again, laughed merrily. "Roy, you are priceless."

"I got the case because I don't want to get the stick all banged up before I got the chance to use it.' '

"Oh, Roy." Her laughter grew. He smiled broadly.

She was now so close he felt bold. Reaching down he lifted the hat box by the string and lightly hefted it.

"What's in it?"

She seemed breathless. "In it?" Then she mimicked, "—Something I made for myself."

"Feels like a hat."

"Maybe a head?" Harriet shook a finger at him.

"Feels more like a hat." A little embarrassed, he set the box down. "Will you come and see me play sometime?" he asked.

She nodded and then he was aware of her leg against his and that she was all but on his lap. His heart slapped against his ribs and he took it all to mean that she had dropped the last of her interest in the Whammer and was putting it on the guy who had buried him.

As they went through a tunnel, Roy placed his arm around her shoulders, and when the train lurched on a curve, casually let his hand fall upon her full breast. The nipple rose between his fingers and before he could resist the impulse he had tweaked it.

Her high-pitched scream lifted her up and twirling like a dancer down the aisle.

Stricken, he rose—had gone too far.

Crooking her arms like broken branches she whirled back to him, her head turned so far around her face hung between her shoulders.

"Look, I'm a twisted tree."

Sam had sneaked out on the squirming, apologetic Mercy, who, with his back to the Whammer—he with a newspaper raised in front of his sullen eyes—had kept up a leechlike prodding about Roy, asking where he had come from (oh, he's just a home town boy), how it was no major league scout had got at him (they did but he turned them down for me) even with the bonus cash that they are tossing around these days (yep), who's his father (like I said, just an old semipro who wanted awful bad to be in the big leagues) and what, for God's sake, does he carry around in that case (that's his bat, Wonderboy). The sportswriter was greedy to know more, hinting he could do great things for the kid, but Sam, rubbing his side where it pained, at last put him off and escaped into the coach to get some shuteye before they hit Chicago, sometime past 1 A.M.

After a long time trying to settle himself comfortably, he fell snoring asleep flat on his back and was at once sucked into a long dream that he had gone thirsty mad for a drink and was threatening the slickers in the car get him a bottle or else. Then this weasel of a Mercy, pretending he was writing on a pad, pointed him out with his pencil and the conductor snapped him up by the seat of his pants and ran his free-wheeling feet lickity-split through the sawdust, giving him the merry heave-ho off the train through the air on a floating trapeze, ploop into a bog where it rained buckets. He thought he better get across the foaming river before it flooded the bridge away so he set out, all bespattered, to cross it, only this queer duck of a doctor in oilskins, an old man with a washable white mustache and a yellow lamp he thrust straight into your eyeballs, swore to him the bridge was gone. You're plumb tootin' crazy, Sam shouted in the storm, I saw it standin' with me own eyes, and he scuffled to get past the geezer, who dropped the light setting the rails afire. They wrestled in the rain until Sam slyly tripped and threw him, and helter-skeltered for the bridge, to find to his crawling horror it was truly down and here he was scatching space till he landed with a splishity-splash in the whirling waters, sobbing (whoa whoa) and the white watchman on the embankment flung him a flare but it was all too late because he heard the roar of the falls below (and restless shifting of the sea) and felt with his red hand where the knife had stabbed him . . .

Roy was dreaming of an enormous mountain—Christ, the size of it—when he felt himself roughly shaken—Sam, he thought, because they were there—only it was Eddie holding a lit candle.

"The fuse blew and I've had no chance to fix it."

"What's the matter?"

"Trou-ble. Your friend has collapsed.' '

Roy hopped out of the berth, stepped into moccasins and ran, with Eddie flying after him with the snuffed wax, into a darkened car where a pool of people under a blue light hovered over Sam, unconscious.

"What happened?" Roy cried.

"Sh," said the conductor, "he's got a raging fever."

"What from?"

"Can't say. We're picking up a doctor."

Sam was lying on a bench, wrapped in blankets with a pillow tucked under his head, his gaunt face broken out in sweat. When Roy bent over him, his eyes opened.

"Hello, kiddo," he said in a cracked voice.

"What hurts you, Sam?"

"Where the washboard banged me—but it don't hurt so much now."

"Oh, Jesus."

"Don't take it so, Roy. I'll be better."

"Save his strength, son," the conductor said. "Don't talk now."

Roy got up. Sam shut his eyes.

The train whistled and ran slow at the next town then came to a draggy halt. The trainman brought a half-dressed doctor in. He examined Sam and straightened up. "We got to get him off and to the hospital."

Roy was wild with anxiety but Sam opened his eyes and told him to bend down.

Everyone moved away and Roy bent low.

"Take my wallet outa my rear pocket."

Roy pulled out the stuffed cowhide wallet.

"Now you go to the Stevens Hotel—"

"No, oh no, Sam, not without you."

"Go on, kiddo, you got to. See Clarence Mulligan tomorrow and say I sent you—they are expecting you. Give them everything you have got on the ball—that'll make me happy."

"But, Sam—"

"You got to. Bend lower."

Roy bent lower and Sam stretched his withered neck and kissed him on the chin.

"Do like I say."

"Yes, Sam."

A tear splashed on Sam's nose.

Sam had something more in his eyes to say but but though he tried, agitated, couldn't say it. Then the trainmen came in with a stretcher and they lifted the catcher and handed him down the steps, and overhead the stars were bright but he knew he was dead.

Roy trailed the anonymous crowd out of Northwest Station and clung to the shadowy part of the wall till he had the courage to call a cab.

"Do you go to the Stevens Hotel?" he asked, and the driver without a word shot off before he could rightly be seated, passed a red light and scuttled a cripple across the deserted street. They drove for miles in a shadow-infested, street-lamped jungle.

He had once seen some stereopticon pictures of Chicago and it was a boxed-up ant heap of stone and crumbling wood buildings in a many-miled spreading checkerboard of streets without much open space to speak of except the railroads, stockyards, and the shore of a windy lake. In the Loop, the offices went up high and the streets were jampacked with people, and he wondered how so many of them could live together in any one place. Suppose there was a fire or something and they all ran out of their houses to see—how could they help but trample all over themselves? And Sam had warned him against strangers, because there were so many bums, sharpers, and gangsters around, people you were dirt to, who didn't know you and didn't want to, and for a dime they would slit your throat and leave you dying in the streets.

"Why did I come here?" he muttered and felt sick for home.

The cab swung into Michigan Avenue, which gave a view of the lake and a white-lit building spiring into the sky, then before he knew it he was standing flatfooted (Christ, the size of it) in front of the hotel, an enormous four-sectioned fortress. He hadn't the nerve to go through the whirling doors but had to because this bellhop grabbed his things—he wrested the bassoon case loose —and led him across the thick-carpeted lobby to a desk where he signed a card and had to count out five of the wallet's pulpy dollars for a room he would give up as soon as he found a house to board in.

But his cubbyhole on the seventeenth floor was neat and private, so after he had stored everything in the closet he lost his nervousness. Unlatching the window brought in the lake breeze. He stared down at the lit sprawl of Chicago, standing higher than he ever had in his life except for a night or two on a mountain. Gazing down upon the city, he felt as if bolts in his knees, wrists, and neck had loosened and he had spread up in height. Here, so high in the world, with the earth laid out in small squares so far below, he knew he would go in tomorrow and wow them with his fast one, and they would know him for the splendid pitcher he was.

The telephone rang. He was at first scared to answer it. In a strange place, so far from everybody he knew, it couldn't possibly be for him.

It rang again. He picked up the phone and listened.

"Hello, Roy? This is Harriet."

He wasn't sure he had got it right. "Excuse me?"

"Harriet Bird, silly."

"Oh, Harriet." He had completely forgotten her.

"Come down to my room," she giggled, "and let me say welcome to the city."

"You mean now?"

"Right away." She gave him the room number.

"Sure." He meant to ask her how she knew he was here but she had hung up.

Then he was elated. So that's how they did it in the city. He combed his hair and got out his bassoon case. In the elevator a drunk tried to take it away from him but Roy was too strong for him.

He walked—it seemed ages because he was impatient—through a long corridor till he found her number and knocked.

"Come on in."

Opening the door, he was astonished at the enormous room.

Through the white-curtained window the sight of the endless dark lake sent a shiver down his spine.

Then he saw her standing shyly in the far corner of the room, naked under the gossamer thing she wore, held up on her risen nipples and the puffed wedge of hair beneath her white belly. A great weight went off his mind.

As he shut the door she reached into the hat box which lay open next to a vase of white roses on the table and fitted the black feathered hat on her head. A thick veil fell to her breasts. In her hand she held a squat, shining pistol.

He was greatly confused and thought she was kidding but a grating lump formed in his throat and his blood shed ice. He cried out in a gruff voice, "What's wrong here?"

She said sweetly, "Roy, will you be the best there ever was in the game?"

"That's right."

She pulled the trigger (thrum of bull fiddle). The bullet cut a silver line across the water. He sought with his bare hands to catch it, but it eluded him and, to his horror, bounced into his gut. A twisted dagger of smoke drifted up from the gun barrel. Fallen on one knee he groped for the bullet, sickened as it moved, and fell over as the forest flew upward, and she, making muted noises of triumph and despair, danced on her toes around the stricken hero.

To the Coast

After passing his driver's test and getting his license, Levin was giving some thought to calling Avis Fliss, if at all feasible, when an attractive girl in one of his classes, Nadalee Hammerstad, began to haunt the surprised forefront of his mind. One day as they were sitting together in his office, discussing her latest theme—she had come in to ask about her grades—Nadalee, imperceptibly leaning forward, nuzzled her hard little breast against Levin's lonely elbow. He moved his arm as if bitten although somehow managing not to be abrupt, at the same time considering the touch unintentional—someone else wouldn't have noticed. He continued talking about her paragraphs, and although he could almost not believe it, the breast again caressed. To test whether this was his imagination overworking, Levin kept his arm where it had been, and the girl for the third time gave him this unmistakable sign of her favor as he droned on about her writing, his thoughts in the wild wind. Two minutes later she thanked him for his criticism and left with a happy smile, not the vaguest sign of a blush on her, although Levin glowed as with high fever.

He had noticed her more than once, a slim girl with short dark-brown hair, pretty, with greenish eyes, mature face, and shapely figure. Although her lower lip was thin and she used eyebrow pencil a bit smearily, she had a way with clothes. Whereas the other girls in her class were contented with skirts and sweaters of pastel shades, or blouses, Nadalee fitted into tight dresses and favored bright colors, a blessing on rainy days. The freshman girls smelled of body heat and talcum powder, but she wore a spicy perfume, which when it touched Levin's nostrils, never failed to interest him. When she slid into her seat in the second row he knew it without looking. There was about her a quality of having been and seen, that made the instructor feel he could talk to her. And she wrote well, sometimes imaginatively. He felt let down when she was absent. Still, he paid her no special attention, and had given her not much thought after class until her visit to his office. After that she was in his mind so tenaciously it wearied him.

Nadalee took on a private uniqueness, a nearness and dearness as though he were in love with her. Although he told himself he wasn't, she had in a sense offered love, and love was what Levin wanted. Though he tried diligently to cast her out of his thoughts, she sneaked back in with half her clothes off to incite him to undress the rest of her. He tried to figure out how to achieve an honorable relationship with the girl. If they were elsewhere in another season—if let's say, in the Catskills in July or August, he might with comparatively undisturbed conscience have taken a bite of what she offered. But here in Easchester, at Cascadia College, English 10, Section Y, 11 A.M. MWF, she was his student and he her instructor, in loco parentis, practically a sacred trust. Levin determined to forget the girl, but his determination was affected by hers. Nadalee appeared in class, the day after the time she had upset him in his office, in one of her prettiest dresses, a thickly petticoated affair, white with wine stripes encircling hips, belly and breasts. She crossed and uncrossed her slim young legs enhanced in nylon stockings. On her narrow feet she wore black ballet slippers in which, without much trouble, he could see her on her toes in *Swan Lake*, himself the evil magician. Surely, he thought, this dressing up isn't for me; and though he went on in class as if he knew what he was doing, he could not keep from desiring her—to consume and be consumed. Afterwards, alone in his office, his chest palpitating as though he were contemplating murder, or flying off on a roaring drunk, Levin reread her themes and in one came across a biographical bit he couldn't understand why he had forgotten. When she was eighteen she had spent a summer on her uncle's ranch in Northern California. In the afternoon when it was hot Nadalee rode her horse to a small lake surrounded by pine trees, tossed off shirt and bra, stepped out of levis and underpants, and dived into the cold blue water. Though Levin's legs cramped after a too hasty immersion in cold water, he jumped in after her and spent most of the night swimming with Nadalee.

The next day the sight of her skirt clinging to her thighs was enough to upset him. After once glancing at her, every line lovely, conscious of his relentless consciousness of her he vowed not to look again, and managed not to that morning, but it was worse later when he was alone. Desire butchered him. He beheld his slaughtered face in the mirror and stared at it, wretched. How escape the ferocious lust that enflamed and tormented his thoughts as it corroded his will? Why must Levin's unlived life put him always in peril? Why obsessively seek what was lost—unlived—in the past? He had no wish to be Faust, or Gatsby; or St. Anthony of Somewhere, who to conquer his torment, had nipped off his balls. Levin wanted to be himself, at peace in present time.

He tried various means of self-control: exhortation, rationalization, censorship, obfuscation. One trick was to think of the girl as his daughter. He was her old man and had watched her grow from a thing in dirty diapers. At twelve she was menstruating; on her eighteenth birthday Levin married her off to a successful lawyer, to whom she bore seven children in six years, all boys. Her father, ever a man to be tempted by every damned temptation—life had plugged him full of sockets and it took only a slight breeze to make a connection—was safe and sound in her invasive presence, until by a dirty stroke of fate (try as he would Levin-père could not reverse it) the lawyer expired of a heart attack from overwork. But Nadalee was financially provided for, so Levin went off to Europe to live, traveling from country to country this side the iron curtain. It couldn't be said he didn't enjoy his life, though where exactly was home? Several years later, in Sevilla—he was then fifty-five going on fifty-six—half drunk on val de peñas one festival night before the corrida, he met this masked beauty at a costume ball. One tango led to another, the dance to a sense of fundamental intimacy—what, after all, is a dance? So, whispering together—Levin confessing most of his sins, including advancing age, the señorita saying nothing of importance—they left for his suite at the Hilton. First they ate. George, the fine waiter, served wild asparagus, a plate of cold meats, manchiego cheese and some dry white capri, iced in buckets; after coffee a bottle of anis del mono, which tasted like licorice and warmed all the way. Then they made love. The masked beauty refused—despite the inconvenience, which she argued was tit for tat for his grizzled beard—to remove her disguise until it was unalterably too late. When he looked at her true face at dawn, he groaned at the misery he had committed. Levin thereupon put out both eyes and threw himself off a high cliff into the shark-infested sea.

He argued with himself: I have evil thoughts, expensive to my spirit; they represent my basest self. I must expunge them by will, no weak thing in man. I must live by responsibility, an invention of mine in me. The girl trusts me, I can't betray her. If I want sex I must be prepared to love, and love may mean marriage. (I live by my nature, not Casanova's.) If I'm not prepared to marry her I'd better stay away. He exhorted himself: teach her only grammar, the principal parts of verbs, spelling, punctuation— nothing not in the syllabus. He would not let the casual brush of a girl's breast against his sleeve seduce him into acting without honor. The self would behave as it must. She would not make a fool of him, much less a worm. He would, in denial, reveal the depth of his strongest, truest strength. Character over lust. By night, after these terrible exertions, including two cold showers, Levin's mind was comparatively calm—he had bludgeoned desire, and though exhausted, beaten half to death by the bloody club he carried against the self, felt more or less at peace.

About a week later, Levin encountered Nadalee, one morning, in the college bookstore. He had been wandering among the book tables and looked up, experiencing overwhelming relief to find her by his side, for he had at once seen her as she was—diminished from a temptress into a nice kid. Levin observed with interest the errors of her face and figure, the thin underlip, too heavily penciled brows; her legs less than slim although not actually skinny, and her childlike ballet-slippered feet. Objectivity, if it did less for her, did more for him. It was her youth that moved me, Levin thought. Also her unexpected favor. He desired those who found him desirable, a too easy response; he must watch this in himself.

Nadalee said she was looking for an entertaining novel and could he suggest one: "It's a gift—a birthday present for guess who?—me, I'm twenty today."

Levin congratulated her. "Twenty, did you say?"

She explained why she was two years older than most freshmen. "You see, I worked in a bank before coming here." But the bank had bored her, so she had quit and registered, with some financial assistance from her father, at Cascadia College. All this was news to Levin, though he tried to sidestep the impression it might be good news. Could good news be bad? Her age, perhaps, explained her maturity. Yet twenty was not too different from eighteen. Before he could decide how different, if different, or where or why different, he hastened to think: she's still too young —ten years between us—a kid. Just look at her feet. Besides I'm her teacher.

Levin found her a novel, tipped his hat, and left for lunch.

Later, to prove he trusted his strength he telephoned her to ask if she liked to walk. "Madly," Nadalee answered. Since she honestly interested him, he had made up his mind it would be better for his nerves if he saw her now and then, in a Platonic relationship. A walk, a bit of a drive here and there, at most a movie in a neighboring town. Company, talk—a blessing under the right circumstances.

They met in the park by the green river. She came in cardigan and skirt, carrying a poplin raincoat; Levin had his on. They wandered along the bank of the Sacajawea. The morning had been gray but this afternoon was blue, infused with light of the invisible sun.

"Don't you just love the day when it's like this?" Nadalee said.

"Very much."

"Look at those clouds in the west. How would you describe them?"

"Vaporous, toiling."

"Tempestuous, like some people's emotions?"

"Whose, for instance?"

"Yours."

"You are observant," he said with a sigh, "mature."

"I'm glad you finally noticed."

Levin bent for a stone to scale on the water but it sank with a plop.

"If you had any idea that I am a little-innocent," she said, watching the ripples in the water, "well, I'm not, if that's what you're worried about. I was once engaged to be married."

The wall he had so painfully built against her, against desire, fell on his head.

He asked in hidden anguish, "Why do you tell me that?"

"Because I am a woman and wish to be treated so."

"By me?"

"Yes, if you must know."

"But why me?" he asked.

"I guess you know I'm different than most of the other girls in your class? I'm tired of college boys. I want real companionship."

"But why me?" Levin said. "There are other men around, graduate students, instructors, some handsome."

"I bet you'd be better looking without your beard."

"No, I wouldn't."

"Anyway, the answer is you happen to appeal to me. I've always liked the intellectual type. I like the way you talk, it's very sincere."

He was humbly grateful to her. They were standing under a tree and impulsively kissed, her young breasts stabbing his chest. They kissed so hard his hat fell off.

Levin said, as they went on, hands locked, "I don't have to tell you Nadalee, the need for absolute secrecy? Many people would not understand or approve this. It could make trouble."

She said she had thought of that and had a scheme for them to spend some time together alone if he agreed. He agreed. Her aunt, Nadalee said, owned a little motel on the coast. She was planning to visit her daughter in Missoula next week-end, and whenever she left she closed up and lit the no-vacancy sign. There wasn't much business at this time of the year, only occasional tourists and some hunters or fishermen. Anyway, Nadalee had promised to look after the place and they could have it to themselves. "We could walk on the beach and the dunes, and picnic and ride around, and just sort of relax. My aunt won't get home till late on Sunday."

Levin resisted every sentence but his imagination was whipped to froth. Who could resist Eden?

Came Friday. He was resolved to go but not necessarily to collect. The fun was having a place to go, companionship, not something he could unfairly get from the girl. He was obliged to treat her responsibly. He would explain this when he got there—she had left by bus that morning but he had a one o'clock to teach; it had been decided they were not to go or come back together. Let's be friends, Levin planned to say. If we can honestly be, later we may think of sex. It will come more pleasurably to friends—a two-fold blessing. That he had reached this conclusion satisfied him. After trimming his beard a half-inch around he drove out of Easchester in a marvelous mood.

For the first time in his life Levin was on the road alone in a car—his own—carried along on his own power, so to say. Three cheers for the pioneers of the auto industry; they had put him on wheels to go where he pleased! He thought with pleasure of the many things he had learned to do in his few months here: had mowed frequent lawns, the grass still green and growing in December; raked a billion leaves, fifty percent from neighboring trees; gathered walnuts in October; picked yellow pears; regularly attended and even cleaned Mrs. B's rumbling sawdust furnace, and so on and what not. Last week he had washed and waxed his car. Levin the handy man; that is to say, man of hands. And here he was with both of them solidly on the wheel, miraculously in motion along the countryside, enjoying the compression of scenery. Heading towards unknown mountains in voyage to the Pacific Ocean, world's greatest. Imagine, Levin from Atlantic to Pacific—who would have thought so only a few years ago?— seeing up close sights he had never seen before: big stone mountains ahead, thick green forests, unexpected farms scattered over the hillsides, the ghostly remains of forest fire, black snags against the sky. Something else new: a little too close for comfort he passed a log truck, surely half a block long, pyramided high with enormous tree trunks, heavily chained, thank God. Here and there millponds were afloat with brown logs, to be fished out and cut into boards. He whizzed past a smoldering, tree-tall furnace shaped like a shuttlecock, a black slash burner that consumed wood waste, its head ablaze at night. He was discovering in person the face of America.

And the weather was better than the newspaper had expected. For short intervals warm sunlight—through thick clouds breaking into sky streams—lit the fields; some harboring sheep, a few with starlings on their backs, picking a living out of the wool. At times the clouds massed darkly, yet the day managed to be cheery, and the bright green winter wheat yielded hidden light. Levin guessed the temperature was around fifty, and this they called onset of winter. It said so on the calendar, and Mrs. Beaty was airing her winter undies and talking of Christmas. Who immersed in Eastern snow and icy winds could guess at Cascadia's pleasant weather? Here, Bucket had told him, spring came sometimes in midwinter; autumn in the right mood might hang on till

January, and at times spring lingered through summer. A season and a half they called it but Levin would not complain. Only a week ago he had caught the odor of a white rose in the best of health on somebody's front lawn. So what if they paid in wetness for the mild climate; the warmth made up for rain, and wasn't it wonderful to be riding to the beach in December? Who but a polar bear would indulge in the Bronx?

He saw stone ascending and discovered himself doing the same. "Holy Moses, I'm up a mountain." As the road turned, his startled sight beheld below a vast forest of pointed conifers, and as he emerged from a corkscrew curve, a mass of peaks—rocks and shadow—extended into the dim distance. "Alps on Alps arise." His heart leapt at the view but when he realized how narrow the ledge he was traveling on, how sheer the drop if he dropped, his heart settled with a wham and he found himself toiling at driving. WARNING, SHARP CURVES. He was sweating to master them as his tires screeched, rolling the wheel as if fighting a storm at sea; to stay on the road yet keep from hitting anything that might come zooming around the bend—ahead invisible till he got there; also to move fast enough to satisfy the irritable pest behind him, sprung up from nowhere and blasting his horn till Levin had a headache. He was doing twenty and considered crawling at ten but didn't dare with this madman behind him. He tried to signal the fiend to stop with the horn, or quell him with a dirty look in the mirror, but no signals worked and he had to keep his eyes glued ahead for fear of losing the slightest sight of the perilous, tortuous road. Another blast of the horn filled him with rage and dismay. He considered stopping and getting out to grapple with his nemesis, but luckily the road widened a few feet, and Levin pulled hard against the side of the cliff to let the monster pass. He furiously shook his fist as a dilapidated Chevy squeezed by, the pee-wee driver with a snip of black mustache, more Chaplin than Hitler, offering a thumbed nose. His dusty license plate read New Jersey—too small world. With no further stomach for tight curves, Levin considered giving his breath a rest, but since no one any longer fastened onto his tail he went his winding way, conscious of abysses deeper than those in dreams, worried that a momentary lapse of attention might send him hurtling into the murderous maw of the forest below, dead, destroyed, never to be seen again. Yet he negotiated each curve as it came, some bent into such unpredictable tormented arcs that it flashed on him he knew for the first time in his life what "straight" meant; and this insight carried him down the mountain onto a peaceful road.

Peaceful for a short happy while, then the grade rose again and his eyes widened in the dusty windshield. But Levin got used to it: Steeplechase, you did what the bear did. There were many mountains and you took them one by one, paying no attention to the rest of the family. Soon the worst seemed over. Descending, Levin was surprised to sail through a momentary hamlet, a cluster of jerry-built, long-unpainted houses around a general store with a dirty gas pump in front. Here too America; you learned as you lived, a refreshing change from books. Out of the townlet and embarked on a broadly winding level road, he hypnotically watched a puff of smoke float up from his radiator and evaporate, Levin at once apprehensive of trouble although he couldn't call it by name. He wondered whether to drive back to the gas pump, but the narrowness of the twisting road made a turn impossible. And he didn't like going back once the plan was to go forward. It was getting late, he was slow. Nadalee was waiting. He studied the hood at intervals, and seeing no more smoke, vowed not to stop until the first service station he hit. By the merest chance his eye caught the progress of the needle of the temperature gauge. It was flirting with HOT. "What'll I do now?" Levin asked himself, trying to recall what the manual that came with the car said, but remembering only confusion. So he drove on till he again spied smoke. The red needle had struck HOT. Fearing fire, he quickly brought the Hudson to a stop on the road and shut off the ignition. A cloud of steam rose from the radiator. Levin, agitated, lifted the hood. He burned his fingers trying to unscrew the water cap, then managed to turn it with a folded handkerchief. A hissing stream of steam and bubbling brown water spilled over, a pox on ex-Dean Feeney. Levin remembered having read about this under BOILING OVER.

Two hours later he was on his way again. The sun was sinking and he was very late. He had been pushed by a pickup truck to a small gas station in a logging village not too far away, whose owner-and-mechanic-on-duty had "gone home for half hour," it said on a stenciled strip of cardboard on the gas pump. Levin fretted as he waited, because he had only twenty dollars in his pocket and Friday was going fast. When at last the man had appeared, he recommended a reverse flush, and though this sounded like a bad poker hand it suited Levin if somebody who knew said so; but the operation took more than an hour, the man wandering off every so often to attend his pump or sell something. Levin walked down the road and sat on a rock watching time hurrying by and nothing he could do about it. He considered trying to call Nadalee to tell her what had happened but gave it up as too complicated. He had estimated—she had—that they would be together by four, but four had come and gone, and with it went some of the beauty of the day and the pleasure of anticipation, because he liked things to work out as planned, time and all. He seriously wondered whether to take this incident as a warning of sorts, yet cheered up when the car was ready, paid twelve dollars courageously, and was again en voyage with a full gas tank and recommended change of oil, although he had changed it last week. He warily watched the temperature gauge, suffering when the needle went up and rejoicing when it settled back. Since the coast was only thirty-five miles away, he gave himself at the very most an hour to get there, counseling calm, the fun was yet to be, Nadalee will wait for me. The road was presently good and he clocked five miles in six minutes. Although the sun had sunk, and shade arose in the fields, a golden-green glow hung in the sky. He enjoyed the stillness, each tree still, the timbered hills multiplying silence. With some misgiving he climbed a new rise. At the first turn of the road a log truck, like a fat worm pulling itself out of a hole in the earth, rumbled forth hauling the largest, most terrifying hunk of wood Levin had ever seen; it looked like a threat to humanity. He pulled the Hudson quickly to the shoulder of the road, holding his foot hard on the brake until the long truck puffed by. When Levin was ready to move he discovered he couldn't his right rear wheel sunk in a ditch.

"I'll die," he muttered after twenty minutes of struggling to free the wheel. Not one car had come by. He pictured himself frozen to death in the Hudson during the night. In the morning they would haul off a stiff corpse; he had read of these things in the paper. Levin desperately figured he had to do something, but the right rear wheel had no respect for reason or will. He was wondering why he had come on this impossible journey when a tractor rattled around the bend and wobbled towards him. It was an old machine, the farmer driving it a wizened man with a small leathery face. He wore a wilted straw hat, and sat up on a high seat, swaying as he sat.

To Levin's astonishment the machine passed by, the farmer lost in thought; he had to yell to get his attention. With a clank the tractor came to a halt, the driver gazing back at Levin as though he couldn't understand where he had risen from.

"Excuse me for bothering you," Levin explained, "but I'm stuck in this ditch."

The farmer in silence got down from the seat, dug a length of rope out of his tool box and knotted it to Levin's front bumper. In less than a minute the Hudson was out of the ditch. It had happened so fast he could hardly believe it.

"Three cheers for the American farmer!"

The farmer smiled wanly. "Say," he said, "could you give me a hand with some trouble I been havin' of my own?"

"Gladly," said Levin, "although I have an important engagement."

He stepped out of the car. The farmer fished in his tool box and came up with a pair of needle-nose pliers.

"Got an achin' tooth here at the back of my mouth. Could you give it a pull with these pliers?"

Levin's muscles tightened to the point of shivers. He saw himself trying to pull the tooth, breaking it, not being able to get it all out, as the man bled, and it ended by his having to drive him to the hospital. Yet he wanted to show his gratitude to the farmer for rescuing him from the ditch.

"Couldn't I drive you to a dentist?" he said. "I'm on my way to the coast."

"Can't stand 'em," the farmer said. "An' I got thirty head of Angus to look after. I'm alone by myself since the missus died."

Opening his mouth he touched a gnarled finger to the offending tooth, a discolored snag.

Levin tried several times to get the pliers gripping the tooth. "Is this it?"

"Feels like. I ain't sure."

He withdrew the pliers from the farmer's mouth and handed them to him. "I'd only hurt you without doing any good."

"Sure hurts anyway," the man said. He tossed the pliers into the tool box and climbed up on his high seat. The tractor rattled down the hill.

"God bless your tooth," Levin called after him. Failed again, he thought.

He started the Hudson and stepped on the gas. "Nadalee, I'm coming."

It was almost six. I've got to make time. He sped along the mountain road, wondering why it was so dark, then hurriedly switched on his lights, gasping as the beams flew forward and were trapped in pools of fog. A sense of doom infected him and he fell to brooding. Where is the fog, in or out? He had slowed to a crawl, every minute convinced he would the very next go shooting into space. Should be stay rooted? If he stopped where he was and escaped being smashed in the rear, he would have to stay put until the fog lifted, if it did, in the morning. If he went on how would he know if he was on the road or off—levitated in space before the ultimate crash, decapitation, dismemberment—what sort of terrible end for a man who had lived through so much in his life and had so many plans?

He drove on with droplets of mist in his beard, at ten miles an hour, and could see only as many feet ahead, frightened by awesome crags that loomed up before him and the fragments of bare rock over his head. Every few seconds he braked, sounding his horn like a wail as he went, by the greatest good luck skirting half-ridden boulders and grotesquely twisted tree trunks whose crowns were shrouded in fog. He had endless visions of disaster, monotonously called himself "idiot" for having invented this purgatorial journey. Levin promised himself he would celebrate if he got out live.

It seemed to him, his nerves pricking through his skin, that he had journeyed for years on an abandoned road, had started as a child but was surely by now somebody's grandpa, his hair turned bone-white, although the face, when he caught a reflected glimpse of it, looked hauntingly dark. He felt he had crawled on for hours, without confidence that he knew which road was presently which, and after a while, with a sense of not much caring. He went where the road went, because it was there; where it ended he would.

He saw then, lit in his headlights, a horse—could it be?—No, this was a mule standing immobile in the road, gazing at something in the night. It slowly came to Levin, for he was worn out, that the mule was not a nightmare; it was real and he was staring at it from a distance of thirty feet; and that the fog had broken into moving patches; the sky glowing with stars, amid them the moon. Yet even as he sighed in unbelievable relief at the lifting of the fog, the mule, like a stone statue, stood broadside on the road, impassable at either end. Ten feet from the animal Levin stopped the car and got out to see what he could do about moving it, offering first a Life Saver, gingerly holding it a foot from the mule's nose, hoping it might mistake the candy for sugar, but its nostrils didn't even mildly twitch. Levin, walking down the road in the glare of his headlights, tore up some wet ferns. He tried holding out a handful but the salad did not tempt the animal. In exasperation he hunted for a rock to bounce off its bony back, but as he was looking, gave up the thought. In the car he cradled his head on his arms folded on the wheel. The horn blast startled the mule. It gave a frightened whinny and took off in an unknown direction.

The moonlit road stretched ahead for visible miles and Levin made fast time. But after he had traveled another twenty-five and still saw no end to his journey, continuing doubts tormented him. Was he on the right road or headed for Mexico or Canada? Would he get there tonight? Would she still be waiting? With these worries he drove through a covered bridge, and as he emerged, saw headlights rising in the distance. Levin pulled to a hasty stop several feet beyond the bridge. After two minutes a car approached. Stepping out of his Hudson, Levin waved both arms and succeeded in flagging down a Dodge of ancient vintage, the driver braking to a screeching stop.

"If you'll pardon me," Levin said, "I'm looking for the coast. How far to go would you say?"

The driver, an old man wearing a large hat and rimless glasses, peered at Levin's limp beard.

"You a Mormon or somethin'?"

"Just a citizen."

"Live in Cascadia?"

"Yes."

The man lifted his hat, and with a finger of the same hand, scratched his veinous bald cranium.

"Beats me," he muttered. "Ain't it t'other way?" He pointed back over Levin's shoulder.

A minute later his car disappeared into the covered bridge.

Levin, about to collapse, tried to figure where he had gone wrong. He guessed in the fog. Somewhere in it he had missed a turn and taken the wrong direction. It served him right for his evil intentions.

As he drove aimlessly on, in sadness contemplating all the failures of his life, the multifarious wrong ways he had gone, the waste of his going, he sniffed a sea smell. Whirling down the window, he smelled again and let out a cry.

The ocean! Either the old geezer hadn't understood his question or was lost himself; maybe he had suspected Levin was a Russian spy.

He beheld in the distance a golden lace of moonlight on the dark bosom of the vast sea.

Ocean in view, oh the joy. "My God, the Pacific!"

He saw himself as stout Cortez—Balboa, that is—gazing down at the water in wild surmise, both eyes moist.

Some minutes later he asked at a service station the way to Nadalee's aunt's place. Though it was about nine when he got there, the motel was dark, no sign lit. But Levin knocked on each cabin door until a light went on in one, and the door fell open.

There stood Nadalee in a sheer nightie.

"Mr. Levin—I mean Seymour."

"Nadalee—I got lost." Before he could say where or why, she had shucked off her garment and her gloriously young body shed light as he hungrily embraced it.

To Kiev

Five months ago, on a mild Friday in early November, before the first snow had snowed on the shtetl, Yakov's father-in-law, a skinny worried man in clothes about to fall apart, who looked as though he had been assembled out of sticks and whipped air, drove up with his skeletal horse and rickety wagon. They sat in the thin cold house—gone to seed two months after Raisl, the faithless wife, had fled—and drank a last glass of tea together. Shmuel, long since sixty, with tousled gray beard, rheumy eyes, and deeply creased forehead—dug into his caftan pocket for half a yellow sugar lump and offered it to Yakov who shook his head. The peddler—he was his daughter's dowry, had had nothing to give so he gave favors, service if possible—sucked tea through sugar but his son-in-law drank his unsweetened. It tasted bitter and he blamed existence. The old man from time to time commented on life without accusing anyone, or asked harmless questions, but Yakov was silent or short with answers.

After he had sipped through half his glass of tea, Shmuel, sighing, said, "Nobody has to be a Prophet to know you're blaming me for my daughter Raisl." He spoke in sadness, wearing a hard hat he had found in a barrel in a neighboring town. When he sweated it stuck to his head, but being a religious man he didn't mind. Otherwise he had on a patched and padded caftan from which his skinny hands hung out. And very roomy shoes, not boots, which he ran in, and around in.

"Who said anything? You're blaming yourself for having brought up a whore."

Shmuel, without a word, pulled out a soiled blue handkerchief and wept.

"So why, if you'll excuse me, did you stop sleeping with her for months? Is that a way to treat a wife?"

"It was more like weeks but how long can a man sleep with a barren woman? I got tired of trying."

"Why didn't you go to the rabbi when I begged you?"

"Let him stay out of my business and I'll stay out of his. All in all he's an ignorant man."

"Charity you were always short of," the peddler said.

Yakov rose, enraged. "Don't talk to me about charity. What have I had all my life? What have I got to give away? I was practically born an orphan—my mother dead ten minutes later, and you know what happened to my poor father. If somebody said Kaddish for them it wasn't me till years later. If they were waiting outside the gates of heaven it was a long cold wait, if they're not still waiting. Throughout my miserable childhood I lived in a stinking orphans' home, barely existing. In my dreams I ate and I ate my dreams. Torah I had little of and Talmud less, though I learned Hebrew because I've got an ear for language. Anyway, I knew the Psalms. They taught me a trade and apprenticed me five minutes after age ten—not that I regret it. So I work—let's call it work—with my hands, and some call me "common" but the truth of it is few people know who is really common. As for those that look like they got class, take another look. Viskover, the Nogid, is in my eyes a common man. All he's got is rubles and when he opens his mouth you can hear them clink. On my own I studied different subjects, and even before I was taken into the army I taught myself a decent Russian, much better than we pick up from the peasants. What little I know I learned on my own—some history and geography, a little science, arithmetic, and a book or two of Spinoza's. Not much but better than nothing."

"Though most is treyf I give you credit—" said Shmuel.

"Let me finish. I've had to dig with my fingernails for a living.

What can anybody do without capital? What they can do I can do but it's not much. I fix what's broken—except in the heart. In this shtetl everything is falling apart—who bothers with leaks in his roof if he's peeking through the cracks to spy on God? And who can pay to have it fixed let's say he wants it, which he doesn't. If he does, half the time I work for nothing. If I'm lucky, a dish of noodles. Opportunity here is born dead. I'm frankly in a foul mood."

Opportunity you don't have to tell me about—"

"They conscripted me for the Russo-Japanese War but it was over before I got in. Thank God. When I got sick they booted me out. An asthmatic Jew wasn't worth the trouble. Thank God. When I got back I scraped again with my broken nails. After a long run-around which started when I met her, I married your daughter, who couldn't get pregnant in five and a half years. She bore me no children so who could I look in the eye? And now she runs off with some stranger she met at the inn—a goy I'm positive. So that's enough—who needs more? I don't want people pitying me or wondering what I did to be so cursed. I did nothing. It was a gift. I'm innocent. I've been an orphan too long. All I have to my name after thirty years in this graveyard is sixteen rubles that I got from selling everything I own. So please don't mention charity because I have no charity to give."

"Charity you can give even when you haven't got. I don't mean money. I meant for my daughter."

"Your daughter deserves nothing."

"She ran from one rabbi to another in every town I took her, but nobody could promise her a child. She ran to the doctors too when she had a ruble, but they told her the same thing. It was cheaper with the rabbis. So she ran away—may God protect her. Even a sinner belongs to Him. She sinned but she was desperate."

"May she run forever."

"She was a true wife to you for years. She shared your every misfortune."

"What she caused she shared. She was a true wife to the last minute, or the last month, or the month before that, and that makes her untrue, a black cholera on her!"

"God forbid," cried Shmuel, rising. "On you!"

Eyes agitated, he thickly cursed the fixer and fled from the house.

Yakov had sold everything but the clothes on his back, which he wore as peasants do—embroidered shirt belted outside his trousers, whose legs were stuffed into wrinkled high boots. And a peasant's worn and patched, brown sheepskin coat, which could, on occasion, smell of sheep. He had kept his tools and a few books: Smirnovsky's *Russian Grammar*, an elementary biology book, *Selections from Spinoza*, and a battered atlas at least twenty-five years old. He had made a small bundle of the books with a piece of knotted twine. The tools were in a flour sack tied at the neck, the crosscut blade protruding. There was also some food in a cone of newspaper. He was leaving behind his few ruined sticks of furniture—a junkman had wanted to be paid to take them—and two sets of cracked dishes, also unsaleable, that Shmuel could do with whatever he wanted—use, ax, or fire—they were worth nothing. Raisl had had two sets for her father's sake, for herself it made not much difference. But in exchange for the horse and wagon the peddler would get a fairly good cow. He could take over his daughter's little dairy business. It could hardly pay less than peddling. He was the only person Yakov knew who peddled nothing and sold it, in bits and slices, for real kopeks. Sometimes he traded nothing for pig bristles, wool, grain, sugar beets, and then sold the peasants dried fish, soap, kerchiefs, candy, in minute quantities. That was his talent and on it he miraculously lived. "He who gave us teeth will give us bread." Yet his breath smelled of nothing—not bread, not anything.

Yakov, in loose clothes and peaked cap, was an elongated nervous man with large ears, stained hard hands, a broad back and tormented face, lightened a bit by gray eyes and brownish hair. His nose was sometimes Jewish, sometimes not. He had to no one's surprise—after Raisl ran away—shaved off his short beard of reddish cast. "Cut off your beard and you no longer resemble your creator," Samuel had warned. Since then he had been admonished by more than one Jew that he looked like a goy but it had caused him neither to mourn nor rejoice. He looked young but felt old and for that he blamed nobody, not even his wife; he blamed fate and spared himself. His nervousness showed in his movements. Generally he moved faster than he had to, considering how little there was to do, but he was always doing something. After all, he was a fixer and had to keep his hands busy.

Dumping his things into the open wagon, a rusty water bucket hanging under it between the back wheels, he was displeased with the appearance of the nag, a naked-looking animal with spindly legs, a brown bony body and large stupid eyes, who got along very well with Shmuel. They asked little from each other and lived in peace. The horse did mostly as he pleased and Shmuel indulged him. After all, what difference did a short delay make in a mad world? Tomorrow he would be no richer. The fixer was irritated with himself for acquiring this decrepit beast, but had thought better a lopsided exchange with Shmuel than getting nothing for the cow from a peasant who coveted her. A father-in-law's blood was thicker than water. Although there was no railroad station anywhere around, and the coachman came for travelers only every second week, Yakov could have got to Kiev without taking over the horse and wagon. Shmuel had offered to drive him the thirty or so versts but the fixer preferred to be rid of him and travel alone. He figured that once he got into the city he could sell the beast and apology-for-dray, if not to a butcher, then at least to a junk dealer for a few rubles.

Dvoira, the dark-uddered cow, was out in the field behind the hut, browsing under a leafless poplar tree, and Yakov went out to her. The white cow raised her head and watched him approach. The fixer patted her lean flank. "Goodbye, Dvoira," he said, "and lots of luck. Give what you got left to Shmuel, also a poor man." He wanted to say more but couldn't. Tearing up some limp yellowing grass, he fed it to the cow, then returned to the horse and wagon. Shmuel had reappeared.

Why does he act as though he were the one who had deserted me?

"I didn't come back to fight with anybody," Shmuel said. "What she did I won't defend—she hurt me as much as she did you. Even more, though when the rabbi says she's now dead my voice agrees but not my heart. First of all she's my only child, and since when do we need more dead? I've cursed her more than once but I ask God not to listen."

"Well, I'm leaving," Yakov said, "take care of the cow."

"Don't leave yet," Shmuel said, his eyes miserable. "If you stay Raisl might come back."

"If she does who's interested?"

"If you had been more patient she wouldn't have left you."

"Five years going on six is enough of patience. I've had enough. I might have waited the legal ten, but she danced off with some dirty stranger, so I've had my fill, thanks."

"Who can blame you?" Shmuel sighed sadly. He asked after a while, "Have you got tobacco for a little cigarette, Yakov?"

"My bag is empty."

The peddler briskly rubbed his dry palms.

"So you haven't, you haven't, but what I don't understand is why you want to bother with Kiev. It's a dangerous city full of churches and anti-Semites."

"I've been cheated from the start," Yakov said bitterly. "What I've been through personally you know already, not to mention living here all my life except for a few months in the army. The shtetl is a prison, no change from the days of Khmelnitsky. It moulders and the Jews moulder in it. Here we're all prisoners, I don't have to tell you, so it's time to try elsewhere I've finally decided. I want to make a living, I want to get acquainted with a bit of the world. I've read a few books in recent years and it's surprising what goes on that none of us knows about. I'm not asking for Tibet but what I saw in St. Petersburg interested me.

Whoever thought of white nights before, but it's a scientific fact; they have them there. When I left the army I thought I would get out of here as soon as possible, but things caught up with me, including your daughter."

"My daughter wanted to run away from here the minute you got married but you wouldn't go."

"It's true," said Yakov, "it was my fault. I thought it couldn't get worse so it must get better. I was wrong both ways so now enough is enough. I'm on my way at last."

"Outside the Pale only wealthy Jews and the professional classes can get residence certificates. The Tsar doesn't want poor Jews all over his land, and Stolypin, may his lungs collapse, urges him on. Ptu!" Shmuel spat through two fingers.

"Since I can't be a professional on account of lack of education I wouldn't mind being wealthy. As the saying goes, I'd sell my last shirt to be a millionaire. Maybe, by luck, I'll make my fortune in the outside world."

"What's in the world," Shmuel said, "is in the shtetl—people, their trials, worries, circumstances. But here at least God is with us."

"He's with us till the Cossacks come galloping, then he's elsewhere. He's in the outhouse, that's where he is."

The peddler grimaced but let the remark pass. "Almost fifty thousand Jews live in Kiev," he said, "restricted to a few districts, and all in the way of the first blow that falls if a new pogrom should come. And it will fall faster in the larger places than it falls here. When we hear their cries we will rush into the woods. Why should you walk straight into the hands of the Black Hundreds, may they hang by their tongues?"

"The truth of it is I'm a man full of wants I'll never satisfy, at least not here. It's time to get out and take a chance. Change your place change your luck, people say."

"Since the last year or so, Yakov, you're a different man. What wants are so important?"

"Those that can't sleep and keep me awake for company. I've

told you what wants: a full stomach now and then. A job that pays rubles, not noodles. Even some education if I can get it, and I don't mean workmen studying Torah after hours. I've had my share of that. What I want to know is what's going on in the world."

"That's all in the Torah, there's no end to it. Stay away from the wrong books, Yakov, the impure."

"There are no wrong books. What's wrong is the fear of them."

Shmuel unstuck his hat and wiped his brow with his handkerchief.

"Yakov, if you want to go to foreign parts, Turks or no Turks, why not to Palestine where a Jew can see Jewish trees and mountains, and breathe the Jewish air? If I had half a chance there's where I'd go."

"All I've had in this miserable town is a beggarly existence. Now I'll try Kiev. If I can live there decently that's what I'll do. If not, I'll make sacrifices, save up, and head for Amsterdam for a boat to America. To sum it up, I have little but I have plans."

"Plans or none you're looking for trouble."

"I've never had to look," said the fixer. "Well, Shmuel, good luck to you. The morning's gone so I'd better go."

He climbed up onto the wagon and reached for the reins.

"I'll ride with you as far as the windmills." Shmuel got up on the seat on the other side.

Yakov touched the nag with a birch switch the old man kept in the holder, a hole bored into the edge of the seat, but the horse, after an initial startled gallop, stopped short and stood motionless in the road.

"Personally I never use it," the peddler remarked. "It's there as a warning. If he dawdles I remind him it's there. He seems to like to hear me talk about it."

"If that's the case I'm better off walking."

"Patience." Shmuel smacked his lips. "Gidap, beauty—he's very vain. Whenever you can afford it, Yakov, feed him oats. Too much grass and he's prone to gas."

"If he's prone to gas let him fart." He flicked the reins.

Yakov didn't look back. The nag moved along a crooked road between black plowed fields with dark round haystacks piled up here and there, the peasant's church visible on the left in the distance; then slowly up the narrow stony cemetery road, a few thin yellow willows amidst the graves, and around a low tomb-stone-covered hill where Yakov's parents, a man and woman in their early twenties, lay buried. He had considered a visit to their weed-strewn graves but hadn't the heart at the last minute. The past was a wound in the head. He thought of Raisl and felt depressed.

The fixer snapped the rod against the nag's ribs but got no increase of motion.

"I'll get to Kiev by Hanukkah."

"If you don't get there it's because God wills it. You won't miss a thing."

A shnorrer in rags called to the fixer from beside a tilted tomb-stone. "Hey, there, Yakov, it's Friday. How about a two-kopek piece for a Sabbath blessing? Charity saves from death."

"Death is the last of my worries."

"Lend me a kopek or two, Yakov," said Shmuel.

"A kopek I haven't earned today."

The shnorrer, a man with ugly feet, called him goy, his mouth twisted, eyes lit in anger.

Yakov spat in the road.

Shmuel said a prayer to ward off evil.

The nag began to trot, drawing the rickety wagon with its swinging bucket banging the axle past the cemetery hill, down the winding road. They drove by the poorhouse, a shabby struc-ture with an addition for orphans, which Yakov averted his eyes from, then clop-clopped across a wooden bridge into the populous section of the town. They passed Shmuel's hut, neither of them looking. A blackened bathhouse with boarded windows stood near a narrow stream and the fixer felt suddenly itchy for a bath, think-ing of himself in the thick steam, slapping his soapened sides with a twig brush as the attendant poured water on his head. God bless soap and water, Raisl used to say. In a few hours the bath-house, steaming from its cracks, would be bulging with Jews washing up for Friday night.

They rattled along a rutted dusty street with thatched cottages on one side, open weedy fields on the other. A big-wigged Jewess, sitting on her doorstep, plucked a bloody-necked hen between her knees, as she cursed out a peasant's sow rooting in the remnants of her potato garden. A pool of blood in the ditch marked the passage of the ritual slaughterer. Further on, a bearded black goat with a twisted horn, tethered to a post, baaed at the horse and charged, but the rope around his neck held and though the post toppled, the goat was thrown on its back. The doors of some of the cottages hung loose, and where there were steps they sagged. Fences buckled and were about to collapse without apparent notice or response, irritating the fixer, who liked things in place and functioning.

Tonight the white candles would gleam from the lit windows. For everybody else.

The horse zigzagged towards the marketplace, and now the quality of the houses improved, some large and attractive, with gardens full of flowers in the summertime.

"Leave it to the lousy rich," the fixer muttered.

Shmuel had nothing to say. His mind, he had often said, had ex-hausted the subject. He did not envy the rich, all he wanted was to share a little of their wealth—enough to live on while he was working hard to earn a living.

The market, a large open square with wooden houses on two sides, some containing first-floor shops, was crowded with peasant carts laden with grains, vegetables, wood, hides and whatnot. Around the stalls and bins mostly women clustered, shopping for the Sabbath. Though the market was his usual hangout, the fixer waved to no one and no one waved to him.

I leave with no regret, he thought. I should have gone years ago.

"Who have you told?" Shmuel asked.

"Who's there to tell? Practically nobody. It's none of their business anyway. Frankly, my heart is heavy—I'll tell the truth but I'm sick of this place."

He had said goodbye to his two cronies, Leibish Polikov and Haskel Dembo. The first had shrugged, the other wordlessly embraced him, and that was that. A butcher holding up by its thick yellow feet a squawking hen beating its wings saw the wagon go by and said something witty to his customers. One of these, a young woman who turned to look, called to Yakov, but by then the wagon was out of the marketplace, scattering some chickens nesting in the ruts of the road and a flock of jabbering ducks, as it clattered on.

They approached the domed synagogue with its iron weathercock, a pock-marked yellow-walled building with an oak door, for the time being resting in peace. It had been sacked more than once. The courtyard was empty except for a black-hatted Jew sitting on a bench reading a folded newspaper in the sunlight. Yakov had rarely been inside the synagogue in recent years yet he easily remembered the long high-ceilinged room with its brass chandeliers, oval stained windows, and the prayer stands with stools and wooden candleholders, where he had spent, for the most part wasted, so many hours.

"Gidap," he said.

At the other side of the town—a shtetl was an island surrounded by Russia—as they came abreast a windmill, its patched fans turning in slow massive motion, the fixer jerked on the reins and the horse clopped to a stop.

"Here's where we part," he said to the peddler.

Shmuel drew out of his pocket an embroidered cloth bag.

"Don't forget these," he said embarrassed. "I found them in your drawer before we left."

In the bag was another containing phylacteries. There was also a prayer shawl and a prayer book. Raisl, before they were married, had made the bag out of a piece of her dress and embroidered it with the tablets of the Ten Commandments.

"Thanks." Yakov tossed the bag among his other things in the wagon.

"Yakov," said Shmuel passionately, "don't forget your God!"

"Who forgets who?" the fixer said angrily. "What do I get from him but a bang on the head and a stream of piss in my face. So what's there to be worshipful about?"

"Don't talk like a meshummed. Stay a Jew, Yakov, don't give up our God."

"A meshummed gives up one God for another. I don't want either. We live in a world where the clock ticks fast while he's on his timeless mountain staring in space. He doesn't see us and he doesn't care. Today I want my piece of bread, not in Paradise."

"Listen to me, Yakov, take my advice. I've lived longer than you. There's a shul in the Podol in Kiev. Go on Shabbos, you'll feel better. 'Blessed are they who put their trust in God.' "

"Where I ought to go is to the Socialist Bund meetings, that's where I should go, not in shul. But the truth of it is I dislike politics, though don't ask me why. What good is it if you're not an activist? I guess it's my nature. I incline toward the philosophical although I don't know much about anything."

"Be careful," Shmuel said, agitated, "we live in the middle of our enemies. The best way to take care is to stay under God's protection. Remember, if He's not perfect, neither are we."

They embraced quickly and Shmuel got down from the wagon.

"Goodbye, sweetheart," he called to the horse. "Good-bye, Yakov, I'll think of you when I say the Eighteen Blessings. If you ever see Raisl, tell her her father is waiting."

Shmuel trudged back towards the synagogue. When he was quite far away Yakov felt a pang for having forgotten to slip him a ruble or two.

"Get on now." The nag flicked an ear, roused itself for a short trot, then slowed to a tired walk.

"It'll be some trip," the fixer thought.

The horse stopped abruptly as a field mouse skittered across the road.

"Gidap, goddamit"—but the nag wouldn't move.

A peasant passed by with a long-horned bullock, prodding the animal with a stick.

"A horse understands a whip," he said across the road in Russian.

Yakov belabored the beast with the birch rod until he drew blood. The nag whinnied but remained tightly immobile on the road. The peasant, after watching awhile, moved on.

"You son-of-a-bitch," said the fixer to the horse, "we'll never get to Kiev."

He was at the point of despair when a brown dog rustling through a blanket of dead leaves under some trees came onto the road, yelping at the horse. The nag hurried forward, Yakov barely grabbing the reins. The dog chased them, barking sharply at the horse's hooves, then at a turn in the road, disappeared. But the wagon rolled on, bucket rattling, its wheels wobbling, the nag trotting as fast as it could.

It clip-clopped along the hard dirt road, on one side of which flowed a mild stream below a sloping embankment; and on the other were the scattered log huts of a peasant village, their roofs covered with rotting straw. Despite poverty and the antics of too many pigs the huts looked better than the shtetl cottages. A bearded peasant chopped wood, a woman pumped water from the village well. They both stopped to stare at him. A verst from his town and he was a stranger in the world.

The horse trotted on, Yukov gazing at the fields, some plowed under, where oats, hay, sugar beets had grown, the haystacks standing dark against the woods. A crow flew slowly over the stubble of a wheatfield. The fixer found himself counting sheep and goats grazing in the communal meadows under lazy thick clouds. It had been a dank and dreary autumn, the dead leaves still hanging on half the trees in the woods around the fields. Last year at this time it had already snowed. Though as a rule he enjoyed the landscape, Yakov felt a weight on him. The buzz and sparkle of summer were gone. In the violet distance the steppe seemed melancholy, endless.

The cut on the horse's flank, though encrusted, still oozed red droplets and drew fleas he switched away without touching the animal. He thought his spirits would rise once he was out of the shtetl but felt no relief. The fixer was troubled by discontent, a deeper sense that he had had no choice about going than he wanted to admit. His few friends were left behind. His habits, his best memories such as they were, were there. But so was his shame. He was leaving because he had earned a worse living—although he hadn't become a gravedigger—than many he knew with fewer brains and less skill. He was leaving because he was childless husband—"alive but dead" the Talmud described such a man—as well as embittered, deserted one. Yet if she had been faithful he would have stayed. Then better she hadn't been. He should be grateful to be escaping from a fruitless life. Still, he was apprehensive of going to a city of strangers—Jews as well as Gentiles, strangers were strangers—in a sense a forbidden place. Holy Kiev, mother of Russian cities! He knew the towns for a dozen versts around but had only once, for a week in summer, been in Kiev. He felt the discontent of strangeness, of not knowing what was where, unable to predict or clearly visualize. All he could think of were the rows of shabby crowded tenements in the Podol. Would he go on in the same useless poverty and drab experience amid masses of Jews as poor as he, or somehow come to a better way of life? How at his age?—already thirty. Jobs for him were always scarce. With just the few rubles in his pocket how long would he last before starving? Why should tomorrow be better than today? Had he earned the privilege?

He had many fears, and since he rarely traveled long distances, had fears of traveling. The soles of his feet itched, which meant, the old wives said: "You will journey to a far-off place." So, good, but would he ever get there? The horse had slowed down again, a black year on its stupid head. Suppose those clouds, grown dark and heavy, cracked open on their undersides and poured

snow upon the world. Would the horse make it? He pictured the
snow falling thickly, in a few minutes turning the road and fields
white so you couldn't see where one ended and the other began,
the wagon filling up with snow. The nag would stop. Yakov might
switch him till his bones gleamed through the blood but the animal was the type that would quietly lie down in the snow to spite
him. "Brother, I'm tired. If you want to go on in this storm, go
in good health. But not me. I'll take sleep and if it's sleep forever,
so much the better. At least the snow is warm." The fixer saw
himself wandering in drifts until he perished.

But the horse said nothing, and it didn't look like snow—or rain
either. It was a brisk day beginning to be windy—it raised the
nag's mane—and though the horse moved leisurely it moved steadily. Yet as they went through a grove of black-branched trees, the
leafless twigs darkly intertwined high above Yakov's head, the
small wood grew gloomy, and the fixer still searching for a change
in the weather became actively nervous again. Shading his eyes
in the queer light, he peered ahead—a winding road, absolutely
snowless. Enough of this, he thought, I'd better eat. As though
it had read his mind the nag came to a stop before he pulled the
reins. Yakov got down off the seat, and taking hold of the bridle,
drew the horse to the side of the road. The horse spread its hind
legs and spattered a yellow stream on the road. Yakov urinated on
some brown ferns. Feeling better, he tore up several handfuls of
dry tussocky grass, and since he could locate no feedbag in the
wagon, fed it in fistfuls to the nag. The horse, its sides heaving,
chewed with its eroded yellow teeth until the grass foamed. The
fixer's stomach rumbled. He sat under a sunlit tree, raised his
sheepskin collar, and opened the food parcel. He ate part of a
cold boiled potato, chewing slowly, then half a cucumber sprinkled with coarse salt, with a piece of sour black bread. Ah, for
some tea, he thought, or if not that, some sweetened hot water.
Yakov fell asleep with his back to the tree, awoke in a hurry, and
climbed up on the wagon.

"It's late, goddamit, come on, move."

The nag wouldn't budge. The fixer reached for the switch. On second thought he climbed down, unhitched the rusty bucket and went looking for water. When he found a little stream the pail leaked, but he offered it, half full, to the horse, who wouldn't drink.

"Games I don't play." Yakov poured out the water, hitched the bucket on the hook under the wagon, and stepped up to the seat. He waved the switch till it whistled. The nag, lowering his ears, moved forward, if one could call it movement. At least is wasn't where it had been before. The fixer again whistled the air with the switch, and the horse, after an indecisive minute, began to trot. The wagon rattled on.

They had gone on a while when the wagon caught up with an old woman, a pilgrim walking slowly in the road, leaning on her long staff, a heavy peasant in black, wearing men's shoes and carrying a knapsack, a thick shawl wrapped around her head.

He drew over to the side to pass her but as he did Yakov called out, "A ride, granny?"

"May Jesus bless you." She had three gray teeth.

Jesus he didn't need. Bad luck, he thought. Yakov helped pull her up to the wagon seat and touched the nag with the birch whip. To his surprise the horse took up his trot. Then as the road turned, the right wheel struck a rock and broke with a crunch. The wagon teetered and sagged at the rear, the left wheel tilted inward.

The old woman crossed herself, slowly climbed down to the road, and walked on with her heavy stick. She did not look back.

Yakov cursed Shmuel for wishing the wagon on him. Jumping to the ground he examined the broken wheel. Its worn metal ring had come off. The wooden rim had caved in, splintering two spokes. The split hub leaked axle grease. He groaned.

After five minutes of stunned emptiness he got his tool sack out of the wagon, untied it and spread out the tools on the road. But with hatchet, saw, plane, tinsmith's shears, tri-square, putty, wire, pointed knife and two awls, the fixer couldn't fix what was broken. Under the best conditions it would take him a day to repair the wheel. He thought of buying one from a peasant if he could get one that fitted, or nearly fitted, but if so where was the peasant? When you didn't need them they were in your beard. Yakov tossed the pieces of broken wheel into the wagon. He tied up his tools and drearily waited for someone to come. Nobody came. He considered returning to the shtetl but remembered he had had enough. The wind was colder, sharper, got under his coat and between the shoulder blades. The sun was setting, the sky turning dark.

If I go slow maybe I can make it on three wheels to the next village.

He tried it, sitting lightly as far to the left on the seat as he could, and begged the nag to take it easy. To his relief they went forward, the back wheel squeaking, for half a verst. He had caught up with the pilgrim and was about to say she couldn't ride when the other rear wheel, grinding thickly against the axle, collapsed, the back of the wagon hitting the road with a crashing thud, the bucket crushed. The horse luched forward, snorted and reared. The fixer, his body tipped at a perilous angle, was paralyzed.

Eventually he got down off the seat. "Who invented my life?" Behind him was the empty treeless steppe, ahead the old woman. She had stopped before a huge wooden crucifix at the side of the road, crossed herself, and then slowly sinking to her knees, began to hit her head against the hard ground. She banged it until Yakov had a headache. The darkening steppe was here uninhabited. He feared fog and a raging wind. Unhitching the horse and drawing him out from under the wooden yoke, Yakov gathered together the reins. He backed the nag to the wagon seat, and climbing up on it, mounted the animal. No sooner up than down. The fixer placed his tool bag, book bundle, and parcels on the tilted seat, wound the reins around him, and remounted the horse. He slung the tools over his shoulder, and with his left hand held the other things as they rested on the horse's back, his right hand grasping the reins. The horse galloped forward. To Yakov's surprise he did not fall off.

They skirted the old woman, prostrate at the cross. He felt foolish and uncertain on the horse but hung on. The nag had slowed to a trot, then to a dejected walk. It stood stock still. Yakov cursed it into eternity and eventually it came to life, once more inching forward. When they were on the move, the fixer, who had never sat on a horse before—he couldn't think why except that he had never had a horse—dreamed of good fortune, accomplishment, affluence. He had a comfortable home, good business—maybe a small factory of some kind—a faithful wife, dark-haired, pretty, and three healthy children, God bless them. But when he was becalmed on the nag he thought blackly of his father-in-law, beat the beast with his fist, and foresaw for himself a useless future. Yakov pleaded with the animal to make haste—it was dark and the steppe wind cut keenly, but freed of the wagon the horse examined the world. He also stopped to crop grass, tearing it audibly with his eroded teeth, and wandering from one side of the road to the other. Once in a while he turned and trotted back a few steps. Yakov, frantic, threatened the switch, but they both knew he had none. In desperation he kicked the beast with his heels. The nag bucked and for a perilous few minutes it was like being in a rowboat on a stormy sea. Having barely survived, Yakov stopped kicking. He considered ditching his goods, hoping the lightened load might speed things up, but didn't dare.

"I'm a bitter man, you bastard horse. Come to your senses or you'll suffer."

It availed him nothing.

By then it was pitch dark. The wind boomed. The steppe was a black sea full of strange voices. Here nobody spoke Yiddish, and the nag, maybe feeling the strangeness of it, began to trot and soon came close to flight. Though the fixer was not a superstitious man he had been a superstitious boy, and he recalled Lilith, Queen of Evil Spirits, and the Fish-witch who tickled travelers to death or otherwise made herself helpful. Ghosts rose like smoke in the Ukraine. From time to time he felt a presence at his back but would not turn. Then a yellow moon rose like a flower growing and lit the empty steppe deep into the shadowy distance. The distance glowed. It'll be a long night, the fixer thought. They galloped through a peasant village, its long-steepled church yellow in moonlight, the squat thatched huts dark, no lights anywhere. Though he smelled woodsmoke he saw none. Yakov considered dismounting, knocking on a strange door and begging for a night's lodging. But he felt that if he got off the horse he would never get back on. He was afraid he might be robbed of his few rubles, so he stayed put and made uncertain progress. The sky was thick with stars, the wind blowing cold in his face. Once he slept momentarily and woke in shivering sweat from a nightmare. He thought he was irretrievably lost, but to his amazement, before him in the distance rose a vast height glowing in dim moonlight and sprinkled sparsely with lights, at the foot of which ran a broad dark river reflecting the half-hidden moon. The nag stopped jogging and it took them an almost endless hour to make the last half verst to the water.

It was freezing cold but the wind was down on the Dnieper. There was no ferry, the boatman said. "Closed down. Closed. Shut." He waved his arms as though talking to a foreigner although Yakov had spoken to him in Russian. That the ferry had stopped running sharpened the fixer's desire to get across the river. He hoped to rent a bed at an inn and wake early to look for work.

"I'll row you across for a ruble," the boatman said.

"Too much," Yakov answered, though deadly tired. "Which way to the bridge?"

"Six or eight versts. A long way for the same thing."

"A ruble," the fixer groaned. "Who's got that much money?"

"You can take it or leave it. It's no easy thing rowing across a dangerous river on a pitch-black night. We might both drown."

"What would I do with my horse?" The fixer spoke more to himself.

"That's none of my business." The boatman, his shoulders like a tree trunk, and wearing a shaggy grizzled beard, blew out one full nostril on a rock, then the other. The white of his right eye was streaked with blood.

"Look, mate, why do you make more trouble than it's worth? Even if I could haul it across, which I can't, the beast will die on you. It doesn't take a long look to see he's on his last legs. Look at him trembling. Listen to him breathing like a gored bull."

"I was hoping to sell him in Kiev."

"What fool would buy a bag of old bones?"

"I thought maybe a horse butcher or someone—at least the skin."

"I say the horse is dead," said the boatman, "but you can save a ruble if you're smart. I'll take him for the cost of the trip. It's a bother to me and I'll be lucky to get fifty kopeks for the carcass, but I'll do you the favor, seeing you're a stranger."

He's only given me trouble, the fixer thought.

He stepped into the rowboat with his bag of tools, books, and other parcels. The boatman untied the boat, dipped both oars into the water and they were off.

The nag, tethered to a paling, watched from the moonlit short.

Like an old Jew he looks, thought the fixer.

The horse whinnied, and when that proved useless, farted loudly.

"I don't recognize the accent you speak," said the boatman, pulling the oars. "It's Russian but from what province?"

"I've lived in Latvia as well as other places," the fixer muttered.

"At first I thought you were a goddam Pole. Pan whosis, Pani whatsis." The boatman laughed, then snickered. "Or maybe a motherfucking Jew. But though you're dressed like a Russian you look more like a German, may the devil destroy them all, excepting yourself and yours of course."

"Latvian," said Yakov.

"Anyway, God save us all from the bloody Jews," the boatman said as he rowed, "those long-nosed, pock-marked, cheating, bloodsucking parasites. They'd rob us of daylight if they could. They foul up earth and air with their body stink and garlic breaths, and Russia will be done to death by the diseases they spread unless we make an end to it. A Jew's a devil—it's a known fact—and if you ever watch one peel off his stinking boot you'll see a split hoof, it's true. I know, for as the Lord is my witness, I saw one with my own eyes. He thought nobody was looking, but I saw his hoof as plain as day."

He stared at Yakov with the bloody eye. The fixer's foot itched but he didn't touch it.

Let him talk, he thought, yet he shivered.

"Day after day they crap up the Motherland," the boatman went on monotonously, "and the only way to save ourselves is to wipe them out. I don't mean kill a Zhid now and then with a blow of the fist or kick in the head, but wipe them all out, which we've sometimes tried but never done as it should be done. I say we ought to call our menfolk together, armed with guns, knives, pitchforks, clubs—anything that will kill a Jew—and when the church bells begin to ring we move on the Zhidy quarter, which you can tell by the stink, routing them out of wherever they're hiding—in attics, cellars, or ratholes—bashing in their brains, stabbing their herring-filled guts, shooting off their snotty noses, no exception made for young or old, because if you spare any they breed like rats and then the job's to do all over again.

"And then when we've slaughtered the whole cursed tribe of them—and the same is done in every province throughout Russia, wherever we can smoke them out—though we've got most of them nice and bunched up in the Pale—we'll pile up the corpses and soak them with benzine and light fires that people will enjoy all over the world. Then when that's done we hose the stinking ashes away and divide the rubles and jewels and silver and furs and all the other loot they stole, or give it back to the poor who it rightfully belongs to anyway. You can take my word—the time's not far off when everything I say, we will do, because our Lord, who they crucified, wants his rightful revenge."

He dropped an oar and crossed himself.

Yakov fought an impulse to do the same. His bag of prayer things fell with a plop into the Dnieper and sank like lead.

Part Two

The Assistant

The early November street was dark though night had ended, but the wind, to the grocer's surprise, already clawed. It flung his apron into his face as he bent for the two milk cases at the curb. Morris Bober dragged the heavy boxes to the door, panting. A large brown bag of hard rolls stood in the doorway along with the sour-faced, gray-haired Poilisheh huddled there, who wanted one.

"What's the matter so late?"

"Ten after six," said the grocer.

"Is cold," she complained.

Turning the key in the lock he let her in. Usually he lugged in the milk and lit the gas radiators, but the Polish woman was impatient. Morris poured the bag of rolls into a wire basket on the counter and found an unseeded one for her. Slicing it in halves, he wrapped it in white store paper. She tucked the roll into her cord market bag and left three pennies on the counter. He rang up the sale on an old noisy cash register, smoothed and put away the bag the rolls had come in, finished pulling in the milk, and stored the bottles at the bottom of the refrigerator. He lit the gas radiator at the front of the store and went into the back to light the one there.

He boiled up coffee in a blackened enamel pot and sipped it, chewing on a roll, not tasting what he was eating. After he had cleaned up he waited; he waited for Nick Fuso, the upstairs tenant, a young mechanic who worked in a garage in the neighborhood. Nick came in every morning around seven for twenty cents' worth of ham and a loaf of bread.

But the front door opened and a girl of ten entered, her face pinched and eyes excited. His heart held no welcome for her.

"My mother says," she said quickly, "can you trust her till tomorrow for a pound of butter, loaf of rye bread and a small bottle of cider vinegar?"

He knew the mother. "No more trust."

The girl burst into tears.

Morris gave her a quarter-pound of butter, the bread and vinegar. He found a penciled spot on the worn counter, near the cash register, and wrote a sum under "Drunk Woman." The total now came to $2.03, which he never hoped to see. But Ida would nag if she noticed a new figure, so he reduced the amount to $1.61. His peace—the little he lived with—was worth forty-two cents.

He sat in a chair at the round wooden table in the rear of the store and scanned, with raised brows, yesterday's Jewish paper that he had already thoroughly read. From time to time he looked absently through the square windowless window cut through the wall, to see if anybody had by chance come into the store. Sometimes when he looked up from his newspaper, he was startled to see a customer standing silently at the counter.

Now the store looked like a long dark tunnel.

The grocer sighed and waited. Waiting he thought he did poorly. When times were bad time was bad. It died as he waited, stinking in his nose.

A workman came in for a fifteen-cent can of King Oscar Norwegian sardines.

Morris went back to waiting. In twenty-one years the store had changed little. Twice he had painted all over, once added new shelving. The old-fashioned double windows at the front a carpenter had made into a large single one. Ten years ago the sign hanging outside fell to the ground but he had never replaced it. Once, when business hit a long good spell, he had had the wooden icebox ripped out and a new white refrigerated showcase put in. The showcase stood at the front in line with the old counter and he often leaned against it as he stared out of the window. Otherwise the store was the same. Years ago it was more a delicatessen; now, though he still sold a little delicatessen, it was more a poor grocery.

A half-hour passed. When Nick Fuso failed to appear, Morris got up and stationed himself at the front window, behind a large cardboard display sign the beer people had rigged up in an otherwise empty window. After a while the hall door opened, and Nick came out in a thick, hand-knitted green sweater. He trotted around the corner and soon returned carrying a bag of groceries. Morris was now visible at the window. Nick saw the look on his face but didn't look long. He ran into the house, trying to make it seem it was the wind that was chasing him. The door slammed behind him, a loud door.

The grocer gazed into the street. He wished fleetingly that he could once more be out in the open, as when he was a boy—never in the house, but the sound of the blustery wind frightened him. He thought again of selling the store but who would buy? Ida still hoped to sell. Every day she hoped. The thought caused him grimly to smile, although he did not feel like smiling. It was an impossible idea so he tried to put it out of his mind. Still, there were times when he went into the back, poured himself a spout of coffee and pleasantly thought of selling. Yet if he miraculously did, where would he go, where? He had a moment of uneasiness as he pictured himself without a roof over his head. There he stood in all kinds of weather, drenched in rain, and the snow froze on his head. No, not for an age had he lived a whole day in the open. As a boy, always running in the muddy, rutted streets of the village, or across the fields, or bathing with the other boys in the river; but as a man, in America, he rarely saw the sky. In the early days when he drove a horse and wagon, yes, but not since his first store. In a store you were entombed.

The milkman drove up to the door in his truck and hurried in, a bull, for his empties. He lugged out a caseful and returned with two half-pints of light cream. Then Otto Vogel, the meat provisions man, entered, a bushy-mustached German carrying a smoked liverwurst and string of wieners in his oily meat basket. Morris paid cash for the liverwurst; from a German he wanted no favors. Otto left with the wieners. The bread driver, new on the route, exchanged three fresh loaves for three stale and walked out without a word. Leo, the cake man, glanced hastily at the package cake on top of the refrigerator and called, "See you Monday, Morris."

Morris didn't answer.

Leo hesitated. "Bad all over, Morris."

"Here is the worst."

"See you Monday."

A young housewife from close by bought sixty-three cents' worth; another came in for forty-one cents'. He had earned his first cash dollar for the day.

Breitbart, the bulb peddler, laid down his two enormous cartons of light bulbs and diffidently entered the back.

"Go in," Morris urged. He boiled up some tea and served it in a thick glass, with a slice of lemon. The peddler eased himself into a chair, derby hat and coat on, and gulped the hot tea, his Adam's apple bobbing.

"So how goes now?" asked the grocer.

"Slow," shrugged Breitbart.

Morris sighed. "How is your boy?"

Breitbart nodded absently, then picked up the Jewish paper and read. After ten minutes he got up, scratched all over, lifted across his thin shoulders the two large cartons tied together with clothesline and left.

Morris watched him go.

The world suffers. *He* felt every schmerz.

At lunchtime Ida came down. She had cleaned the whole house.

Morris was standing before the faded couch, looking out of the rear window at the back yards. He had been thinking of Ephraim.

His wife saw his wet eyes.

"So stop sometime, please." Her own grew wet.

He went to the sink, caught cold water in his cupped palms and dipped his face into it.

"The Italyener," he said, drying himself, "bought this morning across the street."

She was irritated. "Give him for twenty-nine dollars five rooms so he should spit in your face."

"A cold water flat," he reminded her.

"You put in gas radiators."

"Who says he spits? This I didn't say."

"You said something to him not nice?"

"Me?"

"Then why he went across the street?"

"Why? Go ask him," he said angrily.

"How much you took in till now?"

"Dirt."

She turned away.

He absent-mindedly scratched a match and lit a cigarette.

"Stop with the smoking," she nagged.

He took a quick drag, clipped the butt with his thumb nail and quickly thrust it under his apron into his pants pocket. The smoke made him cough. He coughed harshly, his face lit like a tomato. Ida held her hands over her ears. Finally he brought up a gob of phlegm and wiped his mouth with his handkerchief, then his eyes.

"Cigarettes," she said bitterly. "Why don't you listen what the doctor tells you?"

"Doctors," he remarked.

Afterward he noticed the dress she was wearing. "What is the picnic?"

Ida said, embarrassed, "I thought to myself maybe will come today the buyer."

She was fifty-one, nine years younger than he, her thick hair still almost all black. But her face was lined, and her legs hurt when she stood too long on them, although she now wore shoes with arch supports. She had waked that morning resenting the grocer for having dragged her, so many years ago, out of a Jewish neighborhood into this. She missed to this day their old friends and landsleit—lost for parnusseh unrealized. That was bad enough, but on top of their isolation, the endless worry about money embittered her. She shared unwillingly the grocer's fate though she did not show it and her dissatisfaction went no farther than nagging—her guilt that she had talked him into a grocery store when he was in the first year of evening high school, preparing, he had said, for pharmacy. He was, through the years, a hard man to move. In the past she could sometimes resist him, but the weight of his endurance was too much for her now.

"A buyer," Morris grunted, "will come next Purim."

"Don't be so smart. Karp telephoned him."

"Karp," he said in disgust. "Where he telephoned—the cheap-skate?"

"Here."

"When?"

"Yesterday. You were sleeping."

"What did he told him?"

"For sale a store—yours, cheap."

"What do you mean cheap?"

"The key is worth now nothing. For the stock and the fixtures that they are worth also nothing, maybe three thousand, maybe less."

"I paid four."

"Twenty-one years ago," she said irritably. "So don't sell, go in auction."

"He wants the house too?"

"Karp don't know. Maybe."

"Big mouth. Imagine a man that they held him up four times in the last three years and he still don't take in a telephone. What he says ain't worth a cent. He promised me he wouldn't put in a grocery around the corner, but what did he put?—a grocery.

Why does he bring me buyers? Why didn't he keep out the German around the corner?"

She sighed. "He tries to help you now because he feels sorry for you."

"Who needs his sorrow?" Morris said. "Who needs him?"

"So why *you* didn't have the sense to make out of your grocery a wine and liquor store when came out the licenses?"

"Who had cash for stock?"

"So if you don't have, don't talk."

"A business for drunken bums."

"A business is a business. What Julius Karp takes in next door in a day we don't take in in two weeks."

But Ida saw he was annoyed and changed the subject.

"I told you to oil the floor."

"I forgot."

"I asked you special. By now would be dry."

"I will do later."

"Later the customers will walk in the oil and make everything dirty."

"What customers?" he shouted. "Who customers? Who comes in here?"

"Go," she said quietly. "Go upstairs and sleep. I will oil myself."

But he got out the oil can and mop and oiled the floor until the wood shone darkly. No one had come in.

She had prepared his soup. "Helen left this morning without breakfast."

"She wasn't hungry."

"Something worries her."

He said with sarcasm, "What worries her?" Meaning: the store, his health, that most of her meager wages went to keep up payments on the house; that she had wanted a college education but had got instead a job she disliked. Her father's daughter, no wonder she didn't feel like eating.

"If she will only get married," Ida murmured.

"She will get."

"Soon." She was on the verge of tears.

He grunted.

"I don't understand why she don't see Nat Pearl anymore. All summer they went together like lovers."

"A showoff."

"He'll be someday a rich lawyer."

"I don't like him."

"Louis Karp also likes her. I wish she will give him a chance."

"A stupe," Morris said, "like the father."

"Everybody is a stupe but not Morris Bober."

He was staring out at the back yards.

"Eat already and go to sleep," she said impatiently.

He finished the soup and went upstairs. The going up was easier than coming down. In the bedroom, sighing, he drew down the black window shades. He was half asleep, so pleasant was the anticipation. Sleep was his one true refreshment; it excited him to go to sleep. Morris took off his apron, tie and trousers, and laid them on a chair. Sitting at the edge of the sagging wide bed, he unlaced his misshapen shoes and slid under the cold covers in shirt, long underwear and white socks. He nudged his eye into the pillow and waited to grow warm. He crawled toward sleep. But upstairs Tessie Fuso was running the vacuum cleaner, and though the grocer tried to blot the incident out of his mind, he remembered Nick's visit to the German and on the verge of sleep felt bad.

He recalled the bad times he had lived through, but now times were worse than in the past; now they were impossible. His store was always a marginal one, up today, down tomorrow—as the wind blew. Overnight business could go down enough to hurt; yet as a rule it slowly recovered—sometimes it seemed to take forever—went up, not high enough to be really *up*, only not down. When he had first bought the grocery it was all right for the neighborhood; it had got worse as the neighborhood had. Yet even a year ago, staying open seven days a week, sixteen hours a day, he could still eke out a living. What kind of living?—a living; you lived. Now, though he toiled the same hard hours, he was close to bankruptcy, his patience torn. In the past when bad times came he had somehow lived through them, and when good times returned, they more or less returned to him. But now, since the appearance of H. Schmitz across the street ten months ago, all times were bad.

Last year a broken tailor, a poor man with a sick wife, had locked up his shop and gone away, and from the minute of the store's emptiness Morris had felt a gnawing anxiety. He went with hesitation to Karp, who owned the building, and asked him to please keep out another grocery. In this kind of neighborhood one was more than enough. If another squeezed in they would both starve. Karp answered that the neighborhood was better than Morris gave it credit (for schnapps, thought the grocer), but he promised he would look for another tailor or maybe a shoemaker, to rent to. He said so but the grocer didn't believe him. Yet weeks went by and the store stayed empty. Though Ida pooh-poohed his worries, Morris could not overcome his underlying dread. Then one day, as he daily expected, there appeared a sign in the empty store window, announcing the coming of a new fancy delicatessen and grocery.

Morris ran to Karp. "What did you do to me?"

The liquor dealer said with a one-shouldered shrug, "You saw how long stayed empty the store. Who will pay my taxes? But don't worry," he added, "he'll sell more delicatessen but you'll sell more groceries. Wait, you'll see he'll bring you in customers."

Morris groaned; he knew his fate.

Yet as the days went by, the store still sitting empty—emptier, he found himself thinking maybe the new business would never materialize. Maybe the man had changed his mind. It was possible he had seen how poor the neighborhood was and would not attempt to open the new place. Morris wanted to ask Karp if he had guessed right but could not bear to humiliate himself further.

Often after he had locked his grocery at night, he would go secretly around the corner and cross the quiet street. The empty store, dark and deserted, was one door to the left of the corner drugstore; and if no one was looking the grocer would peer through its dusty window, trying to see through shadows whether the emptiness had changed. For two months it stayed the same, and every night he went away reprieved. Then one time—after he saw that Karp was, for once, avoiding him—he spied a web of shelves sprouting from the rear wall, and that shattered the hope he had climbed into.

In a few days the shelves stretched many arms along the other walls, and soon the whole tiered and layered place glowed with new paint. Morris told himself to stay away but he could not help coming nightly to inspect, appraise, then guess the damage, in dollars, to himself. Each night as he looked, in his mind he destroyed what had been built, tried to make it nothing, but the growth was too quick. Every day the place flowered with new fixtures—streamlined counters, the latest refrigerator, fluorescent lights, a fruit stall, a chromium cash register; then from the wholesalers arrived a mountain of cartons and wooden boxes of all sizes, and one night there appeared in the white light a stranger, a gaunt German with a German pompadour, who spent the silent night hours, a dead cigar stuck in his teeth, packing out symmetrical rows of brightly labeled cans, jars, gleaming bottles. Though Morris hated the new store, in a curious way he loved it too, so that sometimes as he entered his own old-fashioned place of business, he could not stand the sight of it; and now he understood why Nick Fuso had that morning run around the corner and crossed the street—to taste the newness of the place and be waited on by Heinrich Schmitz, an energetic German dressed like a doctor, in a white duck jacket. And that was where many of his other customers had gone, and stayed, so that his own poor living was cut in impossible half.

Morris tried hard to sleep but couldn't and grew restless in bed. After another quarter of an hour he decided to dress and go downstairs, but there drifted into his mind, with ease and no sorrow, the form and image of his boy Ephraim, gone so long from him, and he fell deeply and calmly asleep.

Helen Bober squeezed into a subway seat between two women and was on the last page of a chapter when a man dissolved in front of her and another appeared; she knew without looking that Nat Pearl was standing there. She thought she would go on reading, but couldn't, and shut her book.

"Hello, Helen." Nat touched a gloved hand to a new hat. He was cordial but as usual held back something—his future. He carried a fat law book, so she was glad to be protected with a book of her own. But not enough protected, for her hat and coat felt suddenly shabby, a trick of the mind, because on her they would still do.

"Don Quixote"?

She nodded.

He seemed respectful, then said in an undertone, "I haven't seen you a long time. Where've you been keeping yourself?"

She blushed under her clothes.

"Did I offend you in some way or other?"

Both of the women beside her seemed stolidly deaf. One held a rosary in her heavy hand.

"No." The offense was hers against herself.

"So what's the score?" Nat's voice was low, his gray eyes annoyed.

"No score," she murmured.

"How so?"

"You're you, I'm me."

This he considered a minute, then remarked, "I haven't much of a head for oracles."

But she felt she had said enough.

He tried another way. "Betty asks for you."

"Give her my best." She had not meant it but this sounded funny because they all lived on the same block, separated by one house.

Tight-jawed, he opened his book. She returned to hers, hiding her thoughts behind the antics of a madman until memory overthrew him and she found herself ensnared in scenes of summer that she would gladly undo, although she loved the season; but how could you undo what you had done again in the fall, unwillingly willing? Virginity she thought she had parted with without sorrow, yet was surprised by torments of conscience, or was it disappointment at being valued under her expectations? Nat Pearl, handsome, cleft-chinned, gifted, ambitious, had wanted without too much trouble a lay and she, half in love, had obliged and regretted. Not the loving, but that it had taken her so long to realize how little he wanted. Not her, Helen Bober.

Why should he?—magna cum laude, Columbia, now in his second year at law school, she only a high school graduate with a year's evening college credit mostly in lit; he with first-rate prospects, also rich friends he had never bothered to introduce her to; she as poor as her name sounded, with little promise of a better future. She had more than once asked herself if she had meant by her favors to work up a claim on him. Always she denied it. She had wanted, admittedly, satisfaction, but more than that—respect for the giver of what she had to give, had hoped desire would become more than just that. She wanted, simply, a future in love. Enjoyment she had somehow had, felt very moving the freedom of fundamental intimacy with a man. Though she wished for more of the same, she wanted it without aftermath of conscience, or pride, or sense of waste. So she promised herself next time it would go the other way; first mutual love, then loving, harder maybe on the nerves, but easier in memory. Thus she had reasoned, until one night in September, when coming up to see his sister Betty, she had found herself alone in the house with Nat and had done again what she had promised herself she wouldn't. Afterward she fought self-hatred. Since then, to this day, without telling him why, she had avoided Nat Pearl.

Two stations before their stop, Helen shut her book, got up in silence and left the train. On the platform, as the train moved away, she caught a glimpse of Nat standing before her empty seat, calmly reading. She walked on, lacking, wanting, not wanting, not happy.

Coming up the subway steps, she went into the park by a side entrance, and despite the sharp wind and her threadbare coat, took the long way home. The leafless trees left her with unearned sadness. She mourned the long age before spring and feared loneliness in winter. Wishing she hadn't come, she left the park, searching the faces of strangers although she couldn't stand their stares. She went quickly along the Parkway, glancing with envy into the lighted depths of private houses that were, for no reason she could give, except experience, not for her. She promised herself she would save every cent possible and register next fall for a full program at NYU, night.

When she reached her block, a row of faded yellow brick houses, two stories squatting on ancient stores, Sam Pearl, stifling a yawn, was reaching into his corner candy store window to put on the lamp. He snapped the string and the dull glow from the fly-specked globe fell upon her. Helen quickened her step. Sam, always sociable, a former cabbie, bulky, wearing bifocals and chewing gum, beamed at her but she pretended no see. Most of the day he sat hunched over dope sheets spread out on the soda fountain counter, smoking as he chewed gum, making smeary marks with a pencil stub under horses' names. He neglected the store; his wife Goldie was the broad-backed one, yet she did not much complain, because Sam's luck with the nags was exceptional and he had nicely supported Nat in college until the scholarships started rolling in.

Around the corner, through the many-bottled window that blinked in neon "KARP wines and liquors," she glimpsed paunchy Julius Karp, with bushy eyebrows and an ambitious mouth, blowing imaginary dust off a bottle as he slipped a deft fifth of something into a paper bag, while Louis, slightly popeyed son and heir, looking up from clipping to the quick his poor fingernails, smiled amiably upon a sale. The Karps, Pearls and Bobers, representing attached houses and stores, but otherwise detachment, made up the small Jewish segment of this gentile community. They had somehow, her father first, then Karp, later Pearl, drifted together here where no other Jews dwelt, except on the far fringes of the neighborhood. None of them did well and were too poor to move elsewhere until Karp, who with a shoe store that barely made him a living, got the brilliant idea after Prohibition gurgled down the drain and liquor licenses were offered to the public, to borrow cash from a white-bearded rich uncle and put in for one. To everybody's surprise he got the license, though Karp, when asked how, winked a heavy-lidded eye and answered nothing. Within a short time after cheap shoes had become expensive bottles, in spite of the poor neighborhood—or maybe because of it, Helen supposed—he became astonishingly successful and retired his overweight wife from the meager railroad flat above the store to a big house on the Parkway—from which she hardly ever stepped forth—the house complete with two-car garage and Mercury; and at the same time as Karp changed his luck—to hear her father tell it—he became wise without brains.

The grocer, on the other hand, had never altered his fortune, unless degrees of poverty meant alteration, for luck and he were, if not natural enemies, not good friends. He labored long hours, was the soul of honesty—he could not escape his honesty, it was bedrock; to cheat would cause an explosion in him, yet he trusted cheaters—coveted nobody's nothing always got poorer. The harder he worked—his toil was a form of time devouring time—the less he seemed to have. He was Morris Bober and could be nobody more fortunate. With that name you had no sure sense of property, as if it were in your blood and history not to possess, or if by some miracle to own something, to do so on the verge of loss. At the end you were sixty and had less than at thirty. It was, she thought, surely a talent.

Helen removed her hat as she entered the grocery. "Me," she called, as she had from childhood. It meant that whoever was sitting in the back should sit and not suddenly think he was going to get rich.

Morris awoke, soured by the long afternoon sleep. He dressed, combed his hair with a broken comb and trudged downstairs, a heavy-bodied man with sloping shoulders and bushy gray hair in need of a haircut. He came down with his apron on. Although he felt chilly he poured out a cup of cold coffee, and backed against the radiator, slowly sipped it. Ida sat at the table, reading.

"Why you let me sleep so long?" the grocer complained.

She didn't answer.

"Yesterday or today's paper?"

"Yesterday."

He rinsed the cup and set it on the top of the gas range. In the store he rang up "no sale" and took a nickel out of the drawer. Morris lifted the lid of the cash register, struck a match on the underside of the counter, and holding the flame cupped in his palm, peered at the figure of his earnings. Ida had taken in three dollars. Who could afford a paper?

Nevertheless he went for one, doubting the small pleasure he would get from it. What was so worth reading about the world? Through Karp's window, as he passed, he saw Louis waiting on a customer while four others crowded the counter. Der oilem iz a goilem. Morris took the *Forward* from the newsstand and dropped a nickel into the cigar box. Sam Pearl, working over a green racing sheet, gave him a wave of his hammy hand. They never bothered to talk. What did he know about race horses? What did the other know of the tragic quality of life? Wisdom flew over his hard head.

The grocer returned to the rear of his store and sat on the couch, letting the diminishing light in the yard fall upon the paper. He read nearsightedly, with eyes stretched wide, but his thoughts would not let him read long. He put down the newspaper.

"So where is your buyer?" he asked Ida.

Looking absently into the store she did not reply.

"You should sell long ago the store," she remarked after a minute.

"When the store was good, who wanted to sell? After came bad times, who wanted to buy?"

"Everything we did too late. The store we didn't sell in time.

I said, 'Morris, sell now the store.' You said, 'Wait.' What for? The house we bought too late, so we have still a big mortgage that it's hard to pay every month. 'Don't buy,' I said, 'times are bad.' 'Buy,' you said, 'will get better. We will save rent.' "

He answered nothing. If you had failed to do the right thing, talk was useless.

When Helen entered, she asked if the buyer had come. She had forgotten about him but remembered when she saw her mother's dress.

Opening her purse, she took out her pay check and handed it to her father. The grocer, without a word, slipped it under his apron into his pants pocket.

"Not yet," Ida answered, also embarrassed. "Maybe later."

"Nobody goes in the night to buy a store," Morris said. "The time to go is in the day to see how many customers. If this man comes here he will see with one eye the store is dead, then he will run home."

"Did you eat lunch?" Ida asked Helen.

"Yes."

"What did you eat?"

"I don't save menus, Mama."

"Your supper is ready." Ida lit the flame under the pot on the gas range.

"What makes you think he'll come today?" Helen asked her.

"Karp told me yesterday. He knows a refugee that he looks to buy a grocery. He works in the Bronx, so he will be here late."

Morris shook his head.

"He's a young man," Ida went on, "maybe thirty—thirty-two. Karp says he saved a little cash. He can make alterations, buy new goods, fix up modern, advertise a little and make here a nice business."

"Karp should live so long," the grocer said.

"Let's eat." Helen sat at the table.

Ida said she would eat later.

"What about you, Papa?"

"I am not hungry." He picked up his paper.

She ate alone. It would be wonderful to sell out and move but the possibility struck her as remote. If you had lived so long in one place, all but two years of your life, you didn't move out overnight.

Afterward she got up to help with the dishes but Ida wouldn't let her. "Go rest," she said.

Helen took her things and went upstairs.

She hated the drab five-room flat; a gray kitchen she used for breakfast so she could quickly get out to work in the morning. The living room was colorless and cramped; for all its overstuffed furniture of twenty years ago it seemed barren because it was lived in so little, her parents being seven days out of seven in the store; even their rare visitors, when invited upstairs, preferred to remain in the back. Sometimes Helen asked a friend up, but she went to other people's houses if she had a choice. Her bedroom was another impossibility, tiny, dark, despite the two by three foot opening in the wall, through which she could see the living room windows; and at night Morris and Ida had to pass through her room to get to theirs, and from their bedroom back to the bathroom. They had several times talked of giving her the big room, the only comfortable one in the house, but there was no place else that would hold their double bed. The fifth room was a small icebox off the second floor stairs, in which Ida stored a few odds and ends of clothes and furniture. Such was home. Helen had once in anger remarked that the place was awful to live in, and it had made her feel bad that her father had felt so bad.

She heard Morris's slow footsteps on the stairs. He came aimlessly into the living room and tried to relax in a stiff armchair. He sat with sad eyes, saying nothing, which was how he began when he wanted to say something.

When she and her brother were kids, at least on Jewish holidays Morris would close the store and venture forth to Second Avenue to see a Yiddish play, or take the family visiting; but after

Ephraim died he rarely went beyond the corner. Thinking about his life always left her with a sense of the waste of her own.

She looks like a little bird, Morris thought. Why should she be lonely? Look how pretty she looks. Whoever saw such blue eyes?

He reached into his pants pocket and took out a five-dollar bill.

"Take," he said, rising and embarrassedly handing her the money. "You will need for shoes."

"You just gave me five dollars downstairs."

"Here is five more."

"Wednesday was the first of the month, Pa."

"I can't take away from you all your pay."

"You're not taking, I'm giving."

She made him put the five away. He did, with renewed shame. "What did I ever give you? Even your college education I took away."

"It was my own decision not to go, yet maybe I will yet. You can never tell."

"How can you go? You are twenty-three years old."

"Aren't you always saying a person's never too old to go to school?"

"My child," he sighed, "for myself I don't care, for you I want the best but what did I give you?"

"I'll give myself," she smiled. "There's hope."

With this he had to be satisfied. He still conceded her a future.

But before he went down, he said gently, "What's the matter you stay home so much lately? You had a fight with Nat?"

"No." Blushing, she answered, "I don't think we see things in the same way."

He hadn't the heart to ask more.

Going down, he met Ida on the stairs and knew she would cover the same ground.

In the evening there was a flurry of business. Morris's mood quickened and he exchanged pleasantries with the customers. Carl Johnsen, the Swedish painter, whom he hadn't seen in weeks, came in with a wet smile and bought two dollars' worth of beer, cold cuts and sliced Swiss cheese. The grocer was at first worried he would ask to charge—he had never paid what he owed on the books before Morris had stopped giving trust—but the painter had the cash. Mrs. Anderson, an old loyal customer, bought for a dollar. A stranger then came in and left eighty-five cents. After him two more customers appeared. Morris felt a little surge of hope. Maybe things were picking up. But after half-past eight his hands grew heavy with nothing to do. For years he had been the only one for miles around who stayed open at night and had just about made a living from it, but now Schmitz matched him hour for hour. Morris sneaked a little smoke, then began to cough. Ida pounded on the floor upstairs, so he clipped the butt and put it away. He felt restless and stood at the front window, watching the street. He watched a trolley go by. Mr. Lawler, formerly a customer, good for at least a fiver on Friday nights, passed the store. Morris hadn't seen him for months but knew where he was going. Mr. Lawler averted his gaze and hurried along. Morris watched him disappear around the corner. He lit a match and again checked the register—nine and a half dollars, not even expenses.

Julius Karp opened the front door and poked his foolish head in. "Podolsky came?"

"Who Podolsky?"

"The refugee."

Morris said in annoyance, "What refugee?"

With a grunt Karp shut the door behind him. He was short, pompous, a natty dresser in his advanced age. In the past, like Morris, he had toiled long hours in his shoe store, now he stayed all day in silk pajamas until it came time to relieve Louis before supper. Though the little man was insensitive and a blunderer, Morris had got along fairly well with him, but since Karp had rented the tailor shop to another grocer, sometimes they did not speak. Years ago Karp had spent much time in the back of the grocery, complaining of his poverty as if it were a new invention and he its first victim. Since his success with wines and liquors he came in less often, but he still visited Morris more than his welcome entitled him to, usually to run down the grocery and spout unwanted advice. His ticket of admission was his luck, which he gathered wherever he reached, at a loss, Morris thought, to somebody else. Once a drunk had heaved a rock at Karp's window, but it had shattered his. Another time, Sam Pearl gave the liquor dealer a tip on a horse, then forgot to place a bet himself. Karp collected five hundred for his ten-dollar bill. For years the grocer had escaped resenting the man's good luck, but lately he had caught himself wishing on him some small misfortune.

"Podolsky is the one I called up to take a look at your gesheft," Karp answered.

"Who is this refugee, tell me, an enemy yours?"

Karp stared at him unpleasantly.

"Does a man," Morris insisted, "send a friend he should buy such a store that you yourself took away from it the best business?"

"Podolsky ain't you," the liquor dealer replied. "I told him about this place. I said, 'The neighborhood is improving. You can buy cheap and build up this store. It's run down for years, nobody changed anything there for twenty years.'"

"You should live so long how much I changed—" Morris began but he didn't finish, for Karp was at the window, peering nervously into the dark street.

"You saw that gray car that just passed," the liquor dealer said. "This is the third time I saw it in the last twenty minutes." His eyes were restless.

Morris knew what worried him. "Put in a telephone in your store," he advised, "so you will feel better."

Karp watched the street for another minute and worriedly replied, "Not for a liquor store in this neighborhood. If I had a telephone, every drunken bum would call me to make deliveries, and when you go there they don't have a cent."

He opened the door but shut it in afterthought. "Listen, Morris," he said, lowering his voice, "if they come back again, I will lock my front door and put out my lights. Then I will call you from the back window so you can telephone the police."

"This will cost you five cents," Morris said grimly.

"My credit is class A."

Karp left the grocery, disturbed.

God bless Julius Karp, the grocer thought. Without him I would have my life too easy. God made Karp so a poor grocery man will not forget his life is hard. For Karp, he thought, it was miraculously not so hard, but what was there to envy? He would allow the liquor dealer his bottles and gelt just not to be him. Life was bad enough.

At nine-thirty a stranger came in for a box of matches. Fifteen minutes later Morris put out the lights in his window. The street was deserted except for an automobile parked in front of the laundry across the car tracks. Morris peered at it sharply but could see nobody in it. He considered locking up and going to bed, then decided to stay open the last few minutes. Sometimes a person came in at a minute to ten. A dime was a dime.

A noise at the side door which led into the hall frightened him.

"Ida?"

The door opened slowly. Tessie Fuso came in in her housecoat, a homely Italian girl with a big face.

"Are you closed, Mr. Bober?" she asked embarrassedly.

"Come in," said Morris.

"I'm sorry I came through the back way but I was undressed and didn't want to go out in the street."

"Don't worry."

"Please give me twenty cents' ham for Nick's lunch tomorrow."

He understood. She was making amends for Nick's trip around the corner that morning. He cut her an extra slice of ham.

Tessie bought also a quart of milk, package of paper napkins and loaf of bread. When she had gone he lifted the register lid.

Ten dollars. He thought he had long ago touched bottom but now knew there was none.

I slaved my whole life for nothing, he thought.

Then he heard Karp calling him from the rear. The grocer went inside, worn out.

Raising the window he called harshly, "What's the matter there?"

"Telephone the police," cried Karp. "The car is parked across the street."

"What car?"

"The holdupniks."

"There is nobody in this car, I saw myself."

"For God's sake, I tell you call the police. I will pay for the telephone."

Morris shut the window. He looked up the phone number and was about to dial the police when the store door opened and he hurried inside.

Two men were standing at the other side of the counter, with handkerchiefs over their faces. One wore a dirty yellow clotted one, the other's was white. The one with the white one began pulling out the store lights. It took the grocer a half-minute to comprehend that he, not Karp, was their victim.

Morris sat at the table, the dark light of the dusty bulb falling on his head, gazing dully at the few crumpled bills before him, including Helen's check, and the small pile of silver. The gunman with the dirty handkerchief, fleshy, wearing a fuzzy black hat, waved a pistol at the grocer's head. His pimply brow was thick with sweat; from time to time with furtive eyes he glanced into the darkened store. The other, a taller man in an old cap and torn sneakers, to control his trembling leaned against the sink, cleaning his fingernails with a matchstick. A cracked mirror hung behind him on the wall above the sink and every so often he turned to start into it.

"I know damn well this ain't everything you took in," said the heavy one to Morris, in a hoarse, unnatural voice. "Where've you got the rest hid?"

Morris, sick to his stomach, couldn't speak.

"Tell the goddam truth." He aimed the gun at the grocer's mouth.

"Times are bad," Morris muttered.

"You're a Jew lier."

The man at the sink fluttered his hand, catching the other's attention. They met in the center of the room, the other with the cap hunched awkwardly over the one in the fuzzy hat, whispering into his ear.

"No," snapped the heavy one sullenly.

His partner bent lower, whispering earnestly through his handkerchief.

"I say he hid it," the heavy one snarled, "and I'm gonna get it if I have to crack his goddam head."

At the table he whacked the grocer across the face.

Morris moaned.

The one at the sink hastily rinsed a cup and filled it with water. He brought it to the grocer, spilling some on his apron as he raised the cup to his lips.

Morris tried to swallow but managed only a dry sip. His frightened eyes sought the man's but he was looking elsewhere.

"Please," murmured the grocer.

"Hurry up," warned the one with the gun.

The tall one straightened up and gulped down the water. He rinsed the cup and placed it on a cupboard shelf.

He then began to hunt among the cups and dishes there and pulled out the pots on the bottom. Next, he went hurriedly through the drawers of an old bureau in the room, and on hands and knees searched under the couch. He ducked into the store, removed the empty cash drawer from the register and thrust his hand into the slot, but came up with nothing.

Returning to the kitchen he took the other by the arm and whispered to him urgently.

The heavy one elbowed him aside.

"We better scram out of here."

"Are you gonna go chicken on me?"

"That's all the dough he has, let's beat it."

"Business is bad," Morris muttered.

"You Jew ass is bad, you understand?"

"Don't hurt me."

"I will give you your last chance. Where have you got it hid?"

"I am a poor man." He spoke through cracked lips.

The one in the dirty handkerchief raised his gun. The other, staring into the mirror, waved frantically, his black eyes bulging, but Morris saw the blow descend and felt sick of himself, of soured expectations, endless frustration, the years gone up in smoke, he could not begin to count how many. He had hoped for much in America and got little. And because of him Helen and Ida had less. He had defrauded them, he and the bloodsucking store.

He fell without a cry. The end fitted the day. It was his luck, others had better.

During the week that Morris lay in bed with a thickly bandaged head, Ida tended the store fitfully. She went up and down twenty times a day until her bones ached and her head hurt with all her worries. Helen stayed home Saturday, a half-day in her place, and Monday, to help her mother, but she could not risk longer than that, so Ida, who ate in snatches and had worked up a massive nervousness, had to shut the store for a full day, although Morris angrily protested. He needed no attention, he insisted, and urged her to keep open at least half the day or he would lose his remaining few customers; but Ida, short of breath, said she hadn't the strength, her legs hurt. The grocer attempted to get up and pull on his pants but was struck by a violent headache and had to drag himself back to bed.

On the Tuesday the store was closed a man appeared in the neighborhood, a stranger who spent much of his time standing on

Sam Pearl's corner with a toothpick in his teeth, intently observing the people who passed by; or he would drift down the long block of stores, some empty, from Pearl's to the bar at the far end of the street. Beyond that was a freight yard, and in the distance, a bulky warehouse. After an occasional slow beer in the tavern, the stranger turned the corner and wandered past the high-fenced coal yard; he would go around the block until he got back to Sam's candy store. Once in a while the man would walk over to Morris's closed grocery, and with both hands shading his brow, stare through the window; sighing, he went back to Sam's. When he had as much as he could take of the corner he walked around the block again, or elsewhere in the neighborhood.

Helen had pasted a paper on the window of the front door, that said her father wasn't well but the store would open on Wednesday. The man spent a good deal of time studying this paper. He was young, dark-bearded, wore an old brown rain-stained hat, cracked patent leather shoes and a long black overcoat that looked as if it had been lived in. He was tall and not bad looking, except for a nose that had been broken and badly set, unbalancing his face. His eyes were melancholy. Sometimes he sat at the fountain with Sam Pearl, lost in his thoughts, smoking from a crumpled pack of cigarettes he had bought with pennies. Sam, who was used to all kinds of people, and had in his time seen many strangers appear in the neighborhood and as quickly disappear, showed no special concern for the man, though Goldie, after a full day of his presence complained that too much was too much; he didn't pay rent. Sam did notice that the stranger sometimes seemed to be under stress, sighed much and muttered inaudibly to himself. However, he paid the man scant attention—everybody to their own troubles. Other times the stranger, as if he had somehow squared himself with himself, seemed relaxed, even satisfied with his existence. He read through Sam's magazines, strolled around in the neighborhood and when he returned, lit a fresh cigarette as he opened a paper-bound book from the rack in the store. Sam served him coffee when he asked for it, and the stranger, squinting from the smoke of the butt in his mouth, carefully counted out five pennies to pay. Though nobody had asked him he said his name was Frank Alpine and he had lately come from the West, looking for a better opportunity. Sam advised if he could qualify for a chauffeur's license, to try for work as a hack driver. It wasn't a bad life. The man agreed but stayed around as if he was expecting something else to open up. Sam put him down as a moody gink.

The day Ida reopened the grocery the stranger disappeared but he returned to the candy store the next morning, and seating himself at the fountain, asked for coffee. He looked bleary, unhappy, his beard hard, dark, contrasting with the pallor of his face; his nostrils were inflamed and his voice was husky. He looks half in his grave, Sam thought. God knows what hole he slept in last night.

As Frank Alpine was stirring his coffee, with his free hand he opened a magazine lying on the counter, and his eye was caught by a picture in color of a monk. He lifted the coffee cup to drink but had to put it down, and he stared at the picture for five minutes.

Sam, out of curiosity, went behind him with a broom, to see what he was looking at. The picture was of a thin-faced, dark-bearded monk in a coarse brown garment, standing barefooted on a sunny country road. His skinny, hairy arms were raised to a flock of birds that dipped over his head. In the background was a grove of leafy trees; and in the far distance a church in sunlight.

"He looks like some kind of a priest," Sam said cautiously.

"No, it's St. Francis of Assisi. You can tell from that brown robe he's wearing and all those birds in the air. That's the time he was preaching to them. When I was a kid, an old priest used to come to the orphans' home where I was raised, and every time he came he read us a different story about St. Francis. They are clear in my mind to this day."

"Stories are stories," Sam said.

"Don't ask me why I never forgot them."

Sam took a closer squint at the picture. "Talking to the birds? What was he—crazy? I don't say this out of any harm."

The stranger smiled at the Jew. "He was a great man. The way I look at it, it takes a certain kind of a nerve to preach to birds."

"That makes him great, because he talked to birds?"

"Also for other things. For instance, he gave everything away that he owned, every cent, all his clothes off his back. He enjoyed to be poor. He said poverty was a queen and he loved her like she was a beautiful woman."

Sam shook his head. "It ain't beautiful, kiddo. To be poor is dirty work."

"He took a fresh view of things."

The candy store owner glanced again at St. Francis, then poked his broom into a dirty corner. Frank, as he drank his coffee, continued to study the picture. He said to Sam, "Every time I read about somebody like him I get a feeling inside of me I have to fight to keep from crying. He was born good, which is a talent if you have it."

He spoke with embarrassment, embarrassing Sam.

Frank drained his cup and left.

That night as he was wandering past Morris's store he glanced through the door and saw Helen inside, relieving her mother. She looked up and noticed him staring at her through the plate glass. His appearance startled her; his eyes were haunted, hungry, sad; she got the impression he would come in and ask for a handout and had made up her mind to give him a dime, but instead he disappeared.

On Friday, Morris weakly descended the stairs at six A.M., and Ida, nagging, came after him. She had been opening at eight o'clock and had begged him to stay in bed until then, but he had refused, saying he had to give the Poilisheh her roll.

"Why does three cents for a lousy roll mean more to you than another hour sleep?" Ida complained.

"Who can sleep?"

"You need rest, the doctor said."

"Rest I will take in my grave."

She shuddered. Morris said, "For fifteen years she gets here her roll, so let her get."

"All right, but let me open up. I will give her and you go back to bed."

"I stayed in bed too long. Makes me feel weak."

But the woman wasn't there and Morris feared he had lost her to the German. Ida insisted on dragging in the milk boxes, threatening to shout if he made a move for them. She packed the bottles into the refrigerator. After Nick Fuso they waited hours for another customer. Morris sat at the table, reading the paper, occasionally raising his hand gently to feel the bandage around his head. When he shut his eyes he still experienced moments of weakness. By noon he was glad to go upstairs and crawl into bed and he didn't get up until Helen came home.

The next morning he insisted on opening alone. The Poilisheh was there. He did not know her name. She worked somewhere in a laundry and had a little dog called Polaschaya. When she came home at night she took the little Polish dog for a walk around the block. He liked to run loose in the coal yard. She lived in one of the stucco houses nearby. Ida called her die antisemitke, but that part of her didn't bother Morris. She had come with it from the old country, a different kind of anti-Semitism from in America. Sometimes he suspected she needled him a little by asking for a "Jewish roll," and once or twice, with an odd smile, she wanted a "Jewish pickle." Generally she said nothing at all. This morning Morris handed her her roll and she said nothing. She didn't ask him about his bandaged head though her quick beady eyes stared at it, nor why he had not been there for a week; but she put six pennies on the counter instead of three. He figured she had taken a roll from the bag one of the days the store hadn't opened on time. He rang up the six-cent sale.

Morris went outside to pull in the two milk cases. He gripped the boxes but they were like rocks, so he let one go and tugged at the other. A storm cloud formed in his head and blew up to the size of a house. Morris reeled and almost fell into the gutter, but he was caught by Frank Alpine, in his long coat, steadied and led back into the store. Frank then hauled in the milk cases and refrigerated the bottles. He quickly swept up behind the counter and went into the back. Morris, recovered, warmly thanked him.

Frank said huskily, his eyes on his scarred and heavy hands, that he was new to the neighborhood but living here now with a married sister. He had lately come from the West and was looking for a better job.

The grocer offered him a cup of coffee, which he at once accepted. As he sat down Frank placed his hat on the floor at his feet, and he drank the coffee with three heaping spoonfuls of sugar, to get warm quick, he said. When Morris offered him a seeded hard roll, he bit into it hungrily. "Jesus, this is good bread." After he had finished he wiped his mouth with his handkerchief, then swept the crumbs off the table with one hand into the other, and though Morris protested, he rinsed the cup and saucer at the sink, dried them and set them on top of the gas range, where the grocer had got them.

"Much obliged for everything." He had picked up his hat but made no move to leave.

"Once in San Francisco I worked in a grocery store for a couple of months," he remarked after a minute, "only it was one of those supermarket chain store deals."

"The chain store kills the small man."

"Personally I like a small store myself. I might someday have one."

"A store is a prison. Look for something better."

"At least you're your own boss."

"To be a boss of nothing is nothing."

"Still and all, the idea of it appeals to me. The only thing is I would need experience on what goods to order. I mean about brand names, and et cetera. I guess I ought to look for a job in a store and get more experience."

"Try the A&P," advised the grocer.

"I might."

Morris dropped the subject. The man put on his hat.

"What's the matter," he said, staring at the grocer's bandage, "did you have some kind of an accident to your head?"

Morris nodded. He didn't care to talk about it, so the stranger, somehow disappointed, left.

He happened to be in the street very early on Monday when Morris was again struggling with the milk cases. The stranger tipped his hat and said he was off to the city to find a job but he had time to help him pull in the milk. This he did and quickly left. However, the grocer thought he saw him pass by in the other direction about an hour later. That afternoon when he went for his *Forward* he noticed him sitting at the fountain with Sam Pearl. The next morning, just after six, Frank was there to help him haul in the milk bottles and he willingly accepted when Morris, who knew a poor man when he saw one, invited him for coffee.

"How is going now the job?" Morris asked as they were eating.

"So-so," said Frank, his glance shifting. He seemed preoccupied, nervous. Every few minutes he would set down his cup and uneasily look around. His lips parted as if to speak, his eyes took on a tormented expression, but then he shut his jaw as if he had decided it was better never to say what he intended. He seemed to need to talk, broke into sweat—his brow gleamed with it—his pupils widening as he struggled. He looked to Morris like someone who had to retch—no matter where; but after a brutal interval his eyes grew dull. He sighed heavily and gulped down the last of his coffee. After, he brought up a belch. This for a moment satisfied him.

Whatever he wants to say, Morris thought, let him say it to somebody else. I am only a grocer. He shifted in his chair, fearing to catch some illness.

Again the tall man leaned forward, drew a breath and once

more was at the point of speaking, but now a shudder passed through him, followed by a fit of shivering.

The grocer hastened to the stove and poured out a cup of steaming coffee. Frank swallowed it in two terrible gulps. He soon stopped shaking, but looked defeated, humiliated, like somebody, the grocer felt, who had lost out on something he had wanted badly.

"You caught a cold?" he asked sympathetically.

The stranger nodded, scratched up a match on the sole of his cracked shoe, lit a cigarette and sat there, listless.

"I had a rough life," he muttered, and lapsed into silence.

Neither of them spoke. Then the grocer, to ease the other's mood, casually inquired, "Where in the neighborhood lives your sister? Maybe I know her."

Frank answered in a monotone. "I forget the exact address. Near the park somewheres."

"What is her name?"

"Mrs. Garibaldi."

"What kind name is this?"

"What do you mean?" Frank stared at him.

"I mean the nationality?"

"Italian. I am of Italian extraction. My name is Frank Alpine—Alpino in Italian."

The smell of Frank Alpine's cigarette compelled Morris to light his butt. He thought he could control his cough and tried but couldn't. He coughed till he feared his head would pop off. Frank watched with interest. Ida banged on the floor upstairs, and the grocer ashamedly pinched his cigarette and dropped it into the garbage pail.

"She don't like me to smoke," he explained between coughs. "My lungs ain't so healthy."

"Who don't?"

"My wife. It's a catarrh some kind. My mother had it all her life and lived till eighty-four. But they took a picture of my chest last year and found two dried spots. This frightened my wife."

Frank slowly put out his cigarette. "What I started out to say before about my life," he said heavily, "is that I have had a funny one, only I don't mean funny. I mean I've been through a lot. I've been close to some wonderful things—jobs, for instance, education, women, but close is as far as I go." His hands were tightly clasped between his knees. "Don't ask me why, but sooner or later everything I think is worth having gets away from me in some way or other. I work like a mule for what I want, and just when it looks like I am going to get it I make some kind of a stupid move, and everything that is just about nailed down tight blows up in my face."

"Don't throw away your chance for education," Morris advised. "It's the best thing for a young man."

"I could've been a college graduate by now, but when the time came to start going, I missed out because something else turned up that I took instead. With me one wrong thing leads to another and it ends in a trap. I want the moon so all I get is cheese."

"You are young yet."

"Twenty-five," he said bitterly.

"You look older."

"I feel old—damn old."

Morris shook his head.

"Sometimes I think your life keeps going the way it starts out on you," Frank went on. "The week after I was born my mother was dead and buried. I never saw her face, not even a picture. When I was five years old, one day my old man leaves this furnished room where we were staying, to get a pack of butts. He takes off and that was the last I ever saw of him. They traced him years later but by then he was dead. I was raised in an orphans' home and when I was eight they farmed me out to a tough family. I ran away ten times, also from the next people I lived with. I think about my life a lot. I say to myself, 'What do you expect to happen after all of that? Of course, every now and again, you understand, I hit some nice good spots in between, but they are few and far, and usually I end up like I started out, with nothing."

The grocer was moved. Poor boy.

"I've often tried to change the way things work out for me but I don't know how, even when I think I do. I have it in my heart to do more than I can remember." He paused, cleared his throat and said said, "That makes me sound stupid but it's not as easy as that. What I mean to say is that when I need it most something is missing in me, in me or on account of me. I always have this dream where I want to tell somebody something on the telephone so bad it hurts, but then when I am in the booth, instead of a phone being there, a bunch of bananas is hanging on a hook."

He gazed at the grocer then at the floor. "All my life I wanted to accomplish something worthwhile—a thing people will say took a little doing, but I don't. I am too restless—six months in any one place is too much for me. Also I grab at everything too quick—too impatient. I don't do what I have to—that's what I mean. The result is I move into a place with nothing, and I move out with nothing. You understand me?"

"Yes," said Morris.

Frank fell into silence. After a while he said, "I don't understand myself. I don't really know what I'm saying to you or why I am saying it."

"Rest yourself," said Morris.

"What kind of a life is that for a man my age?"

He waited for the grocer to reply—to tell him how to live his life, but Morris was thinking, I am sixty and he talks like me.

"Take some more coffee," he said.

"No, thanks." Frank lit another cigarette and smoked it to the tip. He seemed eased yet not eased, as though he had accomplished something (What? wondered the grocer) yet had not. His face was relaxed, almost sleepy, but he cracked the knuckles of both hands and silently sighed.

Why don't he go home? the grocer thought. I am a working man.

"I'm going." Frank got up but stayed.

"What happened to your head?" he asked again.

Morris felt the bandage. "This Friday before last I had here a holdup."

"You mean they slugged you?"

The grocer nodded.

"Bastards like that ought to die." Frank spoke vehemently.

Morris stared at him.

Frank brushed his sleeve. "You people are Jews, aren't you?"

"Yes," said the grocer, still watching him.

"I always liked Jews." His eyes were downcast.

Morris did not speak.

"I suppose you have some kids?" Frank asked.

"Me?"

"Excuse me for being curious."

"A girl." Morris sighed. "I had once a wonderful boy but he died from an ear sickness that they had in those days."

"Too bad." Frank blew his nose.

A gentleman, Morris thought with a watery eye.

"Is the girl the one that was here behind the counter a couple of nights last week?"

"Yes," the grocer replied, a little uneasily.

"Well, thanks for all the coffee."

"Let me make you a sandwich. Maybe you'll be hungry later."

"No thanks."

The Jew insisted, but Frank felt he had all he wanted from him at the moment.

Left alone, Morris began to worry about his health. He felt dizzy at times, often headachy. Murderers, he thought. Standing before the cracked and faded mirror at the sink he unwound the bandage from his head. He wanted to leave it off but the scar was still ugly, not nice for the customers, so he tied a fresh bandage around his skull. As he did this he thought of that night with bitterness, recalling the buyer who hadn't come, nor had since then, nor ever would. Since his recovery, Morris had not spoken to Karp. Against words the liquor dealer had other words, but silence silenced him.

Afterward the grocer looked up from his paper and was startled to see somebody out front washing his window with a brush on a stick. He ran out with a roar to drive the intruder away, for there were nervy window cleaners who did the job without asking permission, then held out their palms to collect. But when Morris came out of the store he saw the window washer was Frank Alpine.

"Just to show my thanks and appreciation." Frank explained he had borrowed the pail from Sam Pearl and the brush and squeegee from the butcher next door.

Ida then entered the store by the inside door, and seeing the window being washed, hurried outside.

"You got rich all of a sudden?" she asked Morris, her face inflamed.

"He does me a favor," the grocer replied.

"That's right," said Frank, bearing down on the squeegee.

"Come inside, it's cold." In the store Ida asked, "Who is this goy?"

"A poor boy, an Italyener he looks for a job. He gives me a help in the morning with the cases milk."

"If you sold containers like I told you a thousand times, you wouldn't need help."

"Containers leak. I like bottles."

"Talk to the wind," Ida said.

Frank came in blowing his breath on water-reddened fists. "How's it look now, folks, though you can't really tell till I do the inside."

Ida remarked under her breath, "Pay now for your favor."

"Fine," Morris said to Frank. He went to the register and rang up "no sale."

"No, thanks," Frank said, holding up his hand. "For services already rendered."

Ida reddened.

"Another cup coffee?" Morris asked.

"Thanks. Not as of now."

"Let me make you a sandwich?"

"I just ate."

He walked out, threw the dirty water into the gutter, returned the pail and brush, then came back to the grocery. He went behind the counter and into the rear, pausing to rap on the doorjamb.

"How do you like the clean window?" he asked Ida.

"Clean is clean." She was cool.

"I don't want to intrude here but your husband was nice to me, so I just thought maybe I could ask for one more small favor. I am looking for work and I want to try some kind of a grocery job just for size. Maybe I might like it, who knows? It happens I forgot some of the things about cutting and weighing and such, so I am wondering if you would mind me working around here for a couple-three weeks without wages just so I could learn again? It won't cost you a red cent. I know I am a stranger but I am an honest guy. Whoever keeps an eye on me will find that out in no time. That's fair enough, isn't it?"

Ida said, "Mister, isn't here a school."

"What do you say, pop?" Frank asked Morris.

"Because somebody is a stranger don't mean they ain't honest," answered the grocer. "This subject don't interest me. Interests me what you can learn here. Only one thing"—he pressed his hand to his chest—"a heartache."

"You got nothing to lose on my proposition, has he now, Mrs?" Frank said. "I understand he don't feel so hot yet, and if I helped him out a short week or two it would be good for his health, wouldn't it?"

Ida didn't answer.

But Morris said flatly, "No. It's a small, poor store. Three people would be too much."

Frank flipped an apron off a hook behind the door and before either of them could say a word, removed his hat and dropped the loop over his head. He tied the apron strings around him.

"How's that for fit?"

Ida flushed, and Morris ordered him to take it off and put it back on the hook.

"No bad feelings, I hope," Frank said on his way out.

Helen Bober and Louis Karp walked, no hands touching, in the windy dark on the Coney Island boardwalk.

Louis had, on his way home for supper that evening, stopped her in front of the liquor store, on her way in from work.

"How's about a ride in the Mercury, Helen? I never see you much anymore. Things were better in the bygone days in high school."

Helen smiled. "Honestly, Louis, that's so far away." A sense of mourning at once oppressed her, which she fought to a practiced draw.

"Near or far, it's all the same for me." He was built with broad back and narrow head, and despite prominent eyes was presentable. In high school, before he quit, he had worn his wet hair slicked straight back. One day, after studying a picture of a movie actor in the *Daily News,* he had run a part across his head. This was as much change as she had known in him. If Nat Pearl was ambitious, Louis made a relaxed living letting the fruit of his father's investment fall into his lap.

"Anyway," he said, "why not a ride for old-times' sake?"

She thought a minute, a gloved finger pressed into her cheek; but it was a fake gesture because she was lonely.

"For old-times' sake, where?"

"Name your scenery—continuous performance."

"The Island?"

He raised his coat collar. "Brr, it's a cold, windy night. You wanna freeze?"

Seeing her hesitation, he said, "But I'll die game. When'll I pick you up?"

"Ring my bell after eight and I'll come down."

"Check," Louis said. "Eight bells."

They walked to Seagate, where the boardwalk ended. She gazed with envy through a wire fence at the large lit houses fronting the ocean. The Island was deserted, except here and there an open hamburger joint or pinball machine concession. Gone from the sky was the umbrella of rosy light that glowed over the place in summertime. A few cold stars gleamed down. In the distance a dark Ferris wheel looked like a stopped clock. They stood at the rail of the boardwalk, watching the black, restless sea.

All during their walk she had been thinking about her life, the difference between her aloneness now and the fun when she was young and spending every day of summer in a lively crowd of kids on the beach. But as her high school friends had got married, she had one by one given them up; and as others of them graduated from college, envious, ashamed of how little she was accomplishing, she stopped seeing them too. At first it hurt to drop people but after a time it became a not too difficult habit. Now she saw almost no one, occasionally Betty Pearl, who understood, but not enough to make much difference.

Louis, his face reddened by the wind, sensed her mood.

"What's got in you, Helen?" he said, putting his arm around her.

"I can't really explain it. All night I've been thinking of the swell times we had on this beach when we were kids. And do you remember the parties? I suppose I'm blue that I'm no longer seventeen."

"What's so wrong about twenty-three?"

"It's old, Louis. Our lives change so quickly. You know what youth means?"

"Sure I know. You don't catch me giving away nothing for nothing. I got my youth yet."

"When a person is young he's privileged," Helen said, "with all kinds of possibilities. Wonderful things might happen, and when you get up in the morning you feel they will. That's what youth means, and that's what I've lost. Nowadays I feel that every day is like the day before, and what's worse, like the day after."

"So now you're a grandmother?"

"The world has shrunk for me."

"What do you wanna be—Miss Rheingold?"

"I want a larger and better life. I want the return of my possibilities."

"Such as which ones?"

She clutched the rail, cold through her gloves. "Education," she said, "prospects. Things I've wanted but never had."

"Also a man?"

"Also a man."

His arm tightened around her waist. "Talk is too cold, baby, how's about a kiss?"

She brushed his cold lips, then averted her head. He did not press her.

"Louis," she said, watching a far-off light on the water, "what do you want out of your life?"

He kept his arm around her. "The same thing I got—plus."

"Plus what?"

"Plus more, so my wife and family can have also."

"What if she wanted something different than you do?"

"Whatever she wanted I would gladly give her."

"But what if she wanted to make herself a better person, have bigger ideas, live a more worthwhile life? We die so quickly, so helplessly. Life *has* to have some meaning."

"I ain't gonna stop anybody from being better," Louis said, "That's up to them."

"I suppose," she said.

"Say, baby, let's drop this deep philosophy and go trap a hamburger. My stomach complains."

"Just a little longer. It's been ages since I came here this late in the year."

He pumped his arms. "Jesus, this wind, it flies up my pants. At least gimme another kiss." He unbuttoned his overcoat.

She let him kiss her. He felt her breast. Helen stepped back out of his embrace. "Don't, Louis."

"Why not?" He stood there awkwardly, annoyed.

"It gives me no pleasure."

"I suppose I'm the first guy that ever gave it a nip?"

"Are you collecting statistics?"

"Okay," he said, "I'm sorry. You know I ain't a bad guy, Helen."

"I know you're not, but please don't do what I don't like."

"There was a time you treated me a whole lot better."

"That was the past, we were kids."

It's funny, she remembered, how necking made glorious dreams.

"We were older than that, up till the time Nat Pearl started in college, then you got interested in him. I suppose you got him in mind for the future?"

"If I do, I don't know it."

"But he's the one you want, ain't he? I like to know what that stuck up has got beside a college education? I work for my living."

"No, I don't want him, Louis." But she thought, Suppose Nat said I love you? For magic words a girl might do magic tricks.

"So if that's so, what's wrong with me?"

"Nothing. We're friends."

"Friends I got all I need."

"What do you need, Louis?"

"Cut out the wisecracks, Helen. Would it interest you that I would honestly like to marry you?" He paled at his nerve.

She was surprised, touched.

"Thank you," she murmured.

"Thank you ain't good enough. Give me yes or no."

"No, Louis."

"That's what I thought." He gazed blankly at the ocean.

"I never guessed you were at all remotely interested. You go with girls who are so different from me."

"Please, when I go with them you can't see my thoughts."

"No," she admitted.

"I can give you a whole lot better than you got."

"I know you can, but I want a different life from mine now, or yours. I don't want a storekeeper for a husband."

"Wines and liquors ain't exactly pisher groceries."

"I know."

"It ain't because your old man don't like mine?"

"No."

She listened to the wind-driven, sobbing surf. Louis said, "Let's go get the hamburgers."

"Gladly." She took his arm but could tell from the stiff way he walked that he was hurt.

As they drove home on the Parkway, Louis said, "If you can't have everything you want, at least take something. Don't be so goddam proud."

Touché. "What shall I take, Louis?"

He paused. "Take less."

"Less I'll never take."

"People got to compromise."

"I won't with my ideals."

"So what'll you be then, a dried-up prune of an old maid? What's the percentage of that?"

"None."

"So what'll you do?"

"I'll wait. I'll dream. Something will happen."

"Nuts," he said.

He let her off in front of the grocery.

"Thanks for everything."

"You'll make me laugh." Louis drove off.

The store was closed, upstairs dark. She pictured her father asleep after his long day, dreaming of Ephraim. What am I saving myself for? she asked herself. What unhappy Bober fate?

It snowed lightly the next day—too early in the year, complained Ida, and when the snow had melted it snowed again. The grocer remarked, as he was dressing in the dark, that he would shovel after he had opened the store. He enjoyed shoveling snow. It reminded him that he had practically lived in it in his boyhood; but Ida forbade him to exert himself because he still complained of dizziness. Later, when he tried to lug the milk cases through the snow, he found it all but impossible. And there was no Frank Alpine to help him, for he had disappeared after washing the window.

Ida came down shortly after her husband, in a heavy cloth coat, a woolen scarf pinned around her head and wearing galoshes. She shoveled a path through the snow and together they pulled in the milk. Only then did Morris notice that a quart bottle was missing from one of the cases.

"Who took it?" Ida cried.

"How do I know?"

"Did you count yet the rolls?"

"No."

"I told you always to count right away."

"The baker will steal from me? I know him twenty years."

"Count what everybody delivers, I told you a thousand times."

He dumped the rolls out of the basket and counted them. Three were missing and he had sold only one to the Poilisheh. To appease Ida he said they were all there.

The next morning another quart of milk and two rolls were gone. He was worried but didn't tell Ida the truth when she asked him if anything else was missing. He often hid unpleasant news from her because she made it worse. He mentioned the missing bottle to the milkman, who answered, "Morris, I swear I left every bottle in that case. Am I responsible for this lousy neighborhood?"

He promised to cart the milk cases into the vestibule for a few days. Maybe whoever was stealing the bottles would be afraid to go in there. Morris considered asking the milk company for a storage box. Years ago he had had one at the curb, a large wooden box in which the milk was padlocked; but he had given it up after developing a hernia lifting the heavy cases out, so he decided against a box.

On the third day, when a quart of milk and two rolls had again been taken, the grocer, much disturbed, considered calling the police. It wasn't the first time he had lost milk and rolls in this neighborhood. That had happened more than once—usually some poor person stealing a breakfast. For this reason Morris preferred not to call the police but to get rid of the thief by himself. To do it, he would usually wake up very early and wait at his bedroom window in the dark. Then when the man—sometimes it was a woman—showed up and was helping himself to the milk, Morris would quickly raise the window and shout down, "Get outa here, you thief you." The thief, startled—sometimes it was a customer who could afford to buy the milk he was stealing—would drop the bottle and run. Usually he never appeared again—a lost customer cut another way—and the next goniff was somebody else.

So this morning Morris arose at four-thirty, a little before the milk was delivered, and sat in the cold in his long underwear, to wait. The street was heavy with darkness as he peered down. Soon the milk truck came, and the milkman, his breath foggy, lugged the two cases of milk into the vestibule. Then the street was silent again, the night dark, the snow white. One or two people trudged by. An hour later, Witzig, the baker, delivered the rolls, but no one else stopped at the door. Just before six Morris dressed hastily and went downstairs. A bottle of milk was gone, and when he counted the rolls, so were two of them.

He still kept the truth from Ida. The next night she awoke and found him at the window in the dark.

"What's the matter?" she asked, sitting up in bed.

"I can't sleep."

"So don't sit in your underwear in the cold. Come back to bed."

He did as she said. Later, the milk and rolls were missing.

In the store he asked the Polisheh whether she had seen anyone sneak into the vestibule and steal a quart of milk. She stared at him with small eyes, grabbed the sliced roll and slammed the door.

Morris had a theory that the thief lived on the block. Nick Fuso wouldn't do such a thing; if he did Morris would have heard him going down the stairs, then coming up again. The thief was somebody from outside. He sneaked along the street close to the houses, where Morris couldn't see him because of the cornice that hung over the store; then he softly opened the hall door, took the milk, two rolls from the bag, and stole away, hugging the house fronts.

The grocer suspected Mike Papadopolous, the Greek boy who lived on the floor above Karp's store. He had served a reformatory sentence at eighteen. A year later he had in the dead of night climbed down the fire escape overhanging Karp's back yard, boosted himself up on the fence and forced a window into the grocery. There he stole three cartons of cigarettes, and a roll of dimes that Morris had left in the cash register. In the morning, as the grocer was opening the store, Mike's mother, a thin, old-looking woman, returned the cigarettes and dimes to him. She had caught her son coming in with them and had walloped his head with a shoe. She clawed his face, making him confess what he had done. Returning the cigarettes and dimes, she had begged Morris not to have the boy arrested and he had assured her he wouldn't do such a thing.

On this day that he had guessed it might be Mike taking the milk and rolls, shortly after eight A.M., Morris went up the stairs and knocked reluctantly on Mrs. Papadopolous' door.

"Excuse me that I bother you," he said, and told her what had been happening to his milk and rolls.

"Mike work all nights in restaurants," she said. "No come home till nine o'clock in mornings. Sleep all days." Her eyes smoldered. The grocer left.

Now he was greatly troubled. Should he tell Ida and let her call the police? They were bothering him at least once a week with questions about the holdup but had produced nobody. Still, maybe it would be best to call them, for this stealing had gone on for almost a week. Who could afford it? Yet he waited, and that night as he was leaving the store by the side door, which he always padlocked after shutting the front door from inside, he flicked on the cellar light and as he peered down the stairs, his nightly habit, his heart tightened with foreboding that somebody was down there. Morris unlocked the lock, went back into the store and got a hatchet. Forcing his courage, he slowly descended the wooden steps. The cellar was empty. He searched in the dusty storage bins, poked around all over, but there was no sign of anybody.

In the morning he told Ida what was going on and she, calling him big fool, telephoned the police. A stocky, red-faced detective came, Mr. Minogue, from a nearby precinct, who was in charge of investigating Morris's holdup. He was a soft-spoken, unsmiling man, bald, a widower who had once lived in this neighborhood. He had a son Ward, who had gone to Helen's junior high school, a wild boy, always in trouble for manhandling girls. When he saw one he knew playing in front of her house, or on the stoop, he would come swooping down and chase her into the hall. There, no matter how desperately the girl struggled, or tenderly begged him to stop, Ward forced his hand down her dress and squeezed her breast till she screamed. Then by the time her mother came running down the stairs he had ducked out of the hall, leaving the girl sobbing. The detective, when he heard of these happenings, regularly beat up his son, but it didn't do much good. Then one day, about eight years ago, Ward was canned from his job for stealing from the company. His father beat him sick and bloody with his billy and drove him out of the neighborhood. After that, Ward disappeared and nobody knew where he had gone. People felt sorry for the detective, for he was a strict man and they knew what it meant to him to have such a son.

Mr. Minogue seated himself at the table in the rear and listened to Ida's complaint. He slipped on his glasses and wrote in a little black notebook. The detective said he would have a cop watch the store mornings after the milk was delivered, and if there was any more trouble to let him know.

As he was leaving, he said, "Morris, would you recognize Ward Minogue if you happened to see him again? I hear he's been seen around but whereabouts I don't know."

"I don't know," said Morris. "Maybe yes or maybe no. I didn't see him for years."

"If I ever meet up with him," said the detective, "I might bring him in to you for identification."

"What for?"

"I don't know myself—just for possible identification."

Ida said afterward that if Morris had called the police in the first place, he might have saved himself a few bottles of milk that they could hardly afford to lose.

That night, on an impulse, the grocer closed the store an hour later than usual. He snapped on the cellar light and cautiously descended the stairs, gripping his hatchet. Near the bottom he uttered a cry and the hatchet fell from his hands. A man's drawn and haggard face stared up at him in dismay. It was Frank Alpine, gray and unshaven. He had been asleep with his hat and coat on, sitting on a box against the wall. The light had awakened him.

"What do you want here?" Morris cried out.

"Nothing," Frank said dully. "I have just been sleeping in the cellar. No harm done."

"Did you steal from me my milk and rolls?"

"Yes," he confessed. "On account of I was hungry."

"Why didn't you ask me?"

Frank got up. "Nobody has any responsibility to take care of me but myself. I couldn't find any job. I used up every last cent I had. My coat is too thin for this cold and lousy climate. The snow and the rain get in my shoes so I am always shivering. Also, I had no place to sleep. That's why I came down here."

"Don't you stay any more with your sister?"

"I have no sister. That was a lie I told you. I am alone by myself."

"Why you told me you had a sister?"

"I didn't want you to think I was a bum."

Morris regarded the man silently. "Were you ever in prison sometimes?"

"Never, I swear to Christ."

"How you came to me in my cellar?"

"By accident. One night I was walking around in the snow, so I tried the cellar door and found out you left it unlocked, then I started coming down at night about an hour after you closed the store. In the morning, when they delivered the milk and rolls, I sneaked up through the hall, opened the door and took what I needed for breakfast. That's practically all I ate all day. After you came down and got busy with some customer or a salesman, I left by the hallway with the empty milk bottle under my coat. Later I threw it away in a lot. That's all there is to it. Tonight I took a chance and came in while you were still in the back of the store, because I have a cold and don't feel too good."

"How can you sleep in such a cold and drafty cellar?"

"I slept in worse."

"Are you hungry now?"

"I'm always hungry."

"Come upstairs."

Morris picked up his hatchet, and Frank, blowing his nose in his damp handkerchief, followed him up the stairs.

Morris lit a light in the store and made two fat liverwurst sandwiches with mustard, and in the back heated up a can of bean soup. Frank sat at the table in his coat, his hat lying at his feet. He ate with great hunger, his hand trembling as he brought the spoon to his mouth. The grocer had to look away.

As the man was finishing his meal, with coffee and cup cakes, Ida came down in felt slippers and bathrobe.

"What happened?" she asked in fright, when she saw Frank Alpine.

"He's hungry," Morris said.

She guessed at once. "He stole the milk!"

"He was hungry," explained Morris. "He slept in the cellar."

"I was practically starving," said Frank.

"Why didn't you look for a job?' Ida asked.

"I looked all over."

After, Ida said to Frank, "When you finish, please go someplace else." She turned to her husband. "Morris, tell him to go someplace else. We are poor people."

"This he knows."

"I'll go away," Frank said, "as the lady wishes."

"Tonight is already too late," Morris said. "Who wants he should walk all night in the streets?"

"I don't want him here." She was tense.

"Where you want him to go?"

Frank set his coffee cup on the saucer and listened with interest.

"This ain't my business," Ida answered.

"Don't anybody worry," said Frank. "I'll leave in ten minutes' time. You got a cigarette, Morris?"

The grocer went to the bureau and took out of the drawer a crumpled pack of cigarettes.

"It's stale," he apologized.

"Don't make any difference." Frank lit a stale cigarette, inhaling with pleasure.

"I'll go after a short while," he said to Ida.

"I don't like trouble," she explained.

"I won't make any. I might look like a bum in these clothes, but I am not. All my life I lived with good people."

"Let him stay here tonight on the couch," Morris said to Ida.

"No. Give him better a dollar he should go someplace else."

"The cellar would be fine," Frank remarked.

"It's too damp. Also rats."

"If you let me stay there one more night I promise I will get out the first thing in the morning. You don't have to be afraid to trust me. I am an honest man."

"You can sleep here," Morris said.

"Morris, you crazy," shouted Ida.

"I'll work it off for you," Frank said. "Whatever I cost you I'll pay you back. Anything you want me to do, I'll do it."

"We will see," Morris said.

"No," insisted Ida.

But Morris won out, and they went up, leaving Frank in the back, the gas radiator left lit.

"He will clean out the store," Ida said wrathfully.

"Where is his truck?" Morris asked, smiling. Seriously he said, "He's a poor boy. I feel sorry for him."

They went to bed. Ida slept badly. Sometimes she was racked by awful dreams. Then she awoke and sat up in bed, straining to hear noises in the store—of Frank packing huge bags of groceries to steal. But there was no sound. She dreamed she came down in the morning and all the stock was gone, the shelves as barren as the picked bones of dead birds. She dreamed, too, that the Italyener had sneaked up into the house and was peeking through the keyhole of Helen's door. Only when Morris got up to open the store did Ida fall fitfully asleep.

The grocer trudged down the stairs with a dull pain in his head. His legs felt weak. His sleep had not been refreshing.

The snow was gone from the streets and the milk boxes were again lying on the sidewalk near the curb. None of the bottles were missing. The grocer was about to drag in the milk cases when the Poilisheh came by. She went inside and placed three pennies on the counter. He entered with the brown bag of rolls, cut up one and wrapped it. She took it wordlessly and left.

Morris looked through the window in the wall. Frank was asleep on the couch in his clothes, his coat covering him. His beard was black, his mouth loosely open.

The grocer went out into the street, grabbed both milk boxes and yanked. The shape of a black hat blew up in his head, flared into hissing light, and exploded. He thought he was rising but felt himself fall.

Frank dragged him in and laid him on the couch. He ran upstairs and banged on the door. Helen, holding a housecoat over her nightdress, opened it. She suppressed a cry.

"Tell your mother your father just passed out. I called the ambulance."

She screamed. As he ran down the stairs he could hear Ida moaning. Frank hurried into the back of the store. The Jew lay white and motionless on the couch. Frank gently removed his apron. Draping the loop over his own head, he tied the tapes around him.

"I need the experience," he muttered.

Morris had reopened the wound on his head. The ambulance doctor, the same who had treated him after the holdup, said he had got up too soon last time and worn himself out. He again bandaged the grocer's head, saying to Ida, "This time let him lay in bed a good couple of weeks till his strength comes back." "You tell him, doctor," she begged, "he don't listen to me." So the doctor told Morris, and Morris weakly nodded. Ida, in a gray state of collapse, remained with the patient all day. So did Helen, after calling the ladies' underthings concern where she worked. Frank Alpine stayed competently downstairs in the store. At noon Ida remembered him and came down to tell him to leave. Recalling her dreams, she connected him with their new misfortune. She felt that if he had not stayed the night, this might not have happened.

Frank was clean-shaven in the back, having borrowed Morris's safety razor, his thick hair neatly combed, and when she appeared he hopped up to ring open the cash register, showing her a pile of puffy bills.

"Fifteen," he said, "count every one."

She was astonished. "How is so much?"

He explained, "We had a busy morning. A lot of people stopped in to ask about Morris's accident."

Ida had planned to replace him with Helen for the time being, until she herself could take over, but she was now of two minds.

"Maybe you can stay," she faltered, "if you want to, till tomorrow."

"I'll sleep in the cellar, Mrs. You don't have to worry about me. I am as honest as the day."

"Don't sleep in the cellar," she said with a tremble to her voice, "my husband said on the couch. What can anybody steal here? We have nothing."

"How is he now?" Frank asked in a low voice.

She blew her nose.

The next morning Helen went reluctantly to work. Ida came down at ten to see how things were. This time there were only eight dollars in the drawer, but still better than lately. He apologized, "Not so good today, but I wrote down every article I sold so you'll know nothing stuck to my fingers." He produced a list of goods sold, written on wrapping paper. She happened to notice that it began with three cents for a roll. Glancing around, Ida saw he had packed out the few cartons delivered yesterday, swept up, washed the window from the inside and had straightened the cans on the shelves. The place looked a little less dreary.

During the day he also kept himself busy with odd jobs. He cleaned the trap of the kitchen sink, which swallowed water slowly, and in the store fixed a light whose chain wouldn't pull, making useless one lamp. Neither of them mentioned his leaving. Ida, still uneasy, wanted to tell him to go but she couldn't ask Helen to stay home any more, and the prospect of two weeks alone in the store, with her feet and a sick man in the bargain to attend upstairs, was too much for her. Maybe she would let the Italian stay ten days or so. With Morris fairly well recovered there would be no reason to keep him after that. In the meantime he would have three good meals a day and a bed, for being little more than a watchman. What business, after all, did they do here? And while Morris was not around she would change a thing or two she should have done before. So when the milkman stopped by for yesterday's empties, she ordered containers brought from now on. Frank Alpine heartily approved. "Why should we bother with bottles?" he said.

Despite all she had to do upstairs, and her recent good impressions of him, Ida haunted the store, watching his every move. She was worried because, now, not Morris but she was responsible for the man's presence in the store. If something bad happened, it would be her fault. Therefore, though she climbed the stairs often to tend to her husband's needs, she hurried back down, arriving pale and breathless to see what Frank was up to. But anything he happened to be doing was helpful. Her suspicions died slowly, though they never wholly died.

She tried not to be too friendly to him, to make him feel that a distant relationship meant a short one. When they were in the back or for a few minutes together behind the counter she discouraged conversation, took up something to do, or clean, or her paper to read. And in the matter of teaching him the business there was also little to say. Morris had price tags displayed under all items on the shelves, and Ida supplied Frank with a list of prices for meats and salads and for the miscellaneous unmarked things like loose coffee, rice or beans. She taught him how to wrap neatly and efficiently, as Morris had long ago taught her, how to read the scale and to set and handle the electric meat slicer. He caught on quickly; she suspected he knew more than he said he did. He added rapidly and accurately, did not overcut meats or overload the scale on bulk items, as she had urged him not to do, and judged well the length of paper needed to wrap with, and what number bag to pack goods into, conserving the larger bags which cost more money. Since he learned so fast, and since she had seen in him not the least evidence of dishonesty (a hungry man who took milk and rolls, though not above suspicion, was not the same as a thief), Ida forced herself to remain upstairs with more calm, in order to give Morris his medicine, bathe her aching feet and keep up the house, which was always dusty from the coal yard. Yet she felt, whenever she thought of it, always a little troubled at the thought of a stranger's presence below, a goy, after all, and she looked forward to the time when he was gone.

Although his hours were long—six to six, at which time she served him his supper—Frank was content. In the store he was quits with the outside world, safe from cold, hunger and a damp bed. He had cigarettes when he wanted them and was comfortable in clean clothes Morris had sent down, even a pair of pants that fitted him after Ida lengthened and pressed the cuffs. The store was fixed, a cave, motionless. He had all his life been on the move, no matter where he was; here he somehow couldn't be. Here he could stand at the window and watch the world go by, content to be here.

It wasn't a bad life. He woke before dawn. The Polish dame was planted at the door like a statue, distrusting him with beady eyes to open the place in time for her to get to work. Her he didn't like; he would gladly have slept longer. To get up in the middle of the night for three lousy cents was a joke but he did it for the Jew. After packing away the milk containers, turning bottomside up the occasional one that leaked, he swept the store and then the sidewalk. In the back he washed, shaved, had coffee and a sandwich, at first made with meat from a ham or roast pork butt, then after a few days, from the best cut. As he smoked after coffee he thought of everything he could do to improve this dump if it were his. When somebody came in the store he was up with a bound, offering service with a smile. Nick Fuso, on Frank's first day, was surprised to see him there, knowing Morris could not afford a clerk. But Frank said that though the pay was scarce there were other advantages. They spoke about this and that, and when the upstairs tenant learned Frank Alpine was a paisan, he told him to come up and meet Tessie. She cor-

dially invited him for macaroni that same night, and he said he
would come if they let him bring the macs.

Ida, after the first few days, began to go down at her regular hour, around ten, after she had finished the housework; and
she busied herself with writing in a notebook which bills they
had got and which paid. She also wrote out, in a halting hand, a
few meager special-account checks for bills that could not be paid
in cash directly to the drivers, mopped the kitchen floor, emptied
the garbage pail into the metal can on the curb outside and prepared salad if it was needed. Frank watched her shred cabbage on
the meat slicer for coleslaw, which she made in careful quantity,
because if it turned sour it had to be dumped into the garbage.
Potato salad was a bigger job, and she cooked up a large pot of
new potatoes, which Frank helped her peel hot in their steaming
jackets. Every Friday she prepared fish cakes and a panful of
homemade baked beans, first soaking the little beans overnight,
pouring out the water, then spreading brown sugar on top before
baking. Her expression as she dipped in among the soggy beans
pieces of ham from a butt she had cut up caught his eye, and he
felt for her repugnance for hating to touch the ham, and some for
himself because he had never lived this close to Jews before. At
lunchtime there was a little "rush," which meant that a few dirty-
faced laborers from the coal yard and a couple of store clerks
from on the block wanted sandwiches and containers of hot
coffee. But the "rush," for which they both went behind the
counter, petered out in a matter of minutes and then came the
dead hours of the afternoon. Ida said he ought to take some time
off, but he answered that he had nowhere special to go and stayed
in the back, reading the *Daily News* on the couch, or flipping
through some magazines that he had got out of the public library,
which he had discovered during one of his solitary walks in the
neighborhood.

At three, when Ida departed for an hour or so to see if Morris
needed something, and to rest, Frank felt relieved. Alone, he did a
lot of casual eating, sometimes with unexpected pleasure. He

sampled nuts, raisins, and small boxes of stale dates or dried figs, which he liked anyway; he also opened packages of crackers, macaroons, cupcakes and doughnuts, tearing up their wrappers into small pieces and flushing them down the toilet. Sometimes in the middle of eating sweets he would get very hungry for something more substantial, so he made a thick meat and Swiss cheese sandwich on a seeded hard roll spread with mustard, and swallowed it down with a bottle of ice-cold beer. Satisfied, he stopped roaming in the store.

Now and then there were sudden unlooked-for flurries of customers, mostly women, whom he waited on attentively, talking to them about all kinds of things. The drivers, too liked his sociability and cheery manner and stayed to chew the fat. Otto Vogel, once when he was weighing a ham, warned him in a low voice, "Don't work for a Yid, kiddo. They will steal your ass while you are sitting on it." Frank, though he said he didn't expect to stay long, felt embarrassed for being there; then, to his surprise, he got another warning, from an apologetic Jew salesman of paper products, Al Marcus, a prosperous, yet very sick and solemn character who wouldn't stop working. "This kind of a store is a death tomb, positive," Al Marcus said. "Run out while you can. Take my word, if you stay six months, you'll stay forever."

"Don't worry about that," answered Frank.

Alone afterward, he stood at the window, thinking thoughts about his past, and wanting a new life. Would he ever get what he wanted? Sometimes he stared out of the back yard window at nothing at all, or at the clothesline above, moving idly in the wind, flying Morris's scarecrow union suits, Ida's hefty bloomers, modestly folded lengthwise, and her housedresses guarding her daughter's flower-like panties and restless brassières.

In the evening, whether he wanted to or not, he was "off." Ida insisted, fair was fair. She fed him a quick supper and allowed him, with apologies because she couldn't afford more, fifty cents spending money. He occasionally passed the time upstairs with the Fusos or went with them to a picture at the local movie house. Sometimes he walked, in spite of the cold, and stopped off at a poolroom he knew, about a mile and a half from the grocery store. When he got back, always before closing, for Ida wouldn't let him keep a key to the store in his pocket, she counted up the day's receipts, put most of the cash into a small paper bag and took it with her, leaving Frank five dollars to open up with in the morning. After she had gone, he turned the key in the front door lock, hooked the side door through which she had left, put out the store lights and sat in his undershirt in the rear, reading tomorrow's pink-sheeted paper that he had picked off Sam Pearl's stand on his way home. Then he undressed and went restlessly to bed in a pair of Morris's bulky, rarely used, flannel pajamas.

The old dame, he thought with disgust, always hurried him out of the joint before her daughter came down for supper.

The girl was in his mind a lot. He couldn't help it, imagined seeing her in the things that were hanging on the line—he had always had a good imagination. He pictured her as she came down the stairs in the morning; also saw himself standing in the hall after she came home, watching her skirts go flying as she ran up the stairs. He rarely saw her around, had never spoken to her but twice, on the day her father had passed out. She had kept her distance—who could blame her, dressed as he was and what he looked like then? He had the feeling as he spoke to her, a few hurried words, that he knew more about her than anybody would give him credit for. He had got this thought the first time he had ever laid eyes on her, that night he saw her through the grocery window. When she had looked at him he was at once aware of something starved about her, a hunger in her eyes he couldn't forget because it made him remember his own, so he knew how wide open she must be. But he wouldn't try to push anything, for he had heard that these Jewish babes could be troublemakers and he was not looking for any of that now—at least no more than usual; besides, he didn't want to spoil anything before it got started. There were some dames you had to wait for—for them to come to you.

His desire grew to get to know her, he supposed because she had never once come into the store in all the time he was there except after he left at night. There was no way to see and talk to her to her face, and this increased his curiosity. He felt they were both lonely but her old lady kept her away from him as if he had a dirty disease; the result was he grew more impatient to find out what she was like, get to be friends with her for whatever it was worth. So, since she was never around, he listened and watched for her. When he heard her walking down the stairs he went to the front window and stood there waiting for her to come out; he tried to look casual, as if he weren't watching, just in case she happened to glance back and see him; but she never did, as if she liked nothing about the place enough to look back on. She had a pretty face and a good figure, small-breasted, neat, as if she had meant herself to look that way. He liked to watch her brisk, awkward walk till she turned the corner. It was a sexy walk, with a wobble in it, a strange movement, as though she might dart sideways although she was walking forward. Her legs were just a bit bowed, and maybe that was the sexy part of it. She stayed in his mind after she had turned the corner; her legs and small breasts and the pink brassières that covered them. He would be reading something or lying on his back on the couch, smoking, and she would appear in his mind, walking to the corner. He did not have to shut his eyes to see her. Turn around, he said out loud, but in his thoughts she wouldn't.

To see her coming toward him he stood at the lit grocery window at night, but often before he could catch sight of her she was on her way upstairs, or already changing her dress in her room, and his chance was over for the day. She came home about a quarter to six, sometimes a little earlier, so he tried to be at the window around then, which wasn't so easy because that was the time for Morris's few supper customers to come in. So he rarely saw her come home from work, though he always heard her on the stairs. One day things were slower than usual in the store, it was dead at five-thirty, and Frank said to himself, Today I will see her. He combed his hair in the toilet so that Ida wouldn't notice, changed into a clean apron, lit a cigarette, and stood at the window, visible in its light. At twenty to six, just after he had practically shoved a woman out of the joint, a dame who had happened to walk in off the trolley, he saw Helen turn Sam Pearl's corner. Her face was prettier than he had remembered and his throat tightened as she walked to within a couple of feet of him, her eyes blue, her hair, which she wore fairly long, brown, and she had an absent-minded way of smoothing it back off the side of her face. He thought she didn't look Jewish, which was all to the good. But her expression was discontented, and her mouth a little drawn. She seemed to be thinking of something she had no hope of ever getting. This moved him, so that when she glanced up and saw his eyes on her, his face plainly showed his emotion. It must have bothered her because she quickly walked, without noticing him further, to the hall and disappeared inside.

The next morning he didn't see her—as if she had sneaked out on him—and at night he was waiting on somebody when she returned from work; regretfully he heard the door slam behind her. Afterward he felt downhearted; every sight lost to a guy who lived with his eyes was lost for all time. He thought up different ways to meet her and exchange a few words. What he had on his mind to say to her about himself was beginning to weigh on him, though he hadn't clearly figured out the words. Once he thought of coming in on her unexpectedly while she was eating her supper, but then he would have Ida to deal with. He also had the idea of opening the door the next time he saw her and calling her into the store; he could say that some guy had telephoned her, and after that talk about something else, but nobody did call her. She was in her way a lone bird, which suited him fine, though why she should be with her looks he couldn't figure out. He got the feeling that she wanted something big out of life, and this scared him. Still, he tried to think of schemes of getting her inside the store, even planning to ask her something like did she know where her old man kept his saw; only she mightn't like that, her mother being around all day to tell him. He had to watch out not to scare her any farther away than the old dame had done.

For a couple of nights after work he stood in a hallway next door to the laundry across the street in the hope that she would come out to do some errand, then he would cross over, tip his hat and ask if he could keep her company to where she was going. But this did not pay off either, because she didn't leave the house. The second night he waited fruitlessly until Ida put out the lights in the grocery window.

One evening toward the end of the second week after Morris's accident, Frank's loneliness burdened him to the point of irritation. He was eating his supper a few minutes after Helen had returned from work, while Ida happened to be upstairs with Morris. He had seen Helen come round the corner and had nodded to her as she approached the house. Caught by surprise, she half-smiled, then entered the hall. It was then the lonely feeling gripped him. While he was eating, he felt he had to get her into the store before her old lady came down and it was time for him to leave. The only excuse he could think of was to call Helen to answer the phone and after he would say that the guy must've hung up. It was a trick but he had to do it. He warned himself not to, because it would be starting out the wrong way with her and he might someday regret it. He tried to think of a better way but time was pressing him and he couldn't.

Frank got up, went over to the bureau, and took the phone off its cradle. He then walked out into the hall, opened the vestibule door, and holding his breath, pressed the Bober bell.

Ida looked over the banister. "What's the matter?"

"Telephone for Helen."

He could see her hesitate, so he returned quickly to the store. He sat down, pretending to be eating, his heart whamming so hard it hurt. All he wanted, he told himself, was to talk to her a minute so the next time would be easier.

Helen eagerly entered the kitchen. On the stairs she had noticed the excitement that flowed through her. My God, it's gotten to be that a phone call is an event.

If it's Nat, she thought, I might give him another chance.

Frank half-rose as she entered, then sat down.

"Thanks," she said to him as she picked up the phone.

"Hello." While she waited he could hear the buzz in the receiver.

"There's nobody there," she said, mystified.

He laid down his fork. "This girl called you," he said gently.

But when he saw the disappointment in her eyes, how bad she felt, he felt bad.

She gave him a long look. She was wearing a white blouse that showed the firmness of her small breasts. He wet his dry lips, trying to figure out some quick way to square himself, but his mind, usually crowded with all sorts of schemes, had gone blank. He felt very bad, as he had known he would, that he had done what he had. If he had it to do over he wouldn't do it this way.

"Did she leave you her name?" Helen asked.

"No."

"It wasn't Betty Pearl?"

"No."

She absently brushed back her hair. "Did she say anything to you?"

"Only to call you." He paused. "Her voice was nice—like yours. Maybe she didn't get me straight when I said you were upstairs but I would ring your doorbell, and that's why she hung up."

"I don't know why anybody would do that."

Neither did he. He wanted to step clear of his mess but saw no way other than to keep on lying. But lying made their talk useless. When he lied he was somebody else lying to somebody else. It wasn't the two of them as they were. He should have kept that in his mind.

She stood at the bureau, holding the telephone in her hand as if still expecting the buzz to become a voice; so he waited for the same thing, a voice to speak and say he had been telling the truth, that he was a man of fine character. Only that didn't happen either.

He gazed at her with dignity as he considered saying the simple truth, starting from there, come what would, but the thought of confessing what he had done almost panicked him.

"I'm sorry," he said brokenly, but by then she was gone, and he was attempting to fix in his memory what she had looked like so close.

Helen too was troubled. Not only could she not explain why she believed yet did not fully believe him, nor why she had lately become so conscious of his presence among them, though he never strayed from the store, but she was also disturbed by her mother's efforts to keep her away from him. "Eat when he leaves," Ida had said. "I am not used to goyim in my house." This annoyed Helen because of the assumption that she would keel over for somebody just because he happened to be a gentile. It meant, obviously, her mother didn't trust her. If she had been casual about him, Helen doubted she would have paid him any attention to speak of. He was interesting looking, true, but what except a poor grocery clerk? Out of nothing Ida was trying to make something.

Though Ida was still concerned at having the young Italian around the place, she observed with pleased surprise how, practically from the day of his appearance, the store had improved. During the first week there were days when they had taken in from five to seven dollars more than they were averaging daily in the months since summer. And the same held for the second week. The store was of course still a poor store, but with this forty to fifty a week more they might at least limp along until a buyer appeared. She could at first not understand why more people were coming in, why more goods were being sold. True, the same thing had happened before. Without warning, after a

long season of dearth, three or four customers, lost faces, strag-
gled in one day, as if they had been let out of their poor rooms
with a few pennies in their pockets. And others, who had skimped
on food, began to buy more. A storekeeper could tell almost at
once when times were getting better. People seemed less worried
and irritable, less in competition for the little sunlight in the
world. Yet the curious thing was that business, according to most
of the drivers, had not very much improved anywhere. One of
them said that Schmitz around the corner was having his troubles
too; furthermore he wasn't feeling so good. So the sudden pickup
of business in the store, Ida thought, would not have happened
without Frank Alpine. It took her a while to admit this to herself.

The customers seemed to like him. He talked a lot as he waited
on them, sometimes saying things that embarrassed Ida but made
the customers, the gentile housewives, laugh. He somehow drew
in people she had never before seen in the neighborhood, not only
women, men too. Frank tried things that Morris and she could
never do, such as attempting to sell people more than they asked
for, and usually he succeeded. "What can you do with a quarter
of a pound?" he would say. "A quarter is for the birds—not even
a mouthful. Better make it a half." So they would make it a half.
Or he would say, "Here's a new brand of mustard that we just
got in today. It weighs two ounces more than the stuff they sell
you in the supermarkets for the same price. Why don't you give
it a try? If you don't like it, bring it back and I will gargle it."
And they laughed and bought it. This made Ida wonder if Morris
and she were really suited to the grocery business. They had
never been salesmen.

One of the women customers called Frank a supersalesman, a
word that brought a pleased smile to his lips. He was clever and
worked hard. Ida's respect for him reluctantly grew; gradually
she became more relaxed in his presence. Morris was right in recognizing that he was not a bum but a boy who had gone through
bad times. She pitied him for having lived in an orphan asylum.
He did his work quickly, never complained, kept himself neat

and clean now that he had soap and water around, and answered her politely. The one or two times, just lately, that he had briefly talked to Helen in her presence, he had spoken like a gentleman and didn't try to stretch a word into a mouthful. Ida discussed the situation with Morris and they raised his "spending money" from fifty cents a day to five dollars for the week. Despite her good will to him, this worried Ida, but, after all, he was bringing more money into the store, the place looked spic and span—let him keep five dollars of their poor profit. Bad as things still were, he willingly did so much extra around the store—how could they not pay him a little something? Besides, she thought, he would soon be leaving.

Frank accepted the little raise with an embarrassed smile. "You don't have to pay me anything more, Mrs, I said I would work for nothing to make up for past favors from your husband and also to learn the business. Besides that you give me my bed and board, so you don't owe me a thing."

"Take," she said, handing him a crumpled five-dollar bill. He let the money lie on the counter till she urged him to put it into his pocket. Frank felt troubled about the raise because he was earning something for his labor that Ida knew nothing of, for business was a little better than she thought. During the day, while she was not around, he sold at least a buck's worth, or a buck and a half, that he made no attempt to ring up on the register. Ida guessed nothing; the list of sold items he had supplied her with in the beginning they had discontinued as impractical. It wasn't hard for him to scrape up here a bit of change, there a bit. At the end of the second week he had ten dollars in his pocket. With this and the five she gave him he bought a shaving kit, a pair of cheap brown suede shoes, a couple of shirts and a tie or two; he figured that if he stayed around two more weeks he would own an inexpensive suit. He had nothing to be ashamed of, he thought—it was practically his own dough he was taking. The grocer and his wife wouldn't miss it because they didn't know they had it, and they wouldn't have it if it wasn't for his hard work. If he weren't working there, they would have less than they had with him taking what he took.

Thus he settled it in his mind only to find himself remorseful. He groaned, scratching the backs of his hands with his thick nails. Sometimes he felt short of breath and sweated profusely. He talked aloud to himself when he was alone, usually when he was shaving or in the toilet, exhorted himself to be honest. Yet he felt a curious pleasure in his misery, as he had at times in the past when he was doing something he knew he oughtn't to, so he kept on dropping quarters into his pants pocket.

One night he felt very bad about all the wrong he was doing and vowed to set himself straight. If I could do one right thing, he thought, maybe that would start me off; then he thought if he could get the gun and get rid of it he would at least feel better. He left the grocery after supper and wandered restlessly in the foggy streets, feeling cramped in the chest from his long days in the store and because his life hadn't changed much since he had come here. As he passed by the cemetery, he tried to keep out of his mind the memory of the holdup but it kept coming back in. He saw himself sitting with Ward Minogue in the parked car, waiting for Karp to come out of the grocery, but when he did his store lights went out and he hid in the back among the bottles. Ward said to drive quick around the block so they would flush the Jew out, and he would slug him on the sidewalk and take his fat wallet away; but when they got back, Karp's car was gone with him in it, and Ward cursed him into an early grave. Frank said Karp had beat it, so they ought to scram, but Ward sat there with heartburn, watching, with his small eyes, the grocery store, the one lit place on the block besides the candy store on the corner.

"No," Frank urged, "it's just a little joint, I got my doubts if they took in thirty bucks today."

"Thirty is thirty," Ward said. "I don't care if it's Karp or Bober, a Jew is a Jew."

"Why not the candy store?"

Ward made a face. "I can't stand penny candy."

"How do you know his name?" asked Frank.

"Who?"

"The Jew grocer."

"I used to go to school with his daughter. She has a nice ass."

"Then if that's so, he will recognize you."

"Not with a rag around my snoot, and I will rough up my voice. He ain't seen me for eight or nine years. I was a skinny kid then."

"Have it your way. I will keep the car running."

"Come in with me," Ward said. "The block is dead. Nobody will expect a stickup in this dump."

But Frank hesitated. "I thought you said Karp was the one you were out after?"

"I will take Karp some other time. Come on."

Frank put on his cap and crossed the car tracks with Ward Minogue. "It's your funeral," he said, but it was really his own.

He remembered thinking as they went into the store, a Jew is a Jew, what difference does it make? Now he thought, I held him up because he was a Jew. What the hell are they to me so that I gave them credit for it?

But he didn't know the answer and walked faster, from time to time glancing through the spiked iron fence at the shrouded gravestones. Once he felt he was being followed and his heart picked up a hard beat. He hurried past the cemetery and turned right on the first street after it, hugging the stoops of the stone houses as he went quickly down the dark street. When he reached the poolroom he felt relieved.

Pop's poolroom was a dreary four-table joint, owned by a glum old Italian with a blue-veined bald head and droopy hands, who sat close to his cash register.

"Seen Ward yet?" Frank said.

Pop pointed to the rear where Ward Minogue, in his fuzzy black hat and a bulky overcoat, was practicing shots alone at a table. Frank watched him place a black ball at a corner pocket and aim a white at it. Ward leaned tensely forward, his face strained, a dead butt hanging from his sick mouth. He shot but missed. He banged his cue on the floor.

Frank had drifted past the players at the other tables. When Ward looked up and saw him, his eyes lit with fear. The fear drained after he recognized who it was. But his pimply face was covered with sweat.

He spat his butt to the floor. "What have you got on your feet, you bastard, gumshoes?"

"I didn't want to spoil your shot."

"Anyway you did."

"I've been looking for you about a week."

"I was on my vacation." Ward smiled in the corner of his mouth.

"On a drunk?"

Ward put his hand to his chest and brought up a belch. "I wish to hell it was. Somebody tipped my old man I was around here, so I hid out for a while. I had a rough time. My heartburn is acting up." He hung up his cue, then wiped his face with a dirty handkerchief.

"Why don't you go to a doctor?" Frank said.

"The hell with them."

"Some medicine might help you."

"What will help me is if my goddam father drops dead."

"I want to talk to you, Ward," Frank said in a low voice.

"So talk."

Frank nodded toward the players at the next table.

"Come out in the yard," Ward said. "I got something I want to say to you."

Frank followed him out the rear door into a small enclosed back yard with a wooden bench against the building. A weak bulb shone down on them from the top of the doorjamb.

Ward sat down on the bench and lit a cigarette. Frank did the same, from his own pack. He puffed but got no pleasure from the butt, so he threw it away.

"Sit down," said Ward.

Frank sat on the bench. Even in the fog he stinks, he thought.

"What do you want me for?" Ward asked, his small eyes restless.

"I want my gun, Ward, Where is it?"

"What for?"

"I want to throw it in the ocean."

Ward snickered. "Cat got your nuts?"

"I don't want some dick coming around and asking me do I own it."

"I thought you said you bought the rod off a fence."

"That's right."

"Then nobody's got a record of it, so what are you scared of?"

"If you lost it," Frank said, "they trace them even without a record."

"I won't lose it," Ward said. After a minute he ground his cigarette into the dirt. "I will give it back to you after we do this job I have on my mind."

Frank looked at him. "What kind of a job?"

"Karp. I want to stick him up."

"Why Karp?—there are bigger liquor stores."

"I hate that Jew son of a bitch and his popeyed Louis. When I was a kid all I had to do was go near banjo eyes and they would complain to my old man and get me beat up."

"They would recognize you if you go in there."

"Bober didn't. I will use a handkerchief and wear some different clothes. Tomorrow I will go out and pick up a car. All you got to do is drive and I will make the heist."

"You better stay away from that block," Frank warned. "Somebody might recognize you."

Ward moodily rubbed his chest. "All right, you sold me. We will go somewheres else."

"Not with me," Frank said.

"Think it over."

"I've had all I want."

Ward showed his disgust. "The minute I saw you I knew you would puke all over."

Frank didn't answer.

"Don't act so innocent," Ward said angrily. "You're hot, the same as me."

"I know," Frank said.

"I slugged him because he was lying where he hid the rest of the dough," Ward argued.

"He didn't hide it. It's a poor, lousy store."

"I guess you know all about that."

"What do you mean?"

"Can the crud. I know you been working there."

Frank drew a breath. "You following me again, Ward?"

Ward smiled. "I followed you one night after you left the poolroom. I found out you were working for a Jew and living on bird crap."

Frank slowly got up. "I felt sorry for him after you slugged him, so I went back to give him a hand while he was in a weak condition. But I won't be staying there long."

"That was real sweet of you. I suppose you gave him back the lousy seven and a half bucks that was your part of the take?"

"I put it back in the cash register. I told the Mrs the business was getting better."

"I never thought I would meet up with a goddam Salvation Army soldier."

"I did it to quiet my conscience," Frank said.

Ward rose. "That ain't your conscience you are worried about."

"No?"

"It's something else. I hear those Jew girls make nice ripe lays."

Frank went back without his gun.

Helen was with her mother as Ida counted the cash.

Frank stood behind the counter, cleaning his fingernails with his jackknife blade, waiting for them to leave so he could close up.

"I think I'll take a hot shower before I go to bed," Helen said to her mother. "I've felt chilled all night."

"Good night," Ida said to Frank. "I left five dollars change for the morning."

"Good night," said Frank.

They left by the rear door and he heard them go up the stairs. Frank closed the store and went into the back. He thumbed through tomorrow's *News*, then got restless.

After a while he went into the store and listened at the side door; he unlatched the lock, snapped on the cellar light, closed the cellar door behind him so no light would leak out into the hall, then quietly descended the stairs.

He found the air shaft where an old unused dumb-waiter stood, pushed the dusty box back and gazed up the vertical shaft. It was pitch-dark. Neither the Bobers' bathroom window nor the Fusos' showed any light.

Frank struggled against himself but not for long. Shoving the dumb-waiter back as far as it would go, he squeezed into the shaft and then boosted himself up on top of the box. His heart shook him with its beating.

When his eyes got used to the dark he saw that her bathroom window was only a couple of feet above his head. He felt along the wall as high as he could reach and touched a narrow ledge around the air shaft. He thought he could anchor himself on it and see into the bathroom.

But if you do it, he told himself, you will suffer.

Though his throat hurt and his clothes were drenched in sweat, the excitement of what he might see forced him to go up.

Crossing himself, Frank grabbed both of the dumb-waiter ropes and slowly pulled himself up, praying the pulley at the skylight wouldn't squeak too much.

A light went on over his head.

Holding his breath, he crouched motionless, clinging to the swaying ropes. Then the bathroom window was shut with a bang. For a while he couldn't move, the strength gone out of him. He thought he might lose his grip and fall, and he thought of her opening the bathroom window and seeing him lying at the bottom of the shaft in a broken, filthy heap.

It was a mistake to do it, he thought.

But she might be in the shower before he could get a look at her, so, trembling, he began again to pull himself up. In a few minutes he was straddling the ledge, holding onto the ropes to steady himself yet keep his full weight off the wood.

Leaning forward, though not too far, he could see through the uncurtained crossed sash window into the old-fashioned bathroom. Helen was there looking with sad eyes at herself in the mirror. He thought she would stand there forever, but at last she unzipped her housecoat, stepping out of it.

He felt a throb of pain at her nakedness, an overwhelming desire to love her, at the same time an awareness of loss, of never having had what he had wanted most, and other such memories he didn't care to recall.

Her body was young, soft, lovely, the breasts like small birds in flight, her ass like a flower. Yet it was a lonely body in spite of its lovely form, lonelier. Bodies are lonely, he thought, but in bed she wouldn't be. She seemed realer to him now than she had been, revealed without clothes, personal, possible. He felt greedy as he gazed, all eyes at a banquet, hungry so long as he must look. But in looking he was forcing her out of reach, making her into a thing only of his seeing, her eyes reflecting his sins, rotten past, spoiled ideals, his passion poisoned by his shame.

Frank's eyes grew moist and he wiped them with one hand. When he gazed up again she seemed, to his horror, to be staring at him through the window, a mocking smile on her lips, her eyes filled with scorn, pitiless. He thought wildly of jumping, bolting, broken-boned, out of the house; but she turned on the shower and stepped into the tub, drawing the flowered plastic curtain around her.

The window was quickly covered with steam. For this he was relieved, grateful. He let himself down silently. In the cellar, instead of the grinding remorse he had expected to suffer, he felt a moving joy.

On a Saturday morning in December, Morris, after a little more than two impatient weeks upstairs, came down with his head healed. The night before, Ida told Frank he would have to leave in the morning, but when Morris later learned this they had an argument. Although he hadn't said so to Ida, the grocer, after his long layoff, was depressed at the prospect of having to take up his dreary existence in the store. He dreaded the deadweight of hours, mostly sad memories of his lost years of youth. That business was better gave him some comfort but not enough, for he was convinced from all Ida had told him that business was better only because of their assistant, whom he remembered as a stranger with hungry eyes, a man to be pitied. Yet the why of it was simple enough—the store had improved not because this cellar dweller was a magician, but because he was not Jewish. The goyim in the neighborhood were happier with one of their own. A Jew stuck in their throats. Yes, they had, on and off, patronized his store, called him by his first name and asked for credit as if he were obliged to give it, which he had, in the past, often foolishly done; but in their hearts they hated him. If it weren't so, Frank's presence could not have made such a quick difference in income. He was afraid that the extra forty-five dollars weekly would melt away overnight if the Italian left and he vehemently said so to Ida. She, though she feared he was right, still argued that Frank must be let go. How could they, she asked, keep him working seven days a week, twelve hours a day, for a miserable five dollars? It was unjust. The grocer agreed, but why push the boy into the street if he wanted to stay longer? The five dollars, he admitted, was nothing, but what of the bed and board, the free packs of cigarettes, the bottles of beer she said he guzzled in the store? If things went on well, he would offer him more, maybe even a small commission, very small—maybe on all they took in over a hundred and fifty a week, a sum they had not realized since

Schmitz had opened up around the corner; meantime he would give him his Sundays off and otherwise reduce his hours. Since Morris was now able to open the store, Frank could stay in bed till nine. This proposition was no great bargain but the grocer insisted that the man have the chance to take or refuse it.

Ida, a red flush spreading on her neck, said, "Are you crazy, Morris? Even with the forty more that comes in, which we give him away five dollars, our little profit, who can afford to keep him here? Look what he eats. It's impossible."

"We can't afford to keep him but we can't afford to lose him, on account he might improve more the business if he stays," Morris answered.

"How can three people work in such a small store?" she cried.

"Rest your sick feet," he answered. "Sleep longer in the morning and stay more upstairs in the house. Who needs you should be so tired every night?"

"Also," Ida argued, "who wants him in the back all night so we can't go inside after the store is closed when we forget something?"

"This I thought about also. I think I will take off from Nick's rent upstairs a couple dollars and tell him he should give Frank the little room to sleep in. They don't use it for nothing, only storage. There, with plenty blankets he will be comfortable, with a door which it goes right in the hall so he can come in and go out with his own key without bothering anybody. He can wash himself here in the store."

"A couple dollars less from the rent comes also from our poor pocket," Ida replied, pressing her clasped hands to her bosom. "But the most important is I don't want him here on account of Helen. I don't like the way he looks on her."

Morris gazed at her. "So you like maybe how Nat looks on her, or Louis Karp? That's the way they look, the boys. Tell me better, how does she look on him?"

She shrugged stiffly.

"This is what I thought. You know yourself Helen wouldn't

be interested in such a boy. A grocery clerk don't interest her. Does she go out with the salesmen where she works, that they ask her? No. She wants better—so let her have better."

"Will be trouble," she murmured.

He belittled her fears, and when he came down on Saturday morning, spoke to Frank about staying on for a while. Frank had arisen before six and was sitting dejectedly on the couch when the grocer came in. He agreed at once to continue on in the store under the conditions Morris offered.

More animated now, the clerk said he liked the idea of living upstairs near Nick and Tessie; and Morris that day arranged it, in spite of Ida's misgivings, by promising three dollars off their rent. Tessie lugged out of the room a trunk, garment bags and a few odds and ends of furniture; after, she dusted and vacuumed. Between what she offered, and what Morris got out of his bin in the cellar, they supplied a bed with a fairly good mattress, a usable chest of drawers, chair, small table, electric heater and even an old radio Nick had around. Although the room was cold, because it had no radiator and was locked off from the Fusos' gas-heated bedroom, Frank was satisfied. Tessie worried about what would happen if he had to go to the bathroom at night, and Nick talked the matter over with Frank, saying apologetically that she was ashamed to have him go through their bedroom, but Frank said he never woke up at night. Anyway, Nick had a key made to the front door patent lock. He said if Frank ever had to get up he could walk across the hall and let himself in through the front without waking them. And he could also use their bathtub, just so long as he told them when he would want it.

This arrangement suited Tessie. Everyone was satisfied but Ida, who was unhappy with herself for having kept Frank on. She made the grocer promise he would send the clerk away before the summer. Business was always more active in the summertime, so Morris agreed. She asked him to tell Frank at once that he would be let go then, and when the grocer did, the clerk smiled amiably and said the summer was a long ways off but anyway it was all right with him.

The grocer felt his mood change. It was a better mood than he had expected. A few of his old customers had returned. One woman told him that Schmitz was not giving as good service as he once did; he was having trouble with his health and was thinking of selling the store. Let him sell, thought Morris. He thought, let him die, then severely struck his chest.

Ida stayed upstairs most of the day, reluctantly at first, less so as time went by. She came down to prepare lunch and supper—Frank still ate before Helen—or to make a salad when it was needed. She attended to little else in the store; Frank did the cleaning and mopping. Upstairs, Ida took care of the house, read a bit, listened to the Jewish programs on the radio and knitted. Helen bought some wool and Ida knitted her a sweater. In the night, after Frank had gone, Ida spent her time in the store, added up the accounts in her notebook and left with Morris when he closed up.

The grocer got along well with his assistant. They divided tasks and waited on alternate customers, though the waiting in between was still much too long. Morris went up for naps to forget the store. He too urged Frank to take some time off in the afternoon, to break the monotony of the day. Frank, somewhat restless, finally began to. Sometimes he went up to his room and lay on the bed, listening to the radio. Usually he put his coat on over his apron and visited one of the other stores on the block. He liked Giannola, the Italian barber across the street, an old man who had recently lost his wife and and sat in the shop all day, even when it was long past time to go home; the old barber gave a fine haircut. Occasionally Frank dropped in on Louis Karp and gassed with him, but generally Louis bored him. Sometimes he went into the butcher store, next door to Morris, and talked in the back room with Artie, the butcher's son, a blond fellow with a bad complexion who was interested in riding horses. Frank said he might go riding with him sometime but he never did though Artie invited him. Once in a while he drank a beer in the bar on the corner, where he liked Earl, the bartender. Yet when the clerk got back to the grocery he was glad to go in.

When he and Morris were together in the back they spent a lot of time talking. Morris liked Frank's company; he liked to hear about strange places, and Frank told him about some of the cities he had been to, in his long wandering, and some of the different jobs he had worked at. He had passed part of his early life in Oakland, California, but most of it across the bay in a home in San Francisco. He told Morris stories about his hard times as a kid. In this second family the home had sent him to, the man used to work him hard in his machine shop. "I wasn't twelve," Frank said, "and he kept me out of school as long as he could get away with."

After staying with that family for three years, he took off. "Then began my long period of travels." The clerk fell silent, and the ticking clock, on the shelf above the sink, sounded flat and heavy. "I am mostly self-educated," he ended.

Morris told Frank about life in the old country. They were poor and there were pogroms. So when he was about to be conscripted into the czar's army his father said, "Run to America." A landsman, a friend of his father, had sent money for his passage. But he waited for the Russians to call him up, because if you left the district before they had conscripted you, then your father was arrested, fined and imprisoned. If the son got away after induction, then the father could not be blamed; it was the army's responsibility. Morris and his father, a peddler in butter and eggs, planned that he would try to get away on his first day in the barracks.

So on that day, Morris said, he told the sergeant, a peasant with red eyes and a bushy mustache which smelled of tobacco, that he wanted to buy some cigarettes in the town. He felt scared but was doing what his father had advised him to do. The half-drunk sergeant agreed he could go, but since Morris was not yet in uniform he would have to go along with him. It was a September day and had just rained. They walked along a muddy road till they reached the town. There, in an inn, Morris bought cigarettes for himself and the sergeant; then, as he had planned it with his father, he invited the soldier to drink some vodka with him. His stomach became rigid at the chance he was taking. He had never drunk in an inn before, and he had never before tried to deceive anybody to this extent. The sergeant, filling his glass often, told Morris the story of his life, crying when he came to the part where, through forgetfulness, he had not attended his mother's funeral. Then he blew his nose, and wagging a thick finger in Morris's face, warned him if he had any plans to skip, he had better forget them if he expected to live. A dead Jew was of less consequence than a live one. Morris felt a heavy gloom descend on him. In his heart he surrendered his freedom for years to come. Yet once they had left the inn and were trudging in the mud back to the barracks, his hopes rose as the sergeant, in his stupor, kept falling behind. Morris walked slowly on, then the sergeant would cup his hands to his mouth, and cursing, haloo for him to wait. Morris waited. They would go on together, the sergeant muttering to himself, Morris uncertain what would happen next. Then the soldier stopped to urinate into a ditch in the road. Morris pretended to wait but he walked on, every minute expecting a bullet to crash through his shoulders and leave him lying in the dirt, his future with the worms. But then, as if seized by his fate, he began to run. The halooing and cursing grew louder as the red-faced sergeant, waving a revolver, stumbled after him; but when he reached the bend of the tree-lined road where he had last seen Morris, nobody was there but a yellow-bearded peasant driving a nag pulling a load of hay.

Telling this story excited the grocer. He lit a cigarette and smoked without coughing. But when he had finished, when there was no more to say, a sadness settled on him. Sitting in his chair, he seemed a small, lonely man. All the time he had been upstairs his hair had grown bushier and he wore a thick pelt of it at the back of his neck. His face was thinner than before.

Frank thought about the story Morris had just told him. That was the big jig in his life but where had it got him? He had escaped out of the Russian Army to the U.S.A., but once in a store he was like a fish fried in deep fat.

"After I came here I wanted to be a druggist," Morris said. "I went for a year in night school. I took algebra, also German and English. ' "Come," said the wind to the leaves one day, "come over the meadow with me and play." ' This is a poem I learned. But I didn't have the patience to stay in night school, so when I met my wife I gave up my chances." Sighing, he said, "Without education you are lost."

Frank nodded.

"You're still young," Morris said. "A young man without a family is free. Don't do what I did."

"I won't," Frank said.

But the grocer didn't seem to believe him. It made the clerk uncomfortable to see the wet-eyed old bird brooding over him. His pity leaks out of his pants, he thought, but he would get used to it.

When they were behind the counter together, Morris kept an eye on Frank and tried to improve some of the things Ida had taught him. The clerk did very well what he was supposed to. As if ashamed somebody could learn the business so easily, Morris explained to him how different it had been to be a grocer only a few years ago. In those days one was more of a macher, a craftsman. Who was ever called on nowadays to slice up a loaf of bread for a customer, or ladle out a quart of milk?

"Now is everything in containers, jars, or packages. Even hard cheeses that they cut them for hundreds of years by hand come now sliced up in cellophane packages. Nobody has to know anything any more."

"I remember the family milk cans," Frank said, "only my family sent me out to get beer in them."

But Morris said it was a good idea that milk wasn't sold loose any more. "I used to know grocers that they took out a quart or two cream from the top of the can, then they put in water. This water-milk they sold at the regular price."

He told Frank about some other tricks he had seen. "In some stores they bought two kinds loose coffee and two kinds tub butter. One was low grade, the other was medium, but the medium they put half in the medium bin and half in the best. So if you bought the best coffee or the best butter you got medium —nothing else."

Frank laughed. "I'll bet some of the customers came back saying that the best butter tasted better than the medium."

"It's easy to fool people," said Morris.

"Why don't you try a couple of those tricks yourself, Morris? Your amount of profit is small."

Morris looked at him in surprise. "Why should I steal from my customers? Do they steal from me?"

"They would if they could."

"When a man is honest he don't worry when he sleeps. This is more important than to steal a nickel."

Frank nodded.

But he continued to steal. He would stop for a few days then almost with relief go back to it. There were times stealing made him feel good. It felt good to have some change in his pocket, and it felt good to pluck a buck from under the Jew's nose. He would slip it into his pants pocket so deftly that he had to keep himself from laughing. With this money, and what he earned, he bought a suit and hat, and got new tubes for Nick's radio. Now and then, through Sam Pearl, who telephoned it in for him, he laid a two-buck bet on a horse, but as a rule he was careful with the dough. He opened a small savings account in a bank near the library and hid the bankbook under his mattress. The money was for future use.

When he felt pepped up about stealing, it was also because he felt he had brought them luck. If he stopped stealing he bet business would fall off again. He was doing them a favor, at the same time making it a little worth his while to stay on and give them a hand. Taking this small cut was his way of showing himself he had something to give. Besides, he planned to return everything sometime or why would he be marking down the figure of what he took? He kept it on a small card in his shoe. He might someday plunk down a tenner or so on some longshot and then have enough to pay back every lousy cent of what he had taken.

For this reason he could not explain why, from one day to another, he should begin to feel bad about snitching the bucks from Morris, but he did. Sometimes he went around with a quiet grief in him, as if he had just buried a friend and was carrying the fresh grave within himself. This was an old feeling of his. He remembered having had something like it for years back. On days he felt this way he sometimes got headaches and went around muttering to himself. He was afraid to look into the mirror for fear it would split apart and drop into the sink. He was wound up so tight he would spin for a week if the spring snapped. He was full of sudden rages at himself. These were his worst days and he suffered trying to hide his feelings. Yet they had a curious way of ending. The rage he felt disappeared like a windstorm that quietly pooped out, and he felt a sort of gentleness creeping in. He felt gentle to the people who came into the store, especially the kids, whom he gave penny crackers to for nothing. He was gentle to Morris, and the Jew was gentle to him. And he was filled with a quiet gentleness for Helen and no longer climbed the air shaft to spy on her, naked in the bathroom.

And there were days when he was sick to death of everything. He had had it, up to here. Going downstairs in the morning he thought he would gladly help the store burn if it caught on fire. Thinking of Morris waiting on the same lousy customers day after day throughout the years, as they picked out with dirty fingers the same cheap items they ate every day of their flea-bitten lives, then when they were gone, waiting for them to come back again, he felt like leaning over the banister and throwing up. What kind of a man did you have to be born to shut yourself up in an overgrown coffin and never once during the day, so help you, outside of going for your Yiddish newspaper, poke you beak out of the door for a snootful of air? The answer wasn't hard to say—you had to be a Jew. They were born prisoners. That was what Morris was, with his deadly patience, or endurance, or whatever the hell it was; and it explained Al Marcus, the paper products salesman, and that skinny rooster Breitbart, who dragged from store to store his two heavy cartons full of bulbs.

Al Marcus, who had once, with an apologetic smile, warned the clerk not to trap himself in a grocery, was a well-dressed man of forty-six, but he looked, whenever you saw him, as if he had just lapped up cyanide. His face was the whitest Frank had ever seen, and what anybody saw in his eyes if he took a good look, would not help his appetite. The truth of it was, the grocer had confided to Frank, that Al had cancer and was supposed to be dead in his grave a year ago, but he fooled the doctors; he stayed alive if you could call it that. Although he had a comfortable pile, he wouldn't quit working and showed up regularly once a month to take orders for paper bags, wrapping paper and containers. No matter how bad business was, Morris tried to have some kind of little order waiting for him. Al would suck on an unlit cigar, scribble an item or two on a pink page in his metal-covered salesbook, then stand around a few minutes, making small talk, his eyes far away from what he was saying; and after that, tip his hat and take off for the next place. Everybody knew how sick he was, and a couple of the storekeepers earnestly advised him to quit working, but Al, smiling apologetically, took his cigar out of his mouth and said, "If I stay home, somebody in a high hat is gonna walk up the stairs and put a knock on my door. This way let him at least move his bony ass around and try and find me."

As for Breitbart, according to Morris, nine years ago he had owned a good business, but his brother ran it into the ground, gambling, then he took off with what was left of the bank account, persuading Breitbart's wife to come along and keep it company. That left him with a drawerful of bills and no credit; also a not too bright five-year-old boy. Breitbart went bankrupt; his creditors plucked every feather. For months he and the boy lived in a small, dirty furnished room, Breitbart not having the heart to go out to look for work. Times were bad. He went on relief and later took to peddling. He was now in his fifties but his hair had turned white and he acted like an old man. He bought electric bulbs at wholesale and carried two cartons of them slung, with clothesline rope, over his shoulder. Every day, in his crooked shoes, he walked miles, looking into stores and calling out in a mournful voice, "Lights for sale." At night he went home and cooked supper for his Hymie, who played hooky whenever he could from the vocational school where they were making him into a shoemaker.

When Breitbart first came to Morris's neighborhood and dropped into the store, the grocer, seeing his fatigue, offered him a glass of tea with lemon. The peddler eased his rope off his shoulder and set his boxes on the floor. In the back he gulped the hot tea in silence, warming both hands on the glass. And though he had, besides his other troubles, the seven-year itch, which kept him awake half the night, he never complained. After ten minutes he got up, thanked the grocer, fitted the rope onto his lean and itchy shoulder and left. One day he told Morris the story of his life and they both wept.

That's what they live for, Frank thought, to suffer. And the one that has got the biggest pain in the gut and can hold onto it the longest without running to the toilet is the best Jew. No wonder they got on his nerves.

Winter tormented Helen. She ran from it, hid in the house. In the house she revenged herself on December by crossing off the calendar all its days. If Nat would only call, she thought endlessly, but the telephone was deaf and dumb. She dreamed of him nightly, felt deeply in love, famished for him; would gladly have danced into his warm white bed if only he nodded, or she dared ask him to ask her; but Nat never called. She hadn't for a minute glimpsed him since running into him on the subway early in November. He lived around the corner but it might as well be Paradise. So with a sharp-pointed pencil she scratched out each dead day while it still lived.

Though Frank hungered for her company he rarely spoke to her. Now and then he passed her on the street. She murmured hello and walked on with her books, conscious of his eyes following her. Sometimes in the store, as if in defiance of her mother, she stopped to talk for a minute with the clerk. Once he startled her by abruptly mentioning this book he was reading. He longed to ask her to go out with him, but never dared; the old lady's eyes showed distrust of the goings on. So he waited. Mostly he watched for her at the window. He studied her hidden face, sensed her lacks, which deepened his own, but didn't know what to do about it.

December yielded nothing to spring. She awoke to each frozen, lonely day with dulled feeling. Then one Sunday afternoon winter leaned backward for an hour and she went walking. Suddenly she forgave everyone everything. A warmish breath of air was enough to inspire; she was again grateful for living. But the sun soon sank and it snowed pellets. She returned home, leaden. Frank was standing at Sam Pearl's deserted corner but she seemed not to see him though she brushed by. He felt very bad. He wanted her but the facts made a terrible construction. They were Jews and he was not. If he started going out with Helen her mother would throw a double fit and Morris another. And Helen made him feel, from the way she carried herself, even when she seemed most lonely, that she had plans for something big in her life—nobody like F. Alpine. He had nothing, a backbreaking past, had committed a crime against her old man, and in spite of

his touchy conscience, was stealing from him too. How complicated could impossible get?

He saw only one way of squeezing through the stone knot;
start by shoveling out the load he was carrying around in his
mind by admitting to Morris that he was one of the guys that
had held him up. It was a funny thing about that; he wasn't really
sorry they had stuck up a Jew but he hadn't expected to be
sorry that they had picked on this particular one, Bober; yet now
he was. He had not minded, if by mind you meant in expectation, but what he hadn't minded no longer seemed to matter. The
matter was how he now felt, and he now felt bad he had done it.
And when Helen was around he felt worse.

So the confession had to come first—this stuck like a bone
through the neck. From the minute he had tailed Ward Minogue
into the grocery that night, he had got this sick feeling that he
might someday have to vomit up in words, no matter how hard
or disgusting it was to do, the thing he was then engaged in doing. He felt he had known this, in some frightful way, a long time
before he went into the store, before he had met Minogue, or
even come east; that he had really known all his life he would
sometime, through throat blistered with shame, his eyes in the
dirt, have to tell some poor son of a bitch that he was the one
who had hurt or betrayed him. This thought had lived in him
with claws; or like a thirst he could never spit out, a repulsive
need to get out of his system all that had happened—for whatever had happened had happened wrong; to clean it out of his self
and bring in a little peace, a little order; to change the beginning,
beginning with the past that always stupendously stank up the
now—to change his life before the smell of it suffocated him.

Yet when the chance came to say it, when he was alone with
Morris that November morning in the back of the store, as they
were drinking the coffee that the Jew had served him, and the
impulse came on him to spill everything now, *now*, he had strained
to heave it up, but it was like tearing up your whole life, with the
broken roots and blood; and a fear burned in his gut that once

he had got started saying the wrongs he had done he would never leave off until he had turned black; so instead he had told him a few hurried things about how ass-backward his life had gone, which didn't even begin to say what he wanted. He had worked on Morris's pity and left halfway satisfied, but not for long, because soon the need to say it returned and he heard himself groaning, but groans weren't words.

He argued with himself that he was smart in not revealing to the grocer more than he had. Enough was enough; besides, how much of a confession was the Jew entitled to for the seven and a half bucks he had taken, then put back into his cash register drawer, and for the knock on the head he had got from Ward, whom he himself had come with unwillingly? Maybe willing, but not to do what had finally been done. That deserved some consideration, didn't it? Furthermore, he had begged the creep not to hurt anybody, and had later turned him down when he cooked up another scheme of stickup against Karp, who they were out to get in the first place. That showed his good intentions for the future, didn't it? And who was it, after all was said and done, that had waited around shivering in his pants in the dark cold, to pull in Morris's milk boxes, and had worked his ass to a frazzle twelve hours a day while the Jew lay upstairs resting in his bed? And was even now keeping him from starvation in his little rat hole? All that added up to something too.

That was how he argued with himself, but it didn't help for long, and he was soon again fighting out how to jump free of what he had done. He would someday confess it all—he promised himself. If Morris accepted his explanation and solemn apology, it would clear the rocks out of the road for the next move. As for his present stealing from the cash register, he had decided that once he had told the grocer all there was to say about the holdup, he would at the same time start paying back into the drawer, out of his little salary and the few bucks he had put away in the bank, what he had taken, and that would fix that. It wouldn't necessarily mean that Helen Bober would then and there fall for him—the opposite could happen—but if she *did*, he wouldn't feel bad about it.

He knew by heart what he would say to the grocer once he got to say it. One day while they were talking in the back, he would begin, as he had once done, about how his life was mostly made up of lost chances, some so promising he could still not stand to remember them. Well, after certain bad breaks through various causes, mostly his own mistakes—he was piled high with regrets—after many such failures, though he tried every which way to free himself from them, usually he failed; so after a time he gave up and let himself be a bum. He lived in gutters, cellars if he was lucky, slept in lots, ate what the dogs wouldn't, or couldn't, and what he scrounged out of garbage cans. He wore what he found, slept where he flopped and guzzled anything.

By rights this should have killed him, but he lived on, bearded, smelly, dragging himself through the seasons without a hope to go by. How many months he had existed this way he would never know. Nobody kept the score of it. But one day while he lay in some hole he had crawled into, he had this terrific idea that he was really an important guy, and was torn out of his reverie with the thought that he was living this kind of life only because he hadn't known he was meant for something a whole lot better—to do something big, different. He had not till that minute understood this. In the past he had usually thought of himself as an average guy, but there in this cellar it came to him he was wrong. That was why his luck had so often curdled, because he had the wrong idea of what he really was and had spent all his energy trying to do the wrong things. Then when he had asked himself what should he be doing, he had another powerful idea, that he was meant for crime. He had at times teased himself with this thought, but now it wouldn't let go of him. At crime he would change his luck, make adventure, live like a prince. He shivered with pleasure as he conceived robberies, assaults—murders if it had to be—each violent act helping to satisfy a craving that somebody suffer as his own fortune improved. He felt infinitely relieved, believing that if a person figured for himself something big, something different in his life, he had a better chance to get it than some poor jerk who couldn't think that high up.

So he gave up his outhouse existence. He began to work again, got himself a room, saved and bought a gun. Then he headed east, where he figured he could live the way he wanted—where there was money, nightclubs, babes. After a week of prowling around in Boston, not sure where he ought to start off, he hopped a freight to Brooklyn and a couple of days after he got there met Ward Minogue. As they were shooting pool one night, Ward cannily detected the gun on him and made him the proposition that they do a holdup together. Frank welcomed the idea of some kind of start but said he wanted to think about it more. He went to Coney Island, and while sitting on the boardwalk, worrying about what he ought to do, got this oppressive feeling he was being watched. When he turned around it was Ward Minogue. Ward sat down and told him that it was a Jew he planned to rob, so Frank agreed to go with him.

But on the night of the holdup he found himself nervous. In the car Ward sensed it and cursed him. Frank felt he had to stick it out, but the minute they were both in the grocery and tying handkerchiefs around their mouths, the whole idea seemed senseless. He could feel it poop out in his mind. His plans of crime lay down and died. He could hardly breathe in his unhappiness, wanted to rush out into the street and be swallowed up out of existence, but he couldn't let Ward stay there alone. In the back, nauseated by the sight of the Jew's bloodied head, he realized he had made the worst mistake yet, the hardest to wipe out. And that ended his short life of violent crime, another pipe dream, and he was trapped tighter in the tangle of his failures. All this he thought he would someday tell Morris. He knew the Jew well enough to feel sure of his mercy.

Yet there were times when he imagined himself, instead, telling it all to Helen. He wanted to do something that would open her eyes to his true self, but who could be a hero in a grocery store? Telling her would take guts and guts was something. He continued to feel he deserved a better fate, and he would find it if he only once—*once*—did the right thing—the thing to do at the right time. Maybe if they were ever together for any decent amount of time, he would ask her to listen. At first she might be embarrassed, but when he started telling her about his life, he knew she would hear him to the end. After that—who knew? With a dame all you needed was a beginning.

But when the clerk caught himself coldly and saw the sentimentality of his thinking—he was a sentimental wop at heart—he knew he was having another of his hopped-up dreams. What kind of a chance did he think he would have with her after he had admitted the stickup of her old man? So he figured the best thing was to keep quiet. At the same time a foreboding crept into him that if he said nothing now, he would someday soon have a dirtier past to reveal.

A few days after Christmas, on the night of a full moon, Frank, dressed in his new clothes, hurried to the library, about a dozen blocks from the grocery. The library was an enlarged store, well lit, with bulging shelves of books that smelled warm on winter nights. In the rear there were a few large reading tables. It was a pleasant place to come to out of the cold. His guess was good, soon Helen arrived. She wore a red woolen scarf on her head, one end thrown over her shoulder. He was at a table reading. She noticed him as she closed the door behind her; he knew it. They had met here, briefly, before. She had wondered what he read at the table, and once in passing, glanced quickly over his shoulder. She had guessed *Popular Mechanics*, but it was the life of somebody or other. Tonight, as usual, she was aware of his eyes on her as she moved about from shelf to shelf. When, after an hour, she left, he caught a tight hidden glance in his direction. Frank got up and checked out a book. She was halfway down the street before he caught up with her.

"Big moon." He reached up to tip his hat and awkwardly discovered he wasn't wearing any.

"It feels like snow," Helen answered.

He glanced at her to see if she was kidding, then at the sky. It was cloudless, flooded with moonlight.

"Maybe." As they approached the street corner, he remarked, "We could take a walk in the park if it's okay with you."

She shivered at the suggestion, yet turned with a nervous laugh at the corner, and walked by his side. She had said almost nothing to him since the night he had called her to answer the empty phone. Who it had been she would never know; the incident still puzzled her.

Helen felt for him, as they walked, an irritation bordering on something worse. She knew what caused it—her mother, in making every gentile, by definition, dangerous; therefore he and she, together, represented some potential evil. She was also annoyed that his eating eyes were always on her, for he saw, she felt, more than his occasionally trapped gaze revealed. She fought her dislike of him, reasoning it wasn't his fault if her mother had made him into an enemy; and if he was always looking at her, it meant at least he saw something attractive or why would he look? Considering her lonely life, for that she owed him gratitude.

The unpleasant feeling passed and she glanced guardedly up at him. He was walking unmarked in moonlight, innocent of her reaction to him. She felt then—this thought had come to her before—that there might be more to him than she had imagined. She felt ashamed she had never thanked him for the help he had given her father.

In the park the moon was smaller, a wanderer in the white sky. He was talking about winter. "It's funny you mentioned snow before," Frank said. "I was reading about the life of St. Francis in the library, and when you mentioned the snow it made me think about this story where he wakes up one winter night, asking himself did he do the right thing to be a monk. My God, he thought, supposing I met some nice young girl and got married to her and by now I had a wife and a family? That made him feel bad so he couldn't sleep. He got out of his straw bed and went outside the church or monastery or wherever he was staying. The ground was all covered with snow. Out of it he made this snow woman, and he said, 'There, that's my wife.' Then he made two or three kids out of the snow. After, he kissed them all and went inside and laid down in the straw. He felt a whole lot better and fell asleep."

The story surprised and touched her.

"Did you just read that?"

"No. I remember it from the time I was a kid. My head is full of those stories, don't ask me why. A priest used to read them to the orphans in this home I was in, and I guess I never forgot them. They come into my thoughts for no reason at all."

He had had a haircut and in his new clothes was hardly recognizable as her father's baggy-pants assistant who had slept a week in their cellar. Tonight he looked like somebody she had never seen before. His clothes showed taste, and he was, in his way, interesting looking. Without an apron on he seemed younger.

They passed an empty bench. "What do you say if we sit down?" Frank said.

"I'd rather walk."

"Smoke?"

"No."

He lit a cigarette, then caught up with her.

"Sure is some night."

"I want to say thanks for helping my father," Helen said, "You've been very kind. I should have mentioned it before."

"Nobody has to thank me. Your father did me some good favors." He felt uncomfortable.

"Anyway, don't make a career of a grocery," she said. "There's no future in it."

He puffed with a smile on his lips. "Everybody warns me. Don't worry, my imagination is too big for me to get stuck in a grocery. It's only temporary work."

"It isn't what you usually do?"

"No." He set himself to be honest. "I'm just taking a breather, you could call it. I started out wrong and have to change my direction where I am going. The way it happened I landed up in your father's store, but I'm only staying there till I figure out what's my next move."

He remembered the confession he had considered making to her, but the time wasn't ready yet. You could confess as a stranger, and you could confess as a friend.

"I've tried about everything," he said, "now I got to choose one thing and stick with it. I'm tired of being on the move all the time."

"Isn't it a little late for you to be getting started?"

"I'm twenty-five. There are plenty of guys who start that late and some I have read about started later. Age don't mean a thing. It doesn't make you less than anybody else."

"I never said so." At the next empty bench she paused. "We could sit here for a few minutes if you like."

"Sure." Frank wiped the seat with his handkerchief before she sat down. He offered her his cigarettes.

"I said I don't smoke."

"Sorry, I thought you didn't want to smoke while you were walking. Some girls don't like to." He put his pack away.

She noticed the book he was carrying. "What are you reading?"

He showed it to her.

"*The Life of Napoleon*"?

"That's right."

"Why him?"

"Why not—he was great, wasn't he?"

"Others were in better ways."

"I'll read about them too," Frank said.

"Do you read a lot?"

"Sure. I am a curious guy. I like to know why people tick. I like to know the reason they do the things they do, if you know what I mean."

She said she did.

He asked her what book she was reading.

"*The Idiot*. Do you know it?"

"No. What's it about?"

"It's a novel."

"I'd rather read the truth," he said.

"It is the truth."

Helen asked, "Are you a high school graduate?"

He laughed. "Sure I am. Education is free in this country."

She blushed. "It was a silly question."

"I didn't meant any wisecrack," he said quickly.

"I didn't take it as such."

"I went to high school in three different states and finally got finished up at night—in a night school. I planned on going to college but this job came along that I couldn't turn down, so I changed my mind, but it was a mistake."

"I had to help my mother and father out," Helen said, "so I couldn't go either. I've taken courses in NYU at night—mostly lit courses—and I've added up about a year's credit, but it's very hard at night. My work doesn't satisfy me. I would still like to go full time in the day."

He flipped his butt away. "I've been thinking about starting in college lately, even if I am this age. I know a guy who did it."

"Would you go at night?" she asked.

"Maybe, maybe in the day if I could get the right kind of a job—in an all-night cafeteria or something like that, for instance. This guy I just mentioned did that—assistant manager or something. After five or six years he graduated an engineer. Now he's making his pile, working all over the country."

"It's hard doing it that way—very hard."

"The hours are rough but you get used to it. When you got something good to do, sleep is a waste of time."

"It takes years at night."

"Time don't mean anything to me."

"It does to me."

"The way I figure, anything is possible. I always think about the different kinds of chances I have. This has stuck in my mind —don't get yourself trapped in one thing, because maybe you can do something else a whole lot better. That's why I guess I never settled down so far. I've been exploring conditions. I still have some very good ambitions which I would like to see come true. The first step to that, I know for sure now, is to get a good education. I didn't use to think like that, but the more I live the more I do. Now it's always on my mind."

"I've always felt that way," Helen said.

He lit another cigarette, throwing the burnt match away. "What kind of work do you do?"

"I'm a secretary."

"You like it?" He smoked with half-closed eyes. She sensed he knew she didn't care for her job and suspected he had heard her father or mother say so.

After a while, she answered, "No, I don't. The job never changes. And I could live happily without seeing some of those characters I have to deal with all day long, the salesmen, I mean."

"They get fresh?"

"They talk a lot. I'd like to be doing something that feels useful—some kind of social work or maybe teaching. I have no sense of accomplishment in what I'm doing now. Five o'clock comes and at last I go home. That's about all I live for, I guess."

She spoke of her daily routine, but after a minute saw he was only half-listening. He was staring at the moon-drenched trees in the distance, his face drawn, his lit eyes elsewhere.

Helen sneezed, unwound her scarf and wrapped it tightly around her head.

"Shall we go now?"

"Just till I finish my cigarette."

Some fat nerve, she thought.

Yet his face, even with the broken nose, was sensitive in the dark light. What makes me so irritable? She had had the wrong idea of him but it was her own fault, the result of staying so long apart from people.

He drew a long jagged breath.

"Is something the matter?" she asked.

Frank cleared his throat but his voice was hoarse. "No, just something popped into my mind when I was looking at the moon. You know how your thoughts are."

"Nature sets you thinking?"

"I like scenery."

"I walk a lot for that reason."

"I like the sky at night, but you see more of it in the West. Out here the sky is too high, there are too many big buildings."

He squashed his cigarette with his heel and wearily rose, looking now like someone who had parted with his youth.

She got up and walked with him, curious about him. The moon moved above them in the homeless sky.

After a long silence, he said as they were walking, "I like to tell you what I was thinking about."

"Please, you don't have to."

"I feel like talking," he said. "I got to thinking about this carnie outfit I worked for one time when I was about twenty-one. Right after I got the job I fell for a girl in an acrobatic act. She was built something like you—on the slim side, I would say. At first I don't think I rated with her. I think she thought I wasn't a serious type of guy. She was kind of a complicated girl, you know, moody, with lots of problems in her mind that she kept to herself. Well, one day we got to talking and she told me she wanted to be a nun. I said, 'I don't think it will suit you.' 'What do you know about me?' she said. I didn't tell her, although I know people pretty well, don't ask me why, I guess you are born with certain things. Anyway, the whole summer long I was nuts about her but she wouldn't give me another look though there was nobody else around that I saw she went with. 'Is it my age?' I asked her. 'No, but you haven't lived,' she answered me. 'If you only could see in my heart all I have lived through,' I said, but

I have my doubts if she believed me. All we ever did was talk like that. Once in a while I would ask her for a date, not thinking I would ever get one, and I never did. 'Give up,' I said to myself, 'all she is interested in is herself.'

"Then one morning, when it was getting to be around fall and you could smell the season changing, I said to her I was taking off when the show closed. 'Where are you going?' she asked me. I said I was going to look for a better life. She didn't answer anything to that. I said, 'Do you still want to be a nun?' She got red and looked away, then she answered she wasn't sure about that any more. I could see she had changed but I wasn't fool enough to think it was account of me. But I guess it really was, because by accident our hands sort of touched, and when I saw the way she looked at me, it was hard to breathe. My God, I thought, we are both in love. I said to her, 'Honey, meet me here after the show tonight and let's go where we will be alone.' She said yes. Before she left she gave me a quick kiss.

"Anyway, that same afternoon she took off in her old man's jalopy to buy a blouse she had seen in some store window in the last town, but on the way back it started to rain. Exactly what happened I don't know. I guess she misjudged a curve or something and went flying off the road. The jalopy bounced down the hill, and her neck was broken. . . . That's how it ended."

They walked in silence. Helen was moved. But why, she thought, all the sad music?

"I'm awfully sorry."

"It was years ago."

"It was a tragic thing to happen."

"I couldn't expect better," he said.

"Life renews itself."

"My luck stays the same."

"Go on with your plans for an education."

"That's about it," Frank said. "That's what I got to do."

Their eyes met, she felt her scalp prickle.

Then they left the park and went home.

Outside the dark grocery store she quickly said good night.

"I'll stay out a little longer," Frank said. "I like to see the moon."

She went upstairs.

In bed she thought of their walk, wondering how much to believe of what he had told her about his ambitions and plans for college. He could not have said anything to make a better impression on her. And what was the purpose of the sad tale of the carnival girl "built something like you"? Who was he mixing up with his carnival girls? Yet he had told the story simply, without any visible attempt to work on her sympathy. Probably it was a true memory, recalled because he happened to be feeling lonely. She had had her own moonlit memories to contend with. Thinking about Frank, she tried to see him straight but came up with a confusing image: the grocery clerk with the greedy eyes, on top of the ex-carnival hand and future serious college student, a man of possibilities.

On the verge of sleep she sensed a desire on his part to involve her in his life. The aversion she felt for him before returned but she succeeded without too much effort in dispelling it. Thoroughly awake now, she regretted she could not see the sky from her window in the wall, or look down into the street. Who was he making into a wife out of snowy moonlight?

Earnings in the grocery, especially around Christmas and New Year's, continued to rise. For the last two weeks in December Morris averaged an unusual one hundred and ninety. Ida had a new theory to explain the spurt of business: an apartment house had opened for rentals a few blocks away; furthermore, she had heard that Schmitz was not so attentive to his store as he was before. An unmarried storekeeper was sometimes erratic. Morris didn't deny these things but he still attributed their good fortune mostly to his clerk. For reasons that were clear to him the customers liked Frank, so they brought in their friends. As a result, the grocer could once more meet his running expenses, and with pinching and scrimping, even pay off some outstanding bills. Grateful to Frank—who seemed to take for granted the up-swing of business—he planned to pay him more than the measly five dollars they shamefacedly gave him, but cautiously decided to see if the added income would continue in January, when business usually slackened off. Even if he regularly took in two hundred a week, with the slight profit he made he could hardly afford a clerk. Before things were easier they had to take in a minimum of two-fifty or three hundred, an impossibility.

Since, though, the situation was better, Morris told Helen that he wanted her to keep more of her hard-earned twenty-five dollars; he said she must now keep fifteen, and if business stayed as it was maybe he would not need her assistance any more. He hoped so. Helen was overwhelmed at having fifteen a week to spend on herself. She needed shoes badly and could use a new coat—hers was little better than a rag—and a dress or two. And she wanted to put away a few dollars for future tuition at NYU. She felt like her father about Frank—he had changed their luck. Remembering what he had said in the park that night about his ambitions and desire for education, she felt he someday would get what he wanted because he was obviously more than just an ordinary person.

He was often at the library. Almost every time Helen went there she saw him sitting over an open book at one of the tables; she wondered if all he did in his spare time was come here and read. She respected him for it. She herself averaged two weekly visits, each time checking out only a book or two, because it was one of her few pleasures to return for another. Even at her loneliest she liked being among books, although she was sometimes depressed to see how much there was to read that she hadn't. Meeting Frank so often, she was at first uneasy: he haunted the place, for what? But, a library was a library; he came here, as she did, to satisfy certain needs. Like her he read a lot because he was lonely, Helen thought. She thought this after he had told her about the carnival girl. Gradually her uneasiness left her.

Although he left, as a rule, when she did, if she wanted to walk home alone, he did not intrude. Sometimes he rode back on the trolley while she walked. Sometimes she was on the trolley and saw him walking. But generally, so long as the weather was not too bad, they went home together, a couple of times turning off into the park. He told her more about himself. He had lived a different life from most people she had known, and she envied him all the places he had been to. Her own life, she thought, was much like her father's, restricted by his store, his habits, hers. Morris hardly ever journeyed past the corner, except on rare occasions, usually to return something a customer had left on the counter. When Ephraim was alive, when they were kids, her father liked to go bathing Sunday afternoons at Coney Island; and on Jewish holidays they would sometimes see a Yiddish play, or ride on the subway to the Bronx to call on landsleit. But after Ephraim died Morris had for years gone nowhere. Neither had she, for other reasons. Where could she go without a cent? She read with eagerness of far-off places but spent her life close to home. She would have given much to visit Charleston, New Orleans, San Francisco, cities she had heard so much about, but she hardly ever got beyond the borough of Manhattan. Hearing Frank talk of Mexico, Texas, California, other such places, she realized anew the meagerness of her movements: every day but Sunday on the BMT to Thirty-fourth Street and back. Add to that a twice-weekly visit to the library at night. In summer, the same as before, except a few times—usually during her vacation—to Manhattan Beach; also, if she were lucky, to a concert or two at Lewisohn Stadium. Once when she was twenty and worn out, her mother had insisted she go for a week to an inexpensive adult camp in New Jersey. Before that, while in high school, she had traveled to Washington, D. C., with her American history class for a week end of visiting government buildings. So far and no further in the open world. To stick so close to where she had lived her whole life was a crime. His stories made her impatient —she wanted to travel, experience, live.

One night as they were sitting on a bench in an enclosed part of the park beyond the tree-lined plaza, Frank said he had definitely made up his mind to start college in the fall. This excited her, and for hours afterward Helen couldn't stop thinking about it. She imagined all the interesting courses he could take, envied him the worthwhile people he'd meet in his classes, the fun he'd have studying. She pictured him in nice clothes, his hair cut shorter, maybe his nose straightened, speaking a more careful English, interested in music and literature, learning about politics, psychology, philosophy; wanting to know more the more he knew, in this way growing in value to himself and others. She imagined herself invited by him to a campus concert or play, where she would meet his college friends, people of promise. Afterward as they crossed the campus in the dark, Frank would point out the buildings his classes met in, classes taught by distinguished professors. And maybe if she closed her eyes she could see a time—miracle of miracles—when Helen Bober was enrolled here, not just a stranger on the run, pecking at a course or two at night, and tomorrow morning back at Levenspiel's Louisville Panties and Bras. At least he made her dream.

To help him prepare for college Helen said he ought to read some good novels, some of the great ones. She wanted Frank to like novels, to enjoy in them what she did. So she checked out *Madame Bovary, Anna Karenina* and *Crime and Punishment*, all by writers he had barely heard of, but they were very satisfying books, she said. He noticed she handled each yellow-paged volume as though she were holding in her respectful hands the works of God Almighty. As if—according to her—you could read in them everything you couldn't afford not to know—the Truth about Life. Frank carried the three books up to his room, and huddled in a blanket to escape the cold that seeped in through the loose window frames, had rough going. The stories were hard to get into because the people and places were strange to him, their crazy names difficult to hold in his mind and some of the sentences were so godawful complicated he forgot the beginning before he got to the end. The opening pages irritated him as he pushed through forests of odd facts and actions. Though he stared for hours at the words, starting one book, then another, then the third—in the end, in exasperation, he flung them aside.

But because Helen had read and respected these books, it shamed him that he hadn't, so he picked one up from the floor and went back to it. As he dragged himself through the first chapters, gradually the reading became easier and he got interested in the people—their lives in one way or another wounded—some to death. Frank read, at the start, in snatches, then in bursts of strange hunger, and before too long he had managed to finish the books. He had started *Madame Bovary* with some curiosity, but in the end he felt disgusted, wearied, left cold. He did not know why people would want to write about that kind of a dame. Yet he felt a little sorry for her and the way things had happened, till there was no way out of it but her death. *Anna Karenina* was better; she was more interesting and better in bed. He didn't want her to kill herself under the train in the end. Still, although Frank felt he could also take the book or leave it, he was moved at the deep change that came over Levin in the woods just after he had thought of hanging himself. At least he wanted to live. *Crime and Punishment* repelled yet fascinated him, with everybody in the joint confessing to something every time he opened his yap—to some weakness, or sickness, or crime. Raskolnikov, the student, gave him a pain, with all his miseries. Frank first had the idea he must be a Jew and was surprised when he found he wasn't. He felt, in places in the book, even when it excited him, as if his face had been shoved into dirty water in the gutter; in other places, as if he had been on a drunk for a month. He was glad when he was finished with the book, although he liked Sonia, the prostitute, and thought of her for days after he had read it.

Afterward Helen suggested other novels by the same writers, so he would know them better, but Frank balked, saying he wasn't sure that he had understood those he had read. "I'm sure you have," she answered, "if you got to know the people." "I know them," he muttered. But to please her he worked through two more thick books, sometimes tasting nausea on his tongue, his face strained as he read, eyes bright black, frowning, although he usually felt some relief at the end of the book. He wondered what Helen found so satisfying in all this goddamned human misery, and suspected her of knowing he had spied on her in the bathroom and was using the books to punish him for it. But then he thought it was an unlikely idea. Anyway, he could not get out of his thoughts how quick some people's lives went to pot when they had to do it; and he was troubled by the thought of how easy it was for a man to wreck his whole life in a single wrong act. After that the guy suffered forever, no matter what he did to make up for the wrong. At times, as the clerk had sat in his room late at night, a book held stiffly in his reddened hands, his head numb although he wore a hat, he felt a strange falling away from the printed page and had this crazy sensation that he was reading about himself. At first this picked him up but then it deeply depressed him.

One rainy night, as Helen was about to go up to Frank's room to ask him to take back something he had given her that she didn't want, before she could go the phone rang, and Ida hastened out into the hall to call her. Frank, lying on his bed in his room, watching the rainy window, heard her go downstairs. Morris was in the store waiting on someone as Helen came in, but her mother sat in the back over a cup of tea.

"It's Nat," Ida whispered, not moving.

She'll tell herself she isn't listening, thought Helen.

Her first feeling was that she didn't want to talk to the law student, but his voice was warm, which for him meant extended effort, and a warm voice on a wet night was a warm voice. She could easily picture what he looked like as he spoke into the phone. Yet she wished he had called her in December, when she had so desperately wanted him, for now she was again aware of a detachment in herself that she couldn't account for.

"Nobody sees you any more, Helen," Nat began. "Where've you disappeared to?"

"Oh, I've been around," she said, trying to hide a slight tremble in her voice. "And you?"

"Is somebody there where you're talking that you sound so restrained?"

"That's right."

"I thought so. So let me make it quick and clean. Helen, it's been a long time. I want to see you. What do you say if we take in a play this Saturday night? I can stop off for tickets on my way uptown tomorrow."

"Thanks, Nat. I don't think so." She heard her mother sigh.

Nat cleared his throat. "Helen, I honestly want to know how somebody's supposed to defend himself when he hasn't any idea what's in the indictment against him? What kind of a crime have I committed? Yield the details."

"I'm not a lawyer—I don't make indictments."

"So call it a cause—what's the cause? One day we're close to each other, the next I'm alone on an island, holding my hat. What did I do, please tell me?"

"Let's drop this subject."

Here Ida rose and went into the store, softly closing the door behind her. Thanks, thought Helen. She kept her voice low so they wouldn't hear her through the window in the wall.

"You're a funny kid," Nat was saying. "You've got some old-fashioned values about some things. I always told you you punish yourself too much. Why should anybody have such a hot and heavy conscience in these times? People are freer in the twentieth century. Pardon me for saying it but it's true."

She blushed. His insight was to his credit. "My values are my values," she replied.

"What," Nat argued, "would people's lives be like if everybody regretted every beautiful minute of all that happened? Where's the poetry of living?"

"I hope you're alone," she said angrily, "where you're so blithely discussing this subject."

He sounded weary, hurt. "Of course I'm alone. My God, Helen, how low have I fallen in your opinion?"

"I told you what was going on at this end. Up to a minute ago my mother was still in the room."

"I'm sorry, I forgot."

"It's all right now."

"Look, girl," he said affectionately, "the telephone is no place to hash out our personal relations. What do you say if I run upstairs and see you right away? We got to come to some kind of a sensible understanding. I'm not exactly a pig, Helen. What you don't want is your privilege, if I may be so frank. So you don't want, but at least let's be friends and go out once in a while. Let me come up and talk to you."

"Some other time, Nat, I have to do something now."

"For instance?"

"Some other time," she said.

"Why not?" Nat answered amiably.

When he had hung up, Helen stood at the phone, wondering if she had done right. She felt she hadn't.

Ida entered the kitchen. "What did he want—Nat?"

"Just to talk."

"He asked you to go out?"

She admitted it.

"What did you answer him?"

"I said I would some other time."

"What do you mean 'some other time?' " Ida said sharply. "What are you already, Helen, an old lady? What good is it to sit so many nights alone upstairs? Who gets rich from reading? What's the matter with you?"

"Nothing's the matter, Mama." She left the store and went into the hall.

"Don't forget you're twenty-three years old," Ida called after her.

"I won't."

Upstairs her nervousness grew. When she thought what she had to do she didn't want to, yet felt she must.

They had met, she and Frank, last night at the library, the third time in eight days. Helen noticed as they were leaving that he clumsily carried a package she took to contain some shirts or underwear, but on the way home Frank flung away his cigarette, and under a street lamp handed it to her. "Here, this is for you."

"For me? What is it?"

"You'll find out."

She took it half-willingly, and thanked him. Helen carried it awkwardly the rest of the way home, neither of them saying much. She had been caught by surprise. If she had given herself a minute to think, she would have refused it on grounds that it was wise just to stay friends; because, she thought, neither of them really knew the other. But once she had the thing in her hands she hadn't the nerve to ask him to take it back. It was a medium-sized box of some sort with something heavy in it—she guessed a book; yet it seemed too big for a book. As she held it against her breast, she felt a throb of desire for Frank and this disturbed her. About a block from the grocery, nervously saying good night, she went on ahead. This was how they parted when the store window was still lit.

Ida was downstairs with Morris when Helen came into the house, so no questions were asked. She shivered a little as she unwrapped the box on her bed, ready to hide it the minute she heard a footstep on the stairs. Lifting the carton lid, she found two packages in it, each wrapped in white tissue paper and tied with red ribbons with uneven bows, obviously by Frank. When she had untied the first present, Helen gasped at the sight of a long, hand-woven scarf—rich black wool interlaced with gold thread. She was startled to discover that the second present was a red leather copy of Shakespeare's plays. There was no card.

She sat weakly down on the bed. I can't, she told herself. They were expensive things, probably had cost him every penny of the hard-earned money he was saving for college. Even supposing he had enough for that, she still couldn't take his gifts. It wasn't right, and coming from him, it was, somehow, less than not right.

She wanted then and there to go up to his room and leave them at the door with a note, but hadn't the heart to the very night he had given them to her.

The next evening, after a day of worry, she felt she must return them; and now she wished she had done it before Nat had called, then she might have been more relaxed on the phone.

Helen got down on her hands and knees and reached under the bed for the carton with Frank's scarf and book in it. It touched her that he had given her such lovely things—so much nicer than anyone else ever had. Nat, at his best, had produced a half-dozen small pink roses.

For gifts you pay, Helen thought. She drew a deep breath, and taking the box went quietly up the stairs. She tapped hesitantly on Frank's door. He had recognized her step and was waiting behind the door. His fists were clenched, the nails cutting his palms.

When he opened the door and his glance fell on what she was carrying, he frowned as though struck in the face.

Helen stepped awkwardly into the little room, quickly shutting the door behind her. She suppressed a shudder at the smallness and barrenness of the place. On his unmade bed lay a sock he had been trying to mend.

"Are the Fusos home?" she asked in a low voice.

"They went out." He spoke dully, his eyes hopelessly stuck to the things he had given her.

Helen handed him the box with the presents. "Thanks so much, Frank," she said, trying to smile, "but I really don't think I ought to take them. You'll need every cent for your college tuition in the fall."

"That's not the reason you mean," he said.

Her face reddened. She was about to explain that her mother would surely make a scene if she saw his gifts, but instead said, "I can't keep them."

"Why not?"

It wasn't easy to answer and he didn't make it easier, just held the rejected presents in his big hands as if they were living things that had suddenly died.

"I can't," she got out. "You're taste is so nice, I'm sorry."

"Okay," he said wearily. He tossed the box on the bed and the Shakespeare fell to the floor. She stooped quickly to pick it up and was unnerved to see it had opened to "Romeo and Juliet."

"Good night." She left his room and went hastily downstairs. In her room she thought she heard the distant sound of a man crying. She listened tensely, her hand on her throbbing throat, but no longer heard it.

Helen took a shower to relax, then got into a nightgown and housecoat. She picked up a book but couldn't read. She had noticed before signs he might be in love with her, but now she was almost sure of it. Carrying his package as he had walked with her last night, he had been somebody different, though the hat and overcoat were the same. There seemed to be about him a size and potentiality she had not seen before. He did not say love but love was in him. When the insight came to her, at almost the minute he was handing her the package, she had reacted with gooseflesh. That it had gone this far was her own fault. She had warned herself not to get mixed up with him but hadn't obeyed her warning. Out of loneliness she had encouraged him. What else, going so often to the library, knowing he would be there? And she had stopped off with him, on their walks, for pizzas and coffee; had listened to his stories, discussed with him plans for college, talked at length about books he was reading; at the same time she had been concealing these meetings from her father and mother. He knew it, no wonder he had built up hopes.

The strange thing was there were times she felt she liked him very much. He was, in many ways, a worthwhile person, and where a man gave off honest feeling, was she a machine to shut off her own? Yet she knew she mustn't become seriously attracted to him because there would be trouble in buckets. Trouble, thank you, she had had enough of. She wanted now a peaceful life without worry—any more worries. Friends they could be, in a minor key; she might on a moonlit night even hold hands with him, but beyond that nothing. She should have said something of the sort; he would have saved his presents for a better prospect and she would not now be feeling guilt at having hurt him. Yet in a way he had surprised her by his apparent depth of affection. She had not expected anything to happen so quickly, because, for her, things had happened in reverse order. Usually she fell in love first, then the man, if he wasn't Nat Pearl, responded. So the other way around was nice for a change, and she wished it would happen more often, but with the right one. She must go, she decided, less to the library; he would then understand, if he didn't already, and give up any idea of having her love. When he realized what was what he would get over his pain, if he really felt any. But her thoughts gave her no peace, and though she tried often, she could still not concentrate on her books. When Morris and Ida trudged through her room, her light was out and she seemed to be sleeping.

As she left the house for work the next morning, to her dismay she spied the carton containing his presents on top of some greasy garbage bags in the stuffed rubbish can at the curb. The cover of the can apparently had been squeezed down on the box but had fallen off and now lay on the sidewalk. Lifting the carton cover, Helen saw the two gifts, loosely covered with the tissue paper. Angered by the waste, she plucked the scarf and book out of the crushed cardboard box and went quickly into the hall with them. If she took them upstairs Ida would want to know what she had, so she decided to hide them in the cellar. She turned on the light and went quietly down, trying to keep her high heels from clicking on the stairs. Then she removed the tissue paper and hid the presents, neither of which had been harmed, in the bottom drawer of a broken chiffonier in their bin. The dirty tissue paper and red ribbons she rolled up in a sheet of old newspaper, then went upstairs and pressed it into the garbage can. Helen noticed her father at the window, idly watching her. She passed into the store, said good morning, washed her hands and left for work. On the subway she felt despondent.

After supper that night, while Ida was washing dishes, Helen sneaked down into the cellar, got the scarf and book and carried them up to Frank's room. She knocked and nobody answered. She considered leaving them at the door but felt he would throw them away again unless she spoke to him first.

Tessie opened her door. "I heard him go out a while before, Helen." Her eyes were on the things in her hands.

Helen blushed. "Thanks, Tessie."

"Any message?"

"No." She returned to her floor and once more pushed the gifts under her bed. Changing her mind, she put the book and scarf in different bureau drawers, hiding them under her underwear. When her mother came up she was listening to the radio.

"You going someplace tonight, Helen?"

"Maybe, I don't know. Maybe to the library."

"Why so much to the library? You went a couple days ago."

"I go to meet Clark Gable, Mama."

"Helen, don't get fresh."

Sighing, she said she was sorry.

Ida sighed too. "Some people want their children to read more. I want you to read less."

"That won't get me married any faster."

Ida knitted but soon grew restless and went down to the store again. Helen got out Frank's things, packed them in heavy paper she had bought on her way home, tied the bundle with cord, and took the trolley to the library. He wasn't there.

The next night she tried first his room, then when she was able to slip out of the house, again the library, but found him in neither place.

"Does Frank still work here?" she asked Morris in the morning.

"Of course he works."

"I haven't seen him for a while," she said. "I thought he might be gone."

"In the summer he leaves."

"Did he say that?"

"Mama says."

"Does he know?"

"He knows. Why you ask me?"

She said she was just curious.

As Helen came into the hall that evening she heard the clerk descending the stairs and waited for him at the landing. Lifting his hat, he was about to pass when she spoke.

"Frank, why did you throw your two presents into the garbage?"

"What good were they to me?"

"It was a terrible waste. You should have got your money back."

He smiled in the corners of his mouth. "Easy come, easy go."

"Don't joke. I took them out of the rubbish and have them in my room for you. They weren't damaged."

"Thanks."

"Please give them back and get your money. You'll need every penny for the fall."

"Since I was a kid I hate to go back with stuff I bought."

"Then let me have the sales checks and I'll return them during my lunch hour."

"I lost them," he answered.

She said gently, "Frank, sometimes things turn out other than we plan. Don't feel hurt."

"When I don't feel hurt, I hope they bury me."

He left the house, she walked up the stairs.

Over the weekend Helen went back to crossing off the days on the calendar. She found she had crossed nothing since New Year's. She fixed that. On Sunday the weather turned fair and she grew restless. She wished again for Nat to call her; instead his sister did and they walked, in the early afternoon, on the Parkway.

Betty was twenty-seven and resembled Sam Pearl. She was large-boned and on the plain side but made good use of reddish hair and a nice nature. She was in her ideas, Helen thought, somewhat dull. They had not too much in common and saw each other infrequently, but liked to talk once in a while, or go to a movie together. Recently Betty had become engaged to a CPA in her office and was with him most of the time. Now she sported a prosperous diamond ring on her stylish finger. Helen, for once, envied her, and Betty, as if she had guessed, wished her the same good luck.

"And it should happen soon," she said.

"Many thanks, Betty."

After they had gone a few blocks, Betty said, "Helen, I don't like to butt in somebody else's private business but for a long time I wanted to ask you what happened between you and my brother Nat. I once asked him and he gave me double talk."

"You know how such things go."

"I thought you liked him?"

"I did."

"Then why don't you see him any more? Did you have some kind of a fight?"

"No fights. We didn't have the same things in mind."

Betty asked no more. Later, she remarked, "Sometime give him another chance, Helen. Nat really has the makings of a good person. Shep, my boy friend, thinks so too. His worst fault is he thinks his brains entitle him to certain privileges. You'll see, in time he'll get over it."

"I may," Helen said. "We'll see sometime."

They returned to the candy store, where Shep Hirsch, Betty's stout, eyeglassed, future husband was waiting to take her for a drive in his Pontiac.

"Come along, Helen," said Betty.

"With pleasure." Shep tipped his hat.

"Go, Helen," advised Goldie Pearl.

"Thanks, all, from the bottom of my heart," said Helen, "but I have some of my underthings to iron."

Upstairs, she stood at the window, looking out at the back yards. The remnants of last week's dirty snow. No single blade of green, or flower to light the eye or lift the heart. She felt as if she were made of knots and in desperation got on her coat, tied a yellow kerchief around her head and left the house again, not knowing which way to go. She wandered toward the leafless park.

At the approach to the park's main entrance there was a small island in the street, a concrete triangle formed by intersecting avenues. Here people sat on benches during the day and tossed peanuts or pieces of bread to the noisy pigeons that haunted the place. Coming up the block, Helen saw a man squatting by one of the benches, feeding the birds. Otherwise, the island was deserted. When the man rose, the pigeons fluttered up with him, a few landing on his arms and shoulders, one perched on his fingers, pecking peanuts from his cupped palm. Another fat bird sat on his hat. The man clapped his hands when the peanuts were gone and the birds, beating their wings, scattered.

When she recognized Frank Alpine, Helen hesitated. She felt in no mood to see him, but remembering the package hidden in her bureau drawer, determined once and for all to get rid of it. Reaching the corner, she crossed over to the island.

Frank saw her coming and wasn't sure he cared one way or the other. The return of his presents had collapsed his hopes. He had thought that if she ever fell for him it would change his life in the way he wanted it to happen, although at times the very thought of another change, even in this sense of it, made him miserable. Yet what was the payoff, for instance, of marrying a dame like her and having to do with Jews the rest of his life? So he told himself he didn't care one way or the other.

"Hi," Helen said.

He touched his hat. His face looked tired but his eyes were

clear and his gaze steady, as if he had been through something and had beat it. She felt sorry if she had caused him any trouble.

"I had a cold," Frank remarked.

"You should get more sun."

Helen sat down on the edge of the bench, as if she were afraid, he thought, she would be asked to take a lease on it; and he sat a little apart from her. One of the pigeons began to chase another running in circles and landed on its back. Helen looked away but Frank idly watched the birds until they flew off.

"Frank," she said, "I hate to sound like a pest on this subject, but if there's anything I can't stand it's waste. I know you're not Rockefeller, so would you mind giving me the names of the stores where you bought your kind presents so that I can return them? I think I can without the sales checks."

Her eyes, he noticed, were a hard blue, and though he thought it ridiculous, he was a little scared of her, as if she were far too determined, too dead serious for him. At the same time he felt he still liked her. He had not thought so, but with them sitting together like this he thought again that he did. It was in a way a hopeless feeling, yet it was more than that because he did not exactly feel hopeless. He felt, as he sat next to her and saw her worn, unhappy face, that he still had a chance.

Frank cracked his knuckles one by one. He turned to her. "Look, Helen, maybe I try to work too fast. If so, I am sorry. I am the type of a person, who if he likes somebody, has to show it. I like to give her things, if you understand that, though I do know that not everybody likes to take. That's their business. My nature is to give and I couldn't change it even if I wanted. So okay, I am also sorry I got sore and dumped your presents in the can and you had to take them out. But what I want to say is this. Why don't you just go ahead and keep one of those things that I got for you? Let it be a little memory of a guy you once knew that wants to thank you for the good books you told him to read. You don't have to worry that I expect anything for what I give you."

"Frank . . ." she said, reddening.

"Just let me finish. How's this for a deal? If you keep one of those things, I will take the other back to the store and get what I paid for it. What do you say?"

She was not sure what to say, but since she wanted to be finished with it, nodded at his proposal.

"Fine," Frank said. "Now what do you want the most?"

"Well, the scarf is awfully nice, but I'd rather keep the book."

"So keep the book then," he said. "You can give me the scarf anytime you want and I promise I will bring it back."

He lit a cigarette and inhaled deeply.

She considered whether to say good-by, now that the matter had been settled, and go on with her walk.

"You busy now?" he asked.

She guessed a short stroll. "No."

"How about a movie?"

It took her a minute to reply. Was he starting up once more? She felt she must quickly set limits to keep him from again creeping too close. Yet out of respect for his already hurt feelings, she thought it best that she think out exactly what to say and tactfully say it, later on.

"I'll have to be back early."

"So let's go," he said, getting up.

Helen slowly untied her kerchief, then knotted it, and they went off together.

As they walked she kept wondering if she hadn't made a mistake in accepting the book. In spite of what he had said about expecting nothing she felt a gift was a claim, and she wanted none on her. Yet, when, almost without noticing, she once more asked herself if she liked him at all, she had to admit she did a little. But not enough to get worried about; she liked him but not with an eye to the possibility of any deeper feeling. He was not the kind of man she wanted to be in love with. She made that very clear to herself, for among his other disadvantages there was something about him, evasive, hidden. He sometimes appeared to be more than he was, sometimes less. His aspirations, she sensed, were somehow apart from the self he presented normally when he wasn't trying, though he was always more or less trying; therefore when he was trying less. She could not quite explain this to herself, for if he could make himself seem better, broader, wiser when he tried, then he had these things in him because you couldn't make them out of nothing. There was more to him than his appearance. Still, he hid what he had and he hid what he hadn't. With one hand the magician showed his cards, with the other he turned them into smoke. At the very minute he was revealing himself, saying who he was, he made you wonder if it was true. You looked into mirrors and saw mirrors and didn't know what was right or real or important. She had gradually got the feeling that he only pretended to be frank about himself, that in telling so much about his experiences, his trick was to hide his true self. Maybe not purposely—maybe he had no idea he was doing it. She asked herself whether he might have been married already. He had once said he never was. And was there more to the story of the once-kissed, tragic carnival girl? He had said no. If not, what made her feel he had done something—committed himself in a way she couldn't guess?

As they were aproaching the movie theater, a thought of her mother crossed her mind and she heard herself say, "Don't forget I'm Jewish."

"So what?" Frank said.

Inside in the dark, recalling what he had answered her, he felt this elated feeling, as if he had crashed head on through a brick wall but hadn't bruised himself.

She had bitten her tongue but made no reply.

Anyway, by summer he'd be gone.

Ida was very unhappy that she had kept Frank on when she could have got rid of him so easily. She was to blame and she actively worried. Though she had no evidence, she suspected Helen was interested in the clerk. *Something* was going on be-

tween them. She did not ask her daughter what, because a denial
would shame her. And though she had tried she felt she could not
really trust Frank. Yes, he had helped the business, but how much
would they have to pay for it? Sometimes when she came upon
him alone in the store, his expression, she told herself, was sneaky.
He sighed often, muttered to himself, and if he saw he was observed, pretended he hadn't. Whatever he did there was more
in it than he was doing. He was like a man with two minds. With
one he was here, with the other someplace else. Even while he
read he was doing more than reading. And his silence spoke a language she couldn't understand. Something bothered him and Ida
suspected it was her daughter. Only when Helen happened to
come into the store or the back while he was there, did he seem
to relax, become one person. Ida was troubled, although she
could not discover in Helen any response to him. Helen was quiet
in his presence, detached, almost cold to the clerk. She gave him
for his restless eyes, nothing—her back. Yet for this reason, too,
Ida worried.

One night, after Helen had left the house, when her mother
heard the clerk's footsteps going down the stairs, she quickly got
into a coat, wrapped a shawl around her head and trudged through
a sprinkle of snow after him. He walked to the movie house
several blocks away, paid his money, and passed in. Ida was almost
certain that Helen was inside, waiting for him. She returned home
with nails in her heart and found her daughter upstairs, ironing.
Another night she followed Helen to the library. Ida waited across
the street, shivering for almost an hour in the cold, until Helen
emerged, then followed her home. She chided herself for her
suspicions but they would not fly from her mind. Once, listening
from the back, she heard her daughter and the clerk talking about
a book. This annoyed her. And when Helen later happened to
mention that Frank had plans to begin college in the autumn, Ida
felt he was saying that only to get her interested in him.

She spoke to Morris and cautiously asked if he had noticed anything developing between Helen and the clerk.

"Don't be foolish," the grocer replied. He had thought about the possibility, at times felt concerned, but after pondering how different they were, had put the idea out of his head.

"Morris, I am afraid."

"You are afraid of everything, even which it don't exist."

"Tell him to leave now—business is better."

"So is better," he muttered, "but who knows how will be next week. We decided he will stay till summer."

"Morris, he will make trouble."

"What kind trouble will he make?"

"Wait," she said, clasping her hands, "a tragedy will happen."

Her remark at first annoyed, then worried him.

The next morning the grocer and his clerk were sitting at the table, peeling hot potatoes. The pot had been drained of water and dumped on its side; they sat close to the steaming pile of potatoes, hunched over, ripping off the salt-stained skins with small knives. Frank seemed ill at ease. He hadn't shaved and had darb blobs under his eyes. Morris wondered if he had been drinking but there was never any smell of liquor about him. They worked without speaking, each lost in his thoughts.

After a half-hour, Frank squirming restlessly in his chair, remarked, "Say, Morris, suppose somebody asked you what do the Jews believe in, what would you tell them?"

The grocer stopped peeling, unable at once to reply.

"What I like to know is what is a Jew anyway?"

Because he was ashamed of his meager education Morris was never comfortable with such questions, yet he felt he must answer.

"My father used to say to be a Jew all you need is a good heart."

"What do you say?"

"The important thing is the Torah. This is the Law—a Jew must believe in the Law."

"Let me ask you this," Frank went on. "Do you consider yourself a real Jew?"

Morris was startled, "What do you mean if I am a real Jew?"

"Don't get sore about this," Frank said, "But I can give you an argument that you aren't. First thing, you don't go to the synagogue—not that I have ever seen. You don't keep your kitchen kosher and you don't eat kosher. You don't even wear one of those little black hats like this tailor I knew in South Chicago. He prayed three times a day. I even hear the Mrs say you kept the store open on Jewish holidays, it makes no difference if she yells her head off."

"Sometimes," Morris answered, flushing, "to have to eat, you must keep open on holidays. On Yum Kippur I don't keep open. But I don't worry about kosher, which is to me old-fashioned. What I worry is to follow the Jewish Law."

"But all those things are the Law, aren't they? And don't the Law say you can't eat any pig, but I have seen you taste ham."

"This is not important to me if I taste pig or if I don't. To some Jews is this important but not to me. Nobody will tell me that I am not Jewish because I put in my mouth once in a while, when my tongue is dry, a piece ham. But they will tell me, and I will believe them, if I forget the Law. This means to do what is right, to be honest, to be good. This means to other people. Our life is hard enough. Why should we hurt somebody else? For everybody should be the best, not only for you or me. We ain't animals. This is why we need the Law. This is what a Jew believes."

"I think other religions have those ideas too," Frank said. "But tell me why it is that the Jews suffer so damn much, Morris? It seems to me that they like to suffer, don't they?"

"Do you like to suffer? They suffer because they are Jews."

"That's what I mean, they suffer more than they have to."

"If you live, you suffer. Some people suffer more, but not because they want. But I think if a Jew don't suffer for the Law, he will suffer for nothing."

"What do you suffer for, Morris?" Frank said.

"I suffer for you," Morris said calmly.

Frank laid his knife down on the table. His mouth ached. "What do you mean?"

"I mean you suffer for me."

The clerk let it go at that.

"If a Jew forgets the Law," Morris ended, "he is not a good Jew, and not a good man."

Frank picked up his knife and began to tear the skins off the potatoes. The grocer peeled his pile in silence. The clerk asked nothing more.

When the potatoes were cooling, Morris, troubled by their talk, asked himself why Frank had brought up this subject. A thought of Helen, for some reason, crossed his mind.

"Tell me the truth," he said, "why did you ask me such questions?"

Frank shifted in his chair. He answered slowly, "To be truthful to you, Morris, once I didn't have much use for the Jews."

Morris looked at him without moving.

"But that was long ago," said Frank, "before I got to know what they were like. I don't think I understood much about them."

His brow was covered with sweat.

"Happens like this many times," Morris said.

But his confession had not made the clerk any happier.

One afternoon, shortly after lunch, happening to glance at himself in the mirror, Morris saw how bushy his hair was and how thick the pelt on his neck; he felt ashamed. So he said to Frank he was going across the street to the barber. The clerk, studying the racing page of the *Mirror*, nodded. Morris hung up his apron and went into the store to get some change from the cash register. After he took a few quarters out of the drawer, he checked the receipts for the day and was pleased. He left the grocery and crossed the car tracks to the barber shop.

The chair was empty and he didn't have to wait. As Mr. Giannola, who smelled of olive oil, worked on him and they talked,

Morris, though embarrassed at all the hair that had to be cut by the barber, found himself thinking mostly of his store. If it would only stay like this—no Karp's paradise, but at least livable, not the terrible misery of only a few months ago—he would be satisfied. Ida had again been nagging him to sell, but what was the use of selling until things all over got better and he could find a place he would have confidence in? Al Marcus, Breitbart, all the drivers he talked to, still complained about business. The best thing was not to look for trouble but stay where he was. Maybe in the summer, after Frank left, he would sell out and search for a new place.

As he rested in the barber's chair, the grocer, watching through the window his own store, saw with satisfaction that at least three customers had been in since he had sat down. One man left with a large lumpy bag, in which Morris imagined at least six bottles of beer. Also, two women had come out with heavy packages, one carrying a loaded market bag. Figuring, let's say, at least two dollars apiece for the women, he estimated he had taken in a nice fiver and earned his haircut. When the barber unpinned the sheet around him and Morris returned to the grocery, he struck a match over the cash register and peered with anticipation at the figures. To his great surprise he saw that only a little more than three dollars had been added to the sum he had noted on leaving the store. He was stunned. How could it be only three if the bags had been packed tight with groceries? Could it be they contained maybe a couple of boxes of some large item like cornflakes, that came to nothing? He could hardly believe this and felt upset to the point of illness.

In the back he hung up his overcoat, and with fumbling fingers tied his apron strings.

Frank glanced up from the racing page with a smile. "You look different without all the kelp on you, Morris. You look like a sheep that had the wool clipped off it."

The grocer, ashen, nodded.

"What's the matter your face is so pale?"

"I don't feel so good."

"Whyn't you go up then and take your snooze?"

"After."

He shakily poured himself a cup of coffee.

"How's business?" he asked, his back to the clerk.

"So-so," said Frank.

"How many customers you had since I went to the barber?"

"Two or three."

Unable to meet Frank's eye, Morris went into the store and stood at the window, staring at the barber shop, his thoughts in a turmoil, tormented by anxiety. Was the Italyener stealing from the cash register? The customers had come out with stuffed bags, what was there to show for it? Could he have given things on credit? They had told him never to. So what then?

A man entered and Morris waited on him. The man spent forty-one cents. When Morris rang up the sale, he saw it added correctly to the previous total. So the register was not broken. He was now almost certain that Frank had been stealing, and when he asked himself how long, he was numbed.

Frank went into the store and saw the dazed grocer at the window.

"Don't you feel any better, Morris?"

"It will go away."

"Take care of yourself. You don't want to get sick any more."

Morris wet his lips but made no reply. All day he went around, dragging his heart. He had said nothing to Ida, he didn't dare.

For the next few days he carefully watched the clerk. He had decided to give him the benefit of doubt yet not rest till he knew the truth. Sometimes he sat at the table inside, pretending to be reading, but he was carefully listening to each item the customer ordered. He jotted down the prices and when Frank packed the groceries, quickly calculated the approximate sum. After the customer had gone he went idly to the register and secretly examined the amount the clerk had rung up. Always it was near the figure he had figured, a few pennies more or less. So Morris said he would go upstairs for a few minutes, but instead stationed himself in the hall, behind the back door. Peering through a crack in the wood, he could see into the store. Standing here, he added in his head the prices of the items ordered, and later, about fifteen minutes, casually checked the receipts and found totaled there the sum he had estimated. He began to doubt his suspicions. He may have wrongly guessed the contents of the customers' bags when he was at the barber's. Yet he could still not believe they had spent only three dollars; maybe Frank had caught on and was being wary.

Morris then thought, yes, the clerk could have been stealing, but if so it was more his fault than Frank's. He was a grown man with a man's needs and all he was paying him, including his meager commission, was about six or seven dollars a week. True, he got his room and meals free, plus cigarettes, but what was six or seven dollars to anybody in times like these, when a decent pair of shoes cost eight to ten? The fault was therefore his for paying slave wages for a workman's services, including the extra things Frank did, like last week cleaning out the stopped sewer pipe in the cellar with a long wire and so saving five or ten dollars that would surely have gone to the plumber, not to mention how his presence alone had improved the store.

So although he worked on a slim markup, one late afternoon when he and Frank were packing out some cartons of goods that had just been delivered, Morris said to his assistant standing on the stepladder, "Frank, I think from now on till it comes summer I will raise you your wages to straight fifteen dollars without any commission. I would like to pay you more, but you know how much we do here business."

Frank looked down at the grocer. "What for, Morris? The store can't afford to pay me any more than I am getting. If I take fifteen your profits will be shot. Let it go the way it is now. I am satisfied."

"A young man needs more and he spends more."

"I got all I want."

"Let it be like I said."

"I don't want it," said the clerk, annoyed.

"Take," insisted the grocer.

Frank finished his packing then got down, saying he was going to Sam Pearl's. His eyes were averted as he went past the grocer. Morris continued to pack the cans on the shelves. Rather than admit Frank's raise to Ida and start a fuss, he decided to withhold from the register the money he would need to pay him, a little every day so it would not be noticed. He would privately give it to the clerk sometime on Saturday, before Ida handed him his regular wages.

Helen felt herself, despite the strongest doubts, falling in love with Frank. It was a dizzying dance, she didn't want to. The month was cold—it often snowed—she had a rough time, fighting hesitancies, fears of a disastrous mistake. One night she dreamed their house had burned down and her poor parents had nowhere to go. They stood on the sidewalk, wailing in their underwear. Waking, she fought an old distrust of the broken-faced stranger, without success. The stranger had changed, grown unstrange. That was the clue to what was happening to her. One day he seemed unknown, lurking at the far end of an unlit cellar; the next he was standing in sunlight, a smile on his face, as if all she knew of him and all she didn't, had fused into a healed and easily remembered whole. If he was hiding anything, she thought, it was his past pain, his orphanhood and consequent suffering. His eyes were quieter, wiser. His crooked nose fitted his face and his face fitted him. It stayed on straight. He was gentle, waiting for whatever he awaited with a grace she respected. She felt she had changed him and this affected her. That she had willed to stay free of him made little difference now. She felt tender to him, wanted him close by. She had, she thought, changed in changing him.

After she had accepted his gift of a book their relationship had subtly altered. What else, if whenever she read in her Shakespeare, she thought of Frank Alpine, even heard his voice in the plays?

Whatever she read, he crept into her thoughts; in every book he haunted the words, a character in a plot somebody else had invented, as if all associations had only one end. He was, to begin with, everywhere. So, without speaking of it, they met again in the library. That they were meeting among books relieved her doubt, as if she believed, what possible wrong can I do among books, what possible harm can come to me here?

In the library he too seemed surer of himself—though once they were on their way home he became almost remote, strangely watchful, looking back from time to time as though they were being followed, but who or what would follow them? He never took her as far as the store; as before, by mutual consent, she went on ahead, then he walked around the block and entered the hall from the other way so he wouldn't have to go past the grocery window and possibly be seen coming from the direction she had come from. Helen interpreted his caution to mean he sensed victory and didn't want to endanger it. It meant he valued her more than she was altogether sure she wanted to be.

Then one night they walked across a field in the park and turned to one another. She tried to awaken in herself a feeling of danger, but danger was dulled, beyond her, in his arms. Pressed against him, responsive to his touch, she felt the cold ebb out of the night, and a warmth come over her. Her lips parted—she drew from his impassioned kiss all she had long desired. Yet at the moment of sweetest joy she felt again the presence of doubt, almost a touch of illness. This made her sad. The fault was her. It meant she still could not fully accept him. There were still signals signaling no. She had only to think of them and they would work in her, pinching the nerves. On their way home she could not forget the first happiness of their kiss. But why should a kiss become anxiety? Then she saw that his eyes were sad, and she wept when he wasn't looking. Would it never come spring?

She stalled love with arguments, only to be surprised at their swift dissolution; found it difficult to keep her reasons securely nailed down, as they were before. They flew up in the mind, shifted, changed, as if something had altered familiar weights, values, even experience. He wasn't, for instance, Jewish. Not too long ago this was the greatest barrier, her protection against ever taking him seriously; now it no longer seemed such an urgently important thing—how could it in times like these? How could anything be important but love and fulfillment? It had lately come to her that her worry he was a gentile was less for her own sake than for her mother and father. Although she had only loosely been brought up as Jewish she felt loyal to the Jews, more for what they had gone through than what she knew of their history or theology—loved them as a people, thought with pride of herself as one of them; she had never imagined she would marry anybody but a Jew. But she had recently come to think that in such unhappy times—when the odds were so high against personal happiness—to find love was miraculous, and to fulfill it as best two people could was what really mattered. Was it more important to insist a man's religious beliefs be exactly hers (if it was a question of religion), or that the two of them have in common ideals, a desire to keep love in their lives, and to preserve in every possible way what was best in themselves? The less difference among people, the better; thus she settled it for herself yet was dissatisfied for those for whom she hadn't settled it.

But her logic, if it was logic, wouldn't decide a thing for her unhappy parents once they found out what was going on. With Frank enrolled in college maybe some of Ida's doubts of his worth as a person might wither away, but college was not the synagogue, a B.A. not a bar mitzvah; and her mother and even her father with his liberal ideas would insist that Frank had to be what he wasn't. Helen wasn't at all sure she could handle them if it ever came to a showdown. She dreaded the arguments, their tear-stained pleas and her own misery for taking from the small sum of peace they had in the world, adding to the portion of their unhappiness. God knows they had had enough of that. Still, there was just so much time to live, so little of youth among the years; one had to make certain heartbreaking choices. She foresaw the necessity of upholding her own, enduring pain yet keeping to her decisions. Morris and Ida would be grievously hurt, but before too long their pain would grow less and perhaps leave them; yet she could not help but hope her own children would someday marry Jews.

And if she married Frank, her first job would be to help him realize his wish to be somebody. Nat Pearl wanted to be "somebody," but to him this meant making money to lead the life of some of his well-to-do friends at law school. Frank, on the other hand, was struggling to realize himself as a person, a more worthwhile ambition. Though Nat had an excellent formal education, Frank knew more about life and gave the impression of greater potential depth. She wanted him to become what he might, and conceived a plan to support him through college. Maybe she could even see him through a master's degree, once he knew what he wanted to do. She realized this would mean the end of her own vague plans for going to day college, but that was really lost long ago, and she thought she would at last accept the fact once Frank had got what she hadn't. Maybe after he was working, perhaps as an engineer or chemist, she could take a year of college just to slake her thirst. By then she would be almost thirty, but it would be worth postponing having a family to give him a good start and herself a taste of what she had always wanted. She also hoped they would be able to leave New York. She wanted to see more of the country. And if things eventually worked out, maybe Ida and Morris would someday sell the store and come to live near them. They might all live in California, her parents in a little house of their own where they could take life easy and be near their grandchildren. The future offered more in the way of realizable possibilities, Helen thought, if a person dared take a chance with it. The question was, did she?

She postponed making any important decision. She feared most of all the great compromise—she had seen so many of the people she knew settle for so much less than they had always wanted. She feared to be forced to choose beyond a certain point, to accept less of the good life than she had hungered for, appreciably less—to tie up with a fate far short of her ideals. That she mustn't do, whether it meant taking Frank or letting him go. Her constant fear, underlying all others, was that her life would not turn out as she had hoped, or would turn out vastly different. She was willing to change, make substitutions, but she would not part with the substance of her dreams. Well, she would know by summertime what to do. In the meantime Frank went every third night to the library and there she was. But when the old-maid librarian smiled knowingly upon them, Helen felt embarrassed, so they met elsewhere. They met in cafeterias, movie houses, the pizza place—where it was impossible to say much, or hold him or be held. To talk they walked, to kiss they hid.

Frank said he was getting the college bulletins he had written for, and around May he would have a transcript of his high school record sent to whichever place they picked for him to go. He showed he knew she had plans for him. He didn't say much more, for he was always afraid the old jinx would grab hold of him if he opened his mouth a little too wide.

At first he waited patiently. What else was there to do? He had waited and was still waiting. He had been born waiting. But before long, though he tried not to show it, he was beginning to be fed up with his physical loneliness. He grew tired of the frustrations of kissing in doorways, a cold feel on a bench in the park. He thought of her as he had seen her in the bathroom, and the memory became a burden. He was the victim of the sharp edge of his hunger. So he wanted her to the point where he thought up schemes for getting her into his room and in bed. He wanted satisfaction, relief, a stake in the future. She's not yours till she gives it to you, he thought. That's the way they all are. It wasn't always true, but it was true enough. He wanted an end to the torment of coming to a boil, then thank you, no more. He wanted to take her completely.

They met more often now. At a bench on the Parkway, on

street corners—in the wide windy world. When it rained or snowed, they stepped into doorways, or went home.

He complained one night, "What a joke. We leave the same warm house to meet out in the cold here."

She said nothing.

"Forget it," Frank said, looking into her troubled eyes, "we will take it the way it is."

"This is our youth," she said bitterly.

He wanted then to ask her to come to his room but felt she wouldn't, so he didn't ask.

One cold, starry night she led him through the trees in the park near where they usually sat, onto a broad meadow where on summer nights lovers lay in the grass.

"Come on and sit down on the ground for a minute," Frank urged, "there's nobody here now."

But Helen wouldn't.

"Why not?" he asked.

"Not now," she said.

She realized, though he later denied it, that the situation had made him impatient. Sometimes he was moody for hours. She worried, wondering what rusty wound their homelessness had opened in him.

One evening they sat alone on a bench on the Parkway, Frank with his arm around her; but because they were so close to home Helen was jumpy and moved away whenever somebody passed by.

After the third time Frank said, "Listen, Helen, this is no good. Some night we will have to go where we can be inside."

"Where?" she asked.

"Where do you say?"

"I can't say anything, Frank. I don't know."

"How long is this going to keep up like this?"

"As long as we like," she said, smiling faintly, "or as long as we like each other."

"I don't mean it that way. What I am talking about is not having any place private to go to."

She answered nothing.

"Maybe some night we ought to sneak up to my room," he suggested. "We could do it easy enough—I don't mean tonight but maybe Friday, after Nick and Tessie go to the show and your mother is down in the store. I bought a new heater and the room keeps warm. Nobody will know you are there. We would be alone for once. We have never been alone that way."

"I couldn't," Helen said.

"Why?"

"Frank, I can't."

"When will I get a chance to put my arms around you without being an acrobat?"

"Frank," said Helen, "there's one thing I wish to make clear to you. I won't sleep with you now, if that's what you mean. It'll have to wait till I am really sure I love you, maybe till we're married, if we ever are."

"I never asked you to," Frank said. "All I said was for you to come up to my room so we could spend the time more comfortable, not you bucking away from me every time a shadow passes."

He lit a cigarette and smoked in silence.

"I'm sorry." After a minute she said, "I thought I ought to tell you how I feel on this subject. I was going to sometime anyway."

They got up and walked, Frank gnawing his wound.

A cold rain washed the yellow slush out of the gutters. It rained drearily for two days. Helen had promised to see Frank on Friday night but she didn't like the thought of going out in the wet. When she came home from work, and got the chance, she slipped a note under his door, then went down. The note said that if Nick and Tessie did go to the movies, she would try to come up to his room for a while.

At half past seven Nick knocked on Frank's door and asked

him if he wanted to go to the pictures. Frank said no, he thought he had seen the picture that was playing. Nick said good-by and he and Tessie, bundled in raincoats and carrying umbrellas, left the house. Helen waited for her mother to go down to Morris, but Ida complained that her feet hurt, and said she would rest. Helen then went down herself, knowing Frank would hear her on the stairs and figure something had gone wrong. He would understand she could not go up to see him so long as anyone might hear her.

But a few minutes later, Ida came down, saying she felt restless upstairs. Helen then said she intended to drop in on Betty Pearl and might go along with her to the dressmaker who was making her wedding things.

"It's raining," said Ida.

"I know, Mama," Helen answered, hating her deceit.

She went up to her room, got her hat and coat, rubbers and umbrella; then walked down, letting the door bang, as if she had just left the house. She quietly opened it and went on tiptoe up the stairs.

Frank had guessed what was going on and opened his door to her quick tap. She was pale, obviously troubled, but very lovely. He held her hard and could feel her heartbeat against his chest.

She will let me tonight, he told himself.

Helen was still uneasy. It took her a while to quiet her conscience for having lied to her mother. Frank had put out the light and tuned in the radio to soft dance music; now he lay on the bed, smoking. For a time she sat awkwardly in his chair, watching the glow of his cigarette, and when not that, the drops of lit rain on the window, reflecting the street light. But after he had rubbed his butt into an ash tray on the floor, Helen stepped out of her shoes and lay down beside him on the narrow bed, Frank moving over to the wall.

"This is more like it," he sighed.

She lay with closed eyes in his arms, feeling the warmth of the heater like a hand on her back. For a minute she half-dozed, then woke to his kisses. She lay motionless, a little tense, but when he stopped kissing her, relaxed. She listened to the quiet sound of the rain in the street, making it in her mind into spring rain, though spring was weeks away; and within the rain grew all sorts of flowers; and amid the spring flowers, in this flowering dark— a sweet spring night—she lay with him in the open under new stars and a cry rose to her throat. When he kissed her again, she responded with passion.

"Darling."

"I love you, Helen, you are my girl."

They kissed breathlessly, then he undid the buttons of her blouse. She sat up to unhook her brassière but as she was doing it, felt his fingers under her skirt.

Helen grabbed his hand. "Please, Frank. Let's not get that hot and bothered."

"What are we waiting for, honey?" He tried to move his hand but her legs tightened and she swung her feet off the bed.

He pulled her back, pressing her shoulders down. She felt his body trembling on hers and for a fleeting minute thought he might hurt her; but he didn't.

She lay stiff, unresponsive on the bed. When he kissed her again she didn't move. It took a while before he lay back. She saw by the reflected glow of the heater how unhappy he looked.

Helen sat on the edge of the bed, buttoning her blouse.

His hands covered his face. He said nothing but she could feel his body shivering on the bed.

"Christ," he muttered.

"I'm sorry," she said softly. "I told you I wouldn't."

Five minutes passed. Frank slowly sat up. "Are you a virgin, is that what's eating you?"

"I'm not," she said.

"I thought you were," he said, surprised. "You act like one."

"I said I wasn't."

"Then why do you act like one? Don't you know what it does to people?"

"I'm people."

"Then why do you do it for?"

"Because I believe in what I'm doing."

"I thought you said you weren't a virgin?"

"You don't have to be a virgin to have ideals in sex."

"What I don't understand is if you did it before, what's the difference if we do it now?"

"We can't, just because I did," she said, brushing her hair back. "That's the point. I did it and that's why I can't with you now. I wouldn't, that night on the Parkway."

"I don't get it," Frank said.

"Loving should come with love."

"I said I love you, Helen, you heard me say it."

"I mean I have to love you too. I think I do but sometimes I'm not sure."

He fell again into silence. She listened absent-mindedly to the radio but nobody was dancing now.

"Don't be hurt, Frank."

"I'm tired of that," he said harshly.

"Frank," said Helen, "I said I slept with somebody before and the truth of it is, if you want to know, I'm sorry I did. I admit I had some pleasure, but after, I thought it wasn't worth it, only I didn't know at the time I would feel that way, because at the time I didn't know what I wanted. I suppose I felt I wanted to be free, so I settled for sex. But if you're not in love sex isn't being free, so I made a promise to myself that I never would any more unless I really fell in love with somebody. I don't want to dislike myself. I want to be disciplined, and you have to be too if I ask it. I ask it so I might someday love you without reservation.

"Crap," Frank said, but then, to his surprise, the idea seized him. He thought of himself as disciplined, then wished he were. This seemed to him like an old and far-away thought, and he remembered with regret and strange sadness how often he had wished for better control over himself, and how little of it he had achieved.

He said, "I didn't mean to say what I just now did, Helen."

"I know," she answered.

"Helen," he said huskily, "I want you to know I am a very good guy in my heart."

" I don't think otherwise."

"Even when I am bad I am good."

She said she thought she knew what he meant.

They kissed, again and again. He thought there were a whole lot worse things than waiting for something that was going to be good once he got it.

Helen lay back on the bed and dozed, awaking when Nick and Tessie came into their bedroom, talking about the movie they had seen. It was a love story and Tessie had liked it very much. After they undressed and got into bed their double bed creaked. Helen felt bad for Frank but Frank did not seem to feel bad. Nick and Tessie soon fell asleep. Helen, breathing lightly, worrying how she was going to get down to her floor, because if Ida was awake she would hear her on the stairs. But Frank said in a low voice that he would carry her to the vestibule, then she could go up after a few minutes, as if she had just come home from some place.

She put on her coat, hat and rubbers, and was careful to remember her umbrella. Frank carried her down the stairs. There were only his slow, heavy steps going down. And not long after they had kissed good night and he had gone for a walk in the rain, Helen opened the hall door and went up.

Then Ida fell asleep.

Thereafter Helen and Frank met outside the house.

It was snowing in the afternoon, when the front door opened and in came Detective Minogue, pushing before him this stocky hand-cuffed guy, unshaven, and wearing a faded green wind-breaker and denim slacks. He was about twenty-seven, with tired eyes and no hat. In the store he lifted his manacled hands to wipe the snow off his wet hair.

"Where's Morris?" the detective asked the clerk.

"In the back."

"Go on in," said Detective Minogue to the handcuffed man.

They went into the back. Morris was sitting on the couch, stealing a smoke. He hurriedly put out the butt and dropped it into the garbage pail.

"Morris," said the detective, "I think I have got the one who hit you on the head."

The grocer's face turned white as flour. He stared at the man but didn't approach him.

After a minute he muttered, "I don't know if it's him. He had his face covered with a handkerchief."

"He's a big son of a bitch," the detective said. "The one that hit you was big, wasn't he?"

"Heavy," said Morris. "The other was big."

Frank was standing in the doorway, watching.

Detective Minogue turned to him. "Who're you?"

"He's my clerk," explained Morris.

The detective unbuttoned his overcoat and took a clean handkerchief out of his suit pocket. "Do me a favor," he said to Frank. "Tie this around his puss."

"I would rather not," Frank answered.

"As a favor. To save me the trouble of getting hit on the head with his cuffs."

Frank took the handkerchief, and though not liking to, tied it around the man's face, the suspect holding himself stiffly erect.

"How about it now, Morris?"

"I can't tell you," Morris said, embarrassed. He had to sit down.

"You want some water, Morris?" Frank asked.

"No."

"Take your time," said Detective Minogue, "look him over good."

"I don't recognize him. The other acted more rough. He had a rough voice—not nice."

"Say something, son," the detective said.

"I didn't hold this guy up," said the suspect in a dead voice.

"Is that the voice, Morris?"

"No."

"Does he look like the other one—the heavy guy's partner?"

"No, this is a different man."

"How are you so sure?"

"The helper was a nervous man. He was bigger than this one. Also this one has got small hands. The helper had big heavy hands."

"Are you positive? We grabbed him on a job last night. He held up a grocery with another guy who got away."

The detective pulled the handkerchief off the man's face.

"I don't know him," Morris said with finality.

Detective Minogue folded the handkerchief and tucked it into his pocket. He slipped his eyeglasses into a leather case. "Morris, I think I asked you already if you saw my son Ward Minogue around here. Have you yet?"

"No," said the grocer.

Frank went over to the sink and rinsed his mouth with a cup of water.

"Maybe you know him?" the detective asked him.

"No," said the clerk.

"O.K., then." The detective unbuttoned his overcoat. "By the way, Morris, did you ever find out who was stealing your milk that time?"

"Nobody steals any more," said Morris.

"Come on, son," said the detective to the suspect.

The handcuffed man went out of the store into the snow, the detective following him.

Frank watched them get into the police car, sorry for the guy. What if they arrested me now, he thought, although I am not the same guy I once was?

Morris, thinking of the stolen milk bottles, gazed guiltily at his assistant.

Frank happened to notice the size of his hands, then had to go to the toilet.

As he was lying in his bed after supper, thinking about his life, Frank heard footsteps coming up the stairs and someone banged on his door. For a minute his heart hammered with fear, but he got up and forced himself to open the door. Grinning at him from under his fuzzy hat stood Ward Minogue, his eyes small and smeary. He had lost weight and looked worse.

Frank let him in and turned on the radio. Ward sat on the bed, his shoes dripping from the snow.

"Who told you I lived here?" Frank asked.

"I watched you go in the hall, opened the door and heard you go up the stairs," Ward said.

How am I ever going to get rid of this bastard, Frank thought.

"You better stay away from here," he said with a heavy heart. "If Morris recognizes you in that goddamned hat, we will both go to jail."

"I came to visit my popeyed friend, Louis Karp," said Ward. "I wanted a bottle but he wouldn't give it to me because I am short on cash, so I thought my good-looking friend Frank Alpine will lend me some. He's an honest, hard-working bastard."

"You picked the wrong guy. I am poor."

Ward eyed him craftily. "I was sure you'd have saved up a pile by now, stealing from the Jew."

Frank stared at him but didn't answer.

Ward's glance shifted. "Even if you are stealing his chicken feed, it ain't any skin off me. Why I came is this. I got a new job that we can do without any trouble."

"I told you I am not interested in your jobs, Ward."

"I thought you would like to get your gun back, otherwise it might accidentally get lost with your name on it."

Frank rubbed his hands.

"All you got to do is drive," Ward said amiably. "The job is a cinch, a big liquor joint in Bay Ridge. After nine o'clock they only keep one man on. The take will be over three hundred."

"Ward, you don't look to me in any kind of condition to do a stickup. You look more like you need to be in a hospital."

"All I got is a bad heartburn."

"You better take care of yourself."

"You are making me cry."

"Why don't you start going straight?"

"Why don't you?"

"I am trying to."

"Your Jew girl must be some inspiration."

"Don't talk about her, Ward."

"I tailed you last week when you took her in the park. She's a nice piece. How often do you get it?"

"Get the hell out of here."

Ward got up unsteadily. "Hand over fifty bucks or I will fix you good with your Jew boss and your Jew girl. I will write them a letter who did the stickup last November."

Frank rose, his face hard. Taking his wallet out of his pocket, he emptied it on the bed. There were eight single dollar bills. "That's all I have got."

Ward snatched up the money. "I'll be back for more."

"Ward," Frank said through tight teeth, "if you drag your ass up here any more to make trouble, or if you ever follow me and my girl again, or tell Morris anything, the first thing I will do is telephone your old man at the police station and tell him under which rock he can find you. He was in the grocery asking about you today, and if he ever meets up with you, he looks like he will bust your head off."

Ward with a moan spat at the clerk and missed, the gob of spit trickling down the wall.

"You stinking kike," he snarled. Rushing out into the hall, he all but fell down two flights of stairs.

The grocer and Ida ran out to see who was making the racket, but by then Ward was gone.

Frank lay in bed, his eyes closed.

One dark and windy night when Helen left the house late, Ida followed her through the cold streets and across the plaza into the interior of the deserted park, and saw her meet Frank Alpine. There, in an opening between a semicircle of tall lilac shrubs and a grove of dark maples, were a few benches, dimly lit and private, where they liked to come to be alone. Ida watched them sitting together on one of the benches, kissing. She dragged herself home and went upstairs, half-dead. Morris was asleep and she didn't want to wake him, so she sat in the kitchen, sobbing.

When Helen returned and saw her mother weeping at the kitchen table, she knew Ida knew, and Helen was both moved and frightened.

Out of pity she asked, "Mama, why are you crying?"

Ida at last raised her tear-stained face and said in despair, "Why do I cry? I cry for the world. I cry for my life that it went away wasted. I cry for you."

"What have I done?"

"You have killed me in my heart."

"I've done nothing that's wrong, nothing I'm ashamed of."

"You are not ashamed that you kissed a goy?"

Helen gasped. "Did you follow me, Mama?"

"Yes," Ida wept.

"How could you?"

"How could you kiss a goy?"

"I'm not ashamed that we kissed."

She still hoped to avoid an argument. Everything was unsettled, premature.

Ida said, "If you marry such a man your whole life will be poisoned."

"Mama, you'll have to be satisfied with what I now say. I have no plans to marry anybody."

"What kind plans you got then with a man that he kisses you alone in a place where nobody can find you in the park?"

"I've been kissed before."

"But a goy, Helen, an Italyener."

"A man, a human being like us."

"A man is not good enough. For a Jewish girl must be a Jew."

"Mama, it's very late. I don't wish to argue. Let's not wake Papa."

"Frank is not for you. I don't like him. His eyes don't look at a person when he talks to them."

"His eyes are sad. He's had a hard life."

"Let him go and find someplace a shikse that he likes, not a Jewish girl."

"I have to work in the morning. I'm going to bed."

Ida quieted down. When Helen was undressing she came into her room. "Helen," she said, holding back her tears, "the only thing I want for you is the best. Don't make my mistake. Don't make worse and spoil your whole life, with a poor man that he is only a grocery clerk which we don't know about him nothing. Marry somebody who can give you a better life, a nice professional boy with a college education. Don't mix up now with a stranger. Helen, I know what I'm talking. Believe me, I know." She was crying again.

"I'll try my best," Helen said.

Ida dabbed at her eyes with a handkerchief. "Helen, darling, do me one favor."

"What is it? I am very tired."

"Please call up Nat tomorrow. Just to speak to him. Say hello, and if he asks you to go out with him, tell him yes. Give him a chance."

"I gave him one."

"Last summer you enjoyed so much with him. You went to the beach, to concerts. What happened?"

"Our tastes are different," Helen said wearily.

"In the summer you said your tastes were the same."

"I learned otherwise."

"He is a Jewish boy, Helen, a college graduate. Give him another chance."

"All right," said Helen, "now will you go to sleep?"

"Also don't go no more with Frank. Don't let him kiss you, it's not nice."

"I can't promise."

"Please, Helen."

"I said I'd call Nat. Let that be an end of it now. Good night, Mama."

"Good night," Ida said sadly.

Though her mother's suggestion depressed her, Helen called Nat from her office the next day. He was cordial, said he had bought a secondhand car from his future brother-in-law and invited her to go for a drive.

She said she would sometime.

"How about Friday night?" Nat asked.

She was seeing Frank on Friday. "Could you make it Saturday?"

"I happen to have an engagement Saturday, also Thursday—something doing at the law school."

"Then Friday is all right." She agreed reluctantly, thinking it would be best to change the date with Frank, to satisfy her mother.

When Morris came up for his nap that afternoon Ida desperately begged him to send Frank away at once.

"Leave me alone on this subject ten minutes."

"Morris," she said, "last night I went out when Helen went, and I saw she met Frank in the park, and they kissed each the other."

Morris frowned. "He kissed her?"

"Yes."

"She kissed him?"

"I saw with my eyes."

But the grocer, after thinking about it, said wearily, "So what is a kiss? A kiss is nothing."

Ida said furiously, "Are you crazy?"

"He will go away soon," he reminded her. "In the summer."

Tears sprang into her eyes. "By summer could happen here ten times a tragedy."

"What kind tragedy you expecting—murder?"

"Worse," she cried.

His heart turned cold, he lost his temper. "Leave me alone on this subject, for God's sakes."

"Wait," Ida bitterly warned.

On Thursday of that week Julius Karp left Louis in the liquor store and stepped outside to peek through the grocery window to see if Morris was alone. Karp had not set foot in Morris's store since the night of the holdup, and he uneasily considered the reception he might meet if he were to go in now. Usually, after a time of not speaking to one another, it was Morris Bober, by nature unable to hold a grudge, who gave in and spoke to Karp; but this time he had put out of his mind the possibility of seeking out the liquor dealer and re-establishing their fruitless relationship. While in bed during his last convalescence he had thought much of Karp—an unwilling and distasteful thinking—and had discovered he disliked him more than he had imagined. He resented him as a crass and stupid person who had fallen through luck into flowing prosperity. His every good fortune spattered others with misfortune, as if there was just so much luck in the world and what Karp left over wasn't fit to eat. Morris was incensed by thoughts of the long years he had toiled without just reward. Though this was not Karp's fault, it *was* that a delicatessen had moved in across the street to make a poor man poorer. Nor could the grocer forgive him the blow he had taken on the head in his place, who could in health and wealth better afford it. Therefore it gave him a certain satisfaction not to have anything to do with the liquor dealer, though he was every day next door.

Karp, on the other hand, had been content to wait for Morris to loosen up first. He pictured the grocer yielding his aloof silence while he enjoyed the signs of its dissolution, meanwhile pitying the poor Jew his hard luck life—in capital letters. Some were born that way. Whereas Karp in whatever he touched now coined pure gold, if Morris Bober found a rotten egg in the street, it was already cracked and leaking. Such a one needed someone with experience to advise him when to stay out of the rain. But Morris, whether he knew how Karp felt, or not, remained rigidly uncommunicative—offering not so much as a flicker of recognition when on his way to the corner for his daily *Forward*, he passed the liquor dealer standing in front of his store or caught his eye peeking into his front window. As a month passed, now, quickly, almost four, Karp came to the uncomfortable conclusion that although Ida was still friendly to him, he would this time get nothing for free from Morris; he wasn't going to give in. He reacted coldly to this insight, would give back what he got—so let it be indifference. But indifference was not a commodity he was pleased to exchange. For some reason that was not clear to him Karp liked Morris to like him, and it soon rankled that his down-at-the-heels neighbor continued to remain distant. So he had been hit on the head in a holdup, but was the fault Karp's? *He* had taken care—why hadn't Morris, the shlimozel? Why, when he had warned him there were two holdupniks across the street, hadn't he like a sensible person gone first to lock his door, then telephoned the police? Why?—because he was inept, unfortunate.

And because he was, his troubles grew like bananas in bunches. First, in another accident to his hard head, then through employing Frank Alpine. Karp, no fool, knew the makings of a bad situation when he saw it. Frank, whom he had got acquainted with and considered a fly-by-night rolling stone, would soon make trouble—of that he was certain. Morris's fly-specked, worm-eaten shop did not earn half enough to pay for a full-time helper, and it was idiotic extravagance for the grocer, after he was better, to keep the clerk working for him. Karp soon learned from Louis that his estimate of a bad situation was correct. He found out that Frank every so often invested in a bottle of the best stuff, paying, naturally, cash—but whose? Furthermore Sam Pearl, another waster, had mentioned that the clerk would now and then paste a two-dollar bill on some nag's useless nose, from which it blew off in the breeze. This done by a man who was no doubt paid in peanuts added up to only one thing—he stole. Who did he steal from? Naturally from M. Bober, who had anyway nothing— who else? Rockefeller knew how to take care of his millions, but if Morris earned a dime he lost it before he could put it into his torn pocket. It was the nature of clerks to steal from those they were working for. Karp had, as a young man, privately peculated from his employer, a half-blind shoe wholesaler; and Louis, he knew, snitched from him, but by Louis he was not bothered. He was, after all, a son; he worked in the business and would some- day—it shouldn't be too soon—own it. Also, by strict warnings and occasional surprise inventories he held Louis down to a bare minimum—beans. A stranger stealing money was another matter —slimy. It gave Karp gooseflesh to think of the Italian working for him.

And since misfortune was the grocer's lot, the stranger would shovel on more, not less, for it was always dangerous to have a young goy around where there was a Jewish girl. This worked out by an unchangeable law that Karp would gladly have ex- plained to Morris had they been speaking, and saved him serious trouble. That *this* trouble, too, existed he had confirmed twice in the last week. Once he saw Helen and Frank walking on the Park- way under the trees, and another time while driving home past the local movie house, he had glimpsed them coming out after a show, holding hands. Since then he had often thought about them, indeed with anxiety, and felt he would in some way like to as- sist the luckless Bober.

Without doubt Morris kept Frank on to make his life easier, and probably, being Bober, he had no idea what was happening behind his back. Well, Julius Karp would warn him of his daughter's danger. Tactfully he would explain him what was what. After, he would put in a plug for Louis, who, Karp was aware, had long liked Helen but was not sure enough of himself to be successful with her. Swat Louis down and he retreated to tenderize his fingernails with his teeth. In some things he needed a push. Karp felt he could ease his son's way to Helen by making Morris a proposition he had had in the back of his head for almost a year. He would describe Louis' prospects after marriage in terms of cold cash and other advantages, and suggest that Morris speak to Helen on the subject of going with him seriously. If they went together a couple of months—Louis would give her an extravagant good time—and the combination worked out, it would benefit not only the daughter, but the grocer as well, for then Karp would take over Morris's sad gesheft and renovate and enlarge it into a self-service market with the latest fixtures and goods. His tenant around the corner he would eliminate when his lease expired—a sacrifice, but worthwhile. After that, with himself as the silent partner giving practical advice, it would take a marvelous catastrophe to keep the grocer from earning a decent living in his old age.

Karp foresaw that the main problem of this matter would be Helen, whom he knew as a strictly independent yet not unworthy girl, even if she had pretensions to marriage with a professional— although she had got no place with Nat Pearl. To be successful, Nat needed what Louis Karp would have plenty of, not a poor girl. So he had acted in his best interests in gently shooing Helen away when her thoughts got too warm—a fact Karp had picked up from Sam Pearl. Louis, on the other hand, could afford a girl like Helen, and Helen, independent and intelligent, would be good for Louis. The liquor store owner decided that when the opportunity came he would talk turkey to her like a Dutch uncle. He would patiently explain that her only future with Frank would be as an outcast, poorer even than her father and sharing his foolish fate; whereas with Louis she could have what she wanted and more—leave it to her father-in-law. Karp felt that once Frank had gone she would listen to reason and appreciate the good life he was offering her. Twenty-three or -four was a dangerous age for a single girl. At that age she would not get younger; at that age even a goy looked good.

Having observed that Frank had gone into Sam Pearl's place, and that Morris was for the moment alone in the back of his store, Karp coughed clear his throat and stepped inside the grocery. When Morris, emerging from the rear, saw who it after all was, he experienced a moment of vindictive triumph, but this was followed by annoyance that the pest was once more present, and at the same time by an uncomfortable remembrance that Karp never entered unaccompanied by bad news. Therefore he stayed silent, waiting for the liquor dealer, in prosperous sport jacket and gabardine slacks which could not camouflage his protrusive belly nor subtract from the foolishness of his face, to speak; but for once Karp's active tongue lay flat on its back as, embarrassed in recalling the results of his very last visit here, he stared at the visible scar on Morris's head.

In pity for him, the grocer spoke, his tone friendlier than he would have guessed. "So how are you, Karp?"

"Thanks. What have I got to complain?" Beaming, he thrust a pudgy hand across the counter and Morris found himself unwillingly weighing the heavy diamond ring that pressed his fingers.

Since it did not seem sensible to Karp, one minute after their reconciliation, to blurt out news of a calamity concerning Morris's daughter, he fiddled around for words to say and came up with, "How's business?"

Morris had hoped he would ask. "Fine, and every day gets better."

Karp contracted his brows; yet it occurred to him that Morris's business might have improved more than he had guessed, when peering at odd moments through the grocery window, he had discovered a customer or two instead of the usual dense emptiness. Now on the inside after several months, he noticed the store seemed better taken care of, the shelves solidly packed with stock. But if business was better he at once knew why.

Yet he casually asked, "How is this possible? You are maybe advertising in the paper?"

Morris smiled at the sad joke. Where there was no wit money couldn't buy it. "By word of mouth," he remarked, "is the best advertising."

"This is according to what the mouth says."

"It says," Morris answered without shame, "that I got a fine clerk who has pepped me up the business. Instead going down in the winter, every day goes up."

"Your clerk did this?" Karp said, thoughtfully scratching under one buttock.

"The customers like him. A goy brings in goyim."

"New customers?"

"New, old."

"Something else helps you also?"

"Also helps a little the new apartment house that it opened in December."

"Hmm," said Karp, "nothing more?"

Morris shrugged. "I don't think so. I hear your Schmitz don't feel so good and he don't give service like he used to give. Came back a few customers from him, but the most important help to me is Frank."

Karp was astonished. Could it be that the man didn't know what had happened practically under his nose? He then and there saw a God-given opportunity to boot the clerk out of the place forever. "That wasn't Frank Alpine who improved you your business," he said decisively. "That was something else."

Morris smiled slightly. As usual the sage knew every reason for every happening.

But Karp persisted. "How long does he work here?"

"You know when he came—in November."

"And right away the business started to pick up?"

"Little by little."

"This happened," Karp announced with excitement, "not because this goy came here. What did he know about the grocery business? Nothing. Your store improved because my tenant Schmitz got sick and had to close his store part of the day. Didn't you know that?"

"I heard he was sick," Morris answered, his throat tightened, "but the drivers said his old father came to give him a help."

"That's right," Karp said, "but in the middle December he went every morning to the hospital for treatments. First the father stayed in the store, then he got too tired so Schmitz didn't open till maybe nine, ten o'clock, instead of seven. And instead of closing ten o'clock at night, he closed eight. This went on like this till last month, then he couldn't open till eleven o'clock in the morning, and so he lost half a day's business. He tried to sell the store but nobody would buy then. Yesterday he closed up altogether. Didn't somebody mention that to you?"

"One of the customers said," Morris answered, distressed, "but I thought it was temporary."

"He's very sick," said Karp solemnly. "He won't open again."

My God, thought Morris. For months he had watched the store when it was empty and while it was being altered, but never since its opening had he gone past Sam Pearl's corner to look at it. He hadn't the heart to. But why had no one told him that the place had been closing part of the day for more than two months—Ida, Helen? Probably they had gone past it without noticing the door was sometimes closed. In their minds, as in his, it was always open for *his* business.

"I don't say," Karp was saying, "that your clerk didn't help your income, but the real reason things got better is when Schmitz couldn't stay open, some of his customers came here. Naturally, Frank wouldn't tell you that."

Filled with foreboding, Morris reflected on what the liquor dealer had said. "What happened to Schmitz?"

"He has a bad blood disease and lays now in the hospital."

"Poor man," the grocer sighed. Hope wrestled shame as he asked, "Will he give the store in auction?"

Karp was devastating. "What do you mean give in auction? It's a good store. He sold it Wednesday to two up-to-date Norwegian partners and they will open next week a modern fancy grocery and delicatessen. You will see where your business will go."

Morris, with clouded eyes, died slowly.

Karp, to his horror, realized he had shot at the clerk and wounded the grocer. He remarked hastily, "What could I do? I couldn't tell him to go in auction if he had a chance to sell."

The grocer wasn't listening. He was thinking of Frank with a violent sense of outrage, of having been deceived.

"Listen, Morris," Karp said quickly, "I got a proposition for you about your gesheft. Throw out first on his ass this Italyener that he fooled you, then tell Helen that my Louis—"

But when the ghost behind the counter cursed him in a strange tongue for the tidings he had brought, Karp backed out of the store and was swallowed in his own.

After a perilous night at the hands of ancient enemies, Morris escaped from his bed and appeared in the store at five A.M. There he faced the burdensome day alone. The grocer had struggled all night with Karp's terrible news—had tossed around like a red coal why nobody had told him before how sick the German was —maybe one of the salesmen, or Breitbart, or a customer. Probably no one had thought it too important, seeing that Schmitz's store was until yesterday open daily. Sure he was sick, but somebody had already mentioned that, and why should they tell him again if they figured that people got sick but then they got better? Hadn't he himself been sick, but who had talked of it in the neighborhood? Probably nobody. People had their own worries to worry about. As for the news that Schmitz had sold his store, the grocer felt that here he had nothing to complain of— he had been informed at once, like a rock dropped on his skull.

As for what he would do with Frank, after long pondering the situation, thinking how the clerk had acted concerning their increase in business—as if he alone had created their better times—Morris at length decided that Frank had not—as he had assumed when Karp told him the news—tried to trick him into believing that he was responsible for the store's change for the better. The grocer supposed that the clerk, like himself, was probably ignorant of the true reason for their change of luck. Maybe he shouldn't have been, since he at least got out during the day, visited other places on the block, heard news, gossip—maybe he should have known, but Morris felt he didn't, possibly because he wanted to believe he was their benefactor. Maybe that was why he had been too blind to see what he should have seen, too deaf to have heard what he had heard. It was possible.

After his first confusion and fright, Morris had decided he must sell the store—he had by eight o'clock already told a couple of drivers to pass the word around—but he must under no circumstances part with Frank and must keep him here to do all he could to prevent the Norwegian partners, after they had reopened the store, from quickly calling back the customers of Schmitz who were with him now. He couldn't believe that Frank hadn't helped. It had not been proved in the Supreme Court that the German's sickness was the only source of their recent good fortune. Karp said so but since when did Karp speak the word of God? Of course Frank had helped the business—only not so much as they had thought. Ida was not so wrong about that. But maybe Frank could hold onto a few people; the grocer doubted he himself could. He hadn't the energy, the nerve to be alone in the store during another time of change for the worse. The years had eaten away his strength.

When Frank came down he at once noticed that the grocer was not himself, but the clerk was too concerned with his own problems to ask Morris what ailed him. Often since the time Helen had been in his room he had recalled her remark that he must discipline himself and wondered why he had been so moved by the word, why it should now bang around in his head like a stick against a drum. With the idea of self-control came the feeling of the beauty of it—the beauty of a person being able to do things the way he wanted to, to do good if he wanted; and this feeling was followed by regret—of the slow dribbling away, starting long ago, of his character, without him lifting a finger to stop it. But today, as he scraped at his hard beard with a safety razor, he made up his mind to return, bit by bit until all paid up, the hundred and forty-odd bucks he had filched from Morris in the months he had worked for him, the figure of which he had kept for this very purpose written on a card hidden in his shoe.

To clean up the slate in a single swipe, he thought again of telling Morris about his part in the holdup. A week ago he was on the point of getting it past his teeth, had even spoken aloud the grocer's name, but when Morris looked up Frank felt it was useless and said never mind. He was born, he thought, with a worrisome conscience that had never done him too much good, although at times he had liked having the acid weight of it in him because it had made him feel he was at least that different from other people. It made him want to set himself straight so he could build his love for Helen right, so it would stay right.

But when he pictured himself confessing, the Jew listening with a fat ear, he still could not stand the thought of it. Why should he make more trouble for himself than he could now handle, and end by defeating his purpose to fix things up and have a better life? The past was the past and the hell with it. He had unwillingly taken part in a holdup, but he was, like Morris, more of a victim of Ward Minogue. If alone, he wouldn't have done it. That didn't excuse him that he did, but it at least showed his true feelings. So what was there to confess if the whole thing had been sort of an accident? Let bygones be gone. He had no control over the past—could only shine it up here and there and shut up as to the rest. From now on he would keep his mind on tomorrow, and tomorrow take up the kind of life that he saw he valued more than how he had been living. He would change and live in a worthwhile way.

Impatient to begin, he waited to empty the contents of his wallet into the cash drawer. He thought he could try it when Morris was napping; but then for some cockeyed reason, although there was nothing for her to do in the store today, Ida came down and sat in the back with him. She was heavy-faced, dispirited; she sighed often but said nothing, although she acted as if she couldn't stand the sight of him. He knew why, Helen had told him, and he felt uncomfortable, as if he were wearing wet clothes she wouldn't let him take off; but the best thing was to keep his trap shut and let Helen handle her end of it.

Ida wouldn't leave, so he couldn't put the dough back although his itch to do so had grown into impatience. Whenever somebody went into the store Ida insisted on waiting on them, but this last time after she came back she said to Frank, stretched out on the couch with a butt in his mouth, that she wasn't feeling so well and was going up.

"Feel better," he said sitting up, but she didn't reply and at last left. He went quickly into the store, once he was sure she was upstairs. His wallet contained a five-dollar bill and a single, and he planned to put it all back in the register, which would leave him only a few coins in his pocket but tomorrow was payday anyway. After ringing up the six bucks, to erase the evidence of an unlikely sale he rang up "no sale." Frank then felt a surge of joy at what he had done and his eyes misted. In the back he drew off his shoe, got out the card, and subtracted six dollars from the total amount he owed. He figured he could pay it all up in a couple-three months, by taking out of the bank the money—about eighty bucks—that was left there, returning it bit by bit, and when that was all used up, giving back part of his weekly salary till he had the debt squared. The trick was to get the money back without arousing anybody's suspicion he was putting in the drawer more than the business was earning.

While he was still in a good mood over what he had done, Helen called up.

"Frank," she said, "are you alone? If not say wrong number and hang up."

"I am alone."

"Have you seen how nice it is today? I went for a walk at lunchtime and it feels like spring has arrived."

"It's still in February. Don't take your coat off too soon."

"After Washington's Birthday winter loses its heart. Do you smell the wonderful air?"

"Not right now."

"Get outside in the sun," she said, "it's warm and wonderful."

"Why did you call me for?" he asked.

"Must I have an excuse to call?" she said softly.

"You never do."

"I called because I wished I were seeing you tonight instead of Nat."

"You don't have to go out with him if you don't want to."

"I'd better, because of my mother."

"Change it to some other time."

She thought a minute then said she had better to get it over with.

"Do it any way you like."

"Frank, do you think we could meet after I see Nat—maybe at half past eleven, or twelve at the latest? Would you like to meet me then?"

"Sure, but what's it all about?"

"I'll tell you when I see you," she said with a little laugh. "Should we meet on the Parkway or our regular place in front of the lilac trees?"

"Wherever you say. The park is okay."

"I really hate to go there since my mother followed us."

"Don't worry about that, honey." He said, "Have you got something nice to tell me?"

"Very nice," Helen said.

He thought he knew what it was. He thought he would carry her like a bride up to his room, then when it was over carry her down so she could go up alone without fear her mother suspected where she had been.

Just then Morris came into the store so he hung up.

The grocer inspected the figure in the cash register and the satisfying sum there set him sighing. By Saturday they would surely have two-forty or fifty, but it wouldn't be that high any more once the Norwegians opened up.

Noticing Morris peering at the register under the yellow flame of his match, Frank remembered that all he had left on him was about seventy cents. He wished Helen had called him before he had put back the six bucks in the drawer. If it rained tonight they might need a cab to get home from the park, or maybe if they went up in his room she would be hungry after and want a pizza or something. Anyway, he could borrow a buck from her if he needed it. He also thought of asking Louis Karp for a little loan but didn't like to.

Morris went out for his *Forward* and spread it before him on the table, but he wasn't reading. He was thinking how distracted he was about the future. While he was upstairs, he had lain in bed trying to think of ways to cut down his expenses. He had thought of the fifteen dollars weekly he paid Frank and had worried over how large the sum was. He had also thought of Helen being kissed by the clerk, and of Ida's warnings, and all this had worked on his nerves. He seriously considered telling Frank to go but couldn't make the decision to. He wished he had let him go long ago.

Frank had decided he didn't like to ask Helen for any money—it wasn't a nice thing to do with a girl you liked. He thought it was better to take a buck out of the register drawer, out of the amount he had just put back. He wished he had paid back the five and kept himself the one-buck bill.

Morris sneaked a glance at his clerk sitting on the couch. Recalling the time he had sat in the barber's chair, watching the customers coming out of the grocery with big bags, he felt uneasy. I wonder if he steals from me, he thought. The question filled him with dread because he had asked it of himself many times yet had never answered it with certainty.

He saw through the window in the wall that a woman had come into the store. Frank got up from the couch. "I'll take this one, Morris."

Morris spoke to his newspaper. "I got anyway something to clean up in the cellar."

"What have you got there?"

"Something."

When Frank walked behind the counter, Morris went down into the cellar but didn't stay there. He stole up the stairs and stationed himself behind the hall door. Peering through a crack in the wood, he clearly saw the woman and heard her ordering. He added up the prices of the items as she ordered them.

The bill came to $1.81. When Frank rang up the money, the grocer held his breath for a painful second, then stepped inside the store.

The customer, hugging her bag of groceries, was on her way out of the front door. Frank had his hand under his apron, in his pants pocket. He gazed at the grocer with a startled expression. The amount rung up on the cash register was eighty-one cents.

Morris groaned within himself.

Frank, though tense with shame, pretended nothing was wrong. This enraged Morris. "The bill was a dollar more, why did you ring a dollar less?"

The clerk, after a time of long agony, heard himself say, "It's just a mistake, Morris."

"No," thundered the grocer. "I heard behind the hall door how much you sold her. Don't think I don't know you did many times the same thing before."

Frank could say nothing.

"Give it here the dollar," Morris ordered, extending his trembling hand.

Anguished, the clerk tried lying. "You're making a mistake. The register owes me a buck. I ran short on nickels so I got twenty from Sam Pearl with my own dough. After, I accidentally rang up one buck instead of 'no sale.' That's why I took it back this way. No harm done, I tell you."

"This is a lie," cried Morris. "I left inside a roll nickels in case anybody needed." He strode behind the counter, rang "no sale" and held up the roll of nickels. "Tell the truth."

Frank thought, This shouldn't be happening to me, for I am a different person now.

"I was short, Morris," he admitted, "that's the truth of it. I figured I would pay you back tomorrow after I got my pay." He took the crumpled dollar out of his pants pocket and Morris snatched it from his hand.

"Why didn't you ask me to lend you a dollar instead to steal it?"

The clerk realized it hadn't occurred to him to borrow from the grocer. The reason was simple—he had never borrowed, he had always stolen.

"I didn't think about it. I made a mistake."

"Always mistakes," the grocer said wrathfully.

"All my life," sighed Frank.

"You stole from me since the day I saw you."

"I confess to it," Frank said, "but for God's sake, Morris, I swear I was paying it back to you. Even today I put back six bucks. That's why you got so much in the drawer from the time you went up to snooze until now. Ask the Mrs if we took in more than two bucks while you were upstairs. The rest I put in."

He thought of taking off his shoe and showing Morris how carefully he had kept track of the money he had taken, but he didn't want to do that because the amount was so large it might anger the grocer more.

"You put it in," Morris cried, "but it belongs to me. I don't want a thief here." He counted fifteen dollars out of the register. "Here's your week's pay—the last. Please leave now the store."

His anger was gone. He spoke in sadness and fear of tomorrow.

"Give me one last chance," Frank begged, "Morris, please." His face was gaunt, his eyes haunted, his beard like night.

Morris, though moved by the man, thought of Helen.

"No."

Frank stared at the gray and broken Jew and seeing, despite tears in his eyes, that he would not yield, hung up his apron on a hook and left.

The night's new beauty struck Helen with the anguish of loss as she hurried into the lamplit park a half-hour after midnight. That morning as she had stepped into the street, wearing a new dress under her old coat, the fragrant day had moved her to tears and she felt then she was truly in love with Frank. Whatever the future held it couldn't deny her the sense of release and fulfillment she had felt then. Hours later, when she was with Nat Pearl, as they stopped off for a drink at a roadside tavern, then at his insistence drove into Long Island, her thoughts were still on Frank and she was impatient to be with him.

Nat was Nat. He exerted himself tonight, giving out with charm. He talked with charm and was hurt with charm. Unchanged after all the months she hadn't been with him, as they were parked on the dark shore overlooking the starlit Sound, after a few charming preliminaries he had put his arms around her. "Helen, how can we forget what pleasure we had in the past?"

She pushed him away, angered. "It's gone, I've forgotten. If you're so much of a gentleman, Nat, you ought to forget it too. Was a couple of times in bed a mortgage on my future?"

"Helen, don't talk like a stranger. For Pete's sake, be human."

"I *am* human, please remember."

"We were once good friends. My plea is for friendship again."

"Why don't you admit by friendship you mean something different?"

"Helen . . ."

"No."

He sat back at the wheel. "Christ, you have become a suspicious character."

She said, "Things have changed—you must realize."

"Who have they changed for," he asked sullenly, "that dago I hear you go with?"

Her answer was ice.

On the way home he tried to unsay what he had said, but Helen yielded him only a quick good-by. She left him with relief and a poignant sense of all she had wasted of the night.

Worried that Frank had had to wait so long, she hurried across the lit plaza and along a gravel path bordered by tall lilac shrubs, toward their meeting place. As she approached their bench, although she was troubled by a foreboding he would not be there, she couldn't believe it, then was painfully disappointed to find that though others were present—it was true, he wasn't.

Could he have been and gone already? It didn't seem possible; he had always waited before, no matter how late she was. And since she had told him she had something important to say, nothing less than that she now knew she loved him, surely he would want to hear what. She sat down, fearing he had had an accident.

Usually they were alone at this spot, but almost warmish late-February night had brought out company. On a bench diagonally opposite Helen, in the dark under budding branches, sat two young lovers locked in a long kiss. The bench at her left was empty, but on the one beyond that a man was sleeping under a dim lamp. A cat nosed at his shadow and departed. The man woke with a grunt, squinted at Helen, yawned and went back to sleep. The lovers at last broke apart and left in silence, the boy awkwardly trailing the happy girl. Helen deeply envied her, an awful feeling to end the day with.

Glancing at her watch she saw it was already past one. Shivering, she rose, then sat down to wait five last minutes. She felt the stars clustered like a distant weight above her head. Utterly lonely, she regretted the spring-like loveliness of the night; it had gone, in her hands, to waste. She was tired of anticipation, of waiting for nothing.

A man was standing unsteadily before her, heavy, dirty, stinking of whiskey. Helen half-rose, struck with fright.

He flipped off his hat and said huskily, "Don't be afraid of me, Helen. I'm personally a fine guy—son of a cop. You remember me, don't you—Ward Minogue that went to your school? My old man beat me up once in the girls' yard."

Though it was years since she had seen him she recognized Ward, at once recalling the incident of his following a girl into a lavatory. Instinctively Helen raised her arm to protect herself. She kept herself from screaming, or he might grab her. How stupid, she thought, to wait for this.

"I remember you, Ward."

"Could I sit down?"

She hesitated. "All right."

Helen edged as far away from him as she could. He looked half-stupefied. If he made a move she would run, screaming.

"How did you recognize me in the dark?" she asked, pretending to be casual as she glanced stealthily around to see how best to escape. If she could get past the trees, it was then another twenty feet along the shrub-lined path before she could be out in the open. Once on the plaza there would be people around she could appeal to.

God only help me, she thought.

"I saw you a couple of times lately," Ward answered, rubbing his hand slowly across his chest.

"Where?"

"Around. Once I saw you come out of your old man's grocery and I figured it was you. You have still kept your looks," he grinned.

"Thanks. Don't you feel so well?"

"I got gas pains in my chest and a goddam headache."

"In case you want one I have a box of aspirins in my purse."

"No, they make me puke." She noticed that he was glancing toward the trees. She grew more anxious, thought of offering him her purse if he only wouldn't touch her.

"How's your boy friend, Frank Alpine?" Ward asked, with a wet wink.

She said in surprise, "Do you know Frank?"

"He's an old friend of mine," he answered. "He was here lookin' for you."

"Is—he all right?"

"Not so hot," said Ward. "He had to go home."

She got up. "I have to leave now."

But he was standing.

"Good night." Helen walked away from him.

"He told me to give you this paper." Ward thrust his hand into his coat pocket.

She didn't believe him but paused long enough for him to move forward. He grabbed her with astonishing swiftness, smothering her scream with his smelly hand, as he dragged her toward the trees.

"All I want is what you give that wop," Ward grunted.

She kicked, clawed, bit his hand, broke loose. He caught her by her coat collar, ripped it off. She screamed again and ran forward but he pounced upon her and got his arm over her mouth. Ward shoved her hard against a tree, knocking the breath out of her. He held her tightly by the throat as with his other hand he ripped open her coat and tore her dress off the shoulder, exposing her brassière.

Struggling, kicking wildly, she caught him between the legs with her knee. He cried out and cracked her across the face. She felt the strength go out of her and fought not to faint. She screamed but heard no sound.

Helen felt his body shuddering against her. I am disgraced, she thought, yet felt curiously freed of his stinking presence, as if he had dissolved into a can of filth and she had kicked it away. Her legs buckled and she slid to the ground. I've fainted, went through her mind, although she felt she was still fighting him.

Dimly she realized that a struggle was going on near her. She heard the noise of a blow, and Ward Minogue cried out in great pain and staggered away.

Frank, she thought with tremulous joy. Helen felt herself gently lifted and knew she was in his arms. She sobbed in relief. He kissed her eyes and lips and he kissed her half-naked breast. She held him tightly with both arms, weeping, laughing, murmuring she had come to tell him she loved him.

He put her down and they kissed under the dark trees. She tasted whiskey on his tongue and was momentarily afraid.

"I love you, Helen," he murmured, attempting clumsily to cover her breast with the torn dress as he drew her deeper into the dark, and from under the trees onto the star-dark field.

They sank to their knees on the winter earth, Helen urgently whispering, "Please not now, darling," but he spoke of his starved and passionate love, and all the endless heartbreaking waiting. Even as he spoke he thought of her as beyond his reach, forever in the bathroom as he spied, so he stopped her pleas with kisses. . . .

Afterward, she cried, "Dog—uncircumcised dog!"

While Morris was sitting alone in the back the next morning, a boy brought in a pink handbill and left it on the counter. When the grocer picked it up he saw it announced the change of management and reopening on Monday, by Taast and Pederson, of the grocery and fancy delicatessen around the corner. There followed, in large print, a list of specials they were offering during their first week, bargains Morris could never hope to match, because he couldn't afford the loss the Norwegians were planning to take. The grocer felt he was standing in an icy draft blowing from some hidden hole in the store. In the kitchen, though he stood with his legs and buttocks pressed against the gas radiator, it took an age to diminish the chill that had penetrated his bones.

All morning he scanned the crumpled handbill, muttering to himself; he sipped cold coffee, thinking of the future, and off and on, of Frank Alpine. The clerk had left last night without taking his fifteen dollars' wages. Morris thought he would come in for it this morning but, as the hours passed, knew he wouldn't, maybe having left it to make up some of the money he had stolen; yet maybe not. For the thousandth time the grocer wondered if he had done right in ordering Frank to go. True, he had stolen from him, but also true, he was paying it back. His story that he had put six dollars into the register and then found he had left himself without a penny in his pocket was probably the truth, because the sum in the register, when Morris counted it, was more than they usually took in during the dead part of the afternoon when he napped. The clerk was an unfortunate man; yet the grocer was alternately glad and sorry the incident had occurred. He was glad he had finally let him go. For Helen's sake it had had to be done, and for Ida's peace of mind, as well as his own. Still, he felt unhappy to lose his assistant and be by himself when the Norwegians opened up.

Ida came down, puffy-eyed from poor sleep. She felt a hopeless rage against the world. What will become of Helen? she asked herself, and cracked her knuckles against her chest. But when Morris looked up to listen to her complaints, she was afraid to say anything. A half-hour later, aware that something had changed in the store, she thought of the clerk.

"Where is he?" she asked.

"He left," Morris answered.

"Where did he leave?" she said in astonishment.

"He left for good."

She gazed at him. "Morris, what happened, tell me?"

"Nothing," he said, embarrassed. "I told him to leave."

"Why, all of a sudden?"

"Didn't you say you didn't want him here no more?"

"From the first day I saw him, but you always said no."

"Now, I said yes."

"A stone falls off my heart." But she was not satisfied. "Did he move out of the house yet?"

"I don't know."

"I will go and ask the upstairske."

"Leave her alone. We will know when he moves."

"When did you tell him to leave?"

"Last night."

"So why didn't you tell me last night?" she said angrily. "Why you told me he went early to the movies?"

"I was nervous."

"Morris," she asked in fright. "Did something else happen? Did Helen—"

"Nothing happened."

"Does she know he left?"

"I didn't tell her. Why she went so early to work this morning?"

"She went early?"

"Yes."

"I don't know," Ida said uneasily.

He produced the handbill. "This is why I feel bad."

She glanced at it, not comprehending.

"The German," he explained. "They bought him out, two Norwegians."

She gasped. "When?"

"This week. Schmitz is sick. He lays now in the hospital."

"I told you," Ida said.

"You told me?"

"Vey is mir. I told you after Christmas—when improved more the business. I told you the drivers said the German was losing customers. You said no, Frank improved the business. A goy brings in goyim, you said. How much strength I had to argue with you?"

"Did you tell me he kept closed in the morning his store?"

"Who said? I didn't know this."

"Karp told me."

"Karp was here?"

"He came on Thursday to tell me the good news."

"What good news?"

"That Schmitz sold out."

"Is this good news?" she asked.

"Maybe to him but not to me."

"You didn't tell me he came."

"I tell you now," he said irritably. "Schmitz sold out. Monday will open two Norwegians. Our business will go to hell again. We will starve here."

"Some helper you had," she said with bitterness. "Why didn't you listen to me when I said let him go?"

"I listened," he said wearily.

She was silent, then asked, "So when Karp told you Schmitz sold his store you told Frank to leave?"

"The next day."

"Thank God."

"See if you say next week 'Thank God.' "

"What is this got to do with Frank? Did he help us?"

"I don't know."

"You don't know," she said shrilly. "You just told me you said he should leave when you found out where came our business."

"I don't know," he said miserably, "I don't know where it came."

"It didn't come from him."

"Where it came I don't worry any more. Where will it come next week I worry." He read aloud the specials the Norwegians were offering.

She squeezed her hands white. "Morris, we must sell the store."

"So sell." Sighing, Morris removed his apron. "I will take my rest."

"It's only half past eleven."

"I feel cold." He looked depressed.

"Eat something first—your soup."

"Who can eat?"

"Drink a hot glass tea."

"No."

"Morris," she said quietly, "don't worry so much. Something will happen. We will always have to eat."

He made no reply, folded the handbill into a small square and took it upstairs with him.

The rooms were cold. Ida always shut off the radiators when she went down and lit them again in the late afternoon about an hour before Helen returned. Now the house was too cold. Morris turned on the stopcock of the bedroom radiator, then found he had no match in his pocket. He got one in the kitchen.

Under the covers he felt shivery. He lay under two blankets and a quilt yet shivered. He wondered if he was sick but soon fell asleep. He was glad when he felt sleep come over him, although it brought night too quickly. But if you slept it was night, that's how things were. Looking, that same night, from the street into his store, he beheld Taast and Pederson—one with a small blond mustache, the other half-bald, a light shining on his head—standing behind *his* counter, poking into *his* cash register. The grocer rushed in but they were gabbing in German and paid no attention to his gibbering Yiddish. At that moment Frank came out of the back with Helen. Though the clerk spoke a musical Italian, Morris recognized a dirty word. He struck his assistant across the face and they wrestled furiously on the floor, Helen screaming mutely. Frank dumped him heavily on his back and sat on his poor chest. He thought his lungs would burst. He tried hard to cry out but his voice cracked his throat and no one would help. He considered the possibility of dying and would have liked to.

Tessie Fuso dreamed of a tree hit by thunder and knocked over; she dreamed she heard someone groan terribly and awoke in fright, listened, then went back to sleep. Frank Alpine, at the dirty end of a long night, awoke groaning. He awoke with a shout—awake, he thought, forever. His impulse was to leap out of bed and rush down to the store; then he remembered that Morris had thrown him out. It was a gray, dreary winter morning. Nick had gone to work and Tessie, in her bathrobe, was sitting in the kitchen, drinking coffee. She heard Frank cry out again but had just discovered that she was pregnant, so did nothing more than wonder at his nightmare.

He lay in bed with the blankets pulled over his head, trying to smother his thoughts but they escaped and stank. The more he smothered them the more they stank. He smelled garbage in the bed and couldn't move out of it. He couldn't because he was it—the stink in his own broken nose. What you did was how bad you smelled. Unable to stand it he flung the covers aside and struggled to dress but couldn't make it. The sight of his bare feet utterly disgusted him. He thirsted for a cigarette but couldn't light one for fear of seeing his hand. He shut his eyes and lit a match. The match burned his nose. He stepped on the lit match with his bare feet and danced in pain.

Oh my God, why did I do it? Why did I ever do it? Why did I do it?

His thoughts were killing him. He couldn't stand them. He sat on the edge of the twisted bed, his thoughtful head ready to bust in his hands. He wanted to run. Part of him was already in flight, he didn't know where. He just wanted to run. But while he was running, he wanted to be back. He wanted to be back with Helen, to be forgiven. It wasn't asking too much. People forgave people—who else? He could explain if she would listen. Explaining was a way of getting close to somebody you had hurt; as if in hurting them you were giving them a reason to love you. He had come, he would say, to the park to wait for her, to hear what she had to tell him. He felt he knew she would say she loved him; it meant they would soon sleep together. This stayed in his mind and he sat there waiting to hear her say it, at the same time in an agony that she never would, that he would lose her the minute she found out why her father had kicked him out of the grocery. What could he tell her about that? He sat for hours trying to think what to say, at last growing famished. At midnight he left to get a pizza but stopped instead in a bar. Then when he saw his face in the mirror he felt a nose-thumbing revulsion. Where have you ever been, he asked the one in the glass, except on the inside of a circle? What have you ever done but always the wrong thing? When he returned to the park, there was Ward Minogue hurting her. He just about killed Ward. Then when he had Helen in his arms, crying, saying at last that she loved him, he had this hopeless feeling it was the end and now he would never see her again. He thought he must love her before she was lost to him. She said no, not to, but he couldn't believe it the same minute she was saying she loved him. He thought, Once I start she will come along with me. So then he did it. He loved her with his love. She should have known that. She should not have gone wild, beat his face with her fists, called him dirty names, run from him, his apologies, pleadings, sorrow.

Oh Jesus, what did I do?

He moaned; had got instead of a happy ending, a bad smell. If he could root out what he had done, smash and destroy it; but it was done, beyond him to undo. It was where he could never lay hands on it any more—in his stinking mind. His thoughts would forever suffocate him. He had failed once too often. He should somewhere have stopped and changed the way he was going, his luck, himself, stopped hating the world, got a decent education, a job, a nice girl. He had lived without will, betrayed every good intention. Had he ever confessed the holdup to Morris? Hadn't he stolen from the cash register till the minute he was canned? In a single terrible act in the park hadn't he murdered the last of his good hopes, the love he had so long waited for— his chance at a future? His goddamned life had pushed him wherever it went; he had led it nowhere. He was blown around in any breath that blew, owned nothing, not even experience to show for the years he had lived. If you had experience you knew at least when to start and where to quit; all he knew was

how to mangle himself more. The self he had secretly considered valuable was, for all he could make of it, a dead rat.
He stank.

This time his shout frightened Tessie. Frank got up on the run
but he had run everywhere. There was no place left to escape to.
The room shrank. The bed was flying up at him. He felt trapped
—sick, wanted to cry but couldn't. He planned to kill himself,
at the same minute had a terrifying insight: that all the while he
was acting like he wasn't, he was really a man of stern morality.

Ida had awakened in the night and heard her daughter crying.
Nat did something to her, she thought wildly, but was ashamed
to go to Helen and beg her to say what. She guessed he had acted
like a lout—it was no wonder Helen had stopped seeing him.
All night she blamed herself for having urged her to go out with
the law student. She fell into an unhappy sleep.

It was growing light when Morris left the flat. Helen dragged
herself out of bed and sat with reddened eyes in the bathroom,
sewing on her coat collar. Once near the office she would give
it to a tailor to fix so the tear couldn't be seen. With her new
dress she could do nothing. Rolling it into a hopeless ball, she
hid it under some things in her bottom bureau drawer. Monday
she would buy one exactly like it and hang it in her closet. Undressing for a shower—her third in hours—she burst into tears at
the sight of her body. Every man she drew to her dirtied her.
How could she have encouraged him? She felt a violent self-
hatred for trusting him, when from the very beginning she had
sensed he was untrustable. How could she have allowed herself
to fall in love with anybody like him? She was filled with loathing
at the fantasy she had created, of making him into what he
couldn't be—educable, promising, kind and good, when he was
no more than a bum. Where were her wits, her sense of elemental
self-preservation?

Under the shower she soaped herself heavily, crying as she
washed. At seven, before her mother awakened, she dressed and

left the house, too sickened to eat. She would gladly have forgotten her life, in sleep, but dared not stay home, dared not be questioned. When she returned from her half-day of work, if he was still there, she would order him to leave or would scream him out of the house.

Coming home from the garage, Nick smelled gas in the hall. He inspected the radiators in his flat, saw they were both lit, then knocked on Frank's door.

After a minute the door opened a crack.

"Do you smell anything?" Nick said, staring at the eye in the crack.

"Mind your goddamned business."

"Are you nuts? I smell gas in the house, it's dangerous."

"Gas?" Frank flung open the door. He was in pajamas, haggard.

"What's the matter, you sick?"

"Where do you smell the gas?"

"Don't tell me you can't smell it."

"I got a bad cold," Frank said hoarsely.

"Maybe it's comin' from the cellar," said Nick.

They ran down a flight and then the odor hit Frank, an acrid stench thick enough to wade through.

"It's coming from this floor," Nick said.

Frank pounded on the door. "Helen, there's gas here, let me in. Helen," he cried.

"Shove it," said Nick.

Frank pushed his shoulder against the door. It was unlocked and he fell in. Nick quickly opened the kitchen window while Frank, in his bare feet, roamed through the house. Helen was not there but he found Morris in bed.

The clerk, coughing, dragged the grocer out of bed and carrying him to the living room, laid him on the floor. Nick closed the stopcock of the bedroom radiator and threw open every window. Frank got down on his knees, bent over Morris, clamped his hands to his sides and pumped.

Tessie ran in in fright, and Nick shouted to her to call Ida. Ida came stumbling up the stairs, moaning, "Oh, my God, oh, my God."

Seeing Morris lying on the floor, his underwear soaked, his face the color of a cooked beet, flecks of foam in the corners of his mouth, she let out a piercing shriek.

Helen, coming dully into the hall, heard her mother's cry. She smelled the gas and ran in terror up the stairs, expecting death.

When she saw Frank in his pajamas bent over her father's back, her throat thickened in disgust. She screamed in fear and hatred.

Frank couldn't look at her, frightened to.

"His eyes just moved," Nick said.

Morris awoke with a massive ache in his chest. His head felt like corroded metal, his mouth horribly dry, his stomach crawling with pain. He was ashamed to find himself stretched out in his long underwear on the floor.

"Morris," cried Ida.

Frank got up, embarrassed at his bare feet and pajamas.

"Papa, Papa." Helen was on her knees.

"Why did you do it for?" Ida yelled in the grocer's ear.

"What happened?" he gasped.

"Why did you do it for?" she wept.

"Are you crazy?" he muttered. "I forgot to light the gas. A mistake."

Helen broke into sobbing, her lips twisted. Frank had to turn his head.

"The only thing that saved him was he got some air," Nick said. "You're lucky this flat ain't windproof, Morris."

Tessie shivered. "It's cold. Cover him, he's sweating."

"Put him in bed," Ida said.

Frank and Nick lifted the grocer and carried him in to his bed. Ida and Helen covered him with blankets and quilt.

"Thanks," Morris said to them. He stared at Frank. Frank looked at the floor.

"Shut the windows," Tessie said. "The smell is gone."

"Wait a little longer," said Frank. He glanced at Helen but her back was to him. She was still crying.

"Why did he do it?" Ida moaned.

Morris gazed long at her, then shut his eyes.

"Leave him rest," Nick advised.

"Don't light any matches for another hour," Frank told Ida.

Tessie closed all but one window and they left. Ida and Helen remained with Morris in the bedroom.

Frank lingered in Helen's room but nothing welcomed him there.

Later he dressed and went down to the store. Business was brisk. Ida came down, and though he begged her not to, shut the store.

That afternoon Morris developed a fever and the doctor said he had to go to the hospital. An ambulance came and took the grocer away, his wife and daughter riding with him.

From his window upstairs, Frank watched them go.

Sunday morning the store was still shut tight. Though he feared to, Frank considered knocking on Ida's door and asking for the key. But Helen might open the door, and since he would not know what to say to her over the doorsill, he went instead down the cellar, and mounting the dumb-waiter, wriggled through the little window in the air shaft, into the store toilet. Once in the back, the clerk shaved and had his coffee. He thought he would stay in the store till somebody told him to scram; and even if they did, he would try in some way to stay longer. That was his only hope left, if there was any. Turning the front door lock, he carried in the milk and rolls and was ready for business. The register was empty, so he borrowed five dollars in change from Sam Pearl, saying he would pay it back from what he took in. Sam wanted to know how Morris was and Frank said he didn't know.

Shortly after half past eight, the clerk was standing at the front window when Ida and her daughter left the house. Helen looked like last year's flower. Observing her, he felt a pang of loss, shame, regret. He felt an unbearable deprivation—that yesterday he had almost had some wonderful thing but today it was gone, all but the misery of remembering it was. Whenever he thought of what he had almost had it made him frantic. He felt like rushing outside, drawing her into a doorway, and declaring the stupendous value of his love for her. But he did nothing. He didn't exactly hide but he didn't show himself, and they soon went away to the subway.

Later he thought he would also go and see Morris in the hospital, as soon as he knew which one he was in—after they got home; but they didn't return till midnight. The store was closed and he saw them from his room, two dark figures getting out of a cab. Monday, the day the Norwegians opened their store, Ida came down at seven A.M. to paste a piece of paper on the door saying Morris Bober was sick and the grocery would be closed till Tuesday or Wednesday. To her amazement, Frank Alpine was standing, in his apron, behind the counter. She entered in anger.

Frank was miserably nervous that Morris or Helen, either or both, had told her all the wrong he had done them, because if they had, he was finished.

"How did you get in here?" Ida asked wrathfully.

He said through the air shaft window. "Thinking of your trouble, I didn't want to bother you about the key, Mrs."

She vigorously forbade him ever to come in that way again. Her face was deeply lined, her eyes weary, mouth bitter, but he could tell that for some miraculous reason she didn't know what he had done.

Frank pulled a handful of dollar bills out of his pants pocket and a little bag of change, laying it all on the counter. "I took in forty-one bucks yesterday."

"You were here yesterday?"

"I got in how I explained you. There was a nice rush around four till about six. We are all out of potato salad."

Her eyes grew tears. He asked how Morris felt.

She touched her wet lids with a handkerchief. "Morris has pneumonia."

"Ah, too bad. Give him my sorrow if you can. How's he coming along out of it?"

"He's a very sick man, he has weak lungs."

"I think I'll go to see him in the hospital."

"Not now," Ida said.

"When he's better. How long do you think he'll be there?"

"I don't know. The doctor will telephone today."

"Look, Mrs," Frank said. "Why don't you stop worrying about the store while Morris is sick and let me take care of it? You know I make no demands."

"My husband told you to go out from the store."

He furtively studied her face but there was no sign of accusation.

"I won't stay very long," he answered. "You don't have to worry about that. I'll stay here till Morris gets better. You'll need every cent for the hospital bills. I don't ask a thing for myself."

"Did Morris tell you why you must leave?"

His heart galloped. Did she or didn't she know? If yes, he would say it was a mistake—deny he had touched a red cent in the register. Wasn't the proof of that in the pile of dough that lay right in front of her eyes on the counter? But he answered, "Sure, he didn't want me to hang around Helen any more."

"Yes, she is a Jewish girl. You should look for somebody else. But he also found out that Schmitz was sick since December and kept closed his store in the mornings, also earlier in the night. This was what improved our income, not you."

She then told Frank that the German had sold out and two Norwegians were opening up today.

Frank flushed. "I knew that Schmitz was sick and kept his store closed sometimes, but that isn't what made your business get better. What did that was how hard I worked building up the trade. And I bet I can keep this place in the same shape it is, even with two Norwegians around the corner or three Greeks. What's more, I bet I can raise the take-in higher."

Though she was half-inclined to believe him, she couldn't.

"Wait, you'll see how smart you are."

"Then let me have a chance to show you. Don't pay me anything, the room and meals are enough."

"What," she asked in desperation, "do you want from us?"

"Just to help out. I have my debt to Morris."

"You have no debt. He has a debt to you that you saved him from the gas."

"Nick smelled it first. Anyway I feel I have a debt to him for all the things he has done for me. That's my nature, when I'm thankful, I'm thankful."

"Please don't bother Helen. She is not for you."

"I won't."

She let him stay. If you were so poor where was your choice?

Taast and Pederson opened up with a horseshoe of spring flowers in their window. Their pink handbills brought them steady business and Frank had plenty of time on his hands. During the day only a few of the regulars came into the grocery. At night, after the Norwegians had closed, the grocery had a spurt of activity, but when Frank pulled the strings of the window lights around eleven, he had only fifteen dollars in the register. He didn't worry too much. Monday was a slow day anyway, and besides, people were entitled to grab off a few specials while they could get them. He figured nobody could tell what difference the Norwegians would make to the business until a couple of weeks had gone by, when the neighborhood was used to them and things settled back to normal. Nobody was going to give specials away that cheap every day. A store wasn't a charity, and when they stopped giving something for nothing, he would match them in service and also prices and get his customers back.

Tuesday was slow, also as usual. Wednesday picked up a little, but Thursday was slow again. Friday was better. Saturday was the best day of the week, although not so good as Saturdays lately. At the end of the week the grocery was close to a hundred short of its recent weekly average. Expecting something like this, Frank had closed up for a half hour on Thursday and taken the trolley to the bank. He withdrew twenty-five dollars from his savings account and put the money into the register, five on Thursday, ten on Friday and ten on Saturday, so that when Ida wrote the figures down in her book each night she wouldn't feel too bad. Seventy-five less for the week wasn't as bad as a hundred.

Morris, better after ten days in the hospital, was brought home in a cab by Ida and Helen and laid to bed to convalesce. Frank, gripping his courage, thought of going up to see him and this time starting out right, right off. He thought of bringing him some fresh baked goods to eat, maybe a piece of cheese cake that he knew the grocer liked, or some apple strudel; but the clerk was afraid it was still too soon and Morris might ask him where he had got the money to buy the cake. He might yell, "You thief, you, the only reason you stay here still is because I am sick upstairs." Yet if Morris felt this way he would already have told Ida what Frank had done. The clerk now was sure he hadn't mentioned it, because she wouldn't have waited this long to pitch him out on his ear. He thought a lot about the way Morris kept things to himself. It was a way a person had if he figured he could be wrong about how he sized up a situtaion. It could be that he might take a different view of Frank in time. The clerk tried to invent reasons why it might be worth the grocer's while, after he got on his feet again, to keep him on in the grocery. Frank felt he would promise anything to stay there. "Don't worry that I ever will steal from you or anybody else any more, Morris. If I do, I hope I drop dead on the spot." He hoped that this promise, and the favor he was doing him by keeping the store open, would convince Morris of his sincerity. Yet he thought he would wait a while longer before going up to see him.

Helen hadn't said anything to anybody about him either and it wasn't hard to understand why. The wrong he had done her was never out of his mind. He hadn't intended wrong but he had done it; now he intended right. He would do anything she wanted, and if she wanted nothing he would do something, what he should do; and he would do it all on his own will, nobody pushing him but himself. He would do it with discipline and with love.

All this time he had snatched only glimpses of her, though his heart was heavy with all he hoped to say. He saw her through the plate glass window—she on the undersea side. Through the green glass she looked drowned, yet never, God help him, lovelier. He felt a tender pity for her, mixed with shame for having made her pitiable. Once, as she came home from work, her eyes happened to look into his and showed disgust. Now I am finished, he thought, she will come in here and tell me to go die some place; but when she looked away she was never there. He was agonized to be so completely apart from her, left apologizing to her shadow, to the floral fragrance she left in the air. To himself he confessed his deed, but not to her. That was the curse of it, to have it to make but who would listen? At times he felt like crying but it made him feel too much like a kid to cry. He didn't like to, did it badly.

Once he met her in the hall. She was gone before he could move his lips. He felt for her a rush of love. He felt, after she had left, that hopelessness was his punishment. He had expected that punishment to be drastic, swift; instead it came slowly—it never came, yet was there.

There was no approach to her. What had happened had put her in another world, no way in.

Early one morning, he stood in the hall till she came down the stairs.

"Helen," he said, snatching off the cloth cap he now wore in the store, "my heart is sorrowful. I want to apologize."

Her lips quivered. "Don't speak to me," she said, in a voice choked with contempt. "I don't want your apologies. I don't want to see you, and I don't want to know you. As soon as my father is better, please leave. You've helped him and my mother and I thank you for that, but you're no help to me. You make me sick."

The door banged behind her.

That night he dreamed he was standing in the snow outside her window. His feet were bare yet not cold. He had waited a long time in the falling snow, and some of it lay on his head and had all but frozen his face; but he waited longer until, moved by pity, she opened the window and flung something out. It floated down; he thought it was a piece of paper with writing on it but saw that it was a white flower, surprising to see in wintertime. Frank caught it in his hand. As she had tossed the flower out through the partly opened window he had glimpsed her fingers only, yet he saw the light of her room and even felt the warmth of it. Then when he looked again the window was shut tight, sealed with ice. Even as he dreamed, he knew it had never been open. There was no such window. He gazed down at his hand for the flower and before he could see it wasn't there, felt himself wake.

The next day he waited for her at the foot of the stairs, bareheaded in the light that fell on his head from the lamp.

She came down, her frozen face averted.

"Helen, nothing can kill the love I feel for you."

"In your mouth it's a dirty word."

"If a guy did wrong, must he suffer forever?"

"I personally don't care what happens to you."

Whenever he waited at the stairs, she passed without a word, as if he didn't exist. He didn't.

If the store blows away some dark night I might as well be dead, Frank thought. He tried every way to hang on. Business was terrible. He wasn't sure how long the grocery could last or how long the grocer and his wife would let him try to keep it alive. If the store collapsed everything would be gone. But if he kept it going there was always the chance that something might change, and if it did, maybe something else might. If he kept the grocery on its feet till Morris came down, at least he would have a couple of weeks to change how things were. Weeks were nothing because to do what he had to do he needed years.

Taast and Pederson had the specials going week after week. They thought of one come-on after another to keep the customers buying. Frank's customers were disappearing. Some of them now passed him in the street without saying hello. One or two crossed the trolley tracks and walked on the other side of the street, not to have to see his stricken face at the window. He withdrew all he had left in the bank and each week padded the income a little, but Ida saw how bad things were. She was despondent and talked of giving the place over to the auctioneer. This made him frantic. He felt he had to try harder.

He tried out all sorts of schemes. He got specials on credit and sold half the stuff, but then the Norwegians began to sell it cheaper, and the rest remained on his shelves. He stayed open all night for a couple of nights but did not take in enough to pay for the light. Having nothing much to do, he thought he would fix up the store. With all but the last five dollars from the bank account, he bought a few gallons of cheap paint. Then removing the goods from one section of the shelves, he scraped away the mildewed paper on the walls and painted them a nice light yellow. When one section was painted he went to work on the next. After he had finished the walls he borrowed a tall ladder, scraped the ceiling bit by bit and painted it white. He also replaced a few shelves and neatly finished them in dime store varnish. In the end he had to admit that all his work hadn't brought back a single customer.

Though it seemed impossible the store got worse.

"What are you telling Morris about the business?" Frank asked Ida.

"He don't ask me so I don't tell him," she said dully.

"How is he now?"

"Weak yet. The doctor says his lungs are like paper. He reads or he sleeps. Sometimes he listens to the radio."

"Let him rest. It's good for him."

She said again, "Why do you work so hard for nothing? What do you stay here for?"

For love, he wanted to say, but hadn't the nerve. "For Morris."

But he didn't fool her. She would even then have told him to pack and go, although he kept them for the moment off the street, had she not known for a fact that Helen no longer bothered with him. He had probably through some stupidity fallen out of her good graces. Possibly her father's illness had made her more considerate of them. She had been a fool to worry. Yet she now worried because Helen, at her age, showed so little interest in men. Nat had called but she wouldn't go near the phone.

Frank scraped down on expenses. With Ida's permission he had the telephone removed. He hated to do it because he thought Helen might sometime come down to answer it. He also reduced as gas bill by lighting only one of the two radiators downstairs. He kept the one in the front lit so the customers wouldn't feel the cold, but he no longer used the one in the kitchen. He wore a heavy sweater, a vest and a flannel shirt under his apron, and his cap on his head. But Ida, even with her coat on, when she could no longer stand the emptiness of the front, or the freezing back, escaped upstairs. One day she came into the kitchen, and seeing him salting up a soup plate of boiled potatoes for lunch, began to cry.

He thought always of Helen. How could she know what was going on in him? If she ever looked at him again she would see the same guy on the outside. He could see out but nobody could see in.

When Betty Pearl got married Helen didn't go to the wedding. The day before she apologized embarrassedly, said she wasn't feeling too well—blamed her father's illness. Betty said she understood, thinking it had something to do with her brother. "Next time," she remarked with a little laugh, but Helen, seeing she was hurt, felt bad. She reconsidered facing the ceremony, rigmarole, relatives, Nat or no Nat—maybe she could still go; but couldn't bring herself to. She was no fixture for a wedding. They might say to her, "With such a face, go better to a funeral." Though she had many a night wept herself out, her memories kept a hard hold in her mind. Crazy woman, how could she have brought herself to love such a man? How could she have considered marrying someone not Jewish? A total, worthless stranger. Only God had saved her from a disastrous mistake. With such thoughts she lost all feeling for weddings.

Her sleep suffered. Every day she dreaded every night. From bedtime to dawn she eked out only a few wearisome unconscious hours. She dreamed she would soon awake and soon awoke. Awake, she felt sorry for herself, and sorrow, no soporific, induced sorrow. Her mind stamped out endless worries: her father's health, for instance; he showed little interest in recovery. The store, as ever. Ida wept in whispers in the kitchen. "Don't tell Papa." But they would sometime soon have to. She cursed all grocery stores. And worried at seeing nobody, planning no future. Each morning she crossed off the calendar the sleepless day to be. God forbid such days.

Though Helen turned over all but four dollars of her check to her mother and it went into the register, they were always hard up for cash to meet expenses. One day Frank got an idea how he might lay hold of some dough. He thought he would collect an old bill from Carl, the Swedish painter. He knew the painter owed Morris over seventy bucks. He looked for the housepainter every day but Carl did not come in.

One morning Frank was standing at the window when he saw him leave Karp's with a wrapped bottle in his pocket.

Frank ran out and reminded Carl of his old bill. He asked him to pay something on the account.

"This is all fixed up with me and Morris," the painter answered. "Don't stick your dirty nose in."

"Morris is sick, he needs the dough," Frank said.

Carl shoved the clerk aside and went on his way.

Frank was sore. "I'll collect from that drunk bastard."

Ida was in the store, so Frank said he would be back soon. He hung up his apron, got his overcoat and followed Carl to his house. After getting the address, he returned to the grocery. He was still angered at the painter for the way he had acted when he had asked him to pay his bill.

That evening he returned to the shabby four-story tenement and climbed the creaking staircase to the top floor. A thin, dark-haired woman came wearily to the door. She was old until his eyes got used to her face, then he realized she was young but looked old.

"Are you Carl the painter's wife?"

"That's right."

"Could I talk to him?"

"On a job?" she said hopefully.

"No. Something different."

She looked old again. "He hasn't worked for months."

"I just want to talk to him."

She let him into a large room which was a kitchen and living room combined, the two halves separated by an undrawn curtain. In the middle of the living room part stood a kerosene heater that stank. This smell mixed with the sour smell of cabbage cooking. The four kids, a boy about twelve and three younger girls, were in the room, drawing on paper, cutting and pasting. They stared at Frank but silently went on with what they were doing. The clerk didn't feel comfortable. He stood at the window, looking down on the dreary lamplit street. He now figured he would cut the bill in half if the painter would pay up the rest.

The painter's wife covered the sizzling frying pan with a pot lid and went into the bedroom. She came back and said her husband was sleeping.

"I'll wait a while," said Frank.

She went back to her frying. The oldest girl set the table, and they all sat down to eat. He noticed they had left a place for their old man. He would soon have to crawl out of his hole. The mother didn't sit down. Paying no attention to Frank, she poured skim milk out of a container into the kids' glasses, then served each one a frankfurter fried in dough. She also gave everybody a forkful of hot sauerkraut.

The kids ate hungrily, not talking. The oldest girl glanced at Frank then stared at her plate when he looked at her.

When the plates were empty she said, "Is there any more, Mama?"

"Go to bed," said the painter's wife.

Frank had a bad headache from the stink of the heater.

"I'll see Carl some other time," he said. His spit tasted like brass. "I'm sorry he didn't wake up."

He ran back to the store. Under the mattress of his bed he had his last three bucks hidden. He took the bills and ran back to Carl's house. But on the way he met Ward Minogue. His face was yellow and shrunken, as if he had escaped out of a morgue.

"I been looking for you," said Ward. He pulled Frank's revolver out of a paper bag. "How much is this worth to you?"

"Shit."

"I'm sick," sobbed Ward.

Frank gave the three bucks to him and later dropped the gun into a sewer.

He read a book about the Jews, a short history. He had many times seen this book on one of the library shelves and had never taken it down, but one day he checked it out to satisfy his curiosity. He read the first part with interest, but after the Crusades and the Inquisition, when the Jews were having it tough, he had to force himself to keep reading. He skimmed the bloody chapters but read slowly the ones about their civilization and accomplishments. He also read about the ghettos, where the half-starved, bearded prisoners spent their lives trying to figure it out why they were the Chosen People. He tried to figure out why but couldn't. He couldn't finish the book and brought it back to the library.

Some nights he spied on the Norwegians. He would go around the corner without his apron and stand on the step of Sam Pearl's hallway, looking across the street at the grocery and fancy delicatessen. The window was loaded with all kinds of shiny cans. Inside, the store was lit as bright as day. The shelves were tightly packed with appetizing goods that made him feel hungry. And there were always customers inside, although his place was generally empty. Sometimes after the partners locked up and went home, Frank crossed to their side of the street and peered through the window into the dark store, as if he might learn from what he saw in it the secret of all good fortune and so change his luck and his life.

One night after he had closed the store, he took a long walk and stepped into the Coffee Pot, in all-night joint he had been in once or twice.

Frank asked the owner if he needed a man for night work.

"I need a counterman for coffee, short orders, and to wash the few dishes," the owner answered.

"I am your boy," said Frank.

The work was from ten to six A.M. and paid thirty-five dollars. When he got home in the morning, Frank opened the grocery. At the end of a week's working, without ringing it up, he put the thirty-five into the cash register. This, and Helen's wages, kept them from going under.

The clerk slept on the couch in the back of the store during the day. He had rigged up a buzzer that waked him when somebody opened the door. He did not suffer from lack of sleep.

He lived in his prison in a climate of regret that he had turned a good thing into a bad, and this thought, though ancient, renewed the pain in his heart. His dreams were bad, taking place in the park at night. The garbage smell stank in his nose. He groaned his life away, his mouth crammed with words he couldn't speak. Mornings, standing at the store window, he watched Helen go off to work. He was there when she came home. She walked, slightly bowlegged, toward the door, her eyes cast down, blind to his presence. A million things to say, some extraordinary, welled up in him, choked his throat; daily they died. He thought endlessly of escape, but that would be what he always did last—beat it. This time he would stay. They would carry him out in a box. When the walls caved in they could dig for him with shovels.

Once he found a two-by-four pine board in the cellar, sawed off a hunk, and with his jackknife began to carve it into something. To his surprise it turned into a bird flying. It was shaped off balance but with a certain beauty. He thought of offering it to Helen but it seemed too rough a thing—the first he had ever made. So he tried his hand at something else. He set out to carve her a flower and it came out a rose starting to bloom. When it was done it was delicate in the way its petals were opening yet firm as a real flower. He thought about painting it red and giving it to her but decided to leave off the paint. He wrapped the wooden flower in store paper, printed Helen's name on the outside, and a few minutes before she came home from work, taped the package onto the outside of the mailbox in the vestibule. He saw her enter, then heard her go up the stairs. Looking into the vestibule, he saw she had taken his flower.

The wooden flower reminded Helen of her unhappiness. She lived in hatred of herself for having loved the clerk against her better judgment. She had fallen in love, she thought, to escape her predicament. More than ever she felt herself a victim of circumstance—in a bad dream symbolized by the nightmarish store below, and the relentless, scheming presence in it of the clerk, whom she should have shouted out of the house but had selfishly spared.

In the morning, as he aimed a pail of garbage into the can at the curb, Frank saw at the bottom of it his wooden flower.

On the day he had returned from the hospital Morris felt the urge to jump into his pants and run down to the store, but the doctor, after listening to his lungs, then tapping his hairy knuckles across the grocer's chest, said, "You're coming along fine, so what's your big hurry?" To Ida he privately said, "He has to rest, I don't mean maybe." Seeing her fright he explained, "Sixty isn't sixteen." Morris, after arguing a bit, lay back in bed and after that didn't care if he ever stepped into the store again. His recovery was slow.

With reservations, spring was on its way. There was at least more light in the day; it burst through the bedroom windows. But a cold wind roared in the streets, giving him goose pimples in bed; and sometimes, after half a day of pure sunshine, the sky darkened and some rags of snow fell. He was filled with melancholy and spent hours dreaming of his boyhood. He remembered the green fields. Where a boy runs he never forgets. His father, his mother, his only sister whom he hadn't seen in years, gottenyu. The wailing wind cried to him. . . .

The awning flapping below in the street awoke his dread of the grocery. He had not for a long time asked Ida what went on downstairs but he knew without thinking. He knew in his blood. When he consciously thought of it he remembered that the register rang rarely, so he knew again. He heard heavy silence below. What else can you hear from a graveyard whose noiseless tombstones hold down the sick earth? The smell of death seeped up through the cracks in the floor. He understood why Ida did not dare go downstairs but sought anything to do here. Who could stay in such a place but a goy whose heart was stone? The fate of his store floated like a black-feathered bird dimly in his mind; but as soon as he began to feel stronger, the thing grew lit eyes, worrying him no end. One morning as he sat up against a pillow, scanning yesterday's *Forward*, his thoughts grew so wretched that he broke into sweat and his heart beat erratically. Morris heaved aside his covers, strode crookedly out of bed and began hurriedly to dress.

Ida hastened into the bedroom. "What are you doing, Morris
—a sick man?"

"I must go down."

"Who needs you? There is nothing there. Go rest some more."

He fought a greedy desire to get back into bed and live there
but could not quiet his anxiety.

"I must go."

She begged him not to but he wouldn't listen.

"How much he takes in now?" Morris asked as he belted his
trousers.

"Nothing. Maybe seventy-five."

"A week?"

"What else?"

It was terrible but he had feared worse. His head buzzed with
schemes for saving the store. Once he was downstairs he felt he
could make things better. His fear came from being here, not
where he was needed.

"He keeps open all day?"

"From morning till night—why I don't know."

"Why he stays here?" he asked with sudden irritation.

"He stays," she shrugged.

"What do you pay him?"

"Nothing—he says he don't want."

"So what he wants—my bitter blood?"

"He says he wants to help you."

He muttered something to himself. "You watch him sometimes?"

"Why should I watch him?" she said, worried. "He took something from you?"

"I don't want him here no more. I don't want him near Helen."

"Helen don't talk to him."

He gazed at Ida. "What happened?"

"Go ask her. What happened with Nat? She's like you, she
don't tell me anything."

"He's got to leave today. I don't want him here."

"Morris," she said hesitantly, "he gave you good help, believe me. Keep him one more week till you feel stronger."

"No." He buttoned his sweater and despite her pleading went shakily down the stairs.

Frank heard him coming and grew cold.

The clerk had for weeks feared the time the grocer would leave his bed, although in a curious way he had also looked forward to it. He had spent many fruitless hours trying to construct a story that would make Morris relent and keep him on. He had planned to say, "Didn't I starve rather than to spend the money from the holdup, so I could put it back in the register—which I did, though I admit I took a couple of rolls and some milk to keep myself alive?" But he had no confidence in that. He could also proclaim his long service to the grocer, his long patient labor in the store; but the fact that he had stolen from him during all this time spoiled his claim. He might mention that he had saved Morris after he had swallowed a bellyful of gas, but it was Nick who had saved him as much as he. The clerk felt he was without any good appeal to the grocer—that he had used up all his credit with him, but then he was struck by a strange and exciting idea, a possible if impossible ace in the hole. He figured that if he finally sincerely revealed his part in the holdup, he might in the telling of it arouse in Morris a true understanding of his nature, and a sympathy for his great struggle to overcome his past. Understanding his clerk's plight—the meaning of his long service to him— might make the grocer keep him on, so he would again have the chance to square everything with all concerned. As he pondered this idea, Frank realized it was a wild chance that might doom rather than redeem him. Yet he felt he would try it if Morris insisted he had to leave. What could he lose after that? But when the clerk pictured himself saying what he had done and had been forgiven by the grocer, and he tried to imagine the relief he would feel, he couldn't, because his overdue confession wouldn't be complete or satisfying so long as he kept hidden what he had done to his daughter. About that he knew he could never open his mouth, so he felt that no matter what he did manage to say there would always be some disgusting thing left unsaid, some further sin to confess, and this he found utterly depressing.

Frank was standing behind the counter near the cash register, paring his fingernails with his knife blade when the grocer, his face pale, the skin of it loose, his neck swimming in his shirt collar, his dark eyes unfriendly, entered the store through the hall door.

The clerk tipped his cap and edged away from the cash register.

"Glad to see you back again, Morris," he said, regretting he hadn't once gone up to see him in all the days the grocer had been upstairs. Morris nodded coldly and went into the rear. Frank followed him in, fell on one knee, and lit the radiator.

"It's pretty cold here, so I better light this up. I've been keeping it shut off to save on the gas bill."

"Frank," Morris said firmly, "I thank you that you helped me when I took in my lungs so much gas, also that you kept the store open when I was sick, but now you got to go."

"Morris," answered Frank, heavy-hearted, "I swear I never stole another red cent after that last time, and I hope God will strike me dead right here if it isn't the truth."

"This ain't why I want you to go," Morris answered.

"Then why do you?" asked the clerk, flushing.

"You know," the grocer said, his eyes downcast.

"Morris," Frank said, at agonizing last, "I have something important I want to tell you. I tried to tell you before only I couldn't work my nerve up. Morris, don't blame me now for what I once did, because I am now a changed man, but I was one of the guys that held you up that night. I swear to God I didn't want to once I got in here, but I couldn't get out of it. I tried to tell you about it—that's why I came back here in the first place, and the first chance I got I put my share of the money back in the register—but I didn't have the guts to say it. I couldn't look you in the eye. Even now I feel sick about what I am saying, but I'm telling it to you so you will know how much I suffered on account of what I did, and that I am very sorry you were hurt on your head—even though not by me. The thing you got to understand is I am not the same person I once was. I might look so to you, but if you could see what's been going on in my heart you would know I have changed. You can trust me now, I swear it, and that's why I am asking you to let me stay and help you."

Having said this, the clerk experienced a moment of extraordinary relief—a treeful of birds broke into song; but the song was silenced when Morris, his eyes heavy, said, "This I already know, you don't tell me nothing new."

The clerk groaned. "How do you know it?"

"I figured out when I was laying upstairs in bed. I had once a bad dream that you hurt me, then I remembered—"

"But I didn't hurt you," the clerk broke in emotionally. "I was the one that gave you the water to drink. Remember?"

"I remember. I remember your hands. I remember your eyes. This day when the detective brought in here the holdupnik that he didn't hold me up I saw in your eyes that you did something wrong. Then when I stayed behind the hall door and you stole from me a dollar and put it in your pocket, I thought I saw you before in some place but I didn't know where. That day you saved me from the gas I almost recognized you; then when I was laying in bed I had nothing to think about, only my worries and how I threw away my life in this store, then I remembered when you first came here, when we sat at this table, you told me you always did the wrong thing in your life; this minute when I remembered this I said to myself, 'Frank is the one that made on me the holdup.' "

"Morris," Frank said hoarsely, "I am sorry."

Morris was too unhappy to speak. Though he pitied the clerk, he did not want a confessed criminal around. Even if he had reformed, what good would it do to keep him here—another mouth to feed, another pair of eyes to the death watch?

"Did you tell Helen what I did?" sighed Frank.

"Helen ain't interested in you."

"One last chance, Morris," the clerk pleaded.

"Who was the antisimeet that he hit me on the head?"

"Ward Minogue," Frank said after a minute. "He's sick now."

"Ah," sighed Morris, "the poor father."

"We meant to hold Karp up, not you. Please let me stay one more month. I'll pay for my own food and also my rent."

"With what will you pay if I don't pay you—with my debts?"

"I have a little job at night after the store closes. I make a few odd bucks."

"No," said the grocer.

"Morris, you need my help here. You don't know how bad everything is."

But the grocer had set his heart against his assistant and would not let him stay.

Frank hung up his apron and left the store. Later, he bought a suitcase and packed his few things. When he returned Nick's radio, he said good-by to Tessie.

"Where are you going now, Frank?"

"I don't know."

"Are you ever coming back?"

"I don't know. Say good-by to Nick."

Before leaving, Frank wrote a note to Helen, once more saying he was sorry for the wrong he had done her. He wrote she was the finest girl he had ever met. He had bitched up his life. Helen wept over the note but had no thought of answering.

Although Morris liked the improvements Frank had made in the store he saw at once that they had not the least effect on business. Business was terrible. And with Frank's going the income shrank impossibly lower, a loss of ten terrible dollars from the previous week. He thought he had seen the store at its worst but this brought him close to fainting.

"What will we do?" he desperately asked his wife and daughter, huddled in their overcoats one Sunday night in the unheated back of the store.

"What else?" Ida said, "give right away in auction."

"The best thing is to sell even if we have to give away," Morris argued. "If we sell the store we can also make something on the house. Then I can pay my debts and have maybe a couple thousand dollars. But if we give in auction how can I sell the house?"

"So if we sell who will buy?" Ida snapped.

"Can't we auction off the store without going into bankruptcy?" Helen asked.

"If we auction we will get nothing. Then when the store is empty and it stays for rent, nobody will buy the house. There are already two places for rent on this block. If the wholesalers hear I went in auction they will force me in bankruptcy and take away the house also. But if we sell the store, then we can get a better price for the house."

"Nobody will buy," Ida said. "I told you when to sell but you wouldn't listen."

"Suppose you did sell the house and store," Helen asked, "what would you do then?"

"Maybe I could find a small place, maybe a candy store. If I could find a partner we could open up a store in a nice neighborhood."

Ida groaned. "Penny candy I won't sell. Also a partner we had already, he should drop dead."

"Couldn't you look for a job?" Helen said.

"Who will give me at my age a job?" Morris asked.

"You're acquainted with some people in the business," she answered. "Maybe somebody could get you a cashier's job in a supermarket."

"You want your father to stand all day on his feet with his varicose veins?" Ida asked.

"It would be better than sitting in the freezing back of an empty store."

"So what will we do?" Morris asked, but nobody answered.

Upstairs, Ida told Helen that things would be better if she got married.

"Who should I marry, Mama?"

"Louis Karp," said Ida.

The next evening she visited Karp when he was alone in the liquor store and told him their troubles. The liquor dealer whistled through his teeth.

Ida said, "You remember last November you wanted to send us a man by the name Podolsky, a refugee he was interested to go in the grocery business?"

"Yes. He said he would come here but he caught a cold in his chest."

"Did he buy some place a store?"

"Not yet," Karp said cautiously.

"He still wants to buy?"

"Maybe. But how could I recommend him a store like yours?"

"Don't recommend him the store, recommend him the price. Morris will sell now for two thousand cash. If he wants the house we will give him a good price. The refugee is young, he can fix up the business and give the goyim a good competition."

"Maybe I'll call him sometime," Karp remarked. He casually inquired about Helen. Surely she would be getting married soon?

Ida faced the way she hoped the wind was blowing. "Tell Louis not to be so bashful. Helen is lonely and wants to go out with somebody."

Karp coughed into his fist. "I don't see your clerk any more. How is that?" He spoke offhandedly, walking carefully, knowing the size of his big feet.

"Frank," Ida said solemnly, "don't work for us any more. Morris told him to leave, so he left last week."

Karp raised bushy brows. "Maybe," he said slowly, "I will call Podolsky and tell him to come tomorrow night. He works in the day."

"In the morning is the best time. Comes in then a few Morris's old customers."

"I will tell him to take off Wednesday morning," Karp said.

He later told Louis what Ida had said about Helen, but Louis, looking up from clipping his fingernails, said she wasn't his type.

"When you got gelt in your pocket any woman is your type," Karp said.

"Not her."

"We will see."

The next afternoon Karp came into Morris's and speaking as if they were the happiest of friends, advised the grocer: "Let Podolsky look around here but not too long. Also keep your mouth shut about the business. Don't try to sell him anything. When he finishes in here he will come to my house and I will explain him what's what."

Morris, hiding his feelings, nodded. He felt he had to get away from the store, from Karp, before he collapsed. Reluctantly he agreed to do as the liquor dealer suggested.

Early Wednesday morning Podolsky arrived, a shy young man in a thick greenish suit that looked as if it had been made out of a horse blanket. He wore a small foreign-looking hat and carried a loose umbrella. His face was innocent and his eyes glistened with good will.

Morris, uneasy at what he was engaged in, invited Podolsky into the back, where Ida nervously awaited him, but the refugee tipped his hat and said he would stay in the store. He slid into the corner near the door and nothing could drag him out. Luckily, a few customers dribbled in, and Podolsky watched with interest as Morris professionally handled them.

When the store was empty, the grocer tried to make casual talk from behind the counter, but Podolsky, though constantly clearing his throat, had little to say. Overwhelmed by pity for the poor refugee, at what he had in all probability lived through, a man who had sweated blood to save a few brutal dollars, Morris, unable to stand the planned dishonesty, came from behind the counter, and taking Podolsky by the coat lapels, told him ear-

nestly that the store was rundown but that a boy with his health
and strength, with modern methods and a little cash, could build
it up in a reasonable time and make a decent living out of it.

Ida shrilly called from the kitchen she needed the grocer to
help her peel potatoes, but Morris kept on talking till he was
swimming in his sea of woes; then he recalled Karp's warning,
and though he felt more than ever that the liquor dealer was
thoroughly an ass, abruptly broke off the story he was telling. Yet
before he could tear himself away from the refugee, he remarked,
"I could sell for two thousand, but for fixteen-sixteen cash, anybody who wants it can take the store. The house we will talk
about later. Is this reasonable?"

"Why not?" Podolsky murmured, then again clammed up.

Morris retreated into the kitchen. Ida looked at him as if he
had committed murder but did not speak. Two or three more
people appeared, then after ten-thirty the dry trickle of customers
stopped. Ida grew fidgety and tried to think of ways to get
Podolsky out of the place but he stayed on. She asked him to
come into the back for a glass of tea; he courteously refused. She
remarked that Karp must now be anxious to see him; Podolsky
bobbed his head and stayed. He tightened the cloth around his
umbrella stick. Not knowing what else to say she absently promised to leave him all her recipes for salads. He thanked her, to her
surprise, profusely.

From half past ten to twelve nobody approached the store.
Morris went down to the cellar and hid. Ida sat dully in the back.
Podolsky waited in his corner. Nobody saw as he eased himself
and his black umbrella out of the grocery and fled.

On Thursday morning Morris spat on his shoebrush and polished
his shoes. He was wearing his suit. He rang the hall bell for Ida
to come down, then put on his hat and coat, old but neat because
he rarely used them. Dressed, he rang up "no sale" and hesitantly
pocketed eight quarters.

He was on his way to Charlie Sobeloff, an old partner. Years ago, Charlie, a cross-eyed but clever conniver, had come to the grocer with a meager thousand dollars in his pocket, borrowed money, and offered to go into partnership with him—Morris to furnish four thousand—to buy a grocery Charlie had in mind. The grocer disliked Charlie's nervousness and pale cross-eyes, one avoiding what the other looked at; but he was persuaded by the man's nagging enthusiasm and they bought the store. It was a good business, Morris thought, and he was satisfied. But Charlie, who had taken accountancy in night school, said he would handle the books, and Morris, in spite of Ida's warnings, consented, because, the grocer argued, the books were always in front of his eyes for inspection. But Charlie's talented nose had sniffed the right sucker. Morris never looked at the books until, two years after they had bought the place, the business collapsed.

The grocer, stunned, heartbroken, could not at first understand what had happened, but Charlie had figures to prove that the calamity had been bound to occur. The overhead was too high—they had paid themselves too high wages—his fault, Charlie admitted; also profits were low, the price of goods increasing. Morris now knew that his partner had, behind his back, cheated, manipulated, stolen whatever lay loose. They sold the place for a miserable price, Morris going out dazed, cleaned out, whereas Charlie in a short time was able to raise the cash to repurchase and restock the store, which he gradually worked into a thriving self-service business. For years the two had not met, but within the last four or five years, the ex-partner, when he returned from his winters in Miami, for reasons unknown to Morris, sought out the grocer and sat with him in the back, his eyes roving, his ringed fingers drumming on the table as he talked on about old times when they were young. Morris, through the years, had lost his hatred of the man, though Ida still could not stand him, and it was to Charlie Sobeloff that the grocer, with a growing sense of panic, had decided to run for help, a job—anything.

When Ida came down and saw Morris, in his hat and coat,

standing moodily by the door, she said in surprise, "Morris, where you going?"

"I go to my grave," the grocer said.

Seeing he was overwrought, she cried out, clasping her hands to her bosom, "Where do you go, tell me?"

He had the door open. "I go for a job."

"Come back," she cried in anger. "Who will give you?"

But he knew what she would say and was already in the street.

As he went quickly past Karp's he noticed that Louis had five customers—drunkards all—lined up at the counter and was doing a thriving business in brown bottles. *He* had sold only two quarts of milk in four hours. Although it shamed him, Morris wished the liquor store would burn to the ground.

At the corner he paused, overwhelmed by the necessity of choosing a direction. He hadn't remembered that space provided so many ways to go. He chose without joy. The day, though breezy, was not bad—it promised better, but he had little love left for nature. It gave nothing to a Jew. The March wind hastened him along, prodding the shoulders. He felt weightless, unmanned, the victim in motion of whatever blew at his back; wind, worries, debts, Karp, holdupniks, ruin. He did not go, he was pushed. He had the will of a victim, no will to speak of.

"For what I worked so hard for? Where is my youth, where did it go?"

The years had passed without profit or pity. Who could he blame? What fate didn't do to him he had done to himself. The right thing was to make the right choice but he made the wrong. Even when it was right it was wrong. To understand why, you needed an education but he had none. All he knew was he wanted better but had not after all these years learned how to get it. Luck was a gift. Karp had it, a few of his old friends had it, well-to-do men with grandchildren already, while his poor daughter, made in his image, faced—if not actively sought—old-maidhood. Life was meager, the world changed for the worse. America had become too complicated. One man counted for nothing. There were too many stores, depressions, anxieties. What had he escaped to here?

The subway was crowded and he had to stand till a pregnant woman, getting off, signaled him to her seat. He was ashamed to take it but nobody else moved, so he sat down. After a while he began to feel at ease, thought he would be satisfied to ride on like this, provided he never got to where he was going. But he did. At Myrtle Avenue he groaned softly, and left the train.

Arriving at Sobeloff's Self-Service Market, Morris, although he had heard of the growth of the place from Al Marcus, was amazed at its size. Charlie had tripled the original space by buying the building next door and knocking out the wall between the stores, later running an extension three-quarters of the way into the back yards. The result was a huge market with a large number of stalls and shelved sections loaded with groceries. The supermarket was so crowded with people that to Morris, as he peered half-scared through the window, it looked like a department store. He felt a pang, thinking that part of this might now be his if he had taken care of what he had once owned. He would not envy Charlie Sobeloff his dishonest wealth, but when he thought of what he could do for Helen with a little money his regret deepened that he had nothing.

He spied Charlie standing near the fruit stalls, the balabos, surveying the busy scene with satisfaction. He wore a gray Homburg and blue serge suit, but under the unbuttoned suit jacket he had tied a folded apron around his silk-shirted paunch, and wandered around, thus attired, overseeing. The grocer, looking through the window, saw himself opening the door and walking the long half block to where Charlie was standing.

He tried to speak but was unable to, until after so much silence the boss said he was busy, so say it.

"You got for me, Charlie," muttered the grocer, "a job? Maybe a cashier or something? My business is bad, I am going in auction."

Charlie, still unable to look straight at him, smiled. "I got five

steady cashiers but maybe I can use you part time. Hang up your
coat in the locker downstairs and I'll give you directions what
to do."

Morris saw himself putting on a white duck jacket with "Sobeloff's Self-Service" stitched in red over the region of the heart.
He would stand several hours a day at the checking counter,
packing, adding, ringing up the cash into one of Charlie's massive
chromium registers. At quitting time, the boss would come over
to check his money.

"You're short a dollar, Morris," Charlie said with a little
chuckle, "but we will let it go."

"No," the grocer heard himself say. "I am short a dollar, so
I will pay a dollar."

He took several quarters out of his pants pocket, counted four,
and dropped them into his ex-partner's palm. Then he announced
he was through, hung up his starched jacket, slipped on his coat
and walked with dignity to the door. He joined the one at the
window and soon went away.

Morris clung to the edge of a silent knot of men who drifted
along Sixth Avenue, stopping at the employment agency doors
to read impassively the list of jobs chalked up on the blackboard
signs. There were openings for cooks, bakers, waiters, porters,
handymen. Once in a while one of the men would secretly detach
himself from the others and go into the agency. Morris followed
along with them to Forty-fourth Street, where he noted a job
listed for countermen behind a steam counter in a cafeteria. He
went one flight up a narrow staircase and into a room that smelled
of tobacco smoke. The grocer stood there, uncomfortable, until
the big-faced owner of the agency happened to look up over the
roll-top desk he was sitting at.

"You looking for something, mister?"

"Counterman," Morris said.

"You got experience?"

"Thirty years."

The owner laughed. "You're the champ but they want a kid they can pay twenty a week."

"You got something for a man my experience?"

"Can you slice sandwich meat nice and thin?"

"The best."

"Come back next week, I might have something for you."

The grocer continued along with the crowd. At Forty-seventh Street he applied for a waiter's job in a kosher restaurant but the agency had filled the job and forgotten to erase it from their sign.

"So what else you got for me?" Morris asked the manager.

"What work do you do?"

"I had my own store, grocery and delicatessen."

"So why do you ask for waiter?"

"I didn't see for counterman anything."

"How old are you?"

"Fifty-five."

"I should live so long till you see fifty-five again," said the manager. As Morris turned to go the man offered him a cigarette but the grocer said his cough kept him from smoking.

At Fiftieth he went up a dark staircase and sat on a wooden bench at the far end of a long room.

The boss of the agency, a man with a broad back and a fat rear, holding a dead cigar butt between stubby fingers, had his heavy foot on a chair as he talked in a low voice to two gray-hatted Filipinos.

Seeing Morris on the bench he called out, "Whaddye want, pop?"

"Nothing. I sit on account I am tired."

"Go home," said the boss.

He went downstairs and had coffee at a dish-laden table in the Automat.

America.

Morris rode the bus to East Thirteenth Street, where Breitbart lived. He hoped the peddler would be home but only his son

Hymie was. The boy was sitting in the kitchen, eating cornflakes with milk and reading the comics.

"What time comes home papa?" Morris asked.

"About seven, maybe eight," Hymie mumbled.

Morris sat down to rest. Hymie ate, and read the comics. He had big restless eyes.

"How old are you?"

"Fourteen."

The grocer got up. He found two quarters in his pocket and left them on the table. "Be a good boy. Your father loves you."

He got into the subway at Union Square and rode to the Bronx, to the apartment house where Al Marcus lived. He felt sure Al would help him find something. He would be satisfied, he thought, with little, maybe a night watchman's job.

When he rang Al's bell, a well-dressed woman with sad eyes came to the door.

"Excuse me," said Morris. "My name is Mr. Bober. I am an old-time customer Al Marcus's. I came to see him."

"I am Mrs. Margolies, his sister-in-law."

"If he ain't home I will wait."

"You'll wait a long time," she said, "they took him to the hospital yesterday."

Though he knew why he couldn't help asking.

"Can you go on living if you're already dead?"

When the grocer got home in the cold twilight Ida took one look at him and began to cry.

"What did I tell you?"

That night Morris, alone in the store after Ida had gone up to soak her poor feet, felt an uncontrollable craving for some heavy sweet cream. He remembered the delicious taste of bread dipped in rich milk when he was a boy. He found a half-pint bottle of whipping cream in the refrigerator and took it, guiltily, with a loaf of stale white bread, into the back. Pouring some cream into a saucer, he soaked it up with bread, greedily wolfing the cream-laden bread.

A noise in the store startled him. He hid the cream and bread in the gas range.

At the counter stood a skinny man in an old hat and a dark overcoat down to his ankles. His nose was long, throat gaunt, and he wore a wisp of red beard on his bony chin.

"A gut shabos," said the scarecrow.

"A gut shabos," Morris answered, though shabos was a day away.

"It smells here," said the skinny stranger, his small eyes shrewd, "like a open grave."

"Business is bad."

The man wet his lips and whispered, "Insurinks you got—fire insurinks?"

Morris was frightened. "What is your business?"

"How much?"

"How much what?"

"A smart man hears one word but he understand two. How much you got insurinks?"

"Two thousand for the store."

"Feh."

"Five thousand for the house."

"A shame. Should be ten."

"Who needs ten for this house?"

"Nobody knows."

"What do you want here?" Morris asked, irritated.

The man rubbed his skinny, red-haired hands. "What does a macher want?"

"What kind of a macher? What do you make?"

He shrugged slyly. "I make a living." The macher spoke soundlessly. "I make fires."

Morris drew back.

The macher waited with downcast eyes. "We are poor people," he murmured.

"What do you want from me?"

"We are poor people," the macher said, apologetically. "God

loves the poor people but he helps the rich. The insurinks companies are rich. They take away your money and what they give you? Nothing. Don't feel sorry for the insurinks companies."

He proposed a fire. He would make it swiftly, safely, economically—guaranteed to collect.

From his coat pocket he produced a strip of celluloid. "You know what is this?"

Morris, staring at it, preferred not to say.

"Celluloy," hissed the macher. He struck a large yellow match and lit the celluloid. It flared instantly. He held it a second then let it fall to the counter, where it quickly burned itself out. With a *poof* he blew away nothing. Only the stench remained, floating in air.

"Magic," he hoarsely announced. "No ashes. This is why we use celluloy, not paper, not rags. You push a piece in a crack, and the fire burns in a minute. Then when comes the fire marshal and insurinks investigator, what they find?—nothing. For nothing they pay cash—two thousand for the store, five for the house." A smile crawled over his face.

Morris shivered. "You want me I should burn down my house and my store to collect the insurance?"

"I want," said the macher slyly, "tsu you want?"

The grocer fell silent.

"Take," said the macher persuasively, "your family and go for a ride to Cunyiland. When you come back is the job finished. Cost—five hundred." He lightly dusted his fingers.

"Upstairs lives two people," muttered the grocer.

"When they go out?"

"Sometimes to the movies, Friday night." He spoke dully, not sure why he was revealing secrets to a total stranger.

"So let be Friday night. I am not kosher."

"But who's got five hundred dollars?"

The macher's face fell. He sighed deeply. "I will make for two hundred. I will do a good job. You will get six—seven thousand. After, pay me another three hundred."

But Morris had decided. "Impossible."

"You don't like the price?"

"I don't like fires. I don't like monkey business."

The macher argued another half hour and departed reluctantly.

The next night a car pulled up in front of the door, and the grocer watched Nick and Tessie, dressed for a party, get in and drive off. Twenty minutes later Ida and Helen came down to go to a movie. Helen had asked her mother to go with her, and Ida said yes, seeing how restless her daughter was. When he realized that the house was deserted, Morris felt suddenly agitated.

After ten minutes, he went up the stairs, and searched in a camphor-smelling trunk in the small room for a celluloid collar he had once worn. Ida saved everything, but he couldn't locate it. He searched in Helen's bureau drawer and found an envelope full of picture negatives. Discarding several of her as a school girl, Morris took some of boys in bathing suits, nobody he recognized. Hurrying down, he found matches and went into the cellar. He thought that one of the bins would be a good place to start the fire but settled instead on the air shaft. The flames would shoot up in an instant, and through the open toilet window into the store. Gooseflesh crept over him. He figured he could start the fire and wait in the hall. Once the flames had got a good start, he would rush into the street and ring the alarm. He could later say he had fallen asleep on the couch and had been awakened by the smoke. By the time the fire engines came, the house would be badly damaged. The hoses and axes would do the rest.

Morris inserted the celluloid strips into a crack between two boards, on the inside of the dumb-waiter. His hand shook and he whispered to himself as he touched the match to the negatives. Then the flame shot up in a stupefying stench and at once crawled up the wall of the dumb-waiter. Morris watched, hypnotized, then let out a terrible cry. Slapping frantically at the burning negatives, he knocked them to the cellar floor. As he hunted for something with which to beat out the fire in the dumb-waiter, he discovered that the bottom of his apron was burning. He smacked the flames with both hands and then his sweater sleeves began to blaze. He sobbed for God's mercy, and was at once roughly seized from behind and flung to the ground.

Frank Alpine smothered the grocer's burning clothes with his overcoat. He banged out the fire in the dumb-waiter with his shoe.

Morris moaned.

"For Christ sake," Frank pleaded, "take me back here."

But the grocer ordered him out of the house.

Saturday night, about one A.M., Karp's store began to burn.

In the early evening, Ward Minogue had knocked on Frank's door and learned from Tessie that the clerk had moved.

"Where to?"

"I don't know. Ask Mr. Bober," Tessie said, anxious to get rid of him.

Downstairs, Ward peered through the grocery window and seeing Morris, hurriedly withdrew. Though alcohol nauseated him lately, his thirst for a drink was killing him. He thought if he could get a couple of swigs past the nausea he would feel better. But all he had in his pocket was a dime, so he went into Karp's and begged Louis to trust him to a cheap fifth of anything.

"I wouldn't trust you for a fifth of sewer water," Louis said.

Ward grabbed a bottle of wine from the counter and flung it at Louis' head. He ducked but the wine smashed some bottles on the shelf. As Louis, yelling murder, rushed into the street, Ward snatched a bottle of whiskey and ran out of the store and up the block. He had gone past the butcher's when the bottle slipped from under his arm and broke on the sidewalk. Ward looked back with anguish but kept on running.

By the time the cops came Ward had disappeared. After supper that night, Detective Minogue, roaming the cold streets, saw his son in Earl's bar, standing over a beer. The detective went in by the side door but Ward saw him in the mirror and bolted out the front. Although short of breath, driven by great fear, he ran toward the coal yard. Hearing his father behind him, Ward leaped across the rusted chain stretched in front of the loading platform and sped over the cobblestones toward the back of the yard. He scrambled under one of the trucks in the shed.

The detective, calling him filthy names, hunted him in the dark for fifteen minutes. Then he took out his pistol and fired a shot into the shed. Ward, thinking he would be killed, crawled out from under the truck and ran into his father's arms.

Though he pleaded with the detective not to hurt him, crying he had diabetes and would surely get gangrene, his father beat him mercilessly with his billy until Ward collapsed.

Bending over him, the detective yelled, "I told you to stay the hell out of this neighborhood. This is my last warning to you. If I ever see you again, I'll murder you." He dusted his coat and left the coal yard.

Ward lay on the cobblestones. His nose had been gushing blood but it soon stopped. Getting up, he felt so dizzy he wept. He staggered into the shed and climbed into the cab of one of the coal trucks, thinking he would sleep there. But when he lit a cigarette he was overcome with nausea. Ward threw the butt out and waited for the nausea to leave him. When it did he was thirsty again. If he could climb the coal yard fence, then some of the smaller ones beyond it, he would land up in Karp's back yard. He knew from having cased the place once that the liquor store had a barred window in the back, but that the rusty iron bars were old and loose. He thought that if he got his strength back he could force them apart.

He dragged himself over the coal yard fence, then more slowly over the others until he stood at last in Karp's weedy back yard. The liquor store had been closed since midnight and there were no lights burning in the house. Above the dark grocery one of Bober's windows was lit, so he had to be careful or the Jew might hear him.

Twice, at intervals of ten minutes, he tried to bend the bars but failed. The third time, straining till he shook, he slowly forced the inside two apart. The window was unlocked. Ward got his fingertips under it and lifted it with care because it squeaked. When it was open, he squeezed through the bent bars, squirming into the back of the liquor store. Once in there he laughed a little to himself and moved around freely, knowing Karp was too cheap to have a burglar alarm. From the stock in the rear Ward sampled and spat out three different brands of whiskey. Forcing himself, he gurgled down a third of a bottle of gin. In a couple of minutes he forgot his aches and pains and lost the sorrow he had been feeling for himself. He snickered when he imagined Louis' comic puss as he found the empty bottles all over the floor in the morning. Remembering the cash register, Ward staggered out front and rang it open. It was empty. He angrily smashed a whiskey bottle on it. A feeling of nausea gagged him and with a croak he threw up over Karp's counter. Feeling better, he began by the light of the street lamp to smash the whiskey bottles against the cash register.

Mike Papadopolous, whose bedroom was right above the front part of the liquor store, was awakened by the noise. After five minutes he figured something was wrong so he got up and dressed. Ward had, in the meantime, destroyed a whole shelf of bottles, when he felt a hunger to smoke. It took him two minutes to get a match struck and the light touching his butt. He tasted the smoke with pleasure as the flame briefly lit his face, then he shook the match and flipped it over his shoulder. It landed, still burning, in a puddle of alcohol. The fire flew up with a zoom. Ward, lit like a flaming tree, flailed at himself. Screaming, he ran through the back and tried to get out of the window but was caught between the bars and, exhausted, died.

Smelling smoke, Mike came down in a rush and seeing fire in the store, raced to the drugstore corner to turn in the alarm. As he was running back, the plate glass window of the liquor store exploded and a roaring flame boiled up in the place. After Mike had got his mother and the upstairs tenants out of the house, he ran into Bober's hall, shouting there was a fire next door. They were all up—Helen, who had been reading when the window crashed, had run up to call Nick and Tessie. They left the house, bundled in sweaters and overcoats, and stood across the street, huddled together with some passers-by, watching the fire destroy Karp's once prosperous business, then devour the house. Despite the heavy streams of water the firemen poured into the flames, the fire, fed by the blazing alcohol, rose to the roof, and when it was at last smothered, all that was left of Karp's property was a gutted, dripping shell.

As the firemen began with the grappling hooks to tear out the burned fixtures and heave them onto the sidewalk, everybody fell silent. Ida moaned softly, with shut eyes thinking of Morris's burned sweater that she had found in the cellar, and the singed hair she had noticed on his hands. Sam Pearl, lost without his bifocals, mumbled to himself. Nat, hatless, an overcoat on over pajamas, edged close to Helen until he stood by her side. Morris was fighting a tormenting emotion.

A car drew up and parked beyond the drugstore. Karp got out with Louis and they crossed the hose-filled street to their store. Karp took one unbearable look at his former gesheft, and though it was for the most part insured, tottered forward and collapsed. Louis yelled at him to wake up. Two of the firemen carried the stricken liquor dealer to his car, and Louis frantically drove him home.

Afterward Morris couldn't sleep. He stood at his bedroom window in his long underwear, looking down at the pile of burned and broken fixtures on the sidewalk. With a frozen hand the grocer clawed at a live pain in his breast. He felt an overwhelming hatred of himself. He had wished it on Karp—just this. His anguish was terrible.

Sunday, the last of March, was overcast at eight A.M., and there were snow flurries in the air. Winter still spits in my face, thought the weary grocer. He watched the fat wet flakes melt as they touched the ground. It's too warm for snow, he thought, tomorrow will come April. Maybe. He had awakened with a wound, a gap in his side, a hole in the ground he might fall through if he stepped outside where the liquor store had been. But the earth held him up and the odd feeling wore off. It went as he reflected it was no use mourning Karp's loss; his pocketbook would protect him from too much pain. Pain was for poor people. For Karp's tenants the fire was a tragedy, and for Ward Minogue, dead young; maybe also for the detective, but not for Julius Karp. Morris could have used the fire, so Karp had got it for free. Everything to him who has.

As the grocer was thinking this, the liquor dealer, apparently the victim of a sleepless night, appeared in the falling snow and entered the grocery. He wore a narrow-brimmed hat with a foolish little feather in the band and a double-breasted overcoat, but despite his stylish appearance, his eyes, with dark bags under them, were filled with gloom, his complexion pasty, lips blue. Where his forehead had smacked the sidewalk last night he wore a plaster patch—an unhappy figure, the loss of his business the worst that could happen to him. He couldn't stand the vision of dollars he might be taking in, flying daily away. Karp seemed embarrassed, ill. The grocer, his shame awakened, invited him into the back for tea. Ida, also up early, made a fuss over him.

Karp took a hot sip or two of tea, but after setting the cup down, hadn't the strength to lift it from the saucer. After a fidgety silence he spoke. "Morris, I want to buy your house. Also the store." He drew a deep, trembly breath.

Ida let out a stifled cry. Morris was stupefied.

"What for? The business is terrible."

"Not so terrible," cried Ida.

"Don't interest me the grocery business," Karp gloomily replied. "Only the location. Next door," he said, but couldn't go on.

They understood.

He explained it would take months to rebuild his house and place of business. But if he took over Morris's store he could have it refixtured, painted, stocked in a couple of weeks, thus keeping to a minimum his loss of trade.

Morris couldn't believe his ears. He was filled with excitement and dread that somebody would tell him he had just dreamed a dream, or that Karp, fat fish, would turn into a fat bird and fly away, screeching, "Don't you believe me," or in some heartbreaking way change his mind.

So he put his foot on anticipation and kept his mouth shut, but when Karp asked him to name his price the grocer had one ready. "Nine thousand for the house—three down, my equity—and for the store twenty-five hundred cash." After all, bad as it was, the grocery was a going business, and for the refrigerator alone he had paid nine hundred dollars. With trepidation he figured a fair fifty-five hundred in cash in his hands, enough after he had paid his debts to look for a new business. Seeing Ida's astonished expression, he was surprised at his nerve and thought Karp would surely laugh him in the face and offer less—which he would grab anyway; but the liquor dealer listlessly nodded. "I will give you twenty-five hundred for the store, less the auction price of stock and fixtures."

"This is your business," Morris replied.

Karp could not bear to discuss the terms any further. "My lawyer will draw the contract."

When he left the grocery, the liquor dealer vanished in the swirling snow. Ida wept joyfully, while Morris, still stunned, reflected that his luck had changed. So had Karp's, for what Karp had lost he had in a sense gained, as if to make up for the misery the man had caused him in the past. Yesterday he wouldn't have believed how things would balance out today.

The spring snow moved Morris profoundly. He watched it falling, seeing in it scenes of his childhood, remembering things he thought he had forgotten. All morning he watched the shifting snow. He thought of himself, a boy running in it, whooping at blackbirds as they flew from the snowy trees; he felt an irresistible thirst to be out in the open.

"I think I will shovel the snow," he told Ida at lunchtime.

"Go better to sleep."

"It ain't nice for the customers."

"What customers—who needs them?"

"People can't walk in such high snow," he argued.

"Wait, tomorrow it will be melted."

"It's Sunday, it don't look so nice for the goyim that they go to church."

Her voice had an edge to it. "You want to catch pneumonia, Morris?"

"It's spring," he murmured.

"It's winter."

"I will wear my hat and coat."

"Your feet will get wet. You have no galoshes."

"Only five minutes."

"No," she said flatly.

Later, he thought.

All afternoon the snow came softly down and by evening it had reached a depth of six inches. When the snowing stopped, a wind rose and blew clouds of it through the streets. He watched at the front window.

Ida hung over him all day. He didn't get out till late. After closing he had sat relentlessly over a piece of store paper, writing a long list, until she grew impatient.

"Why do you stay so late?"

"I figure the stock for the auctioneer."

"This is Karp's business."

"I must help, he don't know the prices."

Talk of the store's sale relieved her. "Come up soon," she yawned.

He waited until he felt she was asleep, then went down to the cellar for the shovel. He put on his hat and a pair of old gloves and stepped out into the street. To his surprise the wind wrapped him in an icy jacket, his apron flapping noisily. He had expected, the last of March, a milder night. The surprise lingered in his mind but the shoveling warmed him. He kept his back to Karp's burned hole, though with the black turned white it wasn't too hard to look at.

Scooping up a shovelful of snow he heaved it into the street. It turned to dust in mid-air and whirled whitely away.

He recalled the hard winters when he had first come to America. After about fifteen years they turned mild but now they were hard again. It had been a hard life, but now with God's help he would have an easier time.

He flung another load of snow into the street. "A better life," he muttered.

Nick and Tessie came home from somewhere.

"At least put something warm on, Mr. Bober," advised Tessie.

"I'm almost finished," Morris grunted.

"It's your health," said Nick.

The first floor window shot up. Ida stood there in her flannel nightgown, her hair down.

"Are you crazy?" she shouted to the grocer.

"Finished," he answered.

"Without a coat—are you crazy?"

"Took me ten minutes."

Nick and Tessie went into the house.

"Come up now," Ida shouted.

"Finished," Morris cried. He heaved a last angry shovelful into the gutter. A little of the sidewalk remained to be cleaned but now that she was nagging he felt too tired to do it.

Morris dragged the wet shovel into the store. The warmth struck him across the head. He felt himself reeling and had a momentary fright but after a glass of hot tea with lemon felt rested.

As he was drinking the tea it began to snow again. He watched a thousand flakes push at the window, as if they wanted to snow through the glass and in the kitchen. He saw the snow as a moving curtain, and then he saw it in lit single flakes, not touching each other.

Ida banged hard on the floor, so he finally closed and went upstairs.

She was sitting in her bathrobe with Helen in the living room, her eyes dark with anger. "Are you a baby you had to go out in the snow? What's the matter with such a man?"

"I had my hat on. What am I, tissue paper?"

"You had pneumonia," she shouted.

"Mama, lower your voice," Helen said, "they'll hear upstairs."

"Who asked him to shovel snow, for God's sakes?"

"For twenty-two years stinks in my nose this store. I wanted to smell in my lungs some fresh air."

"Not in the ice cold."

"Tomorrow is April."

"Anyway," Helen said, "don't tempt fate, Papa."

"What kind of winter can be in April?"

"Come to sleep." Ida marched off to bed.

He sat with Helen on the couch. Since hearing of Karp's visit that morning she had lost her moodiness, looked again like a happy girl. He thought with sadness how pretty she was. He wanted to give her something—only good.

"How do you feel that I am selling the house and store?" he asked her.

"You know how I feel."

"Tell me anyway."

"Refreshed."

"We will move to a better neighborhood like you like. I will find a better parnusseh. You will keep your wages."

She smiled at him.

"I remember when you were a little baby," Morris said.

She kissed his hand.

"I want the most you should be happy."

"I will be." Her eyes grew wet. "If you only knew all the good things I'd like to give you, Papa."

"You gave me."

"I'll give you better."

"Look how it snows," said Morris.

They watched the snow through the moving windows, then Morris said good night.

"Sleep well," Helen said.

But he lay in bed restless, almost dejected. There was so much to do, so many changes to make and get used to. Tomorrow was the day Karp would bring the deposit. Tuesday the acutioneer would come and they would go over the goods and fixtures. Wednesday they could hold the auction. Thursday, for the first time in almost a generation, he would be without a place of business. Such a long time. After so many years in one place he hated the thought of having to get used to another. He disliked leaving the neighborhood though he hadn't liked it. It made him uncomfortable to be in a strange place. He thought uneasily of having to locate, appraise, and buy a new store. He would prefer to live above the store, but Helen wanted them to take a small apartment, so let it be a small apartment. Once he had the store he would let them look for a place to live. But the store he would have to find himself. What he feared most was that he would make another mistake and again settle in a prison. The possibility of this worried him intensely. Why would the owner want to sell? Would he be an honest man or, underneath, a thief? And once he had bought the place, would business keep up or go down? Would times stay good? Would he make a living? His thoughts exhausted him. He could feel his poor heart running a race against the merciless future.

He fell heavily asleep but awoke in a couple of hours, drenched in hot sweat. Yet his feet were freezing and he knew that if he kept his thoughts on them he would break into shivering. Then his right shoulder began to hurt, and when he forced himself to take a deep breath, his left side pained him. He knew he was sick and was miserably disappointed. He lay in the dark, trying not to think how stupid it had been to shovel the snow. He must have caught a chill. He thought he would not. He thought he was entitled, after twenty-two years, to a few minutes of freedom. Now his plans would have to wait, although Ida could finish the business with Karp and make arrangements with the auctioneer. Gradually he accepted the thought that he had a cold—maybe flu. He considered waking her to call a doctor but who could they call without a telephone? And if Helen got dressed and used Sam Pearl's phone, what an embarrassment that would be, waking up a whole family when she rang their bell; also arousing a doctor out of his precious sleep, who would say after examining him, "Mister, what's all the excitement? You got the flu, so stay in bed." For such advice he didn't need to call a doctor in his nightshirt. He could wait a few hours till morning. Morris dozed but felt fever shake him in his sleep. He awoke with his hair stiff. Maybe he had pneumonia? After a while he grew calmer. He was sick but sickness was nothing new to him. Probably if he hadn't shoveled snow he would have got sick anyway. In the last few days he hadn't felt so well—headachy, weak in the knees. Yet though he tried to resign himself to what had happened, he felt enormously bitter that he had become ill. So he had shoveled snow in the street, but did it have to snow in April? And if it did, did he have to get sick the minute he stepped out into the open air? It frustrated him hopelessly that every move he made seemed to turn into an inevitable thing.

He dreamed of Ephraim. He had recognized him when the dream began by his brown eyes, clearly his father's. Ephraim wore a beanie cut from the crown of an old hat of Morris's, covered with buttons and shiny pins, but the rest of him was in rags. Though he did not for some reason expect otherwise, this and that the boy looked hungry shocked the grocer.

"I gave you to eat three times a day, Ephraim," he explained, "so why did you leave so soon your father?"

Ephraim was too shy to answer, but Morris, in a rush of love for him—a child was so small at that age—promised him a good start in life.

"Don't worry, I'll give you a fine college education."

Ephraim—a gentleman—averted his face as he snickered.

"I give you my word . . ."

The boy disappeared in the wake of laughter.

"Stay alive," his father cried after him.

When the grocer felt himself awaking, he tried to get back into the dream but it easily evaded him. His eyes were wet. He thought of his life with sadness. For his family he had not provided, the poor man's disgrace. Ida was asleep at his side. He wanted to awaken her and apologize. He thought of Helen. It would be terrible if she became an old maid. He moaned a little, thinking of Frank. His mood was of regret. I gave away my life for nothing. It was the thunderous truth.

Was the snow still falling?

Morris died in the hospital, three days later, and was buried the day after in an enormous cemetery—it went on for miles—in Queens. He had been a member of a burial society since coming to America and the services took place in the Society's funeral parlor on the Lower East Side, where the grocer had lived as a young man. At noon in the chapel's antechamber, Ida, gray-faced and in mourning, every minute on the edge of fainting, sat in a high-backed tapestried chair, rocking her head. At her side, wasted, red-eyed from weeping, sat Helen. Landsleit, old friends, drawn by funeral notices in the Jewish morning papers, lamented aloud as they bent to kiss her, dropping pulpy tears on her hands. They sat on folding chairs facing the bereaved and talked in whispers. Frank Alpine stood for a moment, his hat uncomfortably on, in a corner of the room. When the place grew crowded he left and seated himself among the handful of mourners already assembled in the long narrow chapel, dimly lit by thick, yellow wall lamps. The rows of benches were dark and heavy. In the front of the chapel, on a metal stand, lay the grocer's plain wooden coffin.

At one P.M., the gray-haired undertaker, breathing heavily, escorted the widow and her daughter to the front row on the left, not far from the coffin. A wailing began among the mourners. The chapel was a little more than half-full of old friends of the grocer, a few distant relatives, burial society acquaintances, and one or two customers. Breitbart, the bulb peddler, sat, stricken, against the right wall. Charlie Sobeloff, grown heavy-faced and stout, appeared, with Florida tan and sad crossed eye, together with his stylish wife, who sat staring at Ida. The entire Pearl family was present, Betty with her new husband, and Nat, sober, concerned for Helen, wearing a black skull cap. A few rows behind them was Louis Karp, alone and ill at ease among strangers. Also Witzig, the baker, who had served Morris bread and rolls for twenty years. And Mr. Giannola, the barber, and Nick and Tessie Fuso, behind whom Frank Alpine sat. When the bearded rabbi entered the chapel through a side door, Frank took off his hat but quickly put it on again.

The secretary of the Society appeared, a soft-voiced man with little hair, his glasses lit with reflections of the wall lamps, and read from a handwritten paper praise for Morris Bober and lamentation for his loss. When he announced the body could be seen, the undertaker and his assistant, a man in a chauffeur's cap, lifted the coffin lid and a few people came forward. Helen wept profusely at her father's waxen, berouged image, the head wrapped in a prayer shawl, the thin mouth slightly twisted.

Ida flung up both arms, crying in Yiddish at the corpse, "Morris, why didn't you listen to me? You went away and left me with a child, alone in the world. Why did you to it?" She broke into racking sobs and was gently escorted by Helen and the breathless undertaker to her seat, where she pressed her wet face against her daughter's shoulder. Frank went up last. He could see, where the prayer shawl fell back a little, the scar on the grocer's head, but outside of that it wasn't Morris. He felt a loss but it was an old one.

The rabbi then prayed, a stocky man with a pointed black

beard. He stood on the podium near the coffin, wearing an old Homburg, a faded black frock coat over brown trousers, and bulbous shoes. After his prayer in Hebrew, when the mourners were seated, in a voice laden with sorrow he spoke of the dead man.

"My dear friends, I never had the pleasure to meet this good grocery man that he now lays in his coffin. He lived in a neighborhood where I didn't come in. Still and all I talked this morning to people that knew him and I am now sorry I didn't know him also. I would enjoy to speak to such a man. I talked to the bereaved widow, who lost her dear husband. I talked to his poor beloved daughter Helen, who is now without a father to guide her. To them I talked, also to landsleit and old friends, and each and all told me the same, that Morris Bober, who passed away so untimely—he caught double pneumonia from shoveling snow in front of his place of business so people could pass by on the sidewalk—was a man who couldn't be more honest. Such a person I am sorry I didn't meet sometime in my life. If I met him somewhere, maybe when he went to visit in a Jewish neighborhood—maybe at Rosh Hashana or Pesach—I would say to him, 'God bless you, Morris Bober.' Helen, his dear daughter, remembers from when she was a small girl that her father ran two blocks in the snow to give back to a poor Italian lady a nickel that she forgot on the counter. Who runs in wintertime without hat or coat, without rubbers to protect his feet, two blocks in the snow to give back five cents that a customer forgot? Couldn't he wait till she comes in tomorrow? Not Morris Bober, let him rest in peace. He didn't want the poor woman to worry, so he ran after her in the snow. This is why the grocer had so many friends who admi-red him."

The rabbi paused and gazed over the heads of the mourners.

"He was also a very hard worker, a man that never stopped working. How many mornings he got up in the dark and dressed himself in the cold, I can't count. After, he went downstairs to stay all day in the grocery. He worked long long hours. Six o'clock every morning he opened and he closed after ten every night, sometimes later. Fifteen, sixteen hours a day he was in the store, seven days a week, to make a living for his family. His dear wife Ida told me she will never forget his steps going down the stairs each morning, and also in the night when he came up so tired for his few hours' sleep before he will open again the next day the store. This went on for twenty-two years in this store alone, day after day, except the few days when he was too sick. And for this reason that he worked so hard and bitter, in his house, on his table, was always something to eat. So besides honest he was a good provider."

The rabbi gazed down at his prayer book, then looked up.

"When a Jew dies, who asks if he is a Jew? He is a Jew, we don't ask. There are many ways to be a Jew. So if somebody comes to me and says, 'Rabbi, shall we call such a man Jewish who lived and worked among the gentiles and sold them pig meat, trayfe, that we don't eat it, and not once in twenty years comes inside a synagogue, is such a man a Jew, rabbi?' To him I will say, 'Yes, Morris Bober was to me a true Jew because he lived in the Jewish experience, which he remembered, and with the Jewish heart.' Maybe not to our formal tradition—for this I don't excuse him—but he was true to the spirit of our life—to want for others that which he wants also for himself. He followed the Law which God gave to Moses on Sinai and told him to bring to the people. He suffered, he endu-red, but with hope. Who told me this? I know. He asked for himself little—nothing, but he wanted for his beloved child a better existence than he had. For such reasons he was a Jew. What more does our sweet God ask his poor people? So let Him now take care of the widow, to comfort and protect her, and give to the fatherless child what her father wanted her to have. 'Yaskadal v'yiskadash shmey, rabo. B'olmo divro . . .'"

The mourners rose and prayed with the rabbi.

Helen, in her grief, grew restless. He's overdone it, she thought.

I said Papa was honest but what was the good of such honesty if he couldn't exist in this world? Yes, he ran after this poor woman to give her back a nickel but he also trusted cheaters who took away what belonged to him. Poor Papa; being naturally honest, he didn't believe that others come by their dishonesty naturally. And he couldn't hold onto those things he had worked so hard to get. He gave away, in a sense, more than he owned. He was no saint; he was in a way weak, his only true strength in his sweet nature and his understanding. He knew, at least, what was good. And I didn't say he had many friends who admired him. That's the rabbi's invention. People liked him, but who can admire a man passing his life in such a store? He buried himself in it; he didn't have the imagination to know what he was missing. He made himself a victim. He could, with a little more courage, have been more than he was.

Helen prayed for peace on the soul of her dead father.

Ida, holding a wet handkerchief to her eyes, thought, So what if we had to eat? When you eat you don't want to worry whose money you are eating—yours or the wholesalers'. If he had money he had bills; and when he had more money he had more bills. A person doesn't always want to worry if she will be in the street tomorrow. She wants sometimes a minute's peace. But maybe it's my fault, because I didn't let him be a druggist.

She wept because her judgment of the grocer was harsh although she loved him. Helen, she thought, must marry a professional.

When the prayer was done the rabbi left the chapel through the side door, and the coffin was lifted by some of the Society members and the undertaker's assistant, carried on their shoulders outside, and placed in the hearse. The people in the chapel filed out and went home, except Frank Alpine, who sat alone in the funeral parlor.

Suffering, he thought, is like a piece of goods. I bet the Jews could make a suit of clothes out of it. The other funny thing is that there are more of them around than anybody knows about.

In the cemetery it was spring. The snow had melted on all but
a few graves, the air was warm, fragrant. The small group of
mourners following the grocer's coffin were hot in their overcoats. At the Society's plot, crowded with tombstones, two gravediggers had dug a fresh pit in the earth and were standing back,
holding their shovels. As the rabbi prayed over the empty grave—
from up close his beard was thick with gray—Helen rested her
head against the coffin held by the pallbearers.

"Good-by, Papa."

Then the rabbi prayed aloud over the coffin as the gravediggers
lowered it to the bottom of the grave.

"Gently . . . gently."

Ida, supported by Sam Pearl and the secretary of the Society,
sobbed uncontrollably. She bent forward, shouting into the
grave, "Morris, take care of Helen, you hear me, Morris?"

The rabbi, blessing it, tossed in the first shovelful of earth.

"Gently."

Then the diggers began to push in the loose earth around the
grave and as it fell on the coffin the mourners wept aloud.

Helen tossed in a rose.

Frank, standing close to the edge of the grave, leaned forward
to see where the flower fell. He lost his balance, and though flailing his arms, landed feet first on the coffin.

Helen turned her head away.

Ida wailed.

"Get the hell out of there," Nat Pearl said.

Frank scrambled out of the grave, helped by the diggers. I
spoiled the funeral, he thought. He felt pity on the world for harboring him.

At last the coffin was covered, the grave full, running over. The
rabbi said a last short Kaddish. Nat took Helen by the arm and
led her away.

She gazed back once, with grief, then went with him.

Louis Karp was waiting for them in the dark hallway when Ida
and Helen returned from the cemetery.

"Excuse me for bothering you on this sad occasion," he said, holding his hat in his hand, "but I wanna tell you why my father couldn't get to the funeral. He's sick and has to lay flat on his back for the next six weeks or so. The other night when he passed out at the fire, we found out later he had a heart attack. He's lucky he's still alive."

"Vey is mir," muttered Ida.

"The doctor says he's gonna have to retire from here on in," Louis said, with a shrug, "so I don't think he'll wanna buy your house any more. Myself," he added, "I got a job of salesman for a liquor concern."

He said good-by and left them.

"Your father is better off dead," said Ida.

As they toiled up the stairs they heard the dull cling of the register in the store and knew the grocer was the one who had danced on the grocer's coffin.

Frank lived in the back, his clothes hung in a bought closet, sleeping under his overcoat on the couch. He had used their week of mourning, when mother and daughter were confined upstairs, to get the store going. Staying open kept it breathing, but beyond that things were rocky. If not for his thirty-five weekly dollars in the register he would have had to close up. Seeing he paid his little bills, the wholesalers extended credit. People stopped in to say they were sorry Morris was dead. One man said the grocer was the only storekeeper that had ever trusted him for anything. He paid Frank back eleven dollars that he owed Morris. Frank told anybody who asked that he was keeping the business going for the widow. They approved of that.

He gave Ida twelve dollars a week rent and promised her more when times got better. He said when they did, he might buy the store from her, but it would have to be on small installments because he had no money for a down payment. She didn't answer him. She was worried about the future and feared she might starve. She lived on the rent he paid her, plus Nick's rent, and

Helen's salary. Ida now had a little job sewing epaulettes for military uniforms, a bag of which Abe Rubin, a landsman of Morris's, delivered in his car every Monday morning. That brought in another twenty-eight to thirty a month. She rarely went down to the store. To speak to her, Frank had to go upstairs and knock on her door. Once, through Rubin, someone came to look at the grocery and Frank was worried, but the man soon left.

He lived in the future, to be forgiven. On the stairs one morning he said to Helen, "Things are changed. I am not the same guy I was."

"Always," she answered, "you remind me of everything I want to forget."

"Those books you once gave me to read," he said, "did you understand them yourself?"

Helen waked from a bad dream. In the dream she had got up to leave the house in the middle of the night to escape Frank waiting on the stairs; but there he stood under the yellow lamp, fondling his lascivious cap. As she approached his lips formed, "I love you."

"I'll scream if you say it."

She screamed and woke. •

At a quarter to seven she forced herself out of bed, shut off the alarm before it rang and drew off her nightgown. The sight of her body mortified her. What a waste, she thought. She wanted to be a virgin again and at the same time a mother.

Ida was still asleep in the half-empty bed that had for a lifetime served two. Helen brushed her hair, washed, and put on coffee. Standing at the kitchen window, she gazed out at the back yards in flower, feeling sorrow for her father lying in his immovable grave. What had she ever given him, ever done to make his poor life better? She wept for Morris, thinking of his compromises and surrenders. She felt she must do something for herself, accomplish some worthwhile thing or suffer his fate. Only by growing in value as a person could she make Morris's life meaningful, in the sense that she was of him. She must, she thought, in some way eventually earn her degree. It would take years—but was the only way.

Frank stopped waiting for her in the hall. She had cried out one morning, "Why do you force yourself on me?" and it had struck him that his penitence was a hammer, so he withdrew. But he watched her when he could, through an opening in the tissue paper backing of the store window. He watched as if he were seeing for the first time her slender figure, high small breasts, the slim roundness of her hips and the exciting quality of her slightly bowed legs. She always looked lonely. He tried to think what he could ever do for her and all he could think of was to give her something she had no use for, that would end up in the garbage.

The idea of doing something for her seemed as futile as his other thoughts till one day, the tissue paper held a little aside as he watched her impassively entering the house, he had a thought so extraordinary it made the hair on the back of his neck stiffen. He figured the best thing he could do was help her get the college education she had always wanted. There was nothing she wanted more. But where, if she agreed to let him—he doubted it every minute it was in his mind—could he get the money unless he stole it? The more he pondered this plan, the more it excited him until he couldn't stand the possibility it might be impossible.

He carried in his wallet the note Helen had once written him, that she would come up to his room if Nick and Tessie went to the movies, and he read it often.

One day he got another idea. He pasted a sign in the window: "Hot Sandwiches And Hot Soups To Go." He figured he could use his short-order cooking experience to advantage in the grocery. He had some handbills printed, advertising these new things and paid a kid half a buck to deliver them to places where there were working men. He followed the boy for a couple of blocks to see that he didn't dump the papers into a sewer. Before the end of the week a few new people were coming in at lunch and suppertime. They said this was the first time you could get any hot food to take out in the neighborhood. Frank also tried his hand at ravioli and lasagna once a week, making them from recipes he got out of a cookbook in the library. He experimented with baking small pizzas in the gas stove, which he sold for two bits apiece. The pasta and pizzas sold better than the hot sandwiches. People came in for them. He considered putting a table or two in the grocery but there was no room, so all the food had to go.

He got another little break. The milkman told him the two Norwegians had taken to yelling at each other in front of their customers. He said they were making less than they had expected. The store was fine for one man but not for two, so they each wanted to buy the other out. Pederson's nerves couldn't stand the fighting, and Taast bought him out at the end of May and had the place all to himself. But he found that the long hours alone were killing his feet. His wife came in to help out around suppertime; however Taast couldn't stand being away from his family every night, when everyone else was free and at home, so he decided to close at seven-thirty and stop fighting Frank until almost ten. These couple of hours all to himself at night helped Frank. He got back some of the customers who came home from work late, and also the housewives who at the last minute needed something for breakfast. And Frank noticed, from peering into Taast's window after he was closed, that he was no longer so generous with the specials.

The weather turned hot in July. People cooked less, lived more on delicatessen, canned goods, bottled drinks. He sold a lot of beer. His pastas and pizzas went very well. He heard that Taast had tried making pizzas but they were too doughy. Also, instead of using canned soups, Frank made a minestrone of his own that everybody praised; it took time to cook up, but the profit was better. And the new things he was selling pushed other goods along. He now paid Ida ninety a month for rent and the use of her store. She was earning more money on her epaulettes, and did not think so often that she would starve.

"Why do you give me so much?" she asked him when he raised the money to ninety.

"Maybe Helen could keep some of her wages?" he suggested.

"Helen isn't interested any more in you," she said sternly.

He didn't answer her.

But that night after supper—he had treated himself to ham and eggs and now smoked a cigar—Frank cleared the table and sat down to figure out how much it would cost to support Helen in college if she would quit her job and give all her time to education. When he had figured out the tuition from the college catalogues he had collected, he saw he couldn't do it. His heart was heavy. Later he thought maybe he could work it if she went to a free college. He could give her enough for her daily expenses and also to make up whatever money she now gave her mother. He figured that to do it would be a rocky load on his head, but he *had* to do it, it was his only hope; he could think of no other. All he asked for himself was the privilege of giving her something she couldn't give back.

The big thing, exciting yet frightening, was to talk to her, say what he hoped to do. He always had it in mind to say but found it very hard. To speak to her, after all that had happened to them, seemed impossible—opening on peril, disgrace, physical pain. What was the magic word to begin with? He despaired he could ever convince her. She was remote, sinned again, unfeeling, or if she felt, it was disgust of him. He cursed himself for having conceived this mess he couldn't now bring himself to speak of.

One August night after he had seen her come home from work in the company of Nat Pearl, sick of the misery of unmotion, Frank made himself move. He was standing behind the counter piling bottles of beer into a woman's market bag when he caught sight of Helen going by with some books on her arm. She was wearing a new summer dress, red trimmed with black, and the sight of her struck him with renewed hunger. All summer she had wandered at night alone in the neighborhood, trying to out-walk her loneliness. He had been tempted to close up and follow her, but until he had his new idea he could not think what he dared say that she wouldn't run from. Hurrying the customer out of the store, Frank washed, slicked back his hair and quickly changed into a fresh sport shirt. He locked the store and hurried in the direction Helen had gone. The day had been hot but was cooling now and still. The sky was golden green, though below the light was dark. After running a block he remembered something and trudged back to the store. He sat in the back listening to his heart hammering in his ears. In ten minutes he lit a lamp in the store window. The globe drew a ragged moth. Knowing how long she lingered among books, he shaved. Then locking the front door again, he went toward the library. He figured he would wait across the street till she came out. He would cross over and catch up with her on her way home. Before she could even see him, he would speak his piece and be done with it. Yes or no, she could say, and if no, he would shut the joint tomorrow and skiddoo.

He was nearing the library when he glanced up and saw her. She was about half a block away and walking toward him. He stood there not knowing which way to go, dreading to be met by her as lovely as she looked, standing like a crippled dog as she passed him. He thought of running back the way he had come, but she saw him, turned and went in haste the other way; so, reviving an old habit, he was after her, and before she could deny him, had touched her arm. They shivered. Giving her no time to focus her contempt, he blurted out what he had so long saved to say but could not now stand to hear himself speak.

When Helen realized what he was offering her, her heart moved violently. She had known he would follow and speak, but she could never in a thousand years have guessed he would say *this*. Considering the conditions of his existence, she was startled by his continuing ability to surprise her, make God-knows-what-next-move. His staying power mystified and frightened her, because she felt in herself, since the death of Ward Minogue, a waning of outrage. Although she detested the memory of her experience in the park, lately it had come back to her how she had desired that night to give herself to Frank, and might have if Ward hadn't touched her. She had wanted him. If there had been no Ward Minogue, there would have been no assault. If he had made his starved leap in bed she would have returned passion. She had hated him, she thought, to divert hatred from herself.

But her response to his offer was an instantaneous no. She said it almost savagely, to escape any possibility of being directly obligated to him, of another entrapment, nausea.

"I couldn't think of it."

He was astonished to have got this far, to be walking at her side—only it was a night in a different season, and her summer face was gentler than her winter one, her body more womanly; yet it all added up to loss, the more he wanted her the more he had lost.

"In your father's name," he said. "If not for you, then for him."

"What has my father got to do with it?"

"It's his store. Let it support you to go to college like he wanted you to."

"It can't without you. I don't want your help."

"Morris did me a big favor. I can't return it to him but I might to you. Also because I lost myself that night—"

"For God's sake, don't say it."

He didn't, was dumb. They walked dumbly on. To her horror they were coming to the park. Abruptly she went the other way.

He caught up with her. "You could graduate in three years. You wouldn't have any worry about expenses. You could study all you want."

"What would you expect to get from this—virtue?"

"I already said why—I owe something to Morris."

"For what? Taking you into his stinking store and making a prisoner out of you?"

What more could he say? To his misery, what he had done to her father rose in his mind. He had often imagined he would someday tell her, but not now. Yet the wish to say it overwhelmed him. He tried wildly to escape it. His throat hurt, his stomach heaved. He clamped his teeth tight but the words came up in blobs, in a repulsive stream.

He spoke with pain. "I was the one that held him up that time. Minogue and me. Ward picked on him after Karp ran away, but it was my fault too on account of I went in with him."

She screamed and might have gone on screaming but strangers were staring.

"Helen, I swear—"

"You criminal. How could you hit such a gentle person? What harm did he ever do you?"

"I didn't hit him, Ward did. I gave him a drink of water. He saw I didn't want to hurt him. After, I came to work for him to square up what I did wrong. For Christ's sake, Helen, try to understand me."

With contorted face she ran from him.

"I confessed it to him," he shouted after her.

He had managed well in the summer and fall, but after Christmas business dragged, and though his night salary had been raised five bucks, he found it impossible to meet all his expenses. Every penny looked as big as the moon. Once he spent an hour searching for a two-bit piece he had dropped behind the counter. He tore up a loose floor board and was elated to recover more than three dollars in green and grimy coins that Morris had lost during the years.

For himself he spent only for the barest necessities, though his clothes were falling apart. When he could no longer sew up the holes in his undershirts he threw them away and wore none. He soaked his laundry in the sink and hung it to dry in the kitchen.

He was, as a rule, prompt in his payment of jobbers and whole-salers, but during the winter he kept them waiting. One man he held off his neck by threatening to go bankrupt. Another he promised tomorrow. He slipped a couple of bucks to his most important salesman, to calm them at the office. Thus he kept going. But he never missed a payment of rent to Ida. He valued his payments to her because Helen had returned to night college in the fall, and if he didn't give the ninety to Ida, Helen wouldn't have enough for her own needs.

He was always tired. His spine ached as if it had been twisted like a cat's tail. On his night off from the Coffee Pot he slept without moving, dreaming of sleep. In the dead hours at the Coffee Pot, he sat with his head on his arms at the counter, and during the day in the grocery he took cat-naps whenever he could, trusting the buzzer to rouse him, although other noises did not. When he awoke, his eyes were hot and watery, his head like porous lead. He grew thin, his neck scrawny, face bones prominent, his broken nose sharp. He saw life from a continual wet-eyed yawn. He drank black coffee till his stomach turned sour. In the evening he did nothing—read a little. Or he sat in the back with the lights out, smoking, listening to the blues on the radio.

He had other worries, had noticed Nat was hanging around Helen more. A couple of times a week the law student drove her home from work. Now and then, over the week end, they went for a ride at night. Nat would toot his horn in front of the door and she came out dressed up and smiling, neither of them noticing Frank, in open sight. And she had had a new telephone put in upstairs, and once or twice a week he heard it ring. The phone made him jumpy, jealous of Nat. Once on his night off from the Coffee Pot, Frank woke abruptly when Helen and somebody came into the hall. Sneaking into the store and listening at the side door, he could hear them whispering; then they were quiet and he imagined them necking. For hours after, he couldn't get back to sleep, desiring her so. The next week, listening at the door, he discovered the guy she was kissing was Nat. His jealousy ate him good.

She never entered the store. To see her he had to stand at the front window.

"Jesus," he said, "why am I killing myself so?" He gave himself many unhappy answers, the best being that while he was doing this he was doing nothing worse.

But then he took to doing things he had promised himself he never would again. He did them with dread of what he would do next. He climbed up the air shaft to spy on Helen in the bathroom. Twice he saw her disrobe. He ached for her, for the flesh he had lived in a moment. Yet he hated her for having loved him, for to desire what he had once had, and hadn't now, was torture. He swore to himself that he would never spy on her again, but he did. And in the store he took to cheating customers. When they weren't watching the scale he short-weighted them. A couple of times he short-changed an old dame who never knew how much she had in her purse.

Then one day, for no reason he could give, though the reason felt familiar, he stopped climbing up the air shaft to peek at Helen, and he was honest in the store.

One night in January Helen was waiting at the curb for a trolley. She had been studying with a girl in her class and afterward had listened to some records, so she had left later than she had planned. The trolley was late in coming, and though she was cold, she was considering walking home, when she began to feel she was being watched. Looking into the store before which she was standing, she saw nobody there but the counterman resting his head on his arms. As she observed him, trying to figure out why she felt so strange, he raised his sleepy head and she saw in surprise that it was Frank Alpine. He gazed with burning eyes in a bony face, with sad regret, at his reflection in the window, then went drunkenly back to sleep. It took her a minute to realize he hadn't seen her. She felt the momentary return of an old misery, yet the winter night seemed clear and beautiful.

When the trolley came, she took a seat in the rear. Her thoughts were heavy. She remembered Ida saying Frank worked some place at night but the news had meant nothing to her. Now that she had seen him there, groggy from overwork, thin, unhappy, a burden lay on her, because it was no mystery who he was working for. He had kept them alive. Because of him she had enough to go to school at night.

In bed, half-asleep, she watched the watcher. It came to her that he had changed. It's true, he's not the same man, she said to herself. I should have known by now. She had despised him for the evil he had done, without understanding the why of aftermath, or admitting there could be an end to the bad and a beginning of good.

It was a strange thing about people—they could look the same but be different. He had been one thing, low, dirty, but because of something in himself—something she couldn't define, a memory perhaps, an ideal he might have forgotten and then remembered—he had changed into somebody else, no longer what he had been. She should have recognized it before. What he did to me he did wrong, she thought, but since he has changed in his heart he owes me nothing.

On her way to work one morning a week later, Helen, carrying her brief case, entered the grocery and found Frank hidden behind the tissue paper of the window, watching her. He was embarrassed, and she was curiously moved by the sight of his face.

"I came in to thank you for the help you're giving us," she explained.

"Don't thank me," he said.

"You owe us nothing."

"It's just my way."

They were silent, then he mentioned his idea of her going to day college. It would be more satisfying to her than at night.

"No, thank you," Helen said, blushing. "I couldn't think of it, especially not with you working so hard."

"It's no extra trouble."

"No, please."

"Maybe the store might get better, then I could do it on what we take in here?"

"I'd rather not."

"Think about it," Frank said.

She hesitated, then answered she would.

He wanted to ask her if he still had any chance with her but decided to let that wait till a later time.

Before she left, Helen, balancing the brief case on her knee, unsnapped it and took out a leather-bound book. "I wanted you to know I'm still using your Shakespeare."

He watched her walk to the corner, a good-looking girl, carrying his book in her brief case. She was wearing flat-heeled shoes, making her legs slightly more bowed, which for some reason he found satisfying.

The next night, listening at the side door, he heard a scuffle in the hall and wanted to break in and assist her but held himself back. He heard Nat say something harsh, then Helen slapped him and he heard her run upstairs.

"You bitch," Nat called after her.

One morning in the middle of March the grocer was sleeping heavily after a night off from the Coffee Pot, when he was awakened by a pounding on the front door. It was the Polish nut wanting her three-cent roll. She came later these days but still too early. The hell with all that, he thought, I need my sleep. But after a few minutes he grew restless and began to dress. Business still wasn't so hot. Frank washed his face before the cracked mirror. His thick hair needed cutting but it could wait one more week. He thought of growing himself a beard but was afraid it would scare some of the customers away, so he settled for a mustache. He had been letting one grow for two weeks and was surprised at the amount of red in it. He sometimes wondered if his old lady had been a redhead.

Unlocking the door, he let her in. The Polish dame complained he had kept her waiting too long in the cold. He sliced a roll for her, wrapped it, and rang up three cents.

At seven, standing by the window, he saw Nick, a new father, come out of the hall and run around the corner. Frank hid behind the paper and soon saw him return, carrying a bag of groceries he had bought in Taast's store. Nick ducked into the hallway and Frank felt bad.

"I think I will make this joint into a restaurant."

After he had mopped the kitchen floor and swept the store, Breitbart appeared, dragging his heavy boxes. Lowering the cartons of bulbs to the floor, the peddler took off his derby and wiped his brow with a yellowed handkerchief.

"How's it going?" Frank asked.

"Schwer."

Breitbart drank the tea and lemon that Frank cooked up for him, meanwhile reading his *Forward*. After about ten minutes he folded the newspaper into a small, thick square and pushed it into his coat pocket. He lifted the bulbs onto his itchy shoulders and left.

Frank had only six customers all morning. To keep from getting nervous he took out a book he was reading. It was the Bible and he sometimes thought there were parts of it he could have written himself.

As he was reading he had this pleasant thought. He saw St. Francis come dancing out of the woods in his brown rags, a couple of scrawny birds flying around over his head. St. F. stopped in front of the grocery, and reaching into the garbage can, plucked the wooden rose out of it. He tossed it into the air and it turned into a real flower that he caught in his hand. With a bow he gave it to Helen, who had just come out of the house. "Little sister, here is your little sister the rose." From him she took it, although it was with the love and best wishes of Frank Alpine.

One day in April Frank went to the hospital and had himself circumcised. For a couple of days he dragged himself around with a pain between his legs. The pain enraged and inspired him. After Passover he became a Jew.

Part Three

In Love and Prison

S. Levin in Love

At the Bullocks' for cocktails Levin wandered restlessly from one group to another. He listened for a minute with half an ear, then moved on, wondering what he thought he might find in one bunch that he wouldn't in the next. The house was a stylish split-level on a fashionable western hill, whose large wood-paneled living room could hold thirty without trying and did this Sunday evening in the middle of January. Despite the crowd, with the exception of Avis there wasn't an unmarried woman around, and Levin thought that grim fact accounted for his dullish mood. People were pairing him off with her, he had noticed, and this explained, he thought, his recent popularity, if not with Avis. The beard seemed to help, making him in some people's eyes a person he wasn't. They could have it.

After a short stretch in the garden at sunset, Levin, a mouthful of martini held aimlessly in his hand, sat on the sofa between Alma Kuck and Jeannette Bullock, Alma again going on about the British Isles, and Jeannette deathlessly attentive, that rare thing, a beautiful woman who managed to be uninteresting. Pauline said she had never got over the fact she hadn't been to college. Levin noticed that although her legs attracted wherever she sat, she spent five minutes trying to hide them under her skirts, a pity. But she had constructed a lovely garden amid the oaks and fir trees on their property and was said to send everyone a birthday card on his birthday. As Alma talked and Jeannette listened, Levin, escaping from a yawn, had both eyes on Pauline Gilley across the room, standing partly turned from him amid some of the younger wives. She was attractive in a tight black dress. A small veil floating before her eyes from a wisp of hat created a mystery where none had been before. Who was the masked lady? Amazing what entices, Levin thought. Yet when she happened to glance in his direction, her thin-stemmed martini glass like a flower in her fingers, he pretended to be inspecting his new brown shoes. Secretly he continued to watch her. Alma diverted him with a question, and when he got up a minute later and went to Pauline she was gone.

Bullock appeared with his flowing pitcher, dispensing a boffo with every shot. The contents looked like innocent water but packed a hard wallop. People at the party were gay, they enjoyed Bullock's daring pitcher, a departure from the town's mores. Some were beginning to dance, a rarity in faculty houses. To dance, Levin had been told, one usually joined a social dancing club. There were dances the last Friday of each month, with extras for holidays. If Professor Fairchild or ex-Dean Feeney was present at a party, soft drinks and sweet green punch prevailed, but none of the older people having been invited, the host freely poured firewater, an empty glass seeming to threaten his security. Surprising the instructor without a glass, Bullock handed him one and aimed the spout, but Levin, worried by the man's unthinking prodigality, said he had had enough.

"I thought this was a party," George said. When he was drinking he breathed through a half-open mouth, both eyes verging on vacant. But a sweetness descended on him, and he loved on Sundays those he tolerated weekdays. Levin felt that neither of them took to the other. Bullock invited him because he sensed Levin disliked him, and he came because he couldn't afford to turn down an invitation. He got none from Bucket or Fabrikant, whom he liked, nor were they ever present at Bullock's.

"It is," answered Levin, "but I've already had two."

"That was my last batch. This will dissolve the rust on your gonads, if not the gonads. Have three."

Figuring he would abandon the glass, Levin let him fill it.

"Nice party."

George blinked. "Think so? We were late getting off the ground this fall. By now we've usually had three or four big blasts, but Jeannette hasn't been up to it lately—flu plus miscarriage (keep it quiet) et cetera. I also blame the late godawful football season, let it rest. There's nothing like a consistently losing team to put a damper on your entertaining instinct. It depressed Gerald too."

"Is that so?"

"Yep. Everybody expected a bang-up season. *Look* predicted a possible Rose Bowl for us, then the roof caved in. We won three out of ten with some of the best material on the coast. The alumni are sore as hell at Lon Lewis, the head coach, and he'll probably be traded for somebody with a T-formation. I know most of the boys on the squad and I'll tell you it was no inspiration to see their hangdog pusses in class on Monday mornings."

"They're all in your classes?"

"Some are. They have their free choice of instructors."

"I didn't mean they didn't—"

"Anyway," Bullock said, "exit football, enter basketball. We've copped the first four games and look like a shoo-in to take the coast conference. Bought your season ticket?"

"No," said Levin.

"Tough titty. Keep it in mind for next year. Saves you thirty percent. To the future champs." He raised his right hand, crossing fingers.

Levin lifted his glass. Remembering the red bumper-strip on Bullock's station wagon: "Keep Basketball King at Cascadia College," he drank to a better world.

Like raw gin. He had visions of being picked up drunk in town and fined a hundred dollars and costs.

"Gerald is also affected by a losing team?" Levin asked.

"After some of the rough ones he can't talk for an hour."

"Really? Pauline too?"

"She has her moments. Jeannette gets listless."

"Is that why the Gilleys didn't entertain much this fall?"

"It wouldn't surprise me. They like to have people in after a game but didn't do any of that after the shellacking we got from Cal, right off. He's the fan, though she keeps him pretty steady company at the big games. Both she and Jeannette say sports take their minds off their worries, whatever the hell they are. Pauline can be a moody dame, and I suppose having two kids all of a sudden is no picnic. Gerald did some lousy duck shooting in December. I've never seen him so bad. He's been worn out."

"She wears him out?"

Bullock winked. "I didn't say so but she helps, though last year the kids' colds knocked them both for a loop. Erik gets everything in the book plus some unidentified bugs. That was on top of the fact that Gerald hadn't recovered from L'affaire Duffy, the year before."

"It was that bad?"

"He bore the brunt for more than one reason, one being that Orville folds up his tent and goes home at the first sniff of scandal."

"It was really a scandal?"

"It amounted to one. Excuse me," George said, "the place is going dry." He lifted the spout but Levin withdrew his glass.

"Before you go," he said to Bullock, "have you seen where Pauline went?"

George looked vacantly around. "Try the upstairs bedroom. When she gets high she sometimes lies down."

Levin searched the bedrooms and daylight basement but she wasn't there. Back in the party he saw Avis eyeing him. He headed for the kitchen, slipped behind some people, and sliding open the opaque glass door, walked down six steps to the patio.

Levin sighed at the stars and was at once unexpectedly emotional. An odor of flowers assailed him. Because of the season he thought it was pure imagination, the result of more liquor than he should have had. I'm back in summer, Levin thought, or that far forward, why nobody knows. But he knew that even if he were liv-

ing in another time he would be wishing for another time. The
view in the dark, stars through bare-branched oaks, and the
lights of the town below affected him as though he were listening to music. For the first time in years he thirsted for a butt.

Smelling smoke, he looked abruptly around.

In the dim light reflected from the interior of the house he
made out Pauline Gilley standing between fir trees with a cigarette in her hand.

"Did I frighten you, Mr. Levin?" She had been watching him.

He went across the lawn to her. "I was looking for you, Mrs.
Gilley."

He told her he felt bad about that time she had come to see
him. "Excuse me, I was sick."

"Don't you like me?" Pauline asked. Her scent in the cool air
was warm. He wished he could see her eyes through the veil.

"On the contrary—"

She waited.

"—I like you," Levin said.

"Then why didn't you come to dinner Friday night?"

He nervously fingered his beard. "Would you—er—keep it
confidential?"

"I'm awfully good at that."

"Gerald and I had a disagreement and, frankly, I didn't feel
like accepting his hospitality just then."

"It was my hospitality too."

He admitted it.

"What were you annoyed with Gerald about?"

"I would rather not say, some department thing."

She dropped her cigarette in the grass, stepping on it. "That
was a mistake. Now I'm dizzy again."

He was eager to help. "Can I do something for you?"

She said in a throaty voice, "I should never let George get
near me when he's loose with that pitcher. I can't keep track of
how many I've had because he refills after every mouthful."

"For the sport?"

She gazed at the house. "Doesn't it look like a ship from here, and here we are, you and I, on an island in the middle of the sea? Or am I high? Are you?"

"I'm not."

"Excuse me for mentioning it but have you graduated to cocktails? The night we met, you wouldn't have one."

"Just a sip or two for sociability. I'm always saying no."

"Why?"

"Habit."

"What do you do for sin, Mr. Levin?"

Levin guffawed but came to quickly.

Hugging her arms, Pauline looked down at the lights of Easchester. "I should be home now, little Mary was running a temperature when we left, and I know Erik will have something by tomorrow. Have you seen Gerald?"

"No," said Levin. "Why don't you stay a little longer?"

"Should I?"

"There's a bench in the rock garden."

"Just for a short while, I have to get back to my children. I told Zenamae to have them tucked in by seven-thirty but I know they won't be. Erik gets up after he's been put down and goes exploring."

He was surprised, as he followed her across the patio, at her figure from the rear, so much better than he had noticed. The tight dress helped. Her shoulders, long waist and can were very good. Although a bit unsteady she walked with grace.

Where were my eyes? Levin thought.

"Don't be surprised if I fall," said Pauline.

"Let me help you." Levin took her arm and led her to the wooden bench in the rock garden. They sat in the dark, tall trees behind them.

"You look cold." He offered his jacket.

"I'll get my coat."

"I'll get it," Levin said. "You stay here."

"You won't know where it is. I'll be right back, you won't lose me, Mr. Levin," Pauline laughed.

She walked across the grass as though concentrating on not falling.

Five minutes later Levin was certain she wouldn't return. He was staring glumly at the stars as she came across the lawn with a coat over her shoulders.

"I'd've brought yours if I knew where it was," she said. "Why don't you go in and get it? I wouldn't want you to catch another cold."

"I've had this winter's cold."

"Do you plan everything, Mr. Levin?"

"What I can, I plan."

"My plans come to not much."

"Is that so?"

She touched his beard. "Does it keep you warm?"

She's high for sure, Levin thought. The veil irritated him. It hid as much as it revealed.

"I did have another drink," Pauline said. "George sneaked up on me when I was inside. I was feeling better and my defenses were down. I hope I'm not really drunk, Mr. Levin, because when I am I get sick. I don't want to be sick, please."

"Sit here till you feel better."

"My impression of your whiskers that day we met—it was my fault we were late, I was trying to get up my nerve to meet somebody new, would you guess that?—was they were coal black. But they're really a dark shade of brown. Do you know that beards bring out the quality of a man's lips and eyes? You have sensitive lips and kind eyes, Mr. Levin."

"I grew it in a time of doubt," confessed Levin. "When I couldn't look myself in the face."

"Should I become a bearded lady? Unless this veil does the trick. Does it hide me? At least my beastly nose?"

"Ah, but you're a lovely woman."

"How sweet of you. I'm not really lovely but I grow on people. I'd be nicer if I were less superficial and more accomplished. Oh, there's Gerald."

The glass door had opened and Gilley appeared on the veranda above the patio. He stood there for a wavering minute, a red-headed owl peering into the dark.

Levin sat silent, on the verge of disappointment.

But Gilley, probably affected by Bullock's powerful pitcher, blinked without seeing them although staring in their direction. He disappeared into the house.

They were motionless until she spoke. "I'll have to go now. Gerald wants me." Pauline got up but unsteadily sat down. "I feel like hell."

"Sit till you feel better."

A light went on in an upstairs room. It went out, and on in another. They watched it until it was out.

"What did he do that you didn't like?" she asked.

"It wasn't important."

"I'll bet it was."

Levin shrugged.

She did not pursue it. After a while she said, "I remember your saying, the night we met, that you hoped to make better use of your life here. Have you?"

"It's what one always has to do."

"Tell me what you want from life?"

"Order, value, accomplishment, love," said Levin.

"Love last?"

"Love any time."

"Pardon me for asking, but are you unhappy, Mr. Levin?"

"Why that question?"

"That day I came to see you—"

"Not as I have in the past known unhappiness."

"I sensed that."

"What about you?"

Pauline smiled. "I too am conscious of the misuses of my life, how quickly it goes and how little I do. I want more from myself

than I get, probably than I've got. Are we misfits, Mr. Levin?"
Looking at her veil he thought, Take it off.

"Gerald suffers from my nature," she said, "though he's a patient man. With a woman more satisfied with herself, less critical and more appreciative of his good qualities, maybe he would have been a different person." She went on half absently, "Through the years I've known him he's substituted a series of minor gratifications for serious substantial ones. He's partly affected by what he thinks people expect of him, and partly he's reacted as he has because I've urged the opposite. Lately he's developed an intense ambition to follow Orville in as head of the English department."

"Wasn't it always what he wanted?"

"Not so much until the last year or so."

"Ambition is no crime."

"Not if you're strong."

She quickly said, "I wouldn't want to leave the impression Gerald is weak. He isn't, Mr. Levin, I assure you. He's always been an excellent provider, wonderful to me and the children. If you knew him better I'm sure you'd like him."

"I don't dislike him."

Pauline yawned. "Excuse me, I had a restless night."

Levin rose. "Shall we go in?"

But she sat there. "If you're a married woman past thirty you have at that age pretty much what you're going to have. Still, I blame myself for my compromises, and I resist the homogenization of experience and—if I may call it such—intellect. I wish I could do more for myself, I really can't blame Gerald for not wanting to make a career of shoring up my lacks."

He listened with interest, finally sitting again.

"Poor Mr. Levin, you came out for a breath of air and I've told you all I know."

"We could all do with a cause."

Pauline said, "Leo Duffy used to say, 'A good cause is the highest excitement.' "

Levin copied it on a piece of paper and slipped it into his

pocket. "People talk about him but don't say much. Was he a friend of yours?"

He thought for a minute she would raise her veil but Pauline sat with quiet hands. "What have you heard?"

"Not much—that he livened things up."

"Yes, he did. Leo was different and not the slightest bit fake under any circumstances. He was serious about ideas and should have been given a fair chance to defend his. People were irritated with him because he challenged their premises."

"That I guessed."

"I had the highest regard for him."

"I have his office now."

"So I've heard."

She gasped as they were drenched in glaring light. Bullock's garden spotlights had been turned on.

"That's the end of the party. George flushes the garden with those lights." Pauline rose, swayed in her tracks, and again had to sit down, her face so white the veil looked blacker.

"I feel deathly sick. Please, Mr. Levin, call my husband before I pass out."

"Couldn't I get you some coffee?"

"Just get Gerald."

"Let me take you in where you can lie down."

"Tell Gerald to come take me home."

Levin hurried into the house. The party was over, the room deserted except for Leopold and Alma Kuck in overcoats, talking quietly to both Bullocks.

"Pauline isn't feeling so well," Levin said. "Where's Gerald?"

"He'll be down in a jiffy," George said.

"She's in the garden and wants to go home."

The Kucks left. Jeannette saw them to the door.

"The dope is," Bullock said to Levin, "Gerald's in the up-stairs head. I understand they both ate something that didn't agree with them. Maybe I ought to drive her home?"

"You're in no condition to, George," Jeannette said. "I will."

"Don't bother," Levin said. "I will."

He asked George where the toilet was.

"First to the left upstairs. There's another down here if it's for your use."

"Not for mine," said Levin. He raced up the stairs and knocked on the bathroom door. "Gerald, this is Sy. Pauline doesn't feel so well. She wants you to take her home. If you can't, can I?"

Gilley, after a minute, tiredly spoke. "Why don't you do that, Sy? This has caught me by surprise, but I'm sure it's something we ate last night, some Italian stuff with red peppers and olive oil. Plus too much vino. We both got up queasy this morning. Tell her she can expect me soon."

Levin hurried down, found his coat, and returned to the garden. George and Jeannette were there with Pauline.

"I'm awfully sorry," she was saying.

"Some food she ate," Levin said. He helped her to her feet. "Gerald asked me to drive you home."

She felt his beard and giggled. "For a minute I thought you were somebody else."

"Who, for instance?" George said.

"None of your business," said Jeannette.

"I'm awfully sorry, Jeannette," said Pauline.

"It's not your fault."

Levin threw Bullock a dirty look but missed. They left by way of the garden. He helped Pauline into his Hudson and quickly drove off.

She rested her head against his shoulder.

"How do you feel?" Levin asked.

"Awful, but sexy. Do you think George wants to seduce me, Mr. Levin? He pours me such big drinks."

Levin laughed although he felt a headache coming on.

"My one talent," she said, rubbing her head against him, "only lately developed, is that I know people. I know you, Mr. Levin."

"What do you know?"

"Who you really are. And you know me, don't you?"

"I'm not sure."

She sat up. "I've told you about myself but not about my children."

"Later," said Levin.

"At first I didn't want them because I was ashamed a big girl like me couldn't have her own. When we were first married I had some menstrual trouble and the doctor noticed I had a tipped womb. All along I thought that was the reason why, but years later we were both examined and it turned out Gerald had no seeds. He had had the mumps and enflamed testicles when he was twenty-two."

"I don't want to hear about his personal troubles."

"I know I'm drunk, it makes me talkative."

She fell asleep with her head on his shoulders and awoke when the car stopped in front of her house. Pauline sucked a mint before she got out. He attempted to hold her arm as they walked up the flagstone path to the door but she wouldn't let him. In the house while she was paying Zenamae she showed no signs of distress but when the girl was gone she collapsed on the sofa, her hat awry, the veil crawling up one eye.

"Stay with me and hold my hand."

Her dress had risen above her knees. The legs were exciting though the long black shoes were like stiff herrings aimed skyward. Her chest had the topography of an ironing board.

"I'm suddenly terribly hungry. Could you make me a scrambled egg, Mr. Levin?"

That goddamn veil, he thought. On impulse he tried to pluck her hat off but Pauline clasped both hands over her head. "Stop, it's my only defense."

I'd better not start anything, Levin thought.

Upstairs Mary cried. Erik called, "Mommy."

"Mr. Levin," said Pauline, "I entreat you to look after my poor babies." Her head touched the sofa and she sat bolt upright.

"I married a man with no seeds at all."

She fell asleep, her stomach gurgling.

Levin went upstairs to the little girl's room and turned on the light. She stopped crying and stared at him. Her bottle was in the crib so he fed her part of it.

In the next room, through the open door he saw Erik sitting up in his bed. "Who're you?"

"Mr. Levin—the funny man."

"I want a drink."

He went to the bathroom and got the water. Erik drank and lay back. As Levin was covering him the child raised his head and kissed him under the eye.

Mary was asleep. Levin put off the light and listened to the children sleeping. The poor orphans. He burst into tears.

A warm, sunlit day exhaling pure spring startled Levin at the end of January. He had been forewarned of this, but the long habit of Eastern winter kept him from believing the season could go without once punishing by blizzard or lacerating freeze every dweller in its domain. He felt unsettled for it seemed to him the unused winter must return to extract a measure of revenge for dying so young, so little of it had there been: a few months of darkish rain, a week of soft wet snow (crowning the mountains and drawing the hills closer), gone quickly to slush then gone forever; the returned rain broken by nine days of sunlit cold— never below twenty degrees, afternoons warming—which ex- hilarated Levin although his students complained. Maybe a reluctant icicle had hung for a day or two from the roof of Mrs. Beaty's porch. Having as a kid, nose and feet burning, waded many times through snowdrifts, and often worn an overcoat into mid-April, Levin felt now as though he had been reprieved by prestidigitation, not entirely trustworthy, from ice, snow, and wild wind. If winter were already dead it left him with some guilt, as though he had helped murder it, or got something for nothing when they read the will, rare in his life. Yet the thought remained that to be alive was a short season.

Pessimism was momentary. Better enjoy the changes that had

taken place with or without his knowing. Primroses, Mrs. Beaty had showed him, were in flower, had been all winter. At Christmastime, as Levin lay gloomily in bed, daffodil shoots were a stiff two inches above the ground; crocus under January snow. On New Year's day naked jasmine in the backyard by the cherry tree touched the dark world with yellow light; forsythia performed the same feat a few weeks later. Camelias were budding in January; quince and heather in flower, petals touching the stillest air. After the snow Levin had come upon a cluster of violets behind the garage. Rain was lighter, moodier, giving way to broken sunlight. And he enjoyed the lengthened day, seven A.M. now sixthirty. There was as yet little of spring to smell, either because early spring odors were still too subtle for his city-built nose, or the Northwest cool cheated scent, the throb of emotion in the wake of warm fragrance. If this was spring, Levin knew it because he eternally hunted for it, was always nosing out the new season, the new life, "a new birth in freedom."

On this reasonable facsimile of a late March day, a Thursday when Levin had no afternoon classes, although he had planned to return to the office after lunch and grind away at technical reports, the weather tempted him to a country walk to see what nature across the bridge had been busy at without him; and to feel the sun's beneficent hand on his head. He got out of his bureau drawer, where they had lain all winter, his binoculars and *Western Birds, Trees and Flowers.* Since he had read in last night's paper it might rain, he carried his trusty umbrella; and with this armload, tramped to the distant wood rising to the hills. He went by a route he had not tried before, a country road lined with old pussy willow trees, their sticky budding branches massed against the sky. Although Levin rejoiced at the unexpected weather, his pleasure was tempered by a touch of habitual sadness at the relentless rhythm of nature; change ordained by a force that produced, whether he wanted it or not, today's spring, tomorrow's frost, age, death, yet no man's accomplishment; change that wasn't change, in cycles eternal sameness, a repetition he was part of, so how win freedom in and from self? Was this why his life, despite his determined effort to break away from what he had already lived, remained so much the same? And why, constituted as he was and living the experience he engendered, he had not won anything more than short periods of contentment, not decently prolonged to where he could stop asking himself whether he had it or not? If I could only live as I believe, Levin thought. How often have I told myself happiness is not something you flush out in a planned expedition, a hidden complicated grail all at once the beholder's; that it's rather grace settled on the spirit in desire of life. We're here for a short time, often under the worst circumstances—possible that man may someday be blown off the tips of Somebody's Fingers; the battle lost before we knew what we were about, yet how magnanimously beautiful even to have been is. I have many times in differing circumstances told myself this, so why can't I quit worrying if happiness comes and how long lasts, if it does either? Discontent brings neither cold cash nor true love, therefore why not enjoy this tender marvelous day instead of greeting it with news of everything I haven't got?

He was still a distance from the hills when he approached a large wood—call it a forest—that he had come upon before by other routes. On impulse Levin left the road, hopped over a ditch, and crossing a field, entered among the evergreens. Once in the wood he was not entirely at his ease because he was trespassing, and as he went quietly along he worried about possible bears or maybe a snarling cougar or two, though he had heard of none in the vicinity; if there were any he had only an umbrella to defend himself with. Mostly his uneasiness arose from the thought that his life had been lived largely without experience of very many trees, and among them he felt a little unacquainted. Yet to be alone in the forest, this far in, was already a feat for a born city boy who had never been a Boy Scout. Levin took heart. He walked on soft ground among dark conifers, giants and dwarfs, and a large scattering of leafless other trees; but now he recognized fir, cedars, in green skirts touching the ground, blue spruce, and even hemlock, the trees in profusion, their branches interlaced, the forest gloom broken by rays of sunlight dappling the ground. The wood, as he walked, pungent with levitating coolness, suggested endless distance and deepest depth. Levin began to be worried about getting lost if he wandered too far in, and to avoid circular confusion, considered marking his way with bits of torn paper. The mystery of the wood, the presence of unseen life in natural time, and the feeling that few men had been where he presently was, (Levin, woodsman, explorer; he now understood the soul of Natty Bumppo, formerly paper; "Here, D. Boone CILLED A. BAR") caused him to nudge aside anxiety and continue to venture among the trees in shade and sunlight.

As he came out of the woods into a clearing, a yellow-green, rich grassy meadow sloping downward, a flock of robins—from Canada, he had been told, while the Cascadian species was vacationing in California; you were dealing with strangers who looked like friends—scattered noisily over his head. From the wood across the field a bird hidden in a tree screeched at the world. Levin's head was immersed in silence deepened by a drumming in the wood behind, a woody tattoo. After a short bafflement he located with his glasses a bird drilling away near the top of a dead fir. Hurriedly searching for his bird guide, he read with the greatest satisfaction that he had spotted a red-headed woodpecker, never before seen so clearly. The bird spied Levin and flew into the forest. A moment later he turned pages hastily to identify first a Seattle wren, then a very blue, graybellied blue jay, exciting color; and a chickadee, the first he remembered looking at and naming; also a yellow bird he couldn't identify, whose flight above the treeline Levin followed with pleasure until it disappeared into light like a light gone out. Who sees this in Manhattan Isle? None but the gifted. Here the common man rejoiced in what was naturally visible. But being where he was not supposed to be continued to trouble Levin; he turned as if forewarned someone was in the wood behind him; expecting, if not a boot in the pants, at least the forester's hard hand and gruff get the hell off private property. He would run like mad. Instead, he saw Pauline Gilley watching him from amid trees.

She looked like someone he had never expected to see again, or was the thought a trick on himself to protect what was left of unused virginity? Pauline approached as if unwilling, an expression he attributed to an embarrassment of remembrance; then as though she had made peace with herself in mid-voyage, she looked up, smiling at his astonishment. Her raincoat unbuttoned, he took in blouse, gray skirt, long blue socks and walking shoes. He also quickly calculated what she had on underneath, an innovation in their relationship.

Her hair shone in the sun. "I'm sorry I startled you, Mr. Levin. I'm just as surprised to see you."

Levin explained his umbrella; the paper said rain. She smiled at his armload. "Let me help you."

"It's nothing much." Her presence in the wood aroused a renewed momentary sadness, as if he had come too late to the right place, familiar situation of his dreams.

"The day turned out so springlike I left the children with a sitter so I could walk," Pauline said.

"You've been here before—in this wood?"

"Yes, haven't you?"

"No."

"I didn't know you watched birds."

"If you can call it that. Most get away before I know what I've seen."

"You were engrossed when I saw you."

"When I was a kid I used to look out of the window at sparrows on telegraph wires or hopping in the snow."

"I haven't seen you for weeks, Mr. Levin," Pauline said.

"About two, I'd say. Time flies."

"I talked so much at the Bullocks. I don't think I've been that much affected by liquor in years."

"No need to worry, I've forgotten what you said."

"Please don't."

They weren't looking at each other. When their eyes met, although he obsessively expected a veil, there was none, and Levin beheld an expression of such hungry tenderness he could hardly believe it was addressed to him. Enduring many complicated doubts, he dropped his things in the grass. They moved toward each other, their bodies hitting as they embraced.

"Dear God," Pauline murmured. Her kiss buckled his knees. He had not expected wanting so much in so much giving.

Levin warned himself, Take off, kid, and in their deep kiss saw himself in flight, bearded bird, dream figure, but couldn't move.

They parted, breathing heavily, looked at each other as though seeing were drinking—he could have counted twenty—and after mutual hesitation to the point of pain, embraced.

"My darling."

"Pauline." He kept himself from crying love.

Levin clutched at her chest, and seizing nothing, ran his hand the other way. She gripped his fingers, then let go, embracing him tightly.

"Where shall we go?"

"Anywhere."

She took his hand and they went into the woods, Levin glancing back to see where his things were. "Here," she said in the green shade. The evergreens were thick, the ground damp but soft with fir needles and dead leaves.

"Spread your coat." She spread hers over his, then stepped out of her shoes. She removed a black undergarment, the mask unmasked. Lying on the coats, Pauline raised her hips and drew back her skirt, to Levin the most intimate and beautiful gesture ever made for him.

He hung his trousers over the branch of a fir. When he knelt she received him with outstretched arms, gently smoothed his beard, then embraced him with passion as she fixed her rhythm to his.

He was throughout conscious of the marvel of it—in the open forest, nothing less, what triumph!

As she was combing the needles out of her hair the woods turned dark and it began to rain. They waited under Levin's umbrella under an old lichenous elm. If he expected uneasiness after the fact, he felt none. When he searched her eyes for guilt he was distracted by their light and warmth. He held the umbrella over their heads, his arm around her waist. They were resting against the tree trunk, her head on his shoulder. He felt, in gratitude, peace, and tried not to think of what he didn't have to, namely the future.

When she spoke he wished she hadn't. "Please don't worry about anything."

"Worry?"

"I mean if you have any regrets you're not bound to me. There are no obligations. You can leave this minute if you wish."

Levin pictured himself leaving her under the tree in the rain. Later he returned to see if she were there.

"Why speak of regrets? I have none."

"Your eyes seem sad."

"The fix of habit. I'm happy."

"What were you thinking of just now?" she asked.

"Oh you, your quality. I never had it this way before."

"You haven't had many women, have you?"

"Not many."

"I know you've been in love."

"Often—with the wrong kind. One or two made hash of me."

"I'm so sorry."

"My own fault, but that's in the past."

"Poor boy, did you have to connive for sex?"

"Not connive but pleasure never came too easy."

She was silent a minute. "Did this?"

"This is good."

"You respect me?"

"Of course."

"Mrs. Gilley, mother of two?"

"I respect you, Pauline."

They kissed again. She rubbed her head against his. "I'm hungry to know everything about you."

"I've had my bad times."

"Tell me what happened."

Levin was reluctant to speak about the past.

"You never do. I won't ask again."

He said, thick-voiced, half his face crippled, "The emotion of my youth was humiliation. That wasn't only because we were poor. My father was continuously a thief. Always thieving, always caught, he finally died in prison. My mother went crazy and killed herself. One night I came home and found her sitting on the kitchen floor looking at a bloody bread knife."

Pauline leaned her face against him.

"I mourned them but it was a lie. I was in love with an unhappy, embittered woman who had just got rid of me. I mourned the loss of her more than I did them. I was mourning myself. I became a drunk, it was the only fate that satisfied me."

She moaned; Levin trembled.

"I drank, I stank. I was filthy, skin on bone, maybe a hundred ten pounds. My eyes looked as though they had been pissed on. I saw the world in yellow light."

"Please, that's all."

"For two years I lived in self-hatred, willing to part with life. I won't tell you what I had come to. But one morning in somebody's filthy cellar, I awoke under burlap bags and saw my rotting shoes on a broken chair. They were lit in dim sunlight from a shaft or window. I stared at the chair, it looked like a painting, a thing with a value of its own. I squeezed what was left of my brain to understand why this should move me so deeply, why I was crying. Then I thought, Levin, if you were dead there would be no light on your shoes in this cellar. I came to believe what

I had often wanted to, that life is holy. I then became a man of principle."

"Oh, Lev," she said.

"That was the end of my drinking though not of unhappiness. Just when I thought I had discovered what would save me— when I believed it—my senses seemed to die, as though self-redemption wasn't possible because of what I was—my emptiness the sign of my worth. I denied the self for having denied life. I managed to get and hang onto a little job but as a person I was nothing. People speak of emptiness but it was a terrifying fullness, the soul has gas. It isn't exactly apathy, you have feeling but it's buried six feet. I couldn't respond to experience, the thought of love was unbearable. It was my largest and most hopeless loss of self before death."

Her eyes were shut.

"I felt I had come to something worse than drunkenness. This went on for how long I can't say. I lived in stone. My only occasional relief was in reading. I had a small dark room in a rooming house overrun by roaches and bugs. Once a week I burned the bedbugs with a candle through the bedsprings; they popped as they died. One Sunday night after a not otherwise memorable day, as I was reading in this room, I had the feeling I was about to remember everything I had read in my life. The book felt like a slab of marble in my hands. I strained to see if it could possibly be a compendium of every book ever written, describing all experience. I felt I had somewhere read something I must remember. Sensing an affirmation, I jumped up. That I was a free man lit in my mind even as I denied it. I suddenly knew, as though I were discovering it for the first time, that the source of freedom is the human spirit. This had been passed down to me but I had somehow forgotten. More than forgetting—I had lived away from it, had let it drift out of my consciousness. I thought I must get back what belongs to me; then I thought, 'This is how we invent it when it's gone.' Afterwards I experienced an emotion of well being so intense that I've lived on it ever since."

He said no more. Pauline rubbed her wet eyes against his shoulder. "I sensed it. I knew who you were."

"I felt a new identity."

"You became Levin with a beard."

"What was new were my plans for myself."

"I won't interfere with them," she said fervently. "We shan't meet again."

Pauline smoked as they watched the rain let up. "I'd better be getting back."

Levin, gathering up his things, tucked the umbrella under his arm, and they went through the wet woods. He called it a miraculous forest but she laughed and said it was the property of Cascadia College, where they trained foresters.

"Then it's no miracle you came here today?"

"I've often been, on picnics with forestry friends, and sometimes I come alone to walk in the woods."

It worried him they might have been seen, but she seemed unconcerned so he was content. Whosever forest it was, he had gone into it, met her, and they had made love in the open, marvel enough for Levin.

On the road to town, although the sun shone brightly through broken clouds, he opened the umbrella over their heads.

In his room Levin laughed one minute and groaned the next. Breathing heavily, he paced back and forth for hours. Or he stared out of an open window, lost in profuse memory. Sometimes he silently celebrated his performance in the open—his first married woman, sex uncomplicated in a bed of leaves, short hours, good pay. He was invigorated by the experience, one he would not have predicted for himself. A few minutes later he was soberly conscious of this figure within—an old friend with a broken nose warning him against risking his new identity. The new life was very new. Yet he wondered what he could be with her. Could he, with Pauline, be more than he was? Levin thought in terms of experience with her, not necessarily commitment. Hadn't she herself denied he was obligated to her? This could only mean she wanted no serious tie to him. Yet he was glad he had told her about the past; it was a relief to share that with someone.

By night the forest had taken on a dreamlike quality. Was there such a forest? Were the trees still standing? Were they real? Was it Pauline he had met there? He asked himself, Who is she? Extraordinary thing to have been in a woman and not know her. Could he trust her? What did she want from him; why, for instance, Levin? Because her saintly papa had worn whiskers —beard as totem? Was there perhaps some design in her choice of him (Had she purposely followed him into the woods? Impossible!) or was their lovemaking the more or less accidental end of a discontented woman's desire? If not, if she had in one way or another sought him out, what could he offer her, a man at thirty still running after last year's train, far behind in the world? Nothing. To be involved with a married woman—danger by definition, whose behavior he had no way of predicting was no joke. Who could guess what grade *she* would want changed; or what she might whisper to her lawfully-wedded spouse in a moment of tenderness, or hurl at him in hatred. If she threw Levin up to Gilley, farewell Levin. He feared his fate in her hand. Yet if she were concealment itself he knew his relationship to Gilley was changed for all time. This bothered him. Since he disliked him he wanted it to be for a just cause, to wit, Gilley, not because Levin had stolen from him—the primal cheating, result, oppressor hating oppressed. The thought that haunted him most was that the slightest revelation of the act under the tree would mean the worst disaster he could think of: end of future.

During the week, though she was often in his mind, Levin felt he didn't miss her, and probably vice versa. She could never be interested in a man with his kind of past. As he mulled this, he could not be sure he was right—she had seemed more than sympathetic to him, had practically wept. Probably it was closer to truth to think she had wanted the distraction of an affair, had had it, and quits. Or maybe she's now ashamed of it. She's the one with a husband; thank God I have no wife. So fare thee well. Yet too bad, for what's good deserves repeating. He had been thinking it was impossible to live on memory of sexual pleasure, no matter how satisfying. The better the pleasure the more useless the memory.

This was his mood one rainy night, the week after the forest, as he sat in his room. The fire of unseasoned applewood had sizzled out after nine, and Levin, tired of reading, had rebuilt it. He went back to his book but found it hard to concentrate; had to nail down each sentence before he could move to the next. The alternative was to shut the book and think of her. Let me be honest with myself, he thought; if I have her again I must keep romance apart from convenience. Love goes with freedom in my book. He had less than a minute to test his reflection, for there was a sound on the back stairs, and through the blurred glass he saw Pauline about to tap with a key. He rose hastily, his impression that she had been observing him, questioning what— his existence? worth? good sense? Levin momentarily thought of disappearing, but went instead to open the door where she stood. Could a man do less on a rainy night?

Pauline entered quickly. "Did you want me to come?" Her eyes hid from his.

If he said no it wasn't yes, but Levin said yes. Still, it was yes without pain, unless pain could be present without one's knowing, an unlikely procedure.

They kissed and at once parted as if there was much to say, or at least get straight, before they could kiss again. Her face and hands were cold, she had shivered as he held her. Levin hung up her wet raincoat. Pauline stood before the fire in the green dress he remembered from the night he had banged his head. She wore pendant earrings.

"Just let me get my breath back."

But breath she had. What was missing he wasn't sure. She

seemed troubled, said little. Levin guessed what it probably was
—the difference between last time and this. Their meeting in the
woods was accidental. Tonight she must have lied to Gilley when
she left the house. There was, in any case, that house to leave and
this to come to.

For a half hour they watched the fire. She offered no explanation for her mood and he made it a point not to ask. He had dis-
appointing visions of a short sexless evening. At length Pauline
sighed and gave him her hand.

She looked around. "Is there anyone else on this floor?"

"Nobody. Mrs. Beaty sleeps downstairs."

Pauline plucked off her earrings and dropped them into her
purse. She stepped out of her shoes and began to undress. He
did the same though nobody had asked him. The contract was
in the prior act, there in the forest.

In her lace-bosomed slip reflecting the fire she looked at him
with a half-sad smile.

"Do you like me in this?"

"It's a poetic garment."

"You've never seen me naked."

The fact surprised him.

She drew the slip over her head and was naked. Her hips were
slim. She was long waisted, the legs and trunk gracefully propor-
tioned, her arms and shoulders lovely. Naked, she looked unmarried.

But her chest was barren, the flowerlike nipples only slightly
fleshy. He had almost looked away.

"Shall I keep my slip on? Would you like that better?"

"No." He had to watch himself with her.

She pressed down the mattress to see if the bed creaked.

"Are you afraid?" he asked her.

"Dreadfully. I'd die if anyone heard us."

He took her in his arms. "Don't be afraid. The landlady's deaf
when she's asleep. She's asleep now."

She was suddenly passionate, bit his lip. In bed she met him with open mouth. He thought what he must do for her but there was hardly time. "Take me." She came quickly, at the end half singing out as she had in the woods, a sound that sang in him. At its onset he had taken it for sobbing—regret for what she was doing—but it was a halting cry of pleasure. She took him with her before he thought it time to go. He laughed at the ease of it.

Afterwards she asked, her face lit in the glow of a cigarette, "Does 'My young love's rip'ning breasts' mean so much? Does my flat bosom bother you?"

"If it did it doesn't."

"At least I have symmetry," she said. "My roommate in college had a bigger right breast than left."

He was for symmetry.

"And I've never worn falsies, would you want me to?"

"You're not the type."

"What type am I?"

"The type that doesn't wear them."

"Please always be honest with me," Pauline said.

He said he had to or got mangled.

She asked if he always taught himself lessons from experience.

"Almost always."

"My poor Levin."

"I don't like to make the mistakes I've made."

She said, after putting out her cigarette, "What will you teach yourself from us?"

"Something good, I think."

"Something lovely, perhaps enduring?"

He said he thought so.

"Do you think you could fall in love with a woman without breasts?"

"I've never tried."

She said, suddenly, "I shouldn't really be here."

Pauline was at once out of bed. "Gerald's in Marathon tonight. The children are alone because I couldn't get a sitter. I feel like a heel."

But she swept off the bedsheet and tightened it under him. Emptying the ashtray into the fireplace, Pauline aired the room, dressed, and left. Levin was at once asleep.

She visited him not often but often enough. One of her "meetings" was a good enough excuse for a night out. And Gilley assisted by teaching a winter-term weekly extension course for teachers, in Marathon. Usually Pauline walked the dozen blocks to Levin's. When she had the car she parked it about two blocks from the house. Gilley was home from Marathon by eleven. She had left Levin's room at ten-thirty, short but sweet. He could read afterwards without a stray thought, a great convenience. He envisioned a new Utopia, everyone over eighteen sexually satisfied, aggression reduced, peace in the world. Once she came for an hour after Gilley had fallen asleep, worrying Levin. She was no longer dreadfully afraid; the change in her had escaped him. She said she sometimes slept on a couch in Erik's room and Gilley was a heavy sleeper. In the unlikely event he awoke he would not miss her. But Levin asked her not to take chances. She promised, then went frankly on record in extenuation of the chances she took. "Gerald can sometimes be indifferent to me for weeks. He began to be after we found out the true reason why we couldn't have children, although I will admit there are times when it's my fault, when I just don't have the energy."

What a waste, he thought.

The next time they were in bed, after Levin had dozed and waked, she brought up Gerald. "Why don't you like him?"

"I never said I didn't."

"Tell me what happened in the department."

"I told you we didn't agree about some things."

"Be patient with him," she said. "He has good will towards you."

"Let's not talk about him," Levin said.

"He's really been very sweet to me. Sometimes I'm a moody bitch, but he's usually patient and I'd like to be grateful."

He said nothing.

"We weren't doing so badly at first," Pauline said, "then we began to have some nasty spells. He disappointed me in certain ways, some not his fault. I know I disappointed him. We had a very bad time just before we got Erik but it's really been better since the kids came. They've made me as nearly happy as I've been in recent years. Gerald does a lot for us. Lately I've been thinking I'd like to be in love with him again. It was very nice when we first were. Do you think anybody can bring past love alive or is it gone forever once it goes?"

"I don't know."

"Sometimes I've thought that if I were having an affair he might sense I'm being attractive to someone, and it might awaken more of his desire for me. If that happened maybe I would respond. Do you think that could happen?"

"I doubt it," he said.

"So do I," said Pauline.

He interpreted this to mean she wanted pleasure, solace, a momentary change, but no serious involvement with him. Her marriage, deficient as it seemed to him, apparently meant something to her. The situation suited him. If it made their relationship seem less consequential than it might be, on reflection so much the better. If his affair with Pauline inspired Gilley to respond to her, and she to love him for responding, so much the freer Levin's conscience. It wasn't easy to be helpful while enjoying the fruits of another man's wife.

He anticipated her visits, the tap of her key on the glass. They embraced ardently, her hand going for his fly. Levin guessed this was new for her, probably a new way she saw herself. It was new for him. Off came her earrings, then her clothes, without embarrassment. Breasts or none, her woman's wealth satisfied him. When he touched her nipples the effect was electric. She could be a little wild in bed. "Your fingers are fires." He enjoyed her long body, the cool flesh, sex smell, fragrant hair. He enjoyed the possession and adventure, her intensity with detachment. In bed he rarely thought of her as Gilley's wife. If he did he countered conscience with the thought he could break it off by spending the summer in San Francisco. In the fall he could find some excuse not to see her. He could say he had fallen in love and was thinking of getting married.

The forest had shrunk to a double bed. In bed they lived, in bed explored their bodies and history. She often asked him about his life, what he was like at ten, seventeen, twenty.

"A romantic," Levin said.

"That's still in you."

He shrugged. "Almost gone."

"Don't you like it?"

"I've lived too much on air."

"I like that in you."

Then she said, "Is love air?"

"Too often it was."

When he asked about her she asked: Did he find her attractive? Did he like her hair long? Did he like her legs? "I have such big feet." "I'm not pretty, am I?" She said once she didn't think she was interesting. "I've had so few experiences. My life was so prosaically different from yours. It's almost as though I wouldn't go the extra step to make something happen, and not much did."

"You are an interesting woman," Levin said.

"Do you mean as a person or sexually?"

"As a person with sex."

"Is that part of me strong, the sex?"

"Yes."

"I wish I had been more that way when I was young. If I had been confident of myself I might have had a lover or two."

"Didn't you?"

"I was a virgin when I was married."

"After that?"

"I was interested in men but I've never had the sort of relationship we're having."

A minute later she asked, "Tell me what you hear about me?"

"In what way?"

"Any way."

"Jeannette says you're a very fine person."

"She's a very fine person. What does George say?"

"Nothing I remember."

"Avis?"

"She thinks you could do more to help your husband."

"She's right," said Pauline. "Is that all she said?"

"Yes."

"She's had a crush on Gerald for years."

Levin said he had thought so.

He fell asleep. She woke him. "A woman my age is too old for a man yours. Wouldn't you really be better off with a girl of twenty-three or -four?"

His thoughts were scattered and he answered nothing.

She said wearily, "I'd be afraid of intense love now."

She dressed and went down the back stairs.

He expected her nightly all the next week but she didn't come. One day they met by chance on a downtown street.

"Did I say something wrong last time?" Levin asked.

"No, I haven't been myself."

"Not my fault?"

"I've been nervous, nothing new, an effect of periodicity."

"When can you come again?"

After a while she said she would soon.

Pauline reappeared the next night. Usually she was at once affectionate but tonight she sat at the fire, chain smoking. They talked but not about themselves. When he looked directly at her she seemed to look away. Levin assumed she felt guilty and foresaw the end of their affair.

"Suppose we were to break up?" she said.

"It would depend on you."

It grew late. Pauline got up and put on her coat. She looked lonely. Levin, exploring an insight, lifted her and carried her to the bed. She stiff armed him. "You don't dare." He pushed her down.

Afterwards she held his frontispiece. "I'll never let you go, Mr. Micawber."

The next time after making love, Levin experienced a fiery pain in the butt. He broke into a cold sweat and lay apart from her, his body stiff, pretending to be asleep. He shoved his face into the pillow to keep from crying out. For ten brutal minutes he was in torment, then the pain gradually eased. He felt sickly limp but relieved, thankful for his good health. Less than a week later he felt the same agonizing, flaming pain. Though tensed to misery Levin managed to hide it from her although the torture was worse than any he remembered. It moved up the side, then to the scrotum, then back to the butt, a harrowing embarrassment after sex and shameful way to be vulnerable.

After another such spasm he began to dread going to bed with her. At the same time he was disgusted with himself—pure Levin reaction, for every pleasure, pain. He thought of telling Pauline what the trouble was, but for a lover it was a too vital weakness to confess, one which might, if it continued, waken contempt. When she appeared the next time he suggested going for a drive or maybe to a movie in another town. Pauline seemed touched by the suggestion, sweetly agreed, but in one womanly way and another—although he sensed her puzzlement—enticed him into a performance. Levin paid the price of emission, a fiery pain in the ass.

"Aren't you well?" she asked after minutes of silence.

He said he was.

"I feel you haven't been enjoying yourself lately, I can't quite describe it. Has my breath been bad?"

"No."

"Would you like me to come less often, or not at all?"

"No."

She left it at that, perhaps afraid to ask more, obviously worried. When the pain was gone, although they talked affectionately, he saw her watching him. Before she left she clung to him.

On the night of Gilley's next class in Marathon, Levin tried hiding from her. After supper he went to a movie and later drank beer until midnight. She had left a note: "Sorry I missed you." He slept badly, dreamed his whiskers were on fire. It seemed to him he had just fallen asleep when he was awakened by footsteps coming stealthily up the back stairs. These weren't her steps. Levin listened, nailed to the bed, his heart thundering. The steps stopped. He jumped up in wet sweat, fumbled for the light, fell over his shoes, sprang up and flung open the door. Nothing. Rain in swirling light. Someone wandered up the inside stairs. Levin hastily got into a robe before Mrs. Beaty knocked. She stood at the door in her flannel robe, her earpiece in, holding the battery box in her hand. He said he had had a nightmare and fallen out of bed. She said to be careful, she knew a man who had broken his back that way.

Fearing something serious—kidney, bladder, rectal—possibly cancer—and because he was making Pauline so jumpy she went two moody visits without looking at the bed, Levin decided to see a doctor. He had hoped the pain would go without treatment but it was as bad as ever when they went to bed again.

One afternoon he drove to Marathon to someone recommended by Joe Bucket; he didn't want anyone in Easchester to know his business. The doctor, an old man, examined him elaborately with every instrument he could think of except forceps. He made various tests, then pronounced his judgment.

"Tinsion is all I can find."

"My God, what's that?"

"Some sort of tinsion is causing rectal and other spasms, though possibly it's the prostate, but I can't find any evidence. Have you felt like going to the toilet when you have the pain?"

"I've gone."

"Does it help?"

"No."

"No relief or relaxation?"

"Isn't sex supposed to relax you?"

"It is and it isn't. It does and doesn't." The doctor scratched behind his ear. "Is the lady your wife?"

"Yes," he lied.

"Are conditions favorable for intercourse?"

"Yes."

"You aren't worried about your business or any such worries?"

"No."

"Beats me, I'm afraid," said the doctor, "unless you don't like your wife."

Everyman's Freud, thought Levin.

"You might rest up a week."

"I've rested, it comes back."

The doctor wrote out a prescription. "Take one of the little green pills before intercourse. If that doesn't work, take the white pill afterward. The first is a relaxant for your tinsion, it's an antispasmodic. The other is a pain killer. If neither of them work come back and I'll give you an antibiotic."

In the street Levin tore up the prescription and scattered the pieces.

Levin afflicted by mystery: What was the painful egg the rooster was trying to lay? In the middle of driving home a thought he had had but never particularly valued, stalled the car. He was asking himself what he was hiding from: That he too clearly saw her shortcomings and other disadvantages, and was urgently urging himself to drop her before it was too late? That he was tired of the uneasy life, fed up with assignations with the boss's wife, sick up to here with awareness of danger and fear of consequences? Here was truth yet not enough truth. After mulling these and related thoughts, Levin tracking an idea concerning Pauline, fell over one regarding himself: the dissatisfaction he had lately been hiding from, or feeling for an inadmissibly long time, was with him for withholding what he had to give. He then gave birth. Love ungiven had caused Levin's pain. To be unpained he must give what he unwillingly withheld. It was then he jumped up, stalling the car.

Once home, he didn't know what to do with himself. Run twice around the block. Stand on his ear? Dig hard head into concrete sidewalk? Kiss the mirror or hit it with a hammer for imaging the dark-bearded one who ever complicated the infernally complicated? And Einstein, it said in the papers, used the same cake of soap to shave and bathe. Levin sat in his chair, momentarily slept, started while dreaming, bounded up to spend hours staring out of the open window at nothing he particularly saw. He lay on the bed, then rose up as if the sheets were on fire. He left his room to hurry somewhere—anywhere—and awoke to find himself standing on the back stairs. Above the tops of budding trees he watched the flaring, setting sun, wanting to abolish thought, afraid to probe the complexion of the next minute lest it erupt in his face a fact that would alter his existence. But nature —was it?—a bull aiming at a red flag (Levin's vulnerability, the old self's hunger) charged from behind and the Manhattan matador, rarely in control of any contest, felt himself lifted high and plummeted over violet hills toward an unmapped abyss. Through fields of stars he fell in love.

. . . Love? Levin eventually sighed. Is it love or insufficient exercise? Escape, perhaps, or excitement born from the tension of secrecy, wrongdoing? Love? How at all possible if the proposed lover had such profound reservations concerning the game, rules, even players? Consider once more, for instance, her lank frame, comic big tootsies, nose flying, chest bereft of female flowers. He mourned that motherless breast, the lost softness over the heart to pillow a man's head. He had once in frustration nipped at her nipple; she had socked his head with both fists. Levin had never imagined such as she his, her insufficiencies, discontents. Consider too the burden of her ambient: prior claimant, husband-in-law; the paraphernalia of her married life—love her, love her past. With her possibly take kids and their toys. Not for me, he told himself. He wanted no tying down with ropes, long or short, seen or invisible—had to have room to move so he could fruitfully use freedom. If, ecstasied out of his senses he let down his guard —was leapt on by fate—Lord help Levin!

But if he loved her why loved he her? You are comely, my love. Your self is loveliness. You make me rich in feeling. You have grace, character. I trust you. He loved because she had one unforgettable day given herself to a city boy in a forest. And for the continuance of her generosity in bed (was he less generous?) abating desire as she made it grow, taking serious chances (did he not chance as much?). Or was he moved to love because her eyes mirrored Levin when he looked? Or, to drag truth closer, because he was compelled by his being to be in love with her open, honest, intelligent, clearly not very happy self? (Why do I feel I have chosen her because I am her choice?) The catechism made little difference, for he knew fait accompli when accomplished. Who was he kidding, or what pretending to delay or dress in camouflage? "The truth is I love Pauline Gilley." His confession deeply moved him. What an extraordinary only human thing to be in love. What human-woven mystery. As Levin walked the streets under a pale moon he felt he had recovered everything he had ever lost. If life is not so, at least he feels it is. The world changed as he looked. He thought of his unhappy years as though they had endured only minutes, black birds long ago dissolved in night. Gone for all time. He had made too much of past experience, not enough of possibility's new forms forever. In heaven's eye he beheld a seeing rose.

. . . But Levin had long ago warned himself when he arrived at this intensity of feeling—better stop, whoa. Beware the forms of fantasy. He had been, as a youth, a luftmensch, sop of feeling, too easy to hurt because after treading on air he hit the pavement head first. Afterwards, pain-blinded, he groped for pieces of reality. "I've got to keep control of myself. I must always know where I am." He had times without number warned himself, to harden, toughen, put on armor against love.

It snowed heavily.

The snow fell in buffeted veils. It bent shrubs and small evergreens and broke branches everywhere. There hadn't been such a snowfall in years, Mrs. Beaty said. Gilley's Marathon night passed and Pauline did not visit Levin. He accused himself, then blamed the snow, until after three warm days it vanished and she still had not appeared. Had his antics, while avoiding the bed, scared her away? He hungered to call her or write, but she had once asked him not to. Another Marathon night went by and Levin's desperation grew. He felt he had lost her.

When Pauline appeared in his room ten days after he had discovered he loved her, Levin was moved by the glow of her, the lovely form she achieved in being. How love perfects each imperfect thing. What she was was beauty. With breasts she couldn't possibly be the one he loved. I mustn't forget this, he thought, it's worth remembering.

Yet as she entered the room he knew at once—it smote him—that her detachment, almost unconcern—was something more than of the moment; and if desire, no more than that, the little she wanted from him, for which he castigated himself. She scanned his face and finding him fit plucked off her earrings. Hearing no objections to the contrary, she undressed for bed. When he embraced her she stiffened momentarily in his arms. When he spoke of love she whispered she had only an hour. Levin was thinking of forever. He felt he had loved her from the time he had laid eyes on her at the railroad station last summer—years ago. They had looked guardedly at one another. Had she guessed he would love her and turned away as though the thought was burdensome? Could she ever know that before meeting her he had loved the idea of Pauline Gilley? Didn't that make him worthy of her love?

But what had tilted Levin into love had not tipped her. In bed she dispatched the act with an easy cry. He loved her, wanting as he loved. She fell asleep as he lay awake thinking of the unyielding irony of his life.

Afterward she said, "You've been so strange."

He apologized. "I had some trouble but it's gone now."

"Is that the truth?"

"Pauline, the truth is I love you."

She said after silence, "How like a woman to want to love the one you sleep with."

"I do."

She held her hands to her ears.

He shut his mouth, eyes, his life. She dressed and quickly left. He wasn't looking.

Each day passed excruciatingly, he tried not to count. He fought thinking of her, a mockery—she was in every thought. He beat his brains to destroy her place in his mind without maiming himself. How to be, please God, not Levin? How to live loveless or not live? Once more he paid for who he was, a dirty deal.

Late one night she tapped on his window and nervously entered. Levin, putting down a book he couldn't read, faced her with what dignity he could muster, concealing love in his own defense, and the pain her presence invoked.

"I saw your light," she said.

He answered nothing.

"I tried not to come," Pauline said. "It isn't fair to you."

Fair or foul, he would settle for sex.

"Considering what I know about your life—what you've been through—I have no right to love you or expect your love, my poor darling."

He rose with an aching heart.

"I love you," she was saying, "although I try not to. I tried to be fair to you, to Gerald, and my children."

They embraced. She dug her nails into his back. He beat her with his heart.

"I love you, Lev. That's my name for you. Sy is too much like sigh, Lev is closer to love. I love you, I'm sorry, you deserve better."

"I deserve you."

"I should never have let you that day in the woods. But I love the kind of man you are, the kind I have to love."

"I love you willingly, with all my heart."

"Oh, my darling, we must do something with our lives."

My God, thought Levin, "What hath God wrought?"

If Gilley were alive to political affront, he showed not the slightest sign he was aware of a situation that insulted his manhood; and Levin's passion for his wife grew, fed by the secrecy it lived in. His heart was a taut string played hard by love, one further note of longing and it would snap in its face. Secrecy was an intensifying component, another that he saw her rarely now, and lived much in images of desire. At the time of his deepest need (one way of tormenting himself was to imagine spending twenty-four normal hours in her company) Gilley's winter extension course ended and he did not reschedule it for spring. The trout season wouldn't open till April, and freshman recruitment was temporarily over until a last intensive week in May. Gerald was therefore either home with Pauline or out with her. She saw Levin for occasional short visits, but was now hesitant to give as her excuse for going out, non-existent civic meetings. A Mrs. Bowie, whose house she was supposed to be at, had called one night, and Gilley was mystified until Pauline (fresh from love with Levin) said she had remembered the meeting had been postponed and so had dropped in at Jeannette's. She had become again "deathly afraid." It's the town, Levin thought; too tight to maneuver in. Too much is visible to the naked eye. When they met it still took her a while to stop being afraid. She looked sometimes as though it were all too much for her. Levin said that one night but she denied it. "It's just that I sometimes worry what would happen to the children." He had not much thought of them, but now he thought, though not much. She made him promise faithfully never to mention her name to anyone.

Though the Gilleys entertained more frequently now, Pauline thought it best not to invite Levin. "It's hard to pretend no-love

when I feel so much for you." Therefore though they made plans
to be together more often, they saw each other less. As always he
"had" again as have-not; hadn't bargained for this much longing,
this much not having what was his to have. Missing her became
work. He reveried a warm floral time when they'd be inseparably
together, in various stages of dress or undress, bed or board. My
God, if I could only walk in the street with her. He dreamed of
her as his wife, but on her belly was tattooed "Mrs. Gilley." She
wrote him suddenly, a spate of letters in official-looking brown
envelopes, which he was not permitted to answer because Gilley
made a point of going to the box after the mail delivery during
the lunch hour; and Levin, after carrying it in his inside
pocket, reading and rereading it, burned each letter in the fireplace because she had asked him to. The letters he couldn't write
her were a further loss. He was in his heart a poet these days; each
thought of her was crammed with beauty. It's what you don't
say that counts. But she let him telephone if he made sure Gerald
was either at his desk or in class. Levin went into a phone booth
in the Student Union to make his call, his heart thumping like
a hand on a bull fiddle. They exchanged endearment and hung up.
On Saturday mornings she called from downtown, if she could.
If Mrs. Beaty, deaf or not, was too close by, she could tell from
his voice and said goodbye. If not, each praised the other and
both praised love. Afterwards Levin walked unknown distances.

They had met rarely by chance before they became lovers,
but in March, as though for compensation, he began to see her
almost every time he left the house, and he left the house to see
her. Walking downtown he would spot her driving the family
Buick, tall in the seat, her straight hair touching her shoulders,
nose pointing direction—where Levin must go. They met by
accident in the post office, library, market. She greeted him
vaguely and hurried the kids on. He would pass her on the street
and tip his hat. Last fall, when they had met, she had stopped
to exchange a word; he was the one in a hurry. Now her greetings were hesitant, formal. She hid love, a concealment painful to

him. But there were times when for the slightest second her eyes
were in love with him. Sometimes he saw her alone across the
street; he liked her brisk high-heeled walk. Each noticeable new
thing about her was an event: what she wore: a split skirt showing a bit of white slip against her leg. Long dark blue socks awoke
forest memories. He knew when she had washed her hair. Once
in a food market, Gilley and both kids waiting outside in the
car, when Levin approached Pauline dropped a can of tuna fish
she had just taken off the shelf. It rolled along the floor. He bent
for it, remembering the casserole she had ladled into his lap the
night they had met. As he gave her the can their fingers touched
and his heart grew flowers. Leaving the store, she glanced back
at him. He lived on that for a week.

One Saturday morning when she had not telephoned, Levin
hurried downtown hoping for a glimpse of her. Wherever he
went, she wasn't. At noon he was returning in disappointment to
his car when he passed a photographer's shop displaying some
enlarged shots of the Cascadia basketball team in its window. An
intuition stopped Levin and he went to the window. Almost at
once he discovered Pauline in a picture ("Profs and Wives Cheer
Team"), nothing less than revelation. While the photographer
was posing a bridal party in the studio at the rear of the store,
Levin entered, plucked the picture out of the window, folded it
once, and slipped it into his pocket. He drove home in a hurry
and in his room cut out her intense, open, lovely face. Levin then
tore up Gilley, the Bullocks, and the rest of the crowd he had
extracted her from. He kept this little picture of her hidden
among the best thoughts in his notebook and would often gaze
at it.

Now and then he saw her at people's houses, a star, a flower
amid the full-breasted faculty wives. What they lacked she had.
What she hadn't nobody needed. It was high adventure for him
when she walked in, even with Gilley, even if she hardly seemed
to recognize her lover. Better that than not appear; that broke
the night. At these social gatherings talk was small and wit rare,

but hospitality and warmth were undeniable; Levin eagerly laid hold of any invitation that might produce her. He was surprisingly often invited where she was, almost as though people sensed romance and fostered it, though he hoped not. Whenever they met the action was as before: although they had talked together casually in the past, now, as on the street, she gave him little more than hello, how are you? She was no actress. He loved, therefore, behind the eyes; always conscious of what she was doing, when alone, talking to Jeannette, Alma or another woman, or to men and which men, when in the kitchen, on the sofa, or momentarily gone to the bathroom. He must know where she was. From where Levin observed, standing among others apart from her, sitting near her at a dinner table, trying not to stare, or watching from the next room, her face was gentle and luminous, sometimes a little sad; he created her quality as love created him; her loveliness enriching her clothes, the air around her. Once she drew back a lock of hair to adjust a barette and revealed an ear pinned like a jewel to her head. Another time she was wearing her hair in a bun and he whispered, "Your neck is stupendous." Pauline, in spite of herself, laughed. Lord, thought Levin, how beautiful women are, and how hungry my heart is. But how short life, how soon gone. Where will I find the patience to go on hungering? Love entitled him to create her beauty but never to embrace it when he most desired.

They sat in circles and talked; or, depending on the specialty of the house, watched slides, listened to records, or acted charades. He was pleased when his play acting amused her. There was no mood to a party but Levin's own. Once after dancing with her at Bullocks, he followed her into a bedroom. Pauline returned his kiss then drew back. "Please don't when Gerald's around." She walked out as he wiped his lips clean. He felt there was no future in their love, until a few minutes later, when as they met in a momentarily empty hall, she took his hand and pressed it to her cheek.

Although during the evening he could blot Gilley out of his

mind, what most tormented him was their leaving together, Levin locked out, a dirty trick on a lover. At midnight one of the women mentioned her baby sitter, her husband automatically stood up, and the whole company rose in a body. That ended the party, a blow to a bachelor who slept with his beard. Gilley gave his wife the eye and she went for her coat. They left for what lands, what voyages Levin couldn't make. He sometimes walked downtown and ordered a meal, to eat up his hunger.

One night at Bullocks she stayed as far from him as she could. She clung to Gilley, on her fourth drink without George's assistance. He recalled the time she had said she hoped for a revival of Gerald's love. He doesn't deserve it, Levin thought, but he felt she loved short of his love for her—his usual fate. Pauline saw him watching her and went into another room. She stayed apart from him all night. He was embittered, desolate. At midnight when the Bullocks served their elaborate buffet—coffee and cake was the customary nightcap elsewhere—Pauline filled up a plate and brought it to Gilley. He took it with a grin, placing a public arm around her. Levin, jealous of the years and substance of her Gerald had had, put down his glass and went out into the garden. It had begun to drizzle. As he was thinking he would leave from the garden and come around tomorrow for his coat, he heard footsteps on the patio. She was in his arms before he could turn.

"Forgive me, darling, Gerald's been awfully sweet, and I've felt very guilty. At times I hate myself."

"Don't feel bound to me."

"The truth is I do."

"Then don't feel guilty."

"If it were only that easy."

"Is that why you're drinking?"

"To forget you a little."

They kissed. "I'd better go," she said.

He took her hand. "You're so lovely."

"I feel lovely with you."

"My heart aches for you."

"I for you."

"When can you come?"

"I'll try tonight."

"Don't if you feel bad."

Pauline said she would try.

It was past two when she tapped on the glass. She had slept in Erik's room after Gilley had fallen asleep. When Erik called for his water she gave it to him, then changed the baby in her sleep and left. "I can only stay a few minutes."

"Did you take the car?"

"I was afraid of the noise it would make."

"I'll drive you back."

"Not all the way."

But she had not touched her earrings.

"Aren't you going to undress?"

She looked at him then looked away. "I can't tonight. Gerald wanted to and I couldn't say no."

He was struck by a grave sadness.

A few nights later she came in at nine. "I'm supposed to be at a late movie he doesn't want to see, and I've got to be home just after it lets out."

It was a time of fulfillment. Afterwards Levin said, "I hate to see you so scared. We've got to think of something we can do."

"What, for instance?"

"Whatever you say."

"What about your plans?"

"Sometime we'll have to tell him the truth."

"Not yet," she said. Then she said, "Let's wait till summer, than we'll talk about it."

"Why till summer?"

"To see how things go."

"Don't you think we have a future together?"

"Sometimes I do and sometimes not."

"When do you think so?"

"When it suddenly looks possible. I feel calm and see it that way."

"When doesn't it?"

"When I feel you ought to have someone with fewer problems to bring you."

"Forget that. How does it look now?"

"Possible."

"That creates the future," Levin said.

Before she left he asked, "Are you sure you love me?"

"So much it takes me time to think how much. Why do you ask so often?"

"All my life I've been engaged in wanting."

"Love makes a long journey in you."

"Your love inspires me. It always will."

"Don't make me cry, darling," Pauline said.

She left at midnight, it was raining. She had stayed longer than she had intended; but she had taken the precaution of dropping in at the Scowers before, to say she had been there too if Gerald asked anything.

"The lies shame me most," she said.

He lit her way down the stairs with a flashlight and watched her leave the yard, regretting her going. Tonight the room was empty after she had gone. Levin switched off the light and tried to fall quickly asleep. He was beginning to doze when he heard a knock on his door and roused himself.

The landlady, her gray hair in braids, held her battery box in her hand. She was upset.

"I'm sorry, Mr. Levin, but I have my self-respect to think of. I asked Mrs. Gilley not to come here again. I'm sorry for her and I'm sorry for you, but it's not right, and I have the reputation of my house to think of."

He listened with battered heart and stone ear.

"A few nights ago when I awoke to get my medicine I thought I saw her coming out of the alley with you. Since then

I waited up every night, and tonight I missed her going in but I heard her high heels come down your stairs. At first I was going to talk to you, but then I decided to talk to her. She isn't the right person for you, Mr. Levin, and you'll get into real trouble at the college if you go on with her. Whether you do or you don't, I don't want her coming here any more."

"It would have been merciful if you had spoken to me."

"I'm not sure that a married woman carrying on deserves much mercy. I feel sorry for Mr. Gilley."

"What did she say when you spoke to her?"

"All she did was run away."

Levin groaned.

After the old woman went downstairs he felt a furious desperation. What had happened now seemed inevitable. He dressed and left the house. Levin walked in the rain to Pauline's. Her house was dark except for the white tree on the front lawn. He stood across the street, wanting her through walls. Half the night he wandered in the rain.

In the morning he was impatient to call her but Gilley wasn't at his desk during his office hours and Levin did not want to risk it. Later he found a letter in his office mailbox, a blue envelope addressed in block letters. She had never written him here before.

"Just a word, dearest. I suppose you know?—I'm awfully sorry. I was afraid of something like this. I can't tell you how bad I feel, God knows how I'll get through the night. I'm writing this in Erik's room. Call me Thurs. between 9 & 10, no later. I just had to get in touch. I love you. I miss you so. Destroy this. Pauline."

He kissed the letter.

Thursday at nine he called. Hearing her voice made him feel as though they had been separated for years.

"When can I see you?" he asked.

"Lev, I'm frightened to death. Let's be careful. Not for a while is best."

"I could look for another room or maybe a small apartment with a private entrance?"

"If you move now she may tell people. If she lets you stay I doubt she'd talk. Has she said anything to you?"

"Just only what happened. She hasn't asked me to move but we ought to have plans."

"You have plans, Lev."

"I mean in case something happens."

"I don't want anything else to happen, nothing, nothing."

"Don't be scared."

"I was brought up to be."

"If I could just see you."

"Not for a while, please. Just call me Tuesdays and Thursdays, about this time. I may write but please don't you. I'm terribly sorry—I shouldn't have come so often. She wasn't nasty but I felt awful. I'm sorry I'm not somebody else, I mean someone not married. You don't deserve this."

"I deserve you."

"I'd better hang up. I don't want to cry on the phone."

Though he telephoned twice a week for a brief word of love, he saw her only in passing, in motion away from him. He thought of her with such intensity it was like waking when he stopped thinking. So Levin lived, famished, except for the sound of her voice on the phone and an occasional letter to the office, which he dutifully tore up. Beyond the word he lived on memory: her heart easing presence in his arms. Levin inspired, by her embrace, breath, beauty, the smell and feel of her, their consummation, and aftermath, when because of love's possibilities the previous minute's love was deepened. Otherwise hunger.

"I never see you," he said on the phone. "Where are you besides in my heart?"

"Here," she said, "at this end."

"We've got to meet."

"Where would we go?"

"I'll find some place," he said.

"A beautiful place, a forest."

At night Levin haunted her street. After a walk to river, or the hills, he came to her house when it was late and unlikely Gilley would step out with milk bottles or the cat. Levin stood across the street near the flowering plum tree thick with deep-hued pink blossoms. He watched for a touch of Pauline, a glimpse of her dress as she passed the half-shaded window, or whatever morsel luck would let fall into his empty hands.

In his thoughts he crossed the street and entered his house. She was waiting for him. They ate together, then when the kids were in bed, talked, read, listened to music. They went to bed and made love without ache or fear—was there ever such a life? Anyway, it was love and he had it, until he was standing alone across the street as she lay in bed with a stranger . . .

Levin was startled by a touch on the arm. A cop, staring at his beard, said a taxpayer had called and complained of a peeping Tom.

"Not me," said Levin.

"Could I see some I.D.?"

Levin produced his automobile license.

The cop looked at it and returned the card.

"Could you tell me why you're standing here?"

"Resting after a walk. Such a beautiful night."

"Right in the middle of the sidewalk?"

"I love this tree."

"The lady that phoned said you had been here more than an hour. She thought you might be casing one of the houses across the street."

"That long?" said Levin. He left, heavy hearted.

One early spring night when a brimming moon in the white sky gilded houses, trees, and spring flowers, a moon-drenched Levin wandered along Pauline's street and paused at the flowering plum. He crossed the street and stood, hat in hand, a few feet from her partly-open, dark bedroom window. Come to the window for a minute, my dearest, and I'll be content for a month. But no one appeared, though he thought of it often. In the stillness he heard the rhythmic creaking of a bed, and then on the night—a bird, catch it, hold it—the soft cry of a woman at the height of her pleasure.

Gilley, had, in an inspired moment, satisfied her for him.

They made plans to be together but for one reason or another abandoned them. She was afraid they might be seen wherever they met. "It would be absolutely cruel if Gerald found out through gossip." "Am I never to be with you?" "Be patient, Lev." He cursed the day Mrs. Beaty had seen her in the alley. One morning when he was famished for a look at her, she let him watch from down the block as she entered the food market. When she came out, she looked in his direction for several seconds, then walked to her car. This can't go on, he thought.

Learning on Thursday morning that she was going with Gilley to a post-season basketball game on Saturday night, Levin hurried to the Basketball Palace and with luck got a reserved seat in the balcony, facing the faculty section. On Saturday night he was there early, amid an enormous crowd of students and townspeople. Levin spent most of his time scanning faces with his bird-watching binoculars. Once the glasses met a pair directed at him, a hard eye for an eye. A chill ran through him as he recognized the flushed half-bald dome and expressionless features of Dr. Marion Labhart. Levin had sulfurous visions of himself as Arthur Dimmesdale Levin, locked in stocks on a platform in the town square, a red A stapled on his chest, as President Labhart stood over him, preaching a hellfire sermon denouncing communist adulterers, the climax of which was the public firing of Levin out of the college. Next to the president sat Dean Lawrence Seagram of the Liberal Arts Service Division. When Levin first saw him in September the dean was a clean-shaven youngish type; now he was middle-aged and wore a grizzled Van Dyke but at least looked human.

Seeking Pauline, Levin located Gilley with an empty seat at his side, a gap for Levin. Above in the next row were both Bullocks. Levin, focusing on the empty seat, wondered what had happened to Pauline; he waited impatiently for the two-hour sight of her. From a man at his side he learned that Cascadia was playing Los Angeles for the Western Conference Championship. The floor of the court blazed with reflected light, practice went on, and two bands blared. Among the rally girls on the Cascadia side Levin recognized Nadalee Hammerstad. She shook red pompoms, danced and twirled, revealing her slim thighs and frisky black-tighted behind. She performed directly below Pauline's empty seat, and Levin was uneasy at how life related events and people.

When the game started, Pauline had still not come. He consid-- ered running downstairs to telephone to make sure she was a'l right but he was caught in the prevailing excitement and stayed. The L.A. band had antagonized him. Costumed in hard straw hats, red bow ties, shorts and hairy legs, it created a jazz uproar, drowning out the pep songs of the white-skirted Cascadians. If the strategy was to keep their own players hopped up, they did the same for all present, setting Levin's teeth on edge, and arous-ing in him a strong antagonism to the State of California. From the whistle Los Angeles broke into the lead, and Levin, realizing the home town was the underdog, found himself cheering it. For a minute he studied himself with a sour eye yet went on as be-fore.

Though he had not since college watched basketball, he was gripped by the game. More than once he jumped out of his seat to cheer a good play or boo a bad call. What a bad call was he left to the crowd. He shouted encouragement to the players, in particular Whitey Barker, a skinny, long-chested type, a solid C minus student in Levin's last term's class, but on the court, canny, alert, graceful, wise. He defended like a matador enclosing the bull, and on offense hit baskets with every kind of shot. His re-bounding was outstanding. The instructor waving his hat, cheered himself hoarse for his former student—although he suspected the boy had complained to Bullock about the grade he had got, because George had been cold to Levin for a while at the end of the winter term. Peering with his binoculars at the faculty section to study George's face, he discovered Pauline sitting next to Gerald.

A little ashamed of having forgotten her, he focused his glasses and was moved by her drawn face. She had lost weight. He could hear the game going on, ten men thundering back and forth, pitching a ball at two hoops, but now he kept his glasses tightly on her, taking his excitement from her presence. Pauline seemed, after a while, to be squirming this way and that; he realized she had become aware of him and was trying either to shrink or hide from his magnified eyes. Levin lowered his glasses and absent-mindedly watched the last few minutes of play. At the end he did not know who had won.

As he was leaving the Palace he thought he had at least shared the town's big emotion. He would not, if he could, deny them basketball if once in a while the big emotion came from a good book.

Going down the stairs, he overheard one beanied freshman he knew talking to another.

"Did you see that cat with the black whiskers who had those binocks in front of us? That's my comp prof."

"So what?"

"He's supposed to be nuts about some dame. Maybe he could see her naked in those glasses."

When Levin arrived home, he snipped off his beard with scissors and shaved the rest.

When they met, on a street at the southern edge of town, Pauline looked at him in disbelief then wept, though Levin said it wasn't too bad. He had searched long in the mirror, felt ill but lived. Too much face, the eyes still sad candles, blunt bent nose, lips without speech telling all, but the jaw looked stronger, possibly illusion.

"Why did you do it?" she asked. "It had gotten to look so rich and silky. I hope it isn't bad luck."

He waited until she stopped talking about it.

They tried to think where to go to be alone. He suggested the woods or the riverbank but it rained every day and they had to settle for motels near outlying towns. This was during a time Gilley was beginning to go fishing again. Levin registered and she stayed in the car, her face averted. Alone, they kissed, he tasting on her tongue the Scotch she had had to relax her. She was still mistress of the quick lay, and once it was over he dozed by her side, dreaming of her. Longing was long, the consummation brief. Satisfaction bred quick hunger. It saddened him he couldn't be contented for more than minutes. Levin held her in his arms, longing for Pauline. The thought of all the time that would go by before he saw her again oppressed him.

She wanted, of course, not to be nervous but usually was. "I hate motels. Your room was so nice. I felt at home in it." He offered to move to Marathon, where nobody knew them. "That's not good either," she said. "You'd be miles away and I'd have less time to be with you. And after a while, no matter where you lived, somebody would find out I was coming to see you and this would start again."

One night when there was not much time and they had worked themselves into desire in Levin's car, parked by the riverbank, she joked about the back seat, then grew depressed. The result was nothing achieved, his loss, for she seemed soon to feel better, as though she had exchanged nothing for something. He had lost more than a lay. But loss enlarged love, or so they said. And part of the experience of paradise was when it was no longer paradise. This thought had come to him in a former time when he was struggling to accept fate without making less of experience.

She said, as he was driving her to the street where she usually got out and walked home, "I've been thinking if only something very good happened to Gerald it would be easier to think of leaving him. Please don't oppose him for the headship. I'm sure he'll be good at it."

"There are better men around," Levin said.

"Last night I dreamed he found us in bed and took the children away from me."

"That won't happen."

"I always knew I would fall in love again but I wasn't prepared to feel ravaged so soon."

"Love is life."

"I wish you hadn't cut your beard."

"What can I do to make things easier for you?" Levin asked her. "I could stay away for a month, even till summer if you'd feel any better. Then in the summer we could come to a decision."

"Could you stay away that long?"

"I could for you."

"I don't think I could stand it, I'd worry about you."

"What worry?"

"About how you were and if you still loved me."

"You know I would."

"No, I don't want that kind of worry. I'd rather have this."

Afterwards he wanted to send her something—flowers—but what would she say if Gilley asked her where they had come from? So he settled for a pair of gold hoop earrings which he bought for more than he could afford. But when could she wear them except with him, and where would she hide them later? He kept them for her in his notebook drawer.

The next time they talked on the phone she said, "Don't think of me as poor Pauline, think of me as rich. I may have fears but I have you. I have lovely thoughts of you. I want to give you what you haven't had. I want to make up for all you've been through in the past. I want to make you happy with me."

He said he was happy.

In bed, the next time, she failed to achieve satisfaction. Since this was twice in a row Levin was disappointed.

"Don't make anything out of it," she said, "I've been sleeping badly and I'm usually tired. The kids tire me, and it's not easy to live with one man and be always thinking of another. I worry he senses something is wrong. And I worry about the strain on you."

"Don't worry about me."

"Now you have her, now you don't is no life for a man. And I worry about a definite break with Gerald. I guess I was not passionately attached to him but I've never been able to unlove anyone I ever loved."

"We'll settle it in the summer."

"I already have settled it but my nervous system hasn't. That's what flopped just now—not me. But I'll be myself next time."

Next time was in a little hotel about thirty miles out of Easchester—she was insisting they not go back to the motels they had been to. After a while, Pauline, her brow wet, said, "Don't wait for me, I don't think I can."

"Are you sure."

"Come without me."

Finally he did.

"I'm really beat," she said.

"Is that it?"

She said, "Gerald is ardent again. I think he senses something. I told you he might. Sometimes I get so tired of sex."

Now we have truly come to adultery, Levin thought.

"I would have skipped it if you had asked me," he said.

She caressed his beardless face. Her eyes were tired, her nose thin. "Please don't worry. I go through these periods. I was in a bad period with Gerald just before the first time with you. But he's used to me and doesn't seem to mind."

"I mind."

"Don't idealize sex, Lev."

"Not sex, you."

After the fourth fruitless, songless time, one end-of-April night, Levin lay awake while she slept, grinding her teeth. She had looked imperiled. He felt he had to do something to help her or this might get beyond her. Since it was almost certainly too late to start writing around for a new job, if he could get an assistantship somewhere, and Pauline a part-time job, things might work out. But making new plans worried Levin; it was as if those he had come West with had been wrong to begin with. If that was the case would he ever in his life make the right plans? Yet he felt for her a deep tenderness and dreamed of a decent life for them. When he awoke it was almost six-thirty and Pauline was frantic.

They were racing through a thick fir forest. Levin had said he would take her to the Easchester bus station where she could get a cab, and she had in silence agreed, her face calmly locked in fright.

"What will you do if he's awake?" Levin asked.

"I'll lie."

"Could I go in with you?"

"No."

Above the trees the light brightened, yellow, then foggy gold. " 'Tis the rising, not the setting sun,' " he said.

"Who said so?"

"B. Franklin."

"He was wrong."

The fake forest, Levin thought.

As he was speeding out of it, a siren sounded behind them. A state trooper in an unmarked car waved the Hudson to the side.

Levin cursed. Pauline shut her eyes. Any minute he expected to see gray in her hair.

The trooper talked for ten minutes before handing Levin the ticket. Pauline stared ahead, her stomach rumbling. She bent to hide it but couldn't.

Finally they were off again at fifty.

"I'd better go in with you."

"No, please no."

They parted at the Easchester bus station. She hurried into a cab, forgetting goodbye, Until We Meet Again, or even to wave. He watched the taxi turn the corner on a dull gray morning.

Afterwards Levin sweated it out in his room. He had visions of disaster for all, particularly himself. Yes, she loved him, but she also loved Gilley and she loved the kids. If she had loved Levin as he loved her, she would already have made up her mind to leave Gilley. To go on as they had been, would prolong the torture and destroy what was left of the joy of love. He stayed in the house Saturday and Sunday, waiting for a word from her but none came. Only Pauline lived in his thoughts. He thought of her as she had been when they were first in love and how worn out and unhappy she had looked lately. Levin struck himself for the harm he had done her. He promised that if, by some stroke of luck she had got in without Gilley knowing it, he would not see her till summer. The rest would do her good.

When he went to work on Monday morning, after his first desperate glance at Gerald, Levin knew Pauline had got in safely. Out of love he gave her up.

Yakov Bok in Prison

He waits.

The snow turned to rain.

Nothing happened.

Nothing but the long winter; not the indictment.

He felt the change of weather in his head. Spring came but stayed outside the bars. Through the window he heard the shrilling of swallows.

The seasons came faster than the indictment. The indictment was very slow. The thought that it might sometime come made it so slow.

In the spring it rained heavily. He listened to the sound of the rain and liked the thought of the outside wet, but he didn't like the inside wet. Water seeped through the wall on the prison yard side. Lines of wet formed on the cement between the exposed bricks. From an eroded part of the ceiling above the window, water dripped after the rain had stopped. After the rain there was always a puddle on the floor. Sometimes the dripping went on for days. He awakened at night listening to it. Sometimes it stopped for a few minutes and he slept. When the dripping began again he awoke.

I used to sleep through thunder.

He was so nervous, irritable, so oppressed by imprisonment he feared for his sanity. What will I confess to them if I go mad? Each day's oppressive boredom terrified him. The boredom and the nervousness made him think he might go insane.

One day, out of hunger for something to do, for a word to read, he cracked open one of the phylacteries that had been left in the cell. Holding it by the thongs he hit the box against the wall till it burst with a puff of dust. The inside of the phylactery box smelled of old parchment and leather, yet there was a curious human odor to it. It smelled a little like the sweat of the body. The fixer held the broken phylactery to his nose and greedily sucked in the smell. The small black box was divided into four compartments, each containing a tightly rolled little scroll, two with verses from Exodus and two from Deuteronomy. Yakov puzzled out the script, remembering the words faster than he could read. The bondage in Egypt was over, and in one scroll Moses proclaimed the celebration of Passover. Another scroll was the Sh'ma Yisroël. Another enumerated the rewards for loving and serving God and the punishment for not: the loss of heaven, rain, and the fruit of that rain; even life. In each of the four scrolls the people were commanded to obey God and teach his words. "Therefore you shall lay up these my words in your heart and in your soul, and bind them for a sign upon your hand, that they may be frontlets between your eyes." The sign was the phylactery and it was the phylactery that Yakov had broken. He read the scrolls with excitement and sadness and hid them deep in the mattress straw. But one day Zhitnyak, his eye roving at the peephole, caught the fixer absorbed in reading them. He entered the cell and forced him to give them up. The appearance of the four scrolls puzzled the guard, although Yakov showed him the broken phylactery; and Zhitnyak turned them over to the Deputy Warden, who was greatly excited to have this "new evidence."

A few weeks later, Zhitnyak, while in the cell, sneaked the fixer a small green paper-covered New Testament in Russian. The pages were worn and soiled with use. "It's from my old woman," Zhitnyak whispered. "She said to give it to you so you could repent for the wrong you did. Besides, you're always complaining you have nothing to read. Take it but don't tell anyone who gave it to you or I will break your ass. If they ask you say that one of the prisoners in the kitchen slipped it in your pocket without you knowing it, or maybe one of those who empty the shit cans."

"But why the New Testament, why not the Old?" Yakov said.

"The Old won't do you any good at all," Zhitnyak said. "It's long been used out and full of old graybeard Jews crawling around from one mess to the other. Also there's a lot of fucking ing the Old Testament, so how is that religious? If you want to read the true word of God, read the gospels. My old woman told me to tell you that."

Yakov would at first not open the book, having from childhood feared Jesus Christ, as stranger, apostate, mysterious enemy of the Jews. But with the book there his boredom grew deeper and his curiosity stronger. At last he opened it and began to read. He sat at the table reading through the darkness on the page, though not for long periods because he found it hard to concentrate. Yet the story of Jesus fascinated him and he read it in the four gospels. He was a strange Jew, humorless and fanatic, but the fixer liked the teachings and read with pleasure of the healing of lame, blind, and of the epileptics who fell into fire and water. He enjoyed the loaves and fishes and the raising of the dead. In the end he was deeply moved when he read how they spat on him and beat him with sticks; and how he hung on the cross at night. Jesus cried out help to God but God gave no help. There was a man crying out in anguish in the dark, but God was on the other side of his mountain. He heard but he had heard everything. What was there to hear that he hadn't heard before? Christ died and they took him down. The fixer wiped his eyes. Afterwards he thought if that's how it happened and it's part of the Christian religion, and they believe it, how can they keep me in prison, knowing I am innocent? Why don't they have pity and let me go?

Though his memory gave him trouble he tried to learn by heart some of the verses he liked in the gospels. It was a way to keep his mind occupied and his memory alert. Then he would recite to himself what he had learned. One day he began to say verses aloud through the peephole. Zhitnyak, sitting in his chair in the corridor, hacking at a stick with his knife, heard the fixer recite the Beatitudes, listened to the end, then told him to shut his mouth. When Yakov could not sleep at night; or when he had slept a little and was waked by some dream or noise, he passed part of his waking time reciting in the cell, and Kogin as usual kept his ear to the spy hole, breathing audibly. One night, the guard, lately morose with worry, remarked through the door in his deep voice, "How is it that a Jew who killed a Christian child goes around reciting the words of Christ?"

"I never even touched that boy," said the fixer.

"Everybody says you did. They say you had a secret dispensation from a rabbi to go ahead and do it and your conscience wouldn't hurt you. I've heard it said you were a hardworking man, Yakov Bok, but you still could have committed the crime because in your thinking it was no crime to murder a Christian. All that blood and matzo business is an old part of your religion. I've heard about it ever since I was a small boy."

"In the Old Testament we're not allowed to eat blood. It's forbidden," said Yakov. "But what about these words: 'Truly, truly, I say to you, unless you eat the flesh of the Son of man and drink His blood, you have no life in you; he who eats My flesh and drinks My blood has eternal life, and I will raise him up on the last day. For My flesh is food indeed, and My blood is drink indeed. He who eats My flesh and drinks My blood, abides in Me, and I in him.' "

"Ah, that's a different load of fish altogether," said Kogin. "It means the bread and wine and not the real flesh and blood. Besides, how do you know those words that you just said? When the Devil teaches scripture to a Jew they both get it wrong."

"Blood is blood. I said it the way it was written."

"How do you know it?"

"I read it in the Gospel of John."

"What's a Jew doing reading the gospels?"

"I read them to find out what a Christian is."

"A Christian is a man who loves Christ."

"How can anyone love Christ and keep an innocent man suffering in prison?"

"There is no innocent Christ-killer," Kogin said, shutting the disk over the spy hole.

But the next night as the rain droned steadily in the prison yard and drops of water dripped from the ceiling, the guard came to hear what else Yakov had memorized.

"I haven't been in a church in years," Kogin said. "I'm not much of a body for incense and priests but I like to hear the words of Christ."

" 'Which of you convicts me of sin?' " said Yakov. " 'If I tell the truth, why do you not believe me?' "

"Did he say that?"

"Yes."

"Go on to another one."

" 'But it is easier for heaven and earth to pass away, than for one dot of the law to become void.' "

"When you say the words they sound different than I remember them."

"They're the same words."

"Go on to another one."

" 'Judge not, that you be not judged. For with the judgment you pronounce you will be judged and the measure you give will be the measure you get.' "

"That's enough," said Kogin. "I've had enough."

But the next night he brought a candle stub and match.

"Look, Yakov Bok, I know you're hiding a book of the gospels in your cell. How did you get it?"

Yakov said someone had slipped it into his pocket when he went to get his rations in the kitchen.

"Well, maybe, and maybe not," said Kogin, "but since you have the book in there you might as well read me something. I'm bored to my ass out here all alone night after night. What I really am is a family man."

Yakov lit the candle and read to Kogin through the hole in the door. He read him of the trial and suffering of Christ, as the yellow candle flame dipped and sputtered in the damp cell. When he came to where the soldiers pressed a crown of thorns on Jesus' head, the guard sighed.

Then the fixer spoke in an anxious whisper. "Listen, Kogin, could I ask you for a small favor? It isn't much of one. I would like a piece of paper and a pencil stub to write a few words to an acquaintance of mine. Could you lend them to me?"

"You better go fuck yourself, Bok," said Kogin. "I'm onto your Jew tricks."

He took the candle, blew it out, and did not again come to hear the verses of the gospels.

2

Sometimes he caught the scent of spring through the broken window when a breeze that had passed through the flowering bushes and trees left him with a remembrance of green things growing on earth, and his heart ached beyond belief.

One late afternoon in May, or possibly June, after the fixer had been imprisoned more than year, a priest in gray vestments and a black hat appeared in the dark cell, a pale-faced young man with stringy hair, wet lips, and haunted, dark eyes.

Yakov, thinking himself hallucinated, retreated to the wall.

"Who are you? Where do you come from?"

"Your guard opened the door for me," said the priest, nodding, blinking. He coughed, a complex fit it took him a while to get through. "I've been ill," he said, "and once as I lay in bed in a fever I had an extraordinary vision of a man suffering in this prison. Who can it be? I thought, and at once it came to me, it must be the Jew who was arrested for killing the Christian child. I was covered with perspiration and cried out, 'Heavenly Father, I thank you for this sign, for I understand you wish me to be of service to the imprisoned Jew.' When I had recovered from my illness, I wrote at once to your warden asking him to permit me to see you. At first it seemed impossible, but after I had prayed and fasted, it was finally arranged with the Metropolitan's assistance."

Seeing the ragged, bearded fixer in the gloom, standing with his back to the sweating wall, the priest fell to his knees.

"Dear Lord," he prayed, "forgive this poor Hebrew for his sins, and let him forgive us for sinning against him. 'For if you forgive men their trespasses, your heavenly father also will forgive you; but if you do not forgive men their trespasses, neither will your father forgive your trespasses.' "

"I forgive no one."

Approaching the prisoner on his knees, the priest tried to kiss his hand but the fixer snatched it away and retreated into the shadows of the cell.

Groaning, the priest rose, breathing heavily.

"I beg you to listen to me, Yakov Shepsovitch Bok," he wheezed. "I am told by the guard Zhitnyak that you religiously read the gospels. And the guard Kogin says that you have memorized many passages of the words of the true Christ. This is an excellent sign, for it you embrace Christ, you will have truly repented. He will save you from damnation. And if you are converted to the Orthodox faith, your captors will be compelled to reconsider their accusations and ultimately to release you as one of our brothers. Believe me, there is none so dear in the eyes of God as a Jew who admits he is in error and comes willingly to the true faith. If you agree I will begin to instruct you in the Orthodox dogma. The warden has given his permission. He is a broad-minded man."

The fixer stood mute.

"Are you there?" said the priest, peering into the shadows. "Where are you?" he called, blinking uneasily. He coughed with a heavy rasp.

Yakov stood in the dim light, motionless at the table, the prayer shawl covering his head, the phylactery for the arm bound to his brow.

The priest, coughing thickly, his handkerchief held to his mouth, retreated to the metal door and banged on it with his fist. It was quickly opened and he hurried out.

"You'll get yours," said Zhitnyak to the fixer, from the hall.

Afterwards a lamp was brought into the cell and Yakov was stripped of his clothes and searched for the fourth time that day. The Deputy Warden, in a foul mood, kicked at the mattress and found the New Testament in the straw.

"Where the hell did you get this?"

"Somebody must've slipped it to him in the kitchen," said Zhitnyak.

The Deputy Warden floored the fixer with a blow.

He confiscated the phylacteries and Zhitnyak's New Testament but returned in the morning and flung at Yakov a handful of pages that flew all over the cell. They were pages from the Old Testament in Hebrew, and Yakov collected them and patiently put them together. Half the book was missing and some of the pages were covered with muddy brown stains that looked like dry blood.

3

The birch twig broom came apart. He had used it for months and the twigs had worn out on the stone floor. Some had snapped off in the sweeping and he was given nothing to replace them with. Then the frayed cord that bound the twigs wore away and that was the end of the broom. Zhitnyak would not supply twigs or a new cord. Yakov had asked for them, but he took the broomstick away instead.

"That's so you won't hurt yourself, Bok, or try any more of your dirty tricks on anybody else. Some say you clubbed the poor boy unconscious before you stuck him with your knife."

The fixer talked less with the guards, it was less wearying; they said little to him, once in a while a gruff command, or a curse if he was slow. Without the broom his thin routine began to collapse. He tried to hang on to it but now there was no stove to make or tend, or wait to be lit, and he was no longer permitted to go to the kitchen to get his rations. The food was brought to him in the cell, as it had been before. They said he had stolen things from the kitchen. The New Testament Bible, for instance. And a knife had been "found" during an inspection of his cell. That ended the excursions he had looked forward to, sometimes with excited eagerness, twice a day. "It's only right," said the warden. "We can't have a Jew going around flouting the rules. There have been mutterings among some of the other prisoners." What was left of the routine was to be waked by the prison bell in the morning, to eat meagerly not once but twice a day, and three times each day to be searched to desperation.

He had stopped keeping track of time with the long and short splinters. Beyond a year he couldn't go. Time was summer now, when the hot cell stank heavily and the walls sweated. There were mosquitoes, and bugs hitting the walls. Yet, better summer; he feared another winter. And if there was a spring after the winter it would mean two years in prison. And after that? Time blew like a steppe wind into an empty future. There was no end, no event, indictment, trial. The waiting withered him. He was worn thin by the struggle to wait, by the knowledge of his innocence against the fact of his imprisonment; that nothing had been done in a whole year to free him. He was stricken to be so absolutely alone. Oppressed by the heat, eaten by damp cold, eroded by the expectation of an indictment that never came, were his gray bones visible through his skin? His nerves were threads stretched to the instant before snapping. He cried out of the deepest part of him, a narrow pit, but no one appeared or answered, or looked at him or spoke to him, neither friend nor stranger. Nothing changed but his age. If he were tried, convicted, and sentenced to Siberia, that at least would be something to do. He combed his hair and beard until the teeth of the comb fell out. No one would give him another although he begged, wheedled; so he combed with his fingers. He picked his nose obsessively. His flesh, containing girls who had never become women, tempted him, but that upset his stomach. He tried unsuccessfully to keep himself clean.

Yakov read the Old Testament through the stained and muddied pages, chapter by fragmentary chapter. He read each squat letter with care, although often the words were incomprehensible to him. He had forgotten many he once knew, but in the reading and rereading some came back; some were lost forever. The passages he could not understand and the missing pages of the book did not bother him; he knew the sense of the story. What wasn't there he guessed at, or afterwards recalled. At first he read only for a few minutes at a time. The light was bad. His eyes watered and head swam. Then he read longer and faster, gripped by the narrative of the joyous and frenzied Hebrews, doing business, fighting wars, sinning and worshipping—whatever they were doing always engaged in talk with the huffing-puffing God who tried to sound, maybe out of envy, like a human being.

God talks. He has chosen, he says, the Hebrews to preserve him. He covenants, therefore he is. He offers and Israel accepts, or when will history begin? Abraham, Moses, Noah, Jeremiah, Hosea, Ezra, even Job, make their personal covenant with the talking God. But Israel accepts the covenant in order to break it. That's the mysterious purpose: they need the experience. So they worship false Gods; and this brings Yahweh up out of his golden throne with a flaming sword in both hands. When he talks loud history boils. Assyria, Babylonia, Greece, Rome, become the rod of his anger, the rod that breaks the heads of the Chosen People. Having betrayed the covenant with God they have to pay: war, destruction, death, exile—and they take what goes with it. Suffering, they say, awakens repentance, at least in those who can repent. Thus the people of the covenant wear out their sins against the Lord. He then forgives them and offers a new covenant. Why not? This is his nature, everything must begin again, don't ask

him why. Israel, changed yet unchanged, accepts the new covenant in order to break it by worshipping false gods so that they
will ultimately suffer and repent, which they do endlessly. The
purpose of the covenant, Yakov thinks, is to create human experience, although human experience baffles God. God is after all
God; what he is is what he is: God. What does he know about
such things? Has he ever worshipped God? Has he ever suffered?
How much, after all, has he experienced? God envies the Jews:
it's a rich life. Maybe he would like to be human, it's possible,
nobody knows. That's this God, Yahweh, the one who appears
out of clouds, cyclones, burning bushes; talking. With Spinoza's
God it's different. He is the eternal infinite idea of God as discovered in all of Nature. This one says nothing; either he can't
talk or has no need to. If you're an idea what can you say? One
has to find him in the machinations of his own mind. Spinoza had
reasoned him out but Yakov Bok can't. He is, after all, no
philosopher. So he suffers without either the intellectual idea of
God, or the God of the covenant; he had broken the phylactery.
Nobody suffers for him and he suffers for no one except himself.
The rod of God's anger against the fixer is Nicholas II, the Russian Tsar. He punishes the suffering servant for being godless.
  It's a hard life.
  Zhitnyak watched him as he read. "Rock back and forth like
they do in the synagogue," he said through the spy hole. The
fixer rocked back and forth. The Deputy Warden was called to
see. "What else would you expect?" he said as he spat.
  Sometimes Yakov lost sight of the words. They were black
birds with white wings, white birds with black wings. He was
falling in thoughtless thought, a stupefying whiteness. The fixer
lost track of where he was, a forgetting so profound he ached on
coming out of it. This occurred often now and went on for hours.
Once he fell into this state in the morning, sitting at the table
reading the Old Testament, and came back to the present in the
late afternoon, standing naked in the cell, being searched by the
Deputy Warden and Zhitnyak. And he sometimes walked across

Russia without knowing it. It was hard on the feet and had to be controlled because he wore out the soles of his bast shoes and nobody wanted to give him another pair. He walked in his bare feet over a long rocky road and afterwards found both feet battered and blistered. He awoke to find himself walking and it frightened him when he recalled the pain of the surgeon's scalpel. He willed himself to attention when he began to walk. He took a step or two on the long road and awoke in fright.

Yakov reveried the past; the shtetl, the mistakes and failures of his life. One white-mooned night, after a bitter quarrel about something he couldn't remember now, Raisl had left the hut and run in the dark to her father. The fixer, sitting alone, thinking over his bitterness and the falseness of his accusations, had thought of going after her but had gone to sleep instead. After all, he was dead tired doing nothing. The next year the accusation against her had come true, although it wasn't true then. Who had made it come true? If he had run after her then, would he be sitting here now?

He turned often to pages of Hosea and read with fascination the story of this man God had commanded to marry a harlot. The harlot, he had heard it said, was Israel, but the jealousy and anguish Hosea felt was that of a man whose wife had left his bed and board and gone whoring after strangers.

"And let her put away her harlotries from her face, and her
   adulteries from between her breasts;
Lest I strip her naked,
And set her as in the day that she was born,
And make her as the wilderness,
And set her like dry land,
And slay her with thirst.
And I will not have compassion on her children;
For they are the children of harlotry.
For their mother hath played the harlot,
She that conceived them hath done shamefully;

For she said: 'I will go after my lovers,
That give me bread and my water.
My wool and my flax, mine oil and my drink!'
Therefore, behold, I will hedge up thy way with thorns,
And I will make a wall against her,
That she will not find her paths.
And she shall run after her lovers,
   but she shall not overtake them;
And she shall seek them, but shall not find them;
Then shall she say: 'I will go and return to my first husband:
For then was it better with me than now.' "

4

One morning Zhitnyak brought the prisoner a thick letter in a soiled white envelope with a long row of red stamps. The stamps were portraits of the Tsar in military tunic, wearing a medallion of the royal coat of arms, the double-headed eagle. The letter had been opened by the censor and resealed with a strip of gummed paper. It was addressed to "The Murderer of Zhenia Golov" and sent in care of the Prosecuting Attorney of the Superior Court, Plossky District, Kiev.

Yakov's heart palpitated when he took the letter. "Who is it from?"

"The Queen of Sheba," said the guard. "Open and see."

The fixer waited until the guard had gone. He put the letter down on the table to get it out of his hand. He stared at it for five minutes. Could it be the indictment? Would they address it like that? Yakov clumsily ripped open the envelope, tearing it across, and found in it a sixteen-page letter written in Russian in a woman's spidery handwriting. There were blots of ink on every page, many words misspelled, and some heavily crossed out and rewritten.

"Sir," it began, "I am the bereaved and unfortunate mother of the martyred Zhenia Golov, and I take my pen in my hand to beg you to do the right and decent thing. In God's name give an ear to a mother's pleas. I am worn out by the wicked insults and insinuations that have been wrongfully cast on myself by certain worthless people—including certain neighbors I have now cut myself off from, without any proof whatsoever. *On the contrary* with all the proof directed against you, and I beg you to clear the air up by a complete and candid confession. Although I admit your face, when I saw it in my household, didn't look too Jewish, and maybe you really wouldn't commit such a dreadful crime murdering a child and taking out his precious lifeblood if you hadn't been egged on to do it by fanatical Jews—you know the kind I mean. Still you probably did it because they threatened you with death, although maybe you didn't want to, I don't know. But now I know for a certainty that it was these old Jews with long black coats and nasty beards that warned you you had to make the kill and they would hide my child's corpse in the cave when you did. Just the same night before Zheniushka disappeared I dreamed of one of them carrying a satchel, with wild glaring eyes and bright red spots in his beard, and my former neighbor Sofya Shiskovsky told me she had dreamed the same dream that I had on the same night.

"I am asking you to own up because the evidence is all against you. One thing you might not know is that after Zheniushka confided to me you had chased him with a knife in the cemetery, I had you followed by a gentleman friend of mine to find out what other criminal activities you were engaged in. It is a known fact that you were involved in certain illegal acts in secretly dealing with other Jews in the brickyard who pretended they were not Jews, and also in the cellar of the synagogue, where you all met in the Podol District. You smuggled, robbed, and traded in goods that didn't belong to you. Zheniushka found out all about this and other of your illegalities, and that's another reason why you bore him such a violent hatred, and why you had him in your mind as the victim as soon as you were chosen to find one and drain his blood for the Jewish Easter. You also acted as a

fence for this gang of Jews who broke into the homes of the
Gentry as well as in certain commercial stores, and houses in the
Lipki District, where the aristocratic houses are, and took out
all sorts of loot in money, furs and jewels, not to mention other
precious objects of different kinds. Also you paid your gang only
a part of the real price the goods were worth because as the saying is, each Jew cheats the other. Which is nothing new to anybody because the whole world knows they are born criminals. A
Jew wanted to lend a friend of mine money to build a house, but
she went to the priest for advice and he began to tremble and
advised her to take nothing from a cursed Jew, in Christ's name,
because they will defraud and cheat you because it is their nature
and they can't do otherwise. This priest said their Jewish blood
itches when they aren't engaged in evil. If it weren't for that
maybe you would have resisted the murder of a saintly boy when
they egged you to do it. And I suppose you know there have
been attempts to bribe me not to testify against you when your
trial comes. One fat Jew in silk clothes offered me the sum of
40,000 rubles to leave Russia and he would pay me the sum of
another 10,000 rubles, on arriving in Austria, but even if he and
your fellow Jews had offered me 400,000 rubles, I would still spit
in their faces and say *absolutely no* because I prefer the honor
of my good name to 400,000 rubles of Jewish blood money.

"My gentleman friend also saw you spit on the ground one day
when you walked around on the outside of St. Sophia's Cathedral
after spying out the school in the courtyard where Zhenia went.
He saw you turn your head as though you might go blind if you
didn't, when you looked up on the golden crosses on top of the
green domes, and you spat fast so no one should see you, but my
friend saw you. I was also told you practice black magic religious
ceremonies and certain cabalistic superstitions.

"Also, don't think I don't know the sordid part of the story.
Zhenia told me about the times you enticed him to come to your
room in the stable and there with the promise of bonbons and
sweets you got him to open the buttons of his pants and with your

hand caused him intense excitement. There were other lewd
things you performed which I can't even write because I get
very faint. He told me that after you did those awful things you
were afraid he would tell me and I would denounce you to the
police, so you used to give him ten kopeks not to say anything to
anybody. He never did at the time this all happened, although
once he told me about what went on up there, because he was
worried and frightened, but I haven't breathed a word of it to
anyone, not even to my closest neighbors because I was ashamed
to say anything, and also because your crime of murder is enough
to answer for, and you will probably suffer the tortures of the
cursed for that alone. Yet I will honestly and frankly tell you that
if people go on making suspicious and vile remarks about me
behind my back, I will tell all the facts of the case whether I
blush or not to the Prosecuting Attorney who is first of all a
gentleman. I will also tell everybody the sordid things you did
to my child.

"I will petition the Tsar to defend my good name. Besides losing my child I have led an irreproachable life of toil. I have been
an honest person and a pure woman. I have been the best of
mothers even though I was a working woman with no time to
herself and two people to support. Those who say I didn't weep
for my poor boy at his funeral are saying a filthy lie and I will
some day sue someone for libel and character assassination. I
looked after my Zhenia as though he were a prince. I attended
to his clothes and all of his other needs. I cooked special dishes
that he liked most of all, all sorts of pastries and expensive treats.
I was a mother and also a father to him since his own weakling
of a father deserted me. I helped him with his lessons where I
could and encouraged him and said yes when he wanted to be
a priest. He was already in a preparatory church school to prepare for the priesthood when he was murdered. He felt to me the
way I felt to him—he loved me passionately. Rest assured of that.
Mamashka, he said, I only love you. Please, Zheniushka, I begged
him, stay away from those evil Jews. To my sorrow he did not

follow his mother's advice. You are my son's murderer. I urge you as the martyred mother of a martyred child to confess *the whole truth* at once and clear the evil out of the air so that we can breathe again. If you do, at least you won't have to suffer so much in the afterworld.

                                   "Marfa Vladimirovna Golov"

The excitement of receiving the letter had increased in the reading and Yakov's head throbbed at the questions that ran through his mind. Was the trial she had mentioned already on its way or only assumed to be by her? Probably assumed, yet how could he be sure? Anyway the indictment would still have to come, and where was the indictment? What had caused her to write the letter? What were the "wicked insults and insinuations," and the "suspicious and vile remarks" she referred to? And who was making them? Could it be she was being investigated, yet by whom if not Bibikov? Certainly not Grubeshov, yet why had he let the letter, mad as it was, go through to him? Had she written it with his help? Was it to demonstrate the quality of the witness, to show Yakov what he was up against and thus again to warn or threaten him? To say we assure you she will say these things and more you can never guess, and she will convince a jury of people like her, so why not confess now? They were multiplying the accusations and disgusting motives, and would not rest until they had trapped him like a fly in a gluepot; therefore he had better confess before other means of escape were impossible.

Whatever her reason for sending it the letter seemed close to a confession by her, maybe a sign something else was going on. Would he ever know what? The fixer felt his heartbeat in his ears. He looked around for a place to hide the letter, hoping to pass it on to the lawyer, if he ever had one. But the next morning after he had finished eating, the letter was missing from his coat pocket and he suspected he had been doped, or they had got it some other way, possibly while he was being searched. Anyway the letter was gone.

"Can't I send her an answer?" he asked the Deputy Warden

before the next search, and the Deputy Warden said he could if he was willing to admit the wrongs he had done.

That night the fixer saw Marfa, a tallish, scrawny-necked woman with a figure something like Raisl's, enter the cell and without so much as a word begin to undress—the white hat with cherries, the red rose scarf, green skirt, flowery blouse, cotton petticoat, pointed button shoes, red garters, black stockings and soiled frilly drawers. Lying naked on the fixer's mattress, her legs spread apart, she promised many goyish delights if he would confess to the priest at the peephole.

5

One night he awoke hearing someone singing in the cell and when he listened with his whole being the song was in a boy's high sweet voice. Yakov got up to see where the singing was coming from. The child's pale, shrunken, bony face, corroded copper and black, shone from a pit in the corner of the cell. He was dead yet sang how he had been murdered by a black-bearded Jew. He had gone on an errand for his mother and was on his way home through the Jewish section when this hairy, bent-back rabbi caught up with him and offered him a lozenge. The instant the boy put the candy into his mouth he fell to the ground. The Jew lifted him onto his shoulder and hurried to the brickworks. There the boy was laid on the stable floor, tied up, and stabbed until the blood spouted from the orifices of his body. Yakov listened to the end of the song and cried, "Again! Sing it again!" Again he heard the same sweet song the dead child was singing in his grave.

Afterwards the boy, appearing to him naked, his stigmata brightly bleeding, begged, "Please give me back my clothes."

They're trying to unhinge me, the fixer thought, and then they'll say I went mad because I committed the crime. He feared what he might confess if he went crazy; his suffering to defend his innocence would come to nothing as he babbled his guilt and the blood guilt of those who had put him up to it. He strove with himself, struggled, shouted at him to hold tight to sanity, to keep in the dark unsettled center of the mind a candle burning.

A bloody horse with frantic eyes appeared: Shmuel's nag.

"Murderer!" the horse neighed. "Horsekiller! Childkiller! You deserve what you get!"

He beat the nag's head with a log.

Yakov slept often during the day but badly. Sleep left him limp, depressed. He was being watched by many eyes through the spy hole for the minute he went mad. The air throbbed with voices from afar. There was a plot afoot so save him. He had visions of being rescued by the International Jewish Army. They were laying siege to the outer walls. Among the familiar faces, he recognized Berele Margolis, Leib Rosenbach, Dudye Bont, Itzik Shulman, Kalman Kohler, Shloime Pincus, Yose-Moishe Magadov, Pinye Apfelbaum, and Benya Merpetz, all from the orphans' home, although it seemed to him they were long since gone, some dead, some fled—he should have gone with them.

"Wait," he shouted. "Wait."

Then the streets around the prison were noisy, the crowds roaring, chanting, wailing; animals mooing, clucking, grunting. Everyone ran in several directions, feathers floating in the air, *gevalt* they were killing the Jews! A horde of thick-booted, baggy-trousered, sword-swinging Cossacks were galloping in on small ferocious ponies. In the yard the double-eagle banners were unfurled and fluttered in the wind. Nicholas the Second drove in in a coach drawn by six white horses, saluting from both sides the hundreds of Black Hundreds aching to get at the prisoner and hammer nails into his head. Yakov hid in his cell with chest pains and heartburn. The guards were planning to murder him with rat poison. He planned to murder them first. A Zhid shits on Zhitnyak. Kog on Kogin. He barricaded the door with the table and stool, then smashed them against the wall. While they were battering the door down to get at him he sat cross-legged on the floor, mixing blood with unleavened flour. He kicked savagely at the guards lugged him through the corridcr, raining blows on his head.

The fixer crouched in a dark place trying to hold his mind together with a piece of string so he wouldn't confess. But it exploded into a fountain of rotting fruit, one-eyed herrings, birds of Paradise. It exploded into a million stinking words but when he confessed he confessed in Yiddish so the goyim couldn't understand. In Hebrew he recited the Psalms. In Russian he was silent. He slept in fear and waked in fright. In dreams he heard the voices of screaming children. Dressed in a long caftan and round fur hat he hid behind trees, and when a Christian child approached, compulsively chased him. One small-faced boy, a consumptive type, ran from him frantically, his eyes rolling in fright.

"Stop, I love you," the fixer called to him, but the child never looked back.

"Once is enough, Yakov Bok."

Nicholas II appeared, in the white uniform of an admiral of the Russian Navy.

"Little Father," said the fixer on both knees, "you'll never meet a more patriotic Jew. Tears fill my eyes when I see the flag. Also I'm not interested in politics, I want to make a living. Those accusations are all wrong or you've got the wrong man. Live and let live, if you don't mind me saying so. It's a short life when you think of it."

"My dear fellow," said the blue-eyed, pale-faced Tsar in a gentle voice, "don't envy me my throne. Uneasy lies the et cetera. The Zhidy would do well to understand and stop complaining in a whining tongue. The simple fact is there are too many Jews —my how you procreate! Why should Russia be burdened with teeming millions of you? You yourselves are to blame for your troubles, and the pogroms of 1905-6 *outside* the Pale of Settlement, mind you, were proof positive, if proof is needed, that you aren't staying where you were put. The ingestion of this tribe has poisoned Russia. Who ever wanted it? Our revered ancestor Peter the Great, when asked to admit them into Russia, said,

'They are rogues and cheats. I am trying to eradicate evil, not increase it.' Our revered ancestor, the Tsarina Elizabeth Petrovna, said, 'From the enemies of Christ I wish neither gain nor profit.' Hordes of Jews were expelled from one or another part of the Motherland in 1727, 1739, 1742, but still they crawled back and we have been unable to delouse ourselves of them. The worst of it happened, our greatest error, when Catherine the Great took over half of Poland and inherited the whole filthy lot, a million poisoners of wells, spies against us all, cowardly traitors. I always said it was the Poles' plot to ruin Russia."

"Have mercy on me, your Majesty. So far as I'm concerned, I am an innocent man. What have I seen of the world? Please have mercy."

"The Tsar's heart is in God's hands." He stepped into his white sailboat and sailed away on the Black Sea.

Nikolai Maximovitch had lost weight, the girl limped badly and would not look at the fixer. Proshko, Serdiuk and Richter came in on three skittish horses whose droppings were full of oats he longed to get at. Father Anastasy sought to convert him to Roman Catholicism. Marfa Golov, wept dry-eyed and haggard, offered him a bribe to testify against himself; and the Deputy Warden, in the uniform of a naval officer, for personal reasons insisted on continuing the searches. The guards promised the fixer anything if he would open up and name names, and Yakov said he might for a heated cell in wintertime, a daily bowl of noodles and cheese, and a firm clean hair mattress.

Shots were fired.

He passed through time he had no memory of and one day awoke to find himself in the same cell, not a new one with six doors and windows he had dreamed of. It was still hot but he couldn't be sure it was the same summer. The cell seemed the same, possibly a bit smaller, with the same scabby sweating walls. The same wet stone floor. The same stinking straw mattress; its smell had never killed the bugs. The table and three-legged stool were gone. Scattered over the wet floor were pages of the Old

Testament, stained and muddied. He could not find the phylacteries but still wore the ragged prayer shawl. And the last firewood had been removed and the cell hosed down as though to make it fit for him to stay forever.

"How long was I gone?" he asked Zhitnyak.

"You weren't gone. Who says you were gone?"

"Was I sick then?"

"They say you ran a fever."

"What did I say when I ranted and raved?" he asked uneasily.

"Who the hell knows," said the guard impatiently. "I have my own troubles. Try and live on the lousy wages they pay you here. The Deputy Warden listened to you twice a day but couldn't make out heads or tails. He says you have a filthy mind but nobody expected otherwise."

"Am I better now?"

"That's up to you, but if you break another piece of furniture, we'll smash your head."

Though his legs trembled, he stood at the peephole, looking out. Moving the disk aside with his fingers, he stared out into the corridor. A yellow bulb lit the windowless wall. The cells on both sides of him, he remembered, were empty. He had more than once hit a log against the walls but there was never any response. Once an official passing by in the corridor saw his eye staring out and ordered him to shut the hole and move away from the door. After the man had gone Yakov looked out again. All he could see on the left was the chair the guards sat on, Zhitnyak whittling a stick, Kogin sighing, worrying. The other way a dusty bulb lit up a broken barrel against the wall. The fixer stood for hours staring into the corridor. When Zhitnyak came over to look in, he saw the fixer's eyes staring out.

6

One midsummer night, long past midnight, Yakov, too long imprisoned to sleep, was staring out the peephole when his eye throbbed as if it had been touched, and slowly filled with the pained sight of Shmuel.

The fixer cursed himself, withdrew his eye, and tried the other. Whether vision or visitor it looked like Shmuel, though older, shrunken, grayer, a scarecrow with a frightened beard.

The prisoner, in disbelief, heard a whisper. "Yakov, it's you? Here is Shmuel, your father-in-law."

First the Tsar and now Shmuel. Either I'm still crazy or it's another mad dream. Next comes the Prophet Elijah or Jesus Christ.

But the figure of the fragile old man in shirt-sleeves and a hard hat, standing in the yellow light, his fringed garment hanging out under his shirt, persisted.

"Shmuel, don't lie, is it really you?"

"Who else?" said the peddler hoarsely.

"God forbid you're not a prisoner, are you?" the fixer asked in anguish.

"God forbid. I came to see you though I almost didn't. It's erev shabbos but God will forgive me."

Yakov wiped his eyes. "I've dreamed of everybody so why not you? But how did you get in? How did you come here?"

The old man shrugged his thin shoulders.

"We came in circles. I did what they told me. Yakov, for more than a year I tried to find you but nobody knew where. I thought to myself he's gone for good, I'll never see him again. Then one day I bought for a few kopeks a hill of rotting sugar beets from a sick Russian. Don't ask me why but for the first time in my life what I bought for rotten was not all rotten. More than half the beets turned out good, God's gift to a poor man. The sugar company sent some wagons and took them away. Anyway, I sold the beets for forty rubles, my biggest profit since I'm in business. Also I met Fyodor Zhitnyak, the brother of the one here—he peddles in the Kiev market. We got to talking and he knew your name. He told me that for forty rubles he could arrange it so I could speak to you. He spoke to the brother and the brother said yes if I came late at night and wasn't too ambitious. Who's ambitious, so here I am. For forty rubles they will let me stand here just ten minutes, so we must talk fast. Time I've had like dirt my whole life but now it's worth money. Zhitnyak, the brother who's the guard here, changed shifts with another one who took the night off because his son got arrested. That's how it goes, I wish him luck. Anyway, Zhitnyak will wait for ten minutes down the hall by the outside door but he warned me if somebody comes he might have to shoot. He might as well, if they see me I'm lost."

"Shmuel, before I faint from excitement, how did you know I was in prison?"

Shmuel moved his feet restlessly. It wasn't a dance though it looked like one.

"How I know, he asks. I knew because I knew. I know. When it came out in the Yiddish papers last year that a Jew was arrested in Kiev for murdering a Christian child, I thought to myself who can this poor Jew be, it must be my son-in-law Yakov. Then after a year I saw your name in the newspaper. A counterfeiter by the name of Gronfein got sick from his nerves and went around saying that Yakov Bok was in the Kiev prison for killing a Russian child. He saw him there. I tried to find this man but he disappeared and those who are hopeful hope he's alive. Maybe he went to America, that's what they hope. Yakov, maybe you don't know, it's a terrible tumult now all over Russia, and to tell you the truth, the Jews are frightened to death. Only a few know who you are, and some say it's a fake, there's nobody by that name, the goyim made it up to cast suspicion on the Jews. In the shtetl those who never liked you say it serves you right. Some have pity and would like to help you but we can't do a thing till they give you an indictment. When I saw your name in the Jewish paper I wrote you right away a letter and they sent it back—'No such prisoner.' I also sent you a little package, not much in it, just a few little things, but did you ever get it?"

"Poison I got but no package."

"I tried to get in here to see you and nobody would let me till I made my profit on the sugar beets and I met the brother Zhitnyak."

"Shmuel, I'm sorry for your forty rubles. It's a lot of money and what are you getting for it?"

"Money is nothing. I came to see you, but if it paves my way a foot into Paradise it's a fine investment."

"Run, Shmuel," the fixer said, agitated, "get out while you can or they'll shoot you in cold blood and call it a Jewish conspiracy. If that happens I'm doomed forever."

"I'm running," said Shmuel, cracking his knuckles against his bony chest, "but tell me first why they blame you for this terrible crime?"

"Why they blame me? Because I was a stupid ass. I worked for a Russian factory owner in a forbidden district. Also I lived there without telling him my papers were Jewish."

"You see, Yakov, what happens when you shave your beard and forget your God?"

"Don't talk to me about God," Yakov said bitterly. "I want no part of God. When you need him most he's farthest away. Enough is enough. My past I don't have to tell you, but if you knew what I've lived through since I saw you last." He began to say but his voice cracked.

"Yakov," said Shmuel, clasping and unclasping his excitable hands, "we're not Jews for nothing. Without God we can't live. Without the covenant we would have disappeared out of history. Let that be a lesson to you. He's all we have but who wants more?"

"Me. I'll take misery but not forever."

"For misery don't blame God. He gives the food but we cook it."

"I blame him for not existing. Or if he does it's on the moon or stars but not here. The thing is not to believe or the waiting becomes unbearable. I can't hear his voice and never have. I don't need him unless he appears."

"Who are you, Yakov, Moses himself? If you don't hear His voice so let Him hear yours. 'When prayers go up blessings descend.' "

"Scorpions descend, hail, fire, sharp rocks, excrement. For that I don't need God's help, the Russians are enough. All right, once I used to talk to him and answer myself, but what good does it do if I know so little in the first place? I used to mention once in a while the conditions of my life, my struggles, misfortunes, mistakes. On rare occasions I gave him a little good news, but whatever I said he never answered me. Silence I now give back."

"A proud man is dead and blind. How can he hear God? How can he see Him?"

"Who's proud if I ever was? What have I got to be proud of? That I was born without parents? I never made a decent living? My barren wife ran off with a goy? When a boy was murdered in Kiev, out of three million Jews in Russia they arrested me? So I'm not proud. If God exists I'll gladly listen to him. If he doesn't feel like talking let him open the door so I can walk out. I have nothing. From nothing you get nothing. If he wants from me he has to give first. If not a favor at least a sign."

"Don't ask for signs, ask for mercy."

"I've asked for everything and got nothing." The fixer, after a sigh, spoke close to the peephole. " 'In the beginning was the word,' but it wasn't his. That's the way I look at it now. Nature invented itself and also man. Whatever was there was there to begin with. Spinoza said so. It sounds fantastic but it must be true. When it comes down to basic facts, either God is our invention and can't do anything about it, or he's a force in Nature but not in history. A force is not a father. He's a cold wind and try and keep warm. To tell the truth, I've written him off as a dead loss."

"Yakov," said Shmuel, squeezing both hands, "don't talk so fast. Don't look for God in the wrong place, look in the Torah, the law. That's where to look, not in bad books that poison your thoughts."

"As for the law it was invented by man, is far from perfect, and what good is it to me if the Tsar has no use for it? If God can't give me simple respect I'll settle for justice. Uphold the Law! Destroy the Tsar with a thunderbolt! Free me from prison!"

"God's justice is for the end of time."

"I'm not so young any more, I can't wait that long. Neither can the Jews running from pogroms. We're dealing nowadays with the slaughter of large numbers and it's getting worse. God counts in astronomy but where men are concerned all I know is one plus one. Shmuel, let's drop this useless subject. What's the sense of arguing through a little hole where you can barely see part of my face in the dark? Besides, it's a short visit and we're eating up time."

"Yakov," said Shmuel, "He invented light. He created the world. He made us both. The true miracle is belief. I believe in Him. Job said, 'Though he slay me, yet will I trust in Him.' He said more but that's enough."

"To win a lousy bet with the devil he killed off all the servants and innocent children of Job. For that alone I hate him, not to mention ten thousand pogroms. Ach, why do you make me talk fairy tales? Job is an invention and so is God. Let's let it go at that." He stared at the peddler with one eye. "I'm sorry I'm making you feel bad on your expensive time, Shmuel, but take my word for it, it's not easy to be a freethinker in this terrible cell. I say this without pride or joy. Still, whatever reason a man has, he's got to depend on."

"Yakov," said Shmuel, mopping his face with his blue handkerchief, "do me a favor, don't close your heart. Nobody is lost to God if his heart is open."

"What's left of my heart is pure rock."

"Also don't forget repentance," said Shmuel. "This comes first."

Zhitnyak appeared in a great hurry. "That's enough now, it's time to go. Ten minutes is up but you talked longer."

"It felt like two," Shmuel said. "I was just about to say what's on my heart."

"Run, Shmuel," Yakov urged, his mouth pressed to the peep-hole. "Do whatever you can to help me. Run to the newspapers and tell them the police have imprisoned an innocent man. Run to the rich Jews, to Rothschild if necessary. Ask for help, money, mercy, a good lawyer to defend me. Get me out of here before they lay me in my grave."

Shmuel pulled a cucumber out of his pants pocket. "Here's a little pickle I brought you." He attempted to thrust it through the spy hole but Zhitnyak grabbed it.

"None of that," the guard loudly whispered. "Don't try any Jew tricks on me. Also you shut up," he said to Yakov. "You've had your say and that's enough now."

He grabbed Shmuel by the arm. "Hurry up, it's getting to-wards morning."

"Goodbye, Yakov, remember what I told you."

"Raisl," Yakov called after him. "I forgot to ask. Whatever happened to her?"

"I'm running," said Shmuel, holding on to his hat.

Part Four

Stories

The Mourners

Kessler, formerly an egg candler, lived alone on social security. Though past sixty-five, he might have found well-paying work with more than one butter and egg wholesaler, for he sorted and graded with speed and accuracy, but he was a quarrelsome type and considered a trouble maker, so the wholesalers did without him. Therefore, after a time he retired, living with few wants on his old-age pension. Kessler inhabited a small cheap flat on the top floor of a decrepit tenement on the East Side. Perhaps because he lived above so many stairs, no one bothered to visit him. He was much alone, as he had been most of his life. At one time he'd had a family, but unable to stand his wife or children, always in his way, he had after some years walked out on them. He never saw them thereafter, because he never sought them, and they did not seek him. Thirty years had passed. He had no idea where they were, nor did he think much about it.

In the tenement, although he had lived there ten years, he was more or less unknown. The tenants on both sides of his flat on the fifth floor, an Italian family of three middle-aged sons and their wizened mother, and a sullen, childless German couple named Hoffman, never said hello to him, nor did he greet any of them on the way up or down the narrow wooden stairs. Others of the house recognized Kessler when they passed him in the street, but they thought he lived elsewhere on the block. Ignace, the small, bent-back janitor, knew him best, for they had several times played two-handed pinochle; but Ignace, usually the loser because he lacked skill at cards, had stopped going up after a time. He complained to his wife that he couldn't stand the stink there, that the filthy flat with its junky furniture made him sick. The janitor had spread the word about Kessler to the others on the floor, and they shunned him as a dirty old man. Kessler understood this but had contempt for them all.

One day Ignace and Kessler began a quarrel over the way the egg candler piled oily bags overflowing with garbage into the dumb-waiter, instead of using a pail. One word shot off another, and they were soon calling each other savage names, when Kessler slammed the door in the janitor's face. Ignace ran down five flights of stairs and loudly cursed out the old man to his impassive wife. It happened that Gruber, the landlord, a fat man with a consistently worried face, who wore yards of baggy clothes, was in the building, making a check of plumbing repairs, and to him the enraged Ignace related the trouble he was having with Kessler. He described, holding his nose, the smell in Kessler's flat, and called him the dirtiest person he had ever seen. Gruber knew his janitor was exaggerating, but he felt burdened by financial worries which shot his blood pressure up to astonishing heights, so he settled it quickly by saying, "Give him notice." None of the tenants in the house had held a written lease since the war, and Gruber felt confident, in case somebody asked questions, that he could easily justify his dismissal of Kessler as an undesirable tenant. It had occurred to him that Ignace could then slap a cheap coat of paint on the walls and the flat would be let to someone for five dollars more than the old man was paying.

That night after supper, Ignace victoriously ascended the stairs and knocked on Kessler's door. The egg candler opened it, and seeing who stood there, immediately slammed it shut. Ignace shouted through the door, "Mr. Gruber says to give notice. We don't want you around here. Your dirt stinks the whole house." There was silence, but Ignace waited, relishing what he had said. Although after five minutes he still heard no sound, the janitor stayed there, picturing the old Jew trembling behind the locked door. He spoke again, "You got two weeks' notice till the first, then you better move out or Mr. Gruber and myself will throw you out." Ignace watched as the door slowly opened. To his surprise he found himself frightened at the old man's appearance. He looked, in the act of opening the door, like a corpse adjusting his coffin lid. But if he appeared dead, his voice was alive. It rose terrifyingly harsh from his throat, and he sprayed curses over all the years of Ignace's life. His eyes were reddened, his cheeks sunken, and his wisp of beard moved agitatedly. He seemed to be losing weight as he shouted. The janitor no longer had any heart for the matter, but he could not bear so many insults all at once so he cried out, "You dirty old bum, you better get out and don't make so much trouble." To this the enraged Kessler swore they would first have to kill him and drag him out dead.

On the morning of the first of December, Ignace found in his letter box a soiled folded paper containing Kessler's twenty-five dollars. He showed it to Gruber that evening when the landlord came to collect the rent money. Gruber, after a minute of absently contemplating the money, frowned disgustedly.

"I thought I told you to give notice."

"Yes, Mr. Gruber," Ignace agreed. "I gave him."

"That's a helluva chuzpah," said Gruber. "Gimme the keys."

Ignace brought the ring of pass keys, and Gruber, breathing heavily, began the lumbering climb up the long avenue of stairs. Although he rested on each landing, the fatigue of climbing, and his profuse flowing perspiration, heightened his irritation.

Arriving at the top floor he banged his fist on Kessler's door. "Gruber, the landlord. Open up here."

There was no answer, no movement within, so Gruber inserted the key into the lock and twisted. Kessler had barricaded the door with a chest and some chairs. Gruber had to put his shoulder to the door and shove before he could step into the hallway of the badly-lit two-and-a-half-room flat. The old man, his face drained of blood, was standing in the kitchen doorway.

"I warned you to scram outa here," Gruber said loudly. "Move out or I'll telephone the city marshal."

"Mr. Gruber—" began Kessler.

"Don't bother me with your lousy excuses, just beat it." He gazed around. "It looks like a junk shop and it smells like a toilet. It'll take me a month to clean up here."

"This smell is only cabbage that I am cooking for my supper. Wait, I'll open a window and it will go away."

"When you go away, it'll go away." Gruber took out his bulky wallet, counted out twelve dollars, added fifty cents, and plunked the money on top of the chest. "You got two more weeks till the fifteenth, then you gotta be out or I will get a dispossess. Don't talk back talk. Get outa here and go somewhere that they don't know you and maybe you'll get a place."

"No, Mr. Gruber," Kessler cried passionately. "I didn't do nothing, and I will stay here."

"Don't monkey with my blood pressure," said Gruber. "If you're not out by the fifteenth, I will personally throw you on your bony ass."

Then he left and walked heavily down the stairs.

The fifteenth came and Ignace found the twelve fifty in his letter box. He telephoned Gruber and told him.

"I'll get a dispossess," Gruber shouted. He instructed the janitor to write out a note saying to Kessler that his money was refused and to stick it under his door. This Ignace did. Kessler returned the money to the letter box, but again Ignace wrote a note and slipped it, with the money, under the old man's door.

After another day Kessler received a copy of his eviction notice. It said to appear in court on Friday at 10 A.M. to show cause why he should not be evicted for continued neglect and destruction of rental property. The official notice filled Kessler with great fright because he had never in his life been to court. He did not appear on the day he had been ordered to.

That same afternoon the marshal appeared with two brawny assistants. Ignace opened Kessler's lock for them and as they pushed their way into the flat, the janitor hastily ran down the stairs to hide in the cellar. Despite Kessler's wailing and carrying on, the two assistants methodically removed his meager furniture and set it out on the sidewalk. After that they got Kessler out, though they had to break open the bathroom door because the old man had locked himself in there. He shouted, struggled, pleaded with his neighbors to help him, but they looked on in a silent group outside the door. The two assistants, holding the old man tightly by the arms and skinny legs, carried him, kicking and moaning, down the stairs. They sat him in the street on a chair amid his junk. Upstairs, the marshal bolted the door with a lock Ignace had supplied, signed a paper which he handed to the janitor's wife, and then drove off in an automobile with his assistants.

Kessler sat on a split chair on the sidewalk. It was raining and the rain soon turned to sleet, but he still sat there. People passing by skirted the pile of his belongings. They stared at Kessler and he stared at nothing. He wore no hat or coat, and the snow fell on him, making him look like a piece of his dispossessed goods. Soon the wizened Italian woman from the top floor returned to the house with two of her sons, each carrying a loaded shopping bag. When she recognized Kessler sitting amid his furniture, she began to shriek. She shrieked in Italian at Kessler although he paid no attention to her. She stood on the stoop, shrunken, gesticulating with thin arms, her loose mouth working angrily. Her sons tried to calm her, but still she shrieked. Several of the neighbors came down to see who was making the racket. Finally, the two sons, unable to think what else to do, set down their shopping bags, lifted Kessler out of the chair, and carried him up the stairs. Hoffman, Kessler's other neighbor, working with a small triangular file, cut open the padlock, and Kessler was carried into the flat from which he had been evicted. Ignace screeched at everybody, calling them filthy names, but the three men went downstairs and hauled up Kessler's chairs, his broken table, chest, and ancient metal bed. They piled all the furniture into the bedroom. Kessler sat on the edge of the bed and wept. After a while, after the old Italian woman had sent in a soup plate full of hot macaroni seasoned with tomato sauce and grated cheese, they left.

Ignace phoned Gruber. The landlord was eating and the food

turned to lumps in his throat. "I'll throw them all out, the bastards," he yelled. He put on his hat, got into his car and drove through the slush to the tenement. All the time he was thinking of his worries: high repair costs; it was hard to keep the place together; maybe the building would someday collapse. He had read of such things. All of a sudden the front of the building parted from the rest and fell like a breaking wave into the street. Gruber cursed the old man for taking him from his supper. When he got to the house he snatched Ignace's keys and ascended the sagging stairs. Ignace tried to follow, but Gruber told him to stay the hell in his hole. When the landlord was not looking, Ignace crept up after him.

Gruber turned the key and let himself into Kessler's dark flat. He pulled the light chain and found the old man sitting limply on the side of the bed. On the floor at his feet lay a plate of stiffened macaroni.

"What do you think you're doing here?" Gruber thundered. The old man sat motionless.

"Don't you know it's against the law? This is trespassing and you're breaking the law. Answer me."

Kessler remained mute.

Gruber mopped his brow with a large yellowed handkerchief.

"Listen, my friend, you're gonna make lots of trouble for yourself. If they catch you in here you might go to the workhouse. I'm only trying to advise you."

To his surprise Kessler looked at him with wet, brimming eyes.

"What did I did to you?" he bitterly wept. "Who throws out of his house a man that he lived there ten years and pays every month on time his rent? What did I do, tell me? Who hurts a man without a reason? Are you a Hitler or a Jew?" He was hitting his chest with his fist.

Gruber removed his hat. He listened carefully, at first at a loss what to say, but then answered: "Listen, Kessler, it's not personal. I own this house and it's falling apart. My bills are sky high. If the tenants don't take care they have to go. You don't take care and you fight with my janitor, so you have to go. Leave in the morning, and I won't say another word. But if you don't leave the flat, you'll get the heave-ho again. I'll call the marshal."

"Mr. Gruber," said Kessler, "I won't go. Kill me if you want it, but I won't go."

Ignace hurried away from the door as Gruber left in anger. The next morning, after a restless night of worries, the landlord set out to drive to the city marshal's office. On the way he stopped at a candy store for a pack of cigarettes, and there decided once more to speak to Kessler. A thought had occurred to him: he would offer to get the old man into a public home.

He drove to the tenement and knocked on Ignace's door.

"Is the old gink still up there?"

"I don't know if so, Mr. Gruber." The janitor was ill at ease.

"What do you mean you don't know?"

"I didn't see him go out. Before, I looked in his keyhole but nothing moves."

"So why didn't you open the door with your key?"

"I was afraid," Ignace answered nervously.

"What are you afraid?"

Ignace wouldn't say.

A fright went through Gruber but he didn't show it. He grabbed the keys and walked ponderously up the stairs, hurrying every so often.

No one answered his knock. As he unlocked the door he broke into heavy sweat.

But the old man was there, alive, sitting without shoes on the bedroom floor.

"Listen, Kessler," said the landlord, relieved although his head pounded. "I got an idea that, if you do it the way I say, your troubles are over."

He explained his proposal to Kessler, but the egg candler was not listening. His eyes were downcast, and his body swayed slowly sideways. As the landlord talked on, the old man was thinking of what had whirled through his mind as he had sat out on the sidewalk in the falling snow. He had thought through his miserable life, remembering how, as a young man, he had abandoned his family, walking out on his wife and three innocent children, without even in some way attempting to provide for them; without, in all the intervening years—so God help him—once trying to discover if they were alive or dead. How, in so short a life, could a man do so much wrong? This thought smote him to the heart and he recalled the past without end and moaned and tore at his flesh with his fingernails.

Gruber was frightened at the extent of Kessler's suffering. Maybe I should let him stay, he thought. Then as he watched the old man, he realized he was bunched up there on the floor engaged in an act of mourning. There he sat, white from fasting, rocking back and forth, his beard dwindled to a shade of itself.

Something's wrong here—Gruber tried to imagine what and found it all oppressive. He felt he ought to run out, get away, but then saw himself fall and go tumbling down the five flights of stairs; he groaned at the broken picture of himself lying at the bottom. Only he was still there in Kessler's bedroom, listening to the old man praying. Somebody's dead, Gruber muttered. He figured Kessler had got bad news, yet instinctively knew he hadn't. Then it struck him with a terrible force that the mourner was mourning him: it was *he* who was dead.

The landlord was agonized. Sweating brutally, he felt an enormous constricted weight in him that slowly forced itself up, until his head was at the point of bursting. For a full minute he awaited a stroke; but the feeling painfully passed, leaving him miserable.

When after a while, he gazed around the room, it was clean, drenched in daylight and fragrance. Gruber then suffered unbearable remorse for the way he had treated the old man.

At last he could stand it no longer. With a cry of shame he tore the sheet off Kessler's bed, and wrapping it around his bulk, sank heavily to the floor and became a mourner.

Idiots First

The thick ticking of the tin clock stopped. Mendel, dozing in the dark, awoke in fright. The pain returned as he listened. He drew on his cold embittered clothing, and wasted minutes sitting at the edge of the bed.

"Isaac," he ultimately sighed.

In the kitchen, Isaac, his astonished mouth open, held six peanuts in his palm. He placed each on the table. "One . . . two . . . nine."

He gathered each peanut and appeared in the doorway. Mendel, in loose hat and long overcoat, still sat on the bed. Isaac watched with small eyes and ears, thick hair graying the sides of his head.

"Schlaf," he nasally said.

"No," muttered Mendel. As if stifling he rose. "Come, Isaac."

He wound his old watch though the sight of the stopped clock nauseated him.

Isaac wanted to hold it to his ear.

"No, it's late." Mendel put the watch carefully away. In the drawer he found the little paper bag of crumpled ones and fives and slipped it into his overcoat pocket. He helped Isaac on with his coat.

Isaac looked at one dark window, then at the other. Mendel stared at both blank windows.

They went slowly down the darkly lit stairs, Mendel first, Isaac watching the moving shadows on the wall. To one long shadow he offered a peanut.

"Hungrig."

In the vestibule the old man gazed through the thin glass. The

November night was cold and bleak. Opening the door he cautiously thrust his head out. Though he saw nothing he quickly shut the door.

"Ginzburg, that he came to see me yesterday," he whispered in Isaac's ear.

Isaac sucked air.

"You know who I mean?"

Isaac combed his chin with his fingers.

"That's the one, with the black whiskers. Don't talk to him or go with him if he asks you."

Isaac moaned.

"Young people he don't bother so much," Mendel said in afterthought.

It was suppertime and the street was empty but the store windows dimly lit their way to the corner. They crossed the deserted street and went on. Isaac, with a happy cry, pointed to the three golden balls. Mendel smiled but was exhausted when they got to the pawnshop.

The pawnbroker, a red-bearded man with black horn-rimmed glasses, was eating a whitefish at the rear of the store. He craned his head, saw them, and settled back to sip his tea.

In five minutes he came forward, patting his shapeless lips with a large white handkerchief.

Mendel, breathing heavily, handed him the worn gold watch. The pawnbroker, raising his glasses, screwed in his eyepiece. He turned the watch over once. "Eight dollars."

The dying man wet his cracked lips. "I must have thirty-five."

"So go to Rothschild."

"Cost me myself sixty."

"In 1905." The pawnbroker handed back the watch. It had stopped ticking. Mendel wound it slowly. It ticked hollowly.

"Isaac must go to my uncle that he lives in California."

"It's a free country," said the pawnbroker.

Isaac, watching a banjo, snickered.

"What's the matter with him?" the pawnbroker asked.

"So let be eight dollars," muttered Mendel, "but where will I get the rest till tonight?"

"How much for my hat and coat?" he asked.

"No sale." The pawnbroker went behind the cage and wrote out a ticket. He locked the watch in a small drawer but Mendel still heard it ticking.

In the street he slipped the eight dollars into the paper bag, then searched in his pockets for a scrap of writing. Finding it, he strained to read the address by the light of the street lamp.

As they trudged to the subway, Mendel pointed to the sprinkled sky.

"Isaac, look how many stars are tonight."

"Eggs," said Isaac.

"First we will go to Mr. Fishbein, after we will eat."

They got off the train in upper Manhattan and had to walk several blocks before they located Fishbein's house.

"A regular palace," Mendel murmured, looking forward to a moment's warmth.

Isaac stared uneasily at the heavy door of the house.

Mendel rang. The servant, a man with long sideburns, came to the door and said Mr. and Mrs. Fishbein were dining and could see no one.

"He should eat in peace but we will wait till he finishes."

"Come back tomorrow morning. Tomorrow morning Mr. Fishbein will talk to you. He don't do business or charity at this time of the night."

"Charity I am not interested—"

"Come back tomorrow."

"Tell him it's life or death—"

"Whose life or death?"

"So if not his, then mine."

"Don't be such a big smart aleck."

"Look me in my face," said Mendel, "and tell me if I got time till tomorrow morning?"

The servant stared at him, then at Isaac, and reluctantly let them in.

The foyer was a vast high-ceilinged room with many oil paintings on the walls, voluminous silken draperies, a thick flowered rug at foot, and a marble staircase.

Mr. Fishbein, a paunchy bald-headed man with hairy nostrils and small patent leather feet, ran lightly down the stairs, a large napkin tucked under a tuxedo coat button. He stopped on the fifth step from the bottom and examined his visitors.

"Who comes on Friday night to a man that he has guests, to spoil him his supper?"

"Excuse me that I bother you, Mr. Fishbein," Mendel said. "If I didn't come now I couldn't come tomorrow."

"Without more preliminaries, please state your business. I'm a hungry man."

"Hungrig," wailed Isaac.

Fishbein adjusted his pince-nez. "What's the matter with him?"

"This is my son Isaac. He is like this all his life."

Isaac mewled.

"I am sending him to California."

"Mr. Fishbein don't contribute to personal pleasure trips."

"I am a sick man and he must go tonight on the train to my Uncle Leo."

"I never give to unorganized charity," Fishbein said, "but if you are hungry I will invite you downstairs in my kitchen. We having tonight chicken with stuffed derma."

"All I ask is thirty-five dollars for the train ticket to my uncle in California. I have already the rest."

"Who is your uncle? How old a man?"

"Eighty-one years, a long life to him."

Fishbein burst into laughter. "Eighty-one years and you are sending him this halfwit."

Mendel, flailing both arms, cried, "Please, without names."

Fishbein politely conceded.

"Where is open the door there we go in the house," the sick

man said. "If you will kindly give me thirty-five dollars, God will bless you. What is thirty-five dollars to Mr. Fishbein? Nothing. To me, for my boy, is everything."

Fishbein drew himself up to his tallest height.

"Private contributions I don't make—only to institutions. This is my fixed policy."

Mendel sank to his creaking knees on the rug.

"Please, Mr. Fishbein, if not thirty-five, give maybe twenty."

"Levinson!" Fishbein angrily called.

The servant with the long sideburns appeared at the top of the stairs.

"Show this party where is the door—unless he wishes to partake food before leaving the premises."

"For what I got chicken won't cure it," Mendel said.

"This way if you please," said Levinson, descending.

Isaac assisted his father up.

"Take him to an institution," Fishbein advised over the marble balustrade. He ran quickly up the stairs and they were at once outside, buffeted by winds.

The walk to the subway was tedious. The wind blew mournfully. Mendel, breathless, glanced furtively at shadows. Isaac, clutching his peanuts in his frozen fist, clung to his father's side. They entered a small park to rest for a minute on a stone bench under a leafless two-branched tree. The thick right branch was raised, the thin left one hung down. A very pale moon rose slowly. So did a stranger as they approached the bench.

"Gut yuntif," he said hoarsely.

Mendel, drained of blood, waved his wasted arms. Isaac yowled sickly. Then a bell chimed and it was only ten. Mendel let out a piercing anguished cry as the bearded stranger disappeared into the bushes. A policeman came running, and though he beat the bushes with his nightstick, could turn up nothing. Mendel and Isaac hurried out of the little park. When Mendel glanced back the dead tree had its thin arm raised, the thick one down. He moaned.

They boarded a trolley, stopping at the home of a former friend, but he had died years ago. On the same block they went into a cafeteria and ordered two fried eggs for Isaac. The tables were crowded except where a heavy-set man sat eating soup with kasha. After one look at him they left in haste, although Isaac wept.

Mendel had another address on a slip of paper but the house was too far away, in Queens, so they stood in a doorway shivering.

What can I do, he frantically thought, in one short hour?

He remembered the furniture in the house. It was junk but might bring a few dollars. "Come, Isaac." They went once more to the pawnbroker's to talk to him, but the shop was dark and an iron gate—rings and gold watches glinting through it—was drawn tight across his place of business.

They huddled behind a telephone pole, both freezing. Isaac whimpered.

"See the big moon, Isaac. The whole sky is white."

He pointed but Isaac wouldn't look.

Mendel dreamed for a minute of the sky lit up, long sheets of light in all directions. Under the sky, in California, sat Uncle Leo drinking tea with lemon. Mendel felt warm but woke up cold.

Across the street stood an ancient brick synagogue.

He pounded on the huge door but no one appeared. He waited till he had breath and desperately knocked again. At last there were footsteps within, and the synagogue door creaked open on its massive brass hinges.

A darkly dressed sexton, holding a dripping candle, glared at them.

"Who knocks this time of night with so much noise on the synagogue door?"

Mendel told the sexton his troubles. "Please, I would like to speak to the rabbi."

"The rabbi is an old man. He sleeps now. His wife won't let you see him. Go home and come back tomorrow."

"To tomorrow I said goodbye already. I am a dying man."

Though the sexton seemed doubtful he pointed to an old wooden house next door. "In there he lives." He disappeared into the synagogue with his lit candle casting shadows around him.

Mendel, with Isaac clutching his sleeve, went up the wooden steps and rang the bell. After five minutes a big-faced, gray-haired bulky woman came out on the porch with a torn robe thrown over her nightdress. She emphatically said the rabbi was sleeping and could not be waked.

But as she was insisting, the rabbi himself tottered to the door. He listened a minute and said, "Who wants to see me let them come in."

They entered a cluttered room. The rabbi was an old skinny man with bent shoulders and a wisp of white beard. He wore a flannel nightgown and black skullcap; his feet were bare.

"Vey is mir," his wife muttered. "Put on shoes or tomorrow comes sure pneumonia." She was a woman with a big belly, years younger than her husband. Staring at Isaac, she turned away.

Mendel apologetically related his errand. "All I need more is thirty-five dollars."

"Thirty-five?" said the rabbi's wife. "Why not thirty-five thousand? Who has so much money? My husband is a poor rabbi. The doctors take away every penny."

"Dear friend," said the rabbi, "if I had I would give you."

"I got already seventy," Mendel said, heavy-hearted. "All I need more is thirty-five."

"God will give you," said the rabbi.

"In the grave," said Mendel. "I need tonight. Come, Isaac."

"Wait," called the rabbi.

He hurried inside, came out with a fur-lined caftan, and handed it to Mendel.

"Yascha," shrieked his wife, "not your new coat!"

"I got my old one. Who needs two coats for one body?"

"Yascha, I am screaming—"

"Who can go among poor people, tell me, in a new coat?"

"Yascha," she cried, "what can this man do with your coat? He needs tonight the money. The pawnbrokers are asleep."

"So let him wake them up."

"No." She grabbed the coat from Mendel.

He held on to a sleeve, wrestling her for the coat. Her I know, Mendel thought. "Shylock," he muttered. Her eyes glittered.

The rabbi groaned and tottered dizzily. His wife cried out as Mendel yanked the coat from her hands.

"Run," cried the rabbi.

"Run, Isaac."

They ran out of the house and down the steps.

"Stop, you thief," called the rabbi's wife.

The rabbi pressed both hands to his temples and fell to the floor.

"Help!" his wife wept. "Heart attack! Help!"

But Mendel and Isaac ran through the streets with the rabbi's new fur-lined caftan. After them noiselessly ran Ginzburg.

It was very late when Mendel bought the train ticket in the only booth open.

There was no time to stop for a sandwich so Isaac ate his peanuts and they hurried to the train in the vast deserted station.

"So in the morning," Mendel gasped as they ran, "there comes a man that he sells sandwiches and coffee. Eat but get change. When reaches California the train, will be waiting for you on the station Uncle Leo. If you don't recognize him he will recognize you. Tell him I send best regards."

But when they arrived at the gate to the platform it was shut, the light out.

Mendel, groaning, beat on the gate with his fists.

"Too late," said the uniformed ticket collector, a bulky, bearded man with hairy nostrils and a fishy smell.

He pointed to the station clock. "Already past twelve."

"But I see standing there still the train," Mendel said, hopping in his grief.

"It just left—in one more minute."

"A minute is enough. Just open the gate."

"Too late I told you."

Mendel socked his bony chest with both hands. "With my whole heart I beg you this little favor."

"Favors you had enough already. For you the train is gone. You shoulda been dead already at midnight. I told you that yesterday. This is the best I can do."

"Ginzburg!" Mendel shrank from him.

"Who else?" The voice was metallic, eyes glittered, the expression amused.

"For myself," the old man begged, "I don't ask a thing. But what will happen to my boy?"

Ginzburg shrugged slightly. "What will happen happens. This isn't my responsibility. I got enough to think about without worrying about somebody on one cylinder."

"What then is your responsibility?"

"To create conditions. To make happen what happens. I ain't in the anthropomorphic business."

"Whatever business you in, where is your pity?"

"This ain't my commodity. The law is the law."

"Which law is this?"

"The cosmic universal law, god'damit, the one I got to follow myself."

"What kind of a law is it?" cried Mendel. "For God's sake, don't you understand what I went through in my life with this poor boy? Look at him. For thirty-nine years, since the day he was born, I wait for him to grow up, but he don't. Do you understand what this means in a father's heart? Why don't you let him go to his uncle?" His voice had risen and he was shouting.

Isaac mewled loudly.

"Better calm down or you'll hurt somebody's feelings," Ginzburg said with a wink toward Isaac.

"All my life," Mendel cried, his body trembling, "what did I have? I was poor. I suffered from my health. When I worked I worked too hard. When I didn't work was worse. My wife died a young woman. But I didn't ask from anybody nothing. Now I ask a small favor. Be so kind, Mr. Ginzburg."

The ticket collector was picking his teeth with a match stick.

"You ain't the only one, my friend, some got it worse than you. That's how it goes in this country."

"You dog you." Mendel lunged at Ginzburg's throat and began to choke. "You bastard, don't you understand what it means human?"

They struggled nose to nose, Ginzburg, though his astonished eyes bulged, began to laugh. "You pipsqueak nothing. I'll freeze you to pieces."

His eyes lit in rage and Mendel felt an unbearable cold like an icy dagger invading his body, all of his parts shriveling.

Now I die without helping Isaac.

A crowd gathered. Isaac yelped in fright.

Clinging to Ginzburg in his last agony, Mendel saw reflected in the ticket collector's eyes the depth of his terror. But he saw that Ginzburg, staring at himself in Mendel's eyes, saw mirrored in them the extent of his own awful wrath. He beheld a shimmering, starry, blinding light that produced darkness.

Ginzburg looked astounded. "Who me?"

His grip on the squirming old man slowly loosened, and Mendel, his heart barely beating, slumped to the ground.

"Go." Ginzburg muttered, "take him to the train."

"Let pass," he commanded a guard.

The crowd parted. Isaac helped his father up and they tottered down the steps to the platform where the train waited, lit and ready to go.

Mendel found Isaac a coach seat and hastily embraced him. "Help Uncle Leo, Isaakil. Also remember your father and mother."

"Be nice to him," he said to the conductor. "Show him where everything is."

He waited on the platform until the train began slowly to move. Isaac sat at the edge of his seat, his face strained in the direction of his journey. When the train was gone, Mendel ascended the stairs to see what had become of Ginzburg.

The First Seven Years

Feld, the shoemaker, was annoyed that his helper, Sobel, was so insensitive to his reverie that he wouldn't for a minute cease his fanatic pounding at the other bench. He gave him a look, but Sobel's bald head was bent over the last as he worked and he didn't notice. The shoemaker shrugged and continued to peer through the partly frosted window at the near-sighted haze of falling February snow. Neither the shifting white blur outside, nor the sudden deep remembrance of the snowy Polish village where he had wasted his youth could turn his thoughts from Max the college boy, (a constant visitor in the mind since early that morning when Feld saw him trudging through the snowdrifts on his way to school) whom he so much respected because of the sacrifices he had made throughout the years—in winter or direst heat—to further his education. An old wish returned to haunt the shoemaker: that he had had a son instead of a daughter, but this blew away in the snow for Feld, if anything, was a practical man. Yet he could not help but contrast the diligence of the boy, who was a peddler's son, with Miriam's unconcern for an education. True, she was always with a book in her hand, yet when the opportunity arose for a college education, she had said no she would rather find a job. He had begged her to go, pointing out how many fathers could not afford to send their children to college, but she said she wanted to be independent. As for education, what was it, she asked, but books, which Sobel, who diligently read the classics, would as usual advise her on. Her answer greatly grieved her father.

A figure emerged from the snow and the door opened. At the

counter the man withdrew from a wet paper bag a pair of battered shoes for repair. Who he was the shoemaker for a moment had no idea, then his heart trembled as he realized, before he had thoroughly discerned the face, that Max himself was standing there, embarrassedly explaining what he wanted done to his old shoes. Though Feld listened eagerly, he couldn't hear a word, for the opportunity that had burst upon him was deafening.

He couldn't exactly recall when the thought had occurred to him, because it was clear he had more than once considered suggesting to the boy that he go out with Miriam. But he had not dared speak, for if Max said no, how would he face him again? Or suppose Miriam, who harped so often on independence, blew up in anger and shouted at him for his meddling? Still, the chance was too good to let by: all it meant was an introduction. They might long ago have become friends had they happened to meet somewhere, therefore was it not his duty—an obligation—to bring them together, nothing more, a harmless connivance to replace an accidental encounter in the subway, let's say, or a mutual friend's introduction in the street? Just let him once see and talk to her and he would for sure be interested. As for Miriam, what possible harm for a working girl in an office, who met only loud-mouthed salesmen and illiterate shipping clerks, to make the acquaintance of a fine scholarly boy? Maybe he would awaken in her a desire to go to college; if not—the shoemaker's mind at last came to grips with the truth—let her marry an educated man and live a better life.

When Max finished describing what he wanted done to his shoes, Feld marked them, both with enormous holes in the soles which he pretended not to notice, with large white-chalk x's, and the rubber heels, thinned to the nails, he marked with o's, though it troubled him he might have mixed up the letters. Max inquired the price, and the shoemaker cleared his throat and asked the boy, above Sobel's insistent hammering, would he please step through the side door there into the hall. Though surprised, Max did as the shoemaker requested, and Feld went in after him. For a minute they were both silent, because Sobel had stopped banging, and it seemed they understood neither was to say anything until the noise began again. When it did, loudly, the shoemaker quickly told Max why he had asked to talk to him.

"Ever since you went to high school," he said, in the dimly-lit hallway, "I watched you in the morning go to the subway to school, and I said to myself, this is a fine boy that he wants so much an education."

"Thanks," Max said, nervously alert. He was tall and grotesquely thin, with sharply cut features, particularly a beak-like nose. He was wearing a loose, long slushy overcoat that hung down to his ankles, looking like a rug draped over his bony shoulders, and a soggy, old brown hat, as battered as the shoes he had brought in.

"I am a business man," the shoemaker abruptly said to conceal his embarrassment, "so I will explain you right away why I talk to you. I have a girl, my daughter Miriam—she is nineteen—a very nice girl and also so pretty that everybody looks on her when she passes by in the street. She is smart, always with a book, and I thought to myself that a boy like you, an educated boy—I thought maybe you will be interested sometime to meet a girl like this." He laughed a bit when he had finished and was tempted to say more but had the good sense not to.

Max stared down like a hawk. For an uncomfortable second he was silent, then he asked, "Did you say nineteen?"

"Yes."

"Would it be all right to inquire if you have a picture of her?"

"Just a minute." The shoemaker went into the store and hastily returned with a snapshot that Max held up to the light.

"She's all right," he said.

Feld waited.

"And is she sensible—not the flighty kind?"

"She is very sensible."

After another short pause, Max said it was okay with him if he met her.

"Here is my telephone," said the shoemaker, hurriedly handing him a slip of paper. "Call her up. She comes home from work six o'clock."

Max folded the paper and tucked it away into his worn leather wallet.

"About the shoes," he said. "How much did you say they will cost me?"

"Don't worry about the price."

"I just like to have an idea."

"A dollar—dollar fifty. A dollar fifty," the shoemaker said.

At once he felt bad, for he usually charged two twenty-five for this kind of job. Either he should have asked the regular price or done the work for nothing.

Later, as he entered the store, he was startled by a violent clanging and looked up to see Sobel pounding with all his might upon the naked last. It broke, the iron striking the floor and jumping with a thump against the wall, but before the enraged shoemaker could cry out, the assistant had torn his hat and coat from the hook and rushed out into the snow.

So Feld, who had looked forward to anticipating how it would go with his daughter and Max, instead had a great worry on his mind. Without his temperamental helper he was a lost man, especially since it was years now that he had carried the store alone. The shoemaker had for an age suffered from a heart condition that threatened collapse if he dared exert himself. Five years ago, after an attack, it had appeared as though he would have either to sacrifice his business upon the auction block and live on a pittance thereafter, or put himself at the mercy of some unscrupulous employee who would in the end probably ruin him. But just at the moment of his darkest despair, this Polish refugee, Sobel, appeared one night from the street and begged for work. He was a stocky man, poorly dressed, with a bald head that had once been blond, a severely plain face and soft blue eyes prone to tears over the sad books he read, a young man but old—no one would have guessed thirty. Though he confessed he knew nothing of shoemaking, he said he was apt and would work for a very little if Feld taught him the trade. Thinking that with, after all, a landsman, he would have less to fear than from a complete stranger, Feld took him on and within six weeks the refugee rebuilt as good a shoe as he, and not long thereafter expertly ran the business for the thoroughly relieved shoemaker.

Feld could trust him with anything and did, frequently going home after an hour or two at the store, leaving all the money in the till, knowing Sobel would guard every cent of it. The amazing thing was that he demanded so little. His wants were few; in money he wasn't interested—in nothing but books, it seemed—which he one by one lent to Miriam, together with his profuse, queer written comments, manufactured during his lonely rooming house evenings, thick pads of commentary which the shoemaker peered at and twitched his shoulders over as his daughter, from her fourteenth year, read page by sanctified page, as if the word of God were inscribed on them. To protect Sobel, Feld himself had to see that he received more than he asked for. Yet his conscience bothered him for not insisting that the assistant accept a better wage than he was getting, though Feld had honestly told him he could earn a handsome salary if he worked elsewhere, or maybe opened a place of his own. But the assistant answered, somewhat ungraciously, that he was not interested in going elsewhere, and though Feld frequently asked himself what keeps him here? why does he stay? he finally answered it that the man, no doubt because of his terrible experiences as a refugee, was afraid of the world.

After the incident with the broken last, angered by Sobel's behavior, the shoemaker decided to let him stew for a week in the rooming house, although his own strength was taxed dangerously and the business suffered. However, after several sharp nagging warnings from both his wife and daughter, he went finally in search of Sobel, as he had once before, quite recently, when over some fancied slight—Feld had merely asked him not to give

Miriam so many books to read because her eyes were strained and red—the assistant had left the place in a huff, an incident which, as usual, came to nothing for he had returned after the shoemaker had talked to him, and taken his seat at the bench. But this time, after Feld had plodded through the snow to Sobel's house—he had thought of sending Miriam but the idea became repugnant to him—the burly landlady at the door informed him in a nasal voice that Sobel was not at home, and though Feld knew this was a nasty lie, for where had the refugee to go? still for some reason he was not completely sure of—it may have been the cold and his fatigue—he decided not to insist on seeing him. Instead he went home and hired a new helper.

Having settled the matter, though not entirely to his satisfaction, for he had much more to do than before, and so, for example, could no longer lie late in bed mornings because he had to get up to open the store for the new assistant, a speechless, dark man with an irritating rasp as he worked, whom he would not trust with the key as he had Sobel. Furthermore, this one, though able to do a fair repair job, knew nothing of grades of leather or prices, so Feld had to make his own purchases; and every night at closing time it was necessary to count the money in the till and lock up. However, he was not dissatisfied, for he lived much in his thoughts of Max and Miriam. The college boy had called her, and they had arranged a meeting for this coming Friday night. The shoemaker would personally have preferred Saturday, which he felt would make it a date of the first magnitude, but he learned Friday was Miriam's choice, so he said nothing. The day of the week did not matter. What mattered was the aftermath. Would they like each other and want to be friends? He sighed at all the time that would have to go by before he knew for sure. Often he was tempted to talk to Miriam about the boy, to ask whether she thought she would like his type—he had told her only that he considered Max a nice boy and had suggested he call her—but the one time he tried she snapped at him—justly—how should she know?

At last Friday came. Feld was not feeling particularly well so he stayed in bed, and Mrs. Feld thought it better to remain in the bedroom with him when Max called. Miriam received the boy, and her parents could hear their voices, his throaty one, as they talked. Just before leaving, Miriam brought Max to the bedroom door and he stood there a minute, a tall, slightly hunched figure wearing a thick, droopy suit, and apparently at ease as he greeted the shoemaker and his wife, which was surely a good sign. And Miriam, although she had worked all day, looked fresh and pretty. She was a large-framed girl with a well-shaped body, and she had a fine open face and soft hair. They made, Feld thought, a first-class couple.

Miriam returned after 11:30. Her mother was already asleep, but the shoemaker got out of bed and after locating his bathrobe went into the kitchen, where Miriam, to his surprise, sat at the table, reading.

"So where did you go?" Feld asked pleasantly.

"For a walk," she said, not looking up.

"I advised him," Feld said, clearing his throat, "he shouldn't spend so much money."

"I didn't care."

The shoemaker boiled up some water for tea and sat down at the table with a cupful and a thick slice of lemon.

"So how," he sighed after a sip, "did you enjoy?"

"It was all right."

He was silent. She must have sensed his disappointment, for she added, "You can't really tell much the first time."

"You will see him again?"

Turning a page, she said that Max had asked for another date.

"For when?"

"Saturday."

"So what did you say?"

"What did I say?" she asked, delaying for a moment—"I said yes."

Afterwards she inquired about Sobel, and Feld, without exactly knowing why, said the assistant had got another job. Miriam said nothing more and began to read. The shoemaker's conscience did not trouble him; he was satisfied with the Saturday date.

During the week, by placing here and there a deft question, he managed to get from Miriam some information about Max. It surprised him to learn that the boy was not studying to be either a doctor or lawyer but was taking a business course leading to a degree in accountancy. Feld was a little disappointed because he thought of accountants as bookkeepers and would have preferred "a higher profession." However, it was not long before he had investigated the subject and discovered that Certified Public Accountants were highly respected people, so he was thoroughly content as Saturday approached. But because Saturday was a busy day, he was much in the store and therefore did not see Max when he came to call for Miriam. From his wife he learned there had been nothing especially revealing about their meeting. Max had rung the bell and Miriam had got her coat and left with him—nothing more. Feld did not probe, for his wife was not particularly observant. Instead, he waited up for Miriam with a newspaper on his lap, which he scarcely looked at so lost was he in thinking of the future. He awoke to find her in the room with him, tiredly removing her hat. Greeting her, he was suddenly inexplicably afraid to ask anything about the evening. But since she volunteered nothing he was at last forced to inquire how she had enjoyed herself. Miriam began something non-committal but apparently changed her mind, for she said after a minute, "I was bored."

When Feld had sufficiently recovered from his anguished disappointment to ask why, she answered without hesitation, "Because he's nothing more than a materialist."

"What means this word?"

"He has no soul. He's only interested in things."

He considered her statement for a long time but then asked, "Will you see him again?"

"He didn't ask."

"Suppose he will ask you?"

"I won't see him."

He did not argue; however, as the days went by he hoped increasingly she would change her mind. He wished the boy would telephone, because he was sure there was more to him than Miriam, with her inexperienced eye, could discern. But Max didn't call. As a matter of fact he took a different route to school, no longer passing the shoemaker's store, and Feld was deeply hurt.

Then one afternoon Max came in and asked for his shoes. The shoemaker took them down from the shelf where he had placed them, apart from the other pairs. He had done the work himself and the soles and heels were well built and firm. The shoes had been highly polished and somehow looked better than new. Max's Adam's apple went up once when he saw them, and his eyes had little lights in them.

"How much?" he asked, without directly looking at the shoemaker.

"Like I told you before," Feld answered sadly. "One dollar fifty cents."

Max handed him two crumpled bills and received in return a newly-minted silver half dollar.

He left. Miriam had not been mentioned. That night the shoemaker discovered that his new assistant had been all the while stealing from him, and he suffered a heart attack.

Though the attack was very mild, he lay in bed for three weeks. Miriam spoke of going for Sobel, but sick as he was Feld rose in wrath against the idea. Yet in his heart he knew there was no other way, and the first weary day back in the shop thoroughly convinced him, so that night after supper he dragged himself to Sobel's rooming house.

He toiled up the stairs, though he knew it was bad for him, and at the top knocked at the door. Sobel opened it and the shoemaker entered. The room was a small, poor one, with a single window facing the street. It contained a narrow cot, a low table and several stacks of books piled haphazardly around on the floor along the wall, which made him think how queer Sobel was, to be uneducated and read so much. He had once asked him, Sobel, why you read so much? and the assistant could not answer him. Did you ever study in a college someplace? he had asked, but Sobel shook his head. He read, he said, to know. But to know what, the shoemaker demanded, and to know, why? Sobel never explained, which proved he read much because he was queer.

Feld sat down to recover his breath. The assistant was resting on his bed with his heavy back to the wall. His shirt and trousers were clean, and his stubby fingers, away from the shoemaker's bench, were strangely pallid. His face was thin and pale, as if he had been shut in this room since the day he had bolted from the store.

"So when you will come back to work?" Feld asked him.

To his surprise, Sobel burst out, "Never."

Jumping up, he strode over to the window that looked out upon the miserable street. "Why should I come back?" he cried.

"I will raise your wages."

"Who cares for your wages!"

The shoemaker, knowing he didn't care, was at a loss what else to say.

"What do you want from me, Sobel?"

"Nothing."

"I always treated you like you was my son."

Sobel vehemently denied it. "So why you look for strange boys in the street they should go out with Miriam? Why you don't think of me?"

The shoemaker's hands and feet turned freezing cold. His voice became so hoarse he couldn't speak. At last he cleared his throat and croaked, "So what has my daughter got to do with a shoemaker thirty-five years old who works for me?"

"Why do you think I worked so long for you?" Sobel cried out. "For the stingy wages I sacrificed five years of my life so you could have to eat and drink and where to sleep?"

"Then for what?" shouted the shoemaker.

"For Miriam," he blurted—"for her."

The shoemaker, after a time, managed to say, "I pay wages in cash, Sobel," and lapsed into silence. Though he was seething with excitement, his mind was coldly clear, and he had to admit to himself he had sensed all along that Sobel felt this way. He had never so much as thought it consciously, but he had felt it and was afraid.

"Miriam knows?" he muttered hoarsely.

"She knows."

"You told her?"

"No."

"Then how does she know?"

"How does she know?" Sobel said, "because she knows. She knows who I am and what is in my heart."

Feld had a sudden insight. In some devious way, with his books and commentary, Sobel had given Miriam to understand that he loved. The shoemaker felt a terrible anger at him for his deceit.

"Sobel, you are crazy," he said bitterly. "She will never marry a man so old and ugly like you."

Sobel turned black with rage. He cursed the shoemaker, but then, though he trembled to hold it in, his eyes filled with tears and he broke into deep sobs. With his back to Feld, he stood at the window, fists clenched, and his shoulders shook with his choked sobbing.

Watching him, the shoemaker's anger diminished. His teeth were on edge with pity for the man, and his eyes grew moist. How strange and sad that a refugee, a grown man, bald and old with his miseries, who had by the skin of his teeth escaped Hitler's incinerators, should fall in love, when he had got to America, with a girl less than half his age. Day after day, for five years he had sat at his bench, cutting and hammering away, waiting for the girl to become a woman, unable to ease his heart with speech, knowing no protest but desperation.

"Ugly I didn't mean," he said half aloud.

Then he realized that what he had called ugly was not Sobel but Miriam's life if she married him. He felt for his daughter a strange and gripping sorrow, as if she were already Sobel's bride, the wife, after all, of a shoemaker, and had in her life no more than her mother had had. And all his dreams for her—why he had slaved and destroyed his heart with anxiety and labor—all these dreams of a better life were dead.

The room was quiet. Sobel was standing by the window reading, and it was curious that when he read he looked young.

"She is only nineteen," Feld said brokenly. "This is too young yet to get married. Don't ask her for two years more, till she is twenty-one, then you can talk to her."

Sobel didn't answer. Feld rose and left. He went slowly down the stairs but once outside, though it was an icy night and the crisp falling snow whitened the street, he walked with a stronger stride.

But the next morning, when the shoemaker arrived, heavy-hearted, to open the store, he saw he needn't have come, for his assistant was already seated at the last, pounding leather for his love.

Take Pity

Davidov, the census-taker, opened the door without knocking, limped into the room and sat wearily down. Out came his note-book and he was on the job. Rosen, the ex-coffee salesman, wasted, eyes despairing, sat motionless, cross-legged, on his cot. The square, clean but cold room, lit by a dim globe, was sparsely furnished: the cot, a folding chair, small table, old unpainted chests—no closets but who needed them?—and a small sink with a rough piece of green, institutional soap on its holder—you could smell it across the room. The worn black shade over the single narrow window was drawn to the ledge, surprising Davidov.

"What's the matter you don't pull the shade up?" he remarked.

Rosen ultimately sighed. "Let it stay."

"Why? Outside is light."

"Who needs light?"

"What then you need?"

"Light I don't need," replied Rosen.

Davidov, sour-faced, flipped through the closely scrawled pages of his notebook until he found a clean one. He attempted to scratch in a word with his fountain pen but it had run dry, so he fished a pencil stub out of his vest pocket and sharpened it with a cracked razor blade. Rosen paid no attention to the feathery shavings falling to the floor. He looked restless, seemed to be listening to or for something, although Davidov was con-vinced there was absolutely nothing to listen to. It was only when the census-taker somewhat irritably and with increasing loudness repeated a question, that Rosen stirred and identified himself. He was about to furnish an address but caught himself and shrugged.

Davidov did not comment on the salesman's gesture. "So begin," he nodded.

"Who knows where to begin?" Rosen stared at the drawn shade. "Do they know here where to begin?"

"Philosophy we are not interested," said Davidov. "Start in how you met her."

"Who?" pretended Rosen.

"Her," he snapped.

"So if I got to begin, how you know about her already?" Rosen asked triumphantly.

Davidov spoke wearily, "You mentioned before."

Rosen remembered. They had questioned him upon his arrival and he now recalled blurting out her name. It was perhaps something in the air. It did not permit you to retain what you remembered. That was part of the cure, if you wanted a cure.

"Where I met her—?" Rosen murmured. "I met her where she always was—in the back room there in that hole in the wall that was a waste of time for me I went there. Maybe I sold them a half a bag of coffee a month. This is not business."

"In business we are not interested."

"What then you are interested?" Rosen mimicked Davidov's tone.

Davidov clammed up coldly.

Rosen knew they had him where it hurt, so he went on: "The husband was maybe forty, Axel Kalish, a Polish refugee. He worked like a blind horse when he got to America, and saved maybe two—three thousand dollars that he bought with the money this pisher grocery in a dead neighborhood where he didn't have a chance. He called my company up for credit and they sent me I should see. I recommended okay because I felt sorry. He had a wife, Eva, you know already about her, and two darling girls, one five and one three, little dolls, Fega and Surale, that I didn't want them to suffer. So right away I told him, without tricks, 'Kiddo, this is a mistake. This place is a grave. Here they will bury you if you don't get out quick!' "

Rosen sighed deeply.

"So?" Davidov had thus far written nothing, irking the ex-salesman.

"So?—Nothing. He didn't get out. After a couple months he tried to sell but nobody bought, so he stayed and starved. They never made expenses. Every day they got poorer you couldn't look in their faces. 'Don't be a damn fool,' I told him, 'go in bankruptcy.' But he couldn't stand it to lose all his capital, and he was also afraid it would be hard to find a job. 'My God,' I said, 'do anything. Be a painter, a janitor, a junk man, but get out of here before everybody is a skeleton.'

"This he finally agreed with me, but before he could go in auction he dropped dead."

Davidov made a note. "How did he die?"

"On this I am not an expert," Rosen replied. "You know better than me."

"How did he die?" Davidov spoke impatiently. "Say in one word."

"From what he died?—he died, that's all."

"Answer, please, this question."

"Broke in him something. That's how."

"Broke what?"

"Broke what breaks. He was talking to me how bitter was his life, and he touched me on my sleeve to say something else, but the next minute his face got small and he fell down dead, the wife screaming, the little girls crying that it made in my heart pain. I am myself a sick man and when I saw him laying on the floor, I said to myself, 'Rosen, say goodbye, this guy is finished.' So I said it."

Rosen got up from the cot and strayed despondently around the room, avoiding the window. Davidov was occupying the only chair, so the ex-salesman was finally forced to sit on the edge of the bed again. This irritated him. He badly wanted a cigarette but disliked asking for one.

Davidov permitted him a short interval of silence, then leafed impatiently through his notebook. Rosen, to needle the census-taker, said nothing.

"So what happened?" Davidov finally demanded.

Rosen spoke with ashes in his mouth. "After the funeral—" he paused, tried to wet his lips, then went on, "He belonged to a society that they buried him, and he also left a thousand dollars insurance, but after the funeral I said to her, 'Eva, listen to me. Take the money and your children and run away from here. Let the creditors take the store. What will they get?—Nothing.'

"But she answered me, 'Where will I go, where, with my two orphans that their father left them to starve?'

" 'Go anywhere,' I said. 'Go to your relatives.'

"She laughed like laughs somebody who hasn't got no joy. 'My relatives Hitler took away from me.'

" 'What about Axel—surely an uncle somewheres?'

" 'Nobody,' she said. 'I will stay here like my Axel wanted. With the insurance I will buy new stock and fix up the store. Every week I will decorate the window, and in this way gradually will come in new customers—'

" 'Eva, my darling girl—'

" 'A millionaire I don't expect to be. All I want is I should make a little living and take care on my girls. We will live in the back here like before, and in this way I can work and watch them, too.'

" 'Eva,' I said, 'you are a nice-looking young woman, only thirty-eight years. Don't throw away your life here. Don't flush in the toilet—you should excuse me—the thousand poor dollars from your dead husband. Believe me, I know from such stores. After thirty-five years' experience I know a graveyard when I smell it. Go better some place and find a job. You're young yet. Sometime you will meet somebody and get married.'

" 'No, Rosen, not me,' she said. 'With marriage I am finished. Nobody wants a poor widow with two children.'

" 'This I don't believe it.'

" 'I know,' she said.

"Never in my life I saw so bitter a woman's face.

" 'No,' I said. 'No.'

" 'Yes, Rosen, yes. In my whole life I never had anything. In my whole life I always suffered. I don't expect better. This is my life.'

"I said no and she said yes. What could I do? I am a man with only one kidney, and worse than that, that I won't mention it. When I talked she didn't listen, so I stopped to talk. Who can argue with a widow?"

The ex-salesman glanced up at Davidov but the census-taker did not reply. "What happened then?" he asked.

"What happened?" mocked Rosen. "Happened what happens." Davidov's face grew red.

"What happened, happened," Rosen said hastily. "She ordered from the wholesalers all kinds goods that she paid for them cash. All week she opened boxes and packed on the shelves cans, jars, packages. Also she cleaned, and she washed, and she mopped with oil the floor. With tissue paper she made new decorations in the window, everything should look nice—but who came in? Nobody except a few poor customers from the tenement around the corner. And when they came? When was closed the supermarkets and they needed some little item that they forgot to buy, like a quart milk, fifteen cents' cheese, a small can sardines for lunch. In a few months was again dusty the cans on the shelves, and her thousand was gone. Credit she couldn't get except from me, and from me she got because I paid out of my pocket the company. This she didn't know. She worked, she dressed clean, she waited that the store should get better. Little by little the shelves got empty, but where was the profit? They ate it up. When I looked on the little girls I knew what she didn't tell me. Their faces were white, they were thin, they were hungry. She kept the little food that was left, on the shelves. One night I brought in a nice piece sirloin, but I could see from her eyes that she didn't like that I did it. So what else could I do? I have a heart and I am human."

Here the ex-salesman wept.

Davidov pretended not to see though once he peeked.

Rosen blew his nose, then went on more calmly, "When the children were sleeping we sat in the dark there, in the back, and not once in four hours opened the door should come in a customer. 'Eva, for Godsakes, *run away*,' I said.

" 'I have no place to go,' she said.

" 'I will give you where you can go, and please don't say to me no. I am a bachelor, this you know. I got whatever I need and more besides. Let me help you and the children. Money don't interest me. Interests me good health, but I can't buy it. I'll tell you what I will do. Let this place go to the creditors and move into a two-family house that I own, which the top floor is now empty. Rent will cost you nothing. In the meantime you can go and find a job. I will also pay the downstairs lady to take care of the girls—God bless them—until you will come home. With your wages you will buy the food, if you need clothes, and also save a little. This you can use when you get married someday. What do you say?'

"She didn't answer me. She only looked on me in such a way, with such burning eyes, like I was small and ugly. For the first time I thought to myself, 'Rosen, this woman don't like you.'

" 'Thank you very kindly, my friend Mr. Rosen,' she answered me, 'but charity we are not needing. I got yet a paying business, and it will get better when times are better. Now is bad times. When comes again good times will get better the business.'

" 'Who charity?' I cried to her. 'What charity? Speaks to you your husband's a friend.'

" 'Mr. Rosen, my husband didn't have no friends.'

" 'Can't you see that I want to help the children?'

" 'The children have their mother.'

" 'Eva, what's the matter with you?' I said. 'Why do you make sound bad something that I mean it should be good?'

"This she didn't answer. I felt sick in my stomach, and was coming also a headache so I left.

"All night I didn't sleep, and then all of a sudden I figured out a reason why she was worried. She was worried I would ask for some kind payment except cash. She got the wrong man. Anyway, this made me think of something that I didn't think about before. I thought now to ask her to marry me. What did she have to lose? I could take care of myself without any trouble to them. Fega and Surale would have a father he could give them for the movies, or sometime to buy a little doll to play with, and when I died, would go to them my investments and insurance policies.

"The next day I spoke to her.

" 'For myself, Eva, I don't want a thing. Absolutely not a thing. For you and your girls—everything. I am not a strong man, Eva. In fact, I am sick. I tell you this you should understand I don't expect to live long. But even for a few years would be nice to have a little family.'

"She was with her back to me and didn't speak.

"When she turned around again her face was white but the mouth was like iron.

" 'No, Mr. Rosen.'

" 'Why not, tell me?'

" 'I had enough with sick men.' She began to cry. 'Please, Mr. Rosen. Go home.'

"I didn't have strength I should argue with her, so I went home. I went home but hurt me my mind. All day long and all night I felt bad. My back pained me where was missing my kidney. Also too much smoking. I tried to understand this woman but I couldn't. Why should somebody that her two children were starving always say no to a man that he wanted to help her? What did I do to her bad? Am I maybe a murderer she should hate me so much? All that I felt in my heart was pity for her and the children, but I couldn't convince her. Then I went back and begged her she should let me help them, and once more she told me no.

" 'Eva,' I said, 'I don't blame you that you don't want a sick man. So come with me to a marriage broker and we will find you a strong, healthy husband that he will support you and your girls. I will give the dowry.'

"She screamed, 'On this I don't need your help, Rosen!'

"I didn't say no more. What more could I say? All day long, from early in the morning till late in the night she worked like an animal. All day she mopped, she washed with soap and a brush the shelves, the few cans she polished, but the store was still rotten. The little girls I was afraid to look at. I could see in their faces their bones. They were tired, they were weak. Little Surale held with her hand all the time the dress of Fega. Once when I saw them in the street I gave them some cakes, but when I tried the next day to give them something else, the mother shouldn't know, Fega answered me, 'We can't take, Momma says today is a fast day.'

"I went inside. I made my voice soft. 'Eva, on my bended knee, I am a man with nothing in this world. Allow me that I should have a little pleasure before I die. Allow me that I should help you to stock up once more the store.'

"So what did she do? She cried, it was terrible to see. And after she cried, what did she say? She told me to go away and I shouldn't come back. I felt like to pick up a chair and break her head.

"In my house I was too weak to eat. For two days I took in my mouth nothing except maybe a spoon of chicken noodle soup, or maybe a glass tea without sugar. This wasn't good for me. My health felt bad.

"Then I made up a scheme that I was a friend of Axel's who lived in Jersey. I said I owed Axel seven hundred dollars that he lent me this money fifteen years ago, before he got married. I said I did not have the whole money now, but I would send her every week twenty dollars till it was paid up the debt. I put inside the letter two tens and gave it to a friend of mine, also a salesman, he should mail it in Newark so she would not be suspicious who wrote the letters."

To Rosen's surprise Davidov had stopped writing. The book

was full, so he tossed it onto the table, yawned, but listened amiably. His curiosity had died.

Rosen got up and fingered the notebook. He tried to read the small distorted handwriting but could not make out a single word.

"It's not English and it's not Yiddish," he said. "Could it be in Hebrew?"

"No," answered Davidov. "It's an old-fashioned language that they don't use it nowadays."

"Oh?" Rosen returned to the cot. He saw no purpose to going on now that it was not required, but he felt he had to.

"Came back all the letters," he said dully. "The first she opened it, then pasted back again the envelope, but the rest she didn't even open."

" 'Here,' I said to myself, 'is a very strange thing—a person that you can never give her anything.—*But I will give.*'

"I went then to my lawyer and we made out a will that everything I had—all my investments, my two houses that I owned, also furniture, my car, the checking account—every cent would go to her, and when she died, the rest would be left for the two girls. The same with my insurance. They would be my beneficiaries. Then I signed and went home. In the kitchen I turned on the gas and put my head in the stove.

"Let her say now no."

Davidov, scratching his stubbled cheek, nodded. This was the part he already knew. He got up and before Rosen could cry no, idly raised the window shade.

It was twilight in space but a woman stood before the window.

Rosen with a bound was off his cot to see.

It was Eva, staring at him with haunted, beseeching eyes. She raised her arms to him.

Infuriated, the ex-salesman shook his fist.

"Whore, bastard, bitch," he shouted at her. "Go 'way from here. Go home to your children."

Davidov made no move to hinder him as Rosen rammed down the window shade.

The Maid's Shoes

The maid had left her name with the porter's wife. She said she was looking for steady work and would take anything but preferred not to work for an old woman. Still if she had to she would. She was forty-five and looked older. Her face was worn but her hair was black, and her eyes and lips were pretty. She had few good teeth. When she laughed she was embarrassed around the mouth. Although it was cold in early October, that year in Rome, and the chestnut vendors were already bent over their pans of glowing charcoals, the maid wore only a threadbare black cotton dress which had a split down the left side, where about two inches of seam had opened on the hip, exposing her underwear. She had sewn the seam several times but this was one of the times it was open again. Her heavy but well-formed legs were bare and she wore house slippers as she talked to the portinaia; she had done a single day's washing for a signora down the street and carried her shoes in a paper bag. There were three comparatively new apartment houses on the hilly street and she left her name in each of them.

The portinaia, a dumpy woman wearing a brown tweed skirt she had got from an English family that had once lived in the building, said she would remember the maid but then she forgot; she forgot until an American professor moved into a furnished apartment on the fifth floor and asked her to help him find a maid. The portinaia brought him a girl from the neighborhood, a girl of sixteen, recently from Umbria, who came with her aunt. But the professor, Orlando Krantz, did not like the way the aunt played up certain qualities of the girl, so he sent her away. He told the portinaia he was looking for an older woman, someone he wouldn't have to worry about. Then the portinaia thought of the maid who had left her name and address, and she went to her house on the via Appia Antica near the catacombs and told her an American was looking for a maid, mezzo servizio; she would give him her name if the maid agreed to make it worth her while. The maid, whose name was Rosa, shrugged her shoulders and looked stiffly down the street. She said she had nothing to offer the portinaia.

"Look at what I'm wearing," she said. "Look at this junk pile, can you call it a house? I live here with my son and his bitch of a wife who counts every spoonful of soup in my mouth. They treat me like dirt and dirt is all I have to my name."

"In that case I can do nothing for you," the portinaia said. "I have myself and my husband to think of." But she returned from the bus stop and said she would recommend the maid to the American professor if she gave her five thousand lire the first time she was paid.

"How much will he pay?" the maid asked the portinaia.

"I would ask for eighteen thousand a month. Tell him you have to spend two hundred lire a day for carfare."

"That's almost right," Rosa said. "It will cost me forty one way and forty back. But if he pays me eighteen thousand I'll give you five if you sign that's all I owe you."

"I will sign," said the portinaia, and she recommended the maid to the American professor.

Orlando Krantz was a nervous man of sixty. He had mild gray eyes, a broad mouth, and a pointed clefted chin. His round head was bald and he had a bit of a belly, although the rest of him was quite thin. He was a somewhat odd-looking man but an authority in law, the portinaia told Rosa. The professor sat at a table in his study, writing all day, yet was up every half hour on some pretext or other to look nervously around. He worried how things were going and often came out of his study to see. He would watch Rosa working, then went in and wrote. In a half hour he would come out, ostensibly to wash his hands in the bathroom or drink a glass of water, but he was really passing by to see what she was doing. She was doing what she had to. Rosa worked quickly, especially when he was watching. She seemed, he thought, to be unhappy, but that was none of his business. Their lives, he knew, were full of troubles, often sordid; it was best to be detached.

This was the professor's second year in Italy; he had spent the first in Milan, and the second was in Rome. He had rented a large three-bedroom apartment, one of which he used as a study. His wife and daughter, who had returned for a visit to the States in August, would have the other bedrooms; they were due back before not too long. When the ladies returned, he had told Rosa, he would put her on full time. There was a maid's room where she could sleep; indeed, which she already used as her own though she was in the apartment only from nine till four. Rosa agreed to a full time arrangement because it would mean all her meals in and no rent to pay her son and his dog-faced wife.

While they were waiting for Mrs. Krantz and the daughter to arrive, Rosa did the marketing and cooking. She made the professor's breakfast when she came in, and his lunch at once. She offered to stay later than four, to prepare his supper, which he ate at six, but he preferred to take that meal out. After shopping she cleaned the house, thoroughly mopping the marble floors with a wet rag she pushed around with a stick though the floors did not look particularly dusty to him. She also washed and ironed his laundry. She was a good worker, her slippers clip-clopping as she hurried from one room to the next, and she frequently finished up about an hour or so before she was due to go home; so she retired to the maid's room and there read *Tempo* or *Epoca*, or sometimes a love story in photographs, with the words printed in italics under each picture. Often she pulled her bed down and lay in it under blankets, to keep warm. The weather had turned rainy, and now the apartment was uncomfortably cold. The custom of the condominium in this apartment house was not to heat until the fifteenth of November, and if it was cold before then, as it was now, the people of the house had to do the best they could. The cold disturbed the professor, who wrote with his gloves and hat on, and increased his nervousness so that he was out to look at her more often. He wore a heavy blue bathrobe over his clothes; sometimes the bathrobe belt was wrapped around a hot water bottle he had placed against the lower part of his back, under the suit coat. Sometimes he sat on the hot water bag as he wrote, a sight that caused Rosa, when she once saw this, to smile behind her hand. If he left the hot water bag in the dining room after lunch, Rosa asked if she might use it. As a rule he allowed her to, and then she did her work with the rubber bag pressed against her stomach with her elbow. She said she had trouble with her liver. That was why the professor did not mind her going to the maid's room to lie down before leaving, after she had finished her work.

Once after Rosa had gone home, smelling tobacco smoke in the corridor near her room, the professor entered it to investigate. The room was not more than an elongated cubicle with a narrow bed that lifted sideways against the wall; there was also a small green cabinet, and an adjoining tiny bathroom containing a toilet and a sitzbath fed by a cold water tap. She often did the laundry on a washboard in the sitzbath, but never, so far as he knew, had bathed in it. The day before her daughter-in-law's name day she had asked permission to take a hot bath in his tub in the big bathroom, and though he had hesitated a moment, the professor finally said yes. In her room, he opened a drawer at the bottom of the cabinet and found a hoard of cigarette butts in it, the butts he had left in ash trays. He noticed, too, that she had collected his old newspapers and magazines from the waste baskets. She also saved cord, paper bags and rubber bands; also pencil stubs he threw away. After he found that out, he occasionally gave her some meat left over from lunch, and cheese that had gone dry, to take with her. For this she brought him flowers. She also brought a dirty egg or two her daughter-in-law's hen had laid, but he

thanked her and said the yolks were too strong for his taste. He
noticed that she needed a pair of shoes, for those she put on to
go home in were split in several places, and she wore the same
black dress with the tear in it every day, which embarrassed him
when he had to speak to her; however, he thought he would refer
these matters to his wife when she arrived.

As jobs went, Rosa knew she had a good one. The professor
paid well and promptly, and he never ordered her around in the
haughty manner of some of her Italian employers. This one was
nervous and fussy but not a bad sort. His main fault was his silence. Though he could speak a better than passable Italian, he
preferred, when not at work, to sit in an armchair in the living
room, reading. Only two souls in the whole apartment, you would
think they would want to talk to each other once in a while.
Sometimes when she served him a cup of coffee as he read, she
tried to get in a word about her troubles. She wanted to tell him
about her long, impoverished widowhood, how badly her son had
turned out, and what her miserable daughter-in-law was to live
with. But though he listened courteously; though they shared
the same roof, and even the same hot water bottle and bathtub,
they almost never shared speech. He said no more to her than
a crow would, and clearly showed he preferred to be left alone.
So she left him alone and was lonely in the apartment. Working
for foreigners had its advantages, she thought, but it also had
disadvantages.

After a while the professor noticed that the telephone was ringing regularly for Rosa each afternoon during the time she usually
was resting in her room. In the following week, instead of staying in the house until four, after her telephone call she asked
permission to leave. At first she said her liver was bothering her,
but later she stopped giving excuses. Although he did not much
approve of this sort of thing, suspecting she would take advantage
of him if he was too liberal in granting favors, he informed her
that, until his wife arrived, she might leave at three on two afternoons of the week, provided that all her duties were fully dis-

charged. He knew that everything was done before she left but thought he ought to say it. She listened meekly—her eyes aglow, lips twitching—and meekly agreed. He presumed, when he happened to think about it afterwards, that Rosa had a good spot here, by any standard, and she ought soon to show it in her face, change her unhappy expression for one less so. However, this did not happen, for when he chanced to observe her, even on days when she was leaving early, she seemed sadly preoccupied, sighed much, as if something on her heart were weighing her down.

He never asked what, preferring not to become involved in whatever it was. These people had endless troubles, and if you let yourself get involved in them you got endlessly involved. He knew of one woman, the wife of a colleague, who had said to her maid: "Lucrezia, I am sympathetic to your condition but I don't want to hear about it." This, the professor reflected, was basically good policy. It kept employer-employee relationships where they belonged—on an objective level. He was, after all, leaving Italy in April and would never in his life see Rosa again. It would do her a lot more good if, say, he sent her a small check at Christmas, than if he needlessly immersed himself in her miseries now. The professor knew he was nervous and often impatient, and he was sometimes sorry for his nature; but he was what he was and preferred to stay aloof from what did not closely and personally concern him.

But Rosa would not have it so. One morning she knocked on his study door, and when he said avanti, she went in embarrassedly so that even before she began to speak he was himself embarrassed.

"Professore," Rosa said, unhappily, "please excuse me for bothering your work, but I have to talk to somebody."

"I happen to be very busy," he said, growing a little angry. "Can it wait a while?"

"It'll take only a minute. Your troubles hang on all your life but it doesn't take long to tell them."

"Is it your liver complaint?" he asked.

"No. I need your advice. You're an educated man and I'm no more than an ignorant peasant."

"What kind of advice?" he asked impatiently.

"Call it anything you like. The fact is I have to speak to somebody. I can't talk to my son, even if it were possible in this case. When I open my mouth he roars like a bull. And my daughter-in-law isn't worth wasting my breath on. Sometimes, on the roof, when we're hanging the wash, I say a few words to the portinaia, but she isn't a sympathetic person so I have to come to you, I'll tell you why."

Before he could say how he felt about hearing her confidences, Rosa had launched into a story about this middle-aged government worker in the tax bureau, whom she had happened to meet in the neighborhood. He was married, had four children, and sometimes worked as a carpenter after leaving his office at two o'clock each day. His name was Armando; it was he who telephoned her every afternoon. They had met recently on a bus, and he had, after two or three meetings, seeing that her shoes weren't fit to wear, urged her to let him buy her a new pair. She had told him not to be foolish. One could see he had very little, and it was enough that he took her to the movies twice a week. She had said that, yet every time they met he talked about the shoes he wanted to buy her.

"I'm only human," Rosa frankly told the professor, "and I need the shoes badly, but you know how these things go. If I put on his shoes they may carry me to his bed. That's why I thought I would ask you if I ought to take them."

The professor's face and bald head were flushed. "I don't see how I can possibly advise you—"

"You're the educated one," she said.

"However," he went on, "since the situation is still essentially hypothetical, I will go so far as to say you ought to tell this generous gentleman that his responsibilities should be to his own family. He would do well not to offer you gifts, as you will do, not to accept them. If you don't, he can't possibly make any claims upon you or your person. This is all I care to say. Your business is certainly none of mine. Since you have requested advice, I've given it, but I won't say any more."

Rosa sighed. "The truth of it is I could use a pair of shoes. Mine look as though they've been chewed by goats. I haven't had a new pair in six years."

But the professor had nothing more to add.

After Rosa had gone for the day, in thinking about her problem, he decided to buy her a pair of shoes. He was concerned that she might be expecting something of the sort, had planned, so to speak, to have it work out this way. But since this was conjecture only, evidence entirely lacking, he would assume, until proof to the contrary became available, that she had no ulterior motive in asking his advice. He considered giving her five thousand lire to make the purchase of the shoes herself and relieve him of the trouble, but he was doubtful for there was no guarantee she would use the money for the agreed purpose. Suppose she came in the next day, saying she had had a liver attack that had necessitated calling the doctor, who had charged three thousand lire for his visit; therefore would the professor, in view of these unhappy circumstances, supply an additional three thousand for the shoes? That would never do, so the next morning, when the maid was at the grocer's, the professor slipped into her room and quickly traced on paper the outline of her miserable shoe—a distasteful task but he accomplished it quickly. That evening, in a store on the same piazza as the restaurant where he liked to eat, he bought Rosa a pair of brown shoes for fifty-five hundred lire, slightly more than he had planned to spend; but they were a solid pair of ties, walking shoes with a medium heel, a practical gift.

He gave them to Rosa the next day, a Wednesday. He felt a bit embarrassed to be doing that, because he realized that despite his warnings to her, he had permitted himself to meddle in her affairs; but he considered giving her the shoes a psychologically proper move in more ways than one. In presenting her with them he said, "Rosa, I have perhaps a solution to suggest in the matter you discussed with me. Here are a pair of new shoes for you. Tell your friend you must refuse his. And when you do, perhaps it would be advisable also to inform him that you intend to see him a little less frequently from now on."

Rosa was overjoyed at the professor's kindness. She attempted to kiss his hand but he thrust it behind him and at once retired to his study. On Thursday, when he opened the apartment door to her ring, she was wearing his shoes. She carried a large paper bag from which she offered the professor three small oranges still on a branch with green leaves. He said she needn't have bought them but Rosa, smiling half hiddenly in order not to show her teeth, said that she wanted him to see how grateful she was. Later she requested permission to leave at three so she could show Armando her new shoes.

He said dryly, "You may go at that hour if your work is done."

She thanked him profusely. Hastening through her tasks, she left shortly after three, but not before the professor, in his hat, gloves and bathrobe, standing nervously at his open study door as he was inspecting the corridor floor she had just mopped, saw her hurrying out of the apartment, wearing a pair of dressy black needlepoint pumps. This angered him; and when Rosa appeared the next morning, though she begged him not to when he said she had made a fool of him and he was firing her to teach her a lesson, the professor did. She wept, pleading for another chance, but he would not change his mind. So she desolately wrapped up the odds and ends in her room in a newspaper and left, still crying. Afterwards he was upset and very nervous. He could not stand the cold that day and he could not work.

A week later, the morning the heat was turned on, Rosa appeared at the apartment door, and begged to have her job back. She was distraught, said her son had hit her, and gently touched her puffed black-and-blue upper lip. With tears in her eyes, although she didn't cry, Rosa explained it was no fault of hers that she had accepted both pairs of shoes. Armando had given her his pair first; had, out of jealousy of a possible rival, forced her to take them. Then when the professor had kindly offered his pair of shoes, she had wanted to refuse them but was afraid of angering him and losing her job. This was God's truth, so help her St. Peter. She would, she promised, find Armando, whom she had not seen in a week, and return his shoes if the professor would take her back. If he didn't, she would throw herself into the Tiber. He, though he didn't care for talk of this kind, felt a certain sympathy for her. He was disappointed in himself at the way he had handled her. It would have been better to have said a few appropriate words on the subject of honesty and then philosophically dropped the matter. In firing her he had only made things difficult for them both, because, in the meantime he had tried two other maids and found them unsuitable. One stole, the other was lazy. As a result the house was a mess, impossible for him to work in, although the portinaia came up for an hour each morning to clean. It was his good fortune that Rosa had appeared at the door just then. When she removed her coat, he noticed with satisfaction that the tear in her dress had finally been sewn.

She went grimly to work, dusting, polishing, cleaning everything in sight. She unmade beds, then made them, swept under them, mopped, polished head and foot boards, adorned the beds with newly pressed spreads. Though she had just got her job back and worked with her usual efficiency, she worked, he observed, in sadness, frequently sighing, attempting a smile only when his eye was on her. This is their nature, he thought; they have hard lives. To spare her further blows by her son he gave her permission to live in. He offered extra money to buy meat for her supper but she refused it, saying pasta would do. Pasta and green salad was all she ate at night. Occasionally she boiled an artichoke left over from lunch and ate it with oil and vinegar. He invited her to drink the white wine in the cupboard and take fruit. Once in a while she did, always telling what and how much, though he repeatedly asked her not to. The apartment was nicely in order. Though the phone rang, as usual, daily at three, only seldom did she leave the house after she had talked with Armando.

Then one dismal morning Rosa came to the professor and in her distraught way confessed she was pregnant. Her face was lit in despair; her white underwear shone through her black dress.

He felt disgust, blaming himself for having re-employed her.

"You must leave at once," he said, trying to keep his voice from trembling.

"I can't," she said. "My son will kill me. In God's name, help me, professore."

He was infuriated by her stupidity. "Your adventures are none of my responsibility."

"You've got to help me," she moaned.

"Was it this Armando?" he asked almost savagely.

She nodded.

"Have you informed him?"

"Yes."

"What did he say?"

"He says he can't believe it." She tried to smile but couldn't.

"I'll convince him," he said. "Do you have his telephone number?"

She told it to him. He called Armando at his office, identified himself, and asked the government clerk to come at once to the apartment. "You have a grave responsibility to Rosa."

"I have a grave responsibility to my family," Armando answered.

"You might have considered them before this."

"All right, I'll come over tomorrow after work. It's impossible today. I have a carpentering contract to finish up."

"She'll expect you," the professor said.

When he hung up he felt less angry, though still more emotional than he cared to feel. "Are you quite sure of your condition?" he asked her, "that you are pregnant?"

"Yes." She was crying now. "Tomorrow is my son's birthday. What a beautiful present it will be for him to find out his mother's a whore. He'll break my bones, if not with his hands, then with his teeth."

"It hardly seems likely you can conceive, considering your age."

"My mother gave birth at fifty."

"Isn't there a possibility you are mistaken?"

"I don't know. It's never been this way before. After all, I've been a widow—"

"Well, you'd better find out."

"Yes, I want to," Rosa said. "I want to see the midwife in my neighborhood but I haven't got a single lire. I spent all I had left when I wasn't working, and I had to borrow carfare to get here. Armando can't help me just now. He has to pay for his wife's teeth this week. She has very bad teeth, poor thing. That's why I came to you. Could you advance me two thousand of my pay so I can be examined by the midwife?"

I must put an end to this, he thought. After a minute he counted two one thousand lire notes out of his wallet. "Go to her now," he said. He was about to add that if she was pregnant, not to come back, but he was afraid she might do something desperate, or lie to him so she could go on working. He didn't want her around any more. When he thought of his wife and daughter arriving amidst this mess, he felt sick with nervousness. He wanted to get rid of the maid as soon as possible.

The next day Rosa came in at twelve instead of nine. Her dark face was pale. "Excuse me for being late," she murmured. "I was praying at my husband's grave."

"That's all right," the professor said. "But did you go to the midwife?"

"Not yet."

"Why not?" Though angry he spoke calmly.

She stared at the floor.

"Please answer my question."

"I was going to say I lost the two thousand lire on the bus, but after being at my husband's grave I'll tell you the truth. After all, it's bound to come out."

This is terrible, he thought, it's unending. "What did you do with the money?"

"That's what I mean," Rosa sighed. "I bought my son a present. Not that he deserves it but it was his birthday." She burst into tears.

He stared at her a minute, then said, "Please come with me."

The professor left the apartment in his bathrobe, and Rosa followed. Opening the elevator door he stepped inside, holding the door for her. She entered the elevator.

They stopped two floors below. He got out and near-sightedly scanned the names on the brass plates above the bells. Finding the one he wanted, he pressed the button. A maid opened the door and let them in. She seemed frightened at Rosa's expression.

"Is the doctor in?" the professor asked the doctor's maid.

"I will see."

"Please ask him if he'll see me for a minute. I live in the building, two flights up."

"Si, signore." She glanced again at Rosa, then went inside.

The Italian doctor came out, a short middle-aged man with a beard. The professor had once or twice passed him in the cortile of the apartment house. The doctor was buttoning his shirt cuff.

"I am sorry to trouble you, sir," said the professor. "This is my maid, who has been having some difficulty. She would like to determine whether she is pregnant. Can you assist her?"

The doctor looked at him, then at the maid, who had a handkerchief to her eyes.

"Let her come into my office."

"Thank you," said the professor. The doctor nodded.

The professor went up to his apartment. In a half hour the phone rang.

"Pronto."

It was the doctor. "She is not pregnant," he said. "She is frightened. She also has trouble with her liver."

"Can you be certain, doctor?"

"Yes."

"Thank you," said the professor. "If you write her a prescription, please have it charged to me, and also send me your bill."

"I will," said the doctor and hung up.

Rosa came into the apartment. "The doctor told you?" the professor said. "You aren't pregnant."

"It's the Virgin's blessing," said Rosa.

"Indeed, you are lucky." Speaking quietly, he then told her she would have to go. "I'm sorry, Rosa, but I simply cannot be constantly caught up in this sort of thing. It upsets me and I can't work."

"I know." She turned her head away.

The door bell rang. It was Armando, a small thin man in a long gray overcoat. He was wearing a rakish black Borsalino and a slight mustache. He had dark, worried eyes. He tipped his hat to them.

Rosa told him she was leaving the apartment.

"Then let me help you get your things," Armando said. He followed her to the maid's room and they wrapped Rosa's things in newspaper.

When they came out of the room, Armando carrying a shopping bag, Rosa holding a shoe box wrapped in a newspaper, the professor handed Rosa the remainder of her month's wages.

"I'm sorry," he said again, "but I have my wife and daughter to think of. They'll be here in a few days."

She answered nothing. Armando, smoking a cigarette butt, gently opened the door for her and they left together.

Later the professor inspected the maid's room and saw that Rosa had taken all her belongings but the shoes he had given her. When his wife arrived in the apartment, shortly before Thanksgiving, she gave the shoes to the portinaia, who wore them a week, then gave them to her daughter-in-law.

Black Is My Favorite Color

Charity Sweetness sits in the toilet eating her two hard-boiled eggs while I'm having my ham sandwich and coffee in the kitchen. That's how it goes only don't get the idea of ghettoes. If there's a ghetto I'm the one that's in it. She's my cleaning woman from Father Divine and comes in once a week to my small three-room apartment on my day off from the liquor store. "Peace," she says to me, "Father reached on down and took me right up in Heaven." She's a small person with a flat body, frizzy hair, and a quiet face that the light shines out of, and Mama had such eyes before she died. The first time Charity Sweetness came in to clean, a little more than a year and a half, I made the mistake to ask her to sit down at the kitchen table with me and eat her lunch. I was still feeling not so hot after Ornita left but I'm the kind of a man—Nat Lime, forty-four, a bachelor with a daily growing bald spot on the back of my head, and I could lose frankly fifteen pounds—who enjoys company so long as he has it. So she cooked up her two hardboiled eggs and sat down and took a small bite out of one of them. But after a minute she stopped chewing and she got up and carried the eggs in a cup in the bathroom, and since then she eats there. I said to her more than once, "Okay, Charity Sweetness, so have it your way, eat the eggs in the kitchen by yourself and I'll eat when you're done," but she smiles absentminded, and eats in the toilet. It's my fate with colored people.

Although black is still my favorite color you wouldn't know it from my luck except in short quantities even though I do all right in the liquor store business in Harlem, on Eighth Avenue

between 110th and 111th. I speak with respect. A large part of
my life I've had dealings with Negro people, most on a business
basis but sometimes for friendly reasons with genuine feeling
on both sides. I'm drawn to them. At this time of my life I should
have one or two good colored friends but the fault isn't necessarily mine. If they knew what was in my heart towards them,
but how can you tell that to anybody nowadays? I've tried more
than once but the language of the heart either is a dead language
or else nobody understands it the way you speak it. Very few.
What I'm saying is, personally for me there's only one human
color and that's the color of blood. I like a black person if not
because he's black, then because I'm white. It comes to the same
thing. If I wasn't white my first choice would be black. I'm
satisfied to be white because I have no other choice. Anyway, I
got an eye for color. I appreciate. Who wants everybody to be
the same? Maybe it's like some kind of a talent. Nat Lime might
be a liquor dealer in Harlem, but once in the jungle in New
Guinea in the Second War, I got the idea when I shot at a running Jap and missed him, that I had some kind of a talent,
though maybe it's the kind where you have a marvelous idea now
and then but in the end what do they come to? After all, it's a
strange world.

Where Charity Sweetness eats her eggs makes me think about
Buster Wilson when we were both boys in the Williamsburg section of Brooklyn. There was this long block of run-down dirty
frame houses in the middle of a not-so-hot white neighborhood
full of pushcarts. The Negro houses looked to me like they had
been born and died there, dead not long after the beginning of
the world. I lived on the next street. My father was a cutter
with arthritis in both hands, big red knuckles and swollen fingers
so he didn't cut, and my mother was the one who went to work.
She sold paper bags from a second-hand pushcart in Ellery Street.
We didn't starve but nobody ate chicken unless we were sick
or the chicken was. This was my first acquaintance with a lot of
black people and I used to poke around on their poor block. I

think I thought, brother, if there can be like this, what can't there be? I mean I caught an early idea what life was about. Anyway I met Buster Wilson there. He used to play marbles by himself. I sat on the curb across the street, watching him shoot one marble lefty and the other one righty. The hand that won picked up the marbles. It wasn't so much of a game but he didn't ask me to come over. My idea was to be friendly, only he never encouraged, he discouraged. Why did I pick him out for a friend? Maybe because I had no others then, we were new in the neighborhood, from Manhattan. Also I liked his type. Buster did everything alone. He was a skinny kid and his brothers' clothes hung on him like worn-out potato sacks. He was a beanpole boy, about twelve, and I was then ten. His arms and legs were burnt out matchsticks. He always wore a brown wool sweater, one arm half unraveled, the other went down to the wrist. His long and narrow head had a white part cut straight in the short woolly hair, maybe with a ruler there, by his father, a barber but too drunk to stay a barber. In those days though I had little myself I was old enough to know who was better off, and the whole block of colored houses made me feel bad in the daylight. But I went there as much as I could because the street was full of life. In the night it looked different, it's hard to tell a cripple in the dark. Sometimes I was afraid to walk by the houses when they were dark and quiet. I was afraid there were people looking at me that I couldn't see. I liked it better when they had parties at night and everybody had a good time. The musicians played their banjos and saxophones and the houses shook with the music and laughing. The young girls, with their pretty dresses and ribbons in their hair, caught me in my throat when I saw them through the windows.

But with the parties came drinking and fights. Sundays were bad days after the Saturday night parties. I remember once that Buster's father, also long and loose, always wearing a dirty gray Homburg hat, chased another black man in the street with a half-inch chisel. The other one, maybe five feet high, lost his shoe and when they wrestled on the ground he was already bleeding through his suit, a thick red blood smearing the sidewalk. I was frightened by the blood and wanted to pour it back in the man who was bleeding from the chisel. On another time Buster's father was playing in a crap game with two big bouncy red dice, in the back of an alley between two middle houses. Then about six men started fist-fighting there, and they ran out of the alley and hit each other in the street. The neighbors, including children, came out and watched, everybody afraid but nobody moving to do anything. I saw the same thing near my store in Harlem, years later, a big crowd watching two men in the street, their breaths hanging in the air on a winter night, murdering each other with switch knives, but nobody moved to call a cop. I didn't either. Anyway, I was just a young kid but I still remember how the cops drove up in a police paddy wagon and broke up the fight by hitting everybody they could hit with big nightsticks. This was in the days before LaGuardia. Most of the fighters were knocked out cold, only one or two got away. Buster's father started to run back in his house but a cop ran after him and cracked him on his Homburg hat with a club, right on the front porch. Then the Negro men were lifted up by the cops, one at the arms and the other at the feet, and they heaved them in the paddy wagon. Buster's father hit the back of the wagon and fell, with his nose spouting very red blood, on top of three other men. I personally couldn't stand it, I was scared of the human race so I ran home, but I remember Buster watching without any expression in his eyes. I stole an extra fifteen cents from my mother's pocketbook and I ran back and asked Buster if he wanted to go to the movies. I would pay. He said yes. This was the first time he talked to me.

So we went more than once to the movies. But we never got to be friends. Maybe because it was a one-way proposition—from me to him. Which includes my invitations to go with me, my (poor mother's) movie money, Hershey chocolate bars, watermelon slices, even my best Nick Carter and Merriwell books that I spent hours picking up in the junk shops, and that he never gave me back. Once he let me go in his house to get a match so we could smoke some butts we found, but it smelled so heavy, so impossible, I died till I got out of there. What I saw in the way of furniture I won't mention—the best was falling apart in pieces. Maybe we went to the movies all together five or six matinees that spring and in the summertime, but when the shows were over he usually walked home by himself.

"Why don't you wait for me, Buster?" I said. "We're both going in the same direction."

But he was walking ahead and didn't hear me. Anyway he didn't answer.

One day when I wasn't expecting it he hit me in the teeth. I felt like crying but not because of the pain. I spit blood and said, "What did you hit me for? What did I do to you?"

"Because you a Jew bastard. Take your Jew movies and your Jew candy and shove them up your Jew ass."

And he ran away.

I thought to myself how was I to know he didn't like the movies. When I was a man I thought, you can't force it.

Years later, in the prime of my life, I met Mrs. Ornita Harris. She was standing by herself under an open umbrella at the bus stop, crosstown 110th, and I picked up her green glove that she had dropped on the wet sidewalk. It was in the end of November. Before I could ask her was it hers, she grabbed the glove out of my hand, closed her umbrella, and stepped in the bus. I got on right after her.

I was annoyed so I said, "If you'll pardon me, Miss, there's no law that you have to say thanks, but at least don't make a criminal out of me."

"Well, I'm sorry," she said, "but I don't like white men trying to do me favors."

I tipped my hat and that was that. In ten minutes I got off the bus but she was already gone.

Who expected to see her again but I did. She came into my store about a week later for a bottle of scotch.

"I would offer you a discount," I told her, "but I know you

don't like a certain kind of a favor and I'm not looking for a slap
in the face."

Then she recognized me and got a little embarrassed.

"I'm sorry I misunderstood you that day."

"So mistakes happen."

The result was she took the discount. I gave her a dollar off.

She used to come in about every two weeks for a fifth of Haig
and Haig. Sometimes I waited on her, sometimes my helpers,
Jimmy or Mason, also colored, but I said to give the discount.
They both looked at me but I had nothing to be ashamed. In the
spring when she came in we used to talk once in a while. She was
a slim woman, dark but not the most dark, about thirty years I
would say, also well built, with a combination nice legs and a
good-size bosom that I like. Her face was pretty, with big eyes
and high cheek bones, but lips a little thick and nose a little broad.
Sometimes she didn't feel like talking, she paid for the bottle, less
discount, and walked out. Her eyes were tired and she didn't
look to me like a happy woman.

I found out her husband was once a window cleaner on the big
buildings, but one day his safety belt broke and he fell fifteen
stories. After the funeral she got a job as a manicurist in a Times
Square barber shop. I told her I was a bachelor and lived with
my mother in a small three-room apartment on West Eighty-third
near Broadway. My mother had cancer, and Ornita said she was
very sorry.

One night in July we went out together. How that happened
I'm still not so sure. I guess I asked her and she didn't say no.
Where do you go out with a Negro woman? We went to the
Village. We had a good dinner and walked in Washington Square
Park. It was a hot night. Nobody was surprised when they saw
us, nobody looked at us like we were against the law. If they
looked maybe they saw my new lightweight suit that I bought
yesterday and my shiny bald spot when we walked under a lamp,
also how pretty she was for a man of my type. We went in a
movie on West Eighth Street. I didn't want to go in but she said

she had heard about the picture. We went in like strangers and we came out like strangers. I wondered what was in her mind and I thought to myself, whatever is in there it's not a certain white man that I know. All night long we went together like we were chained. After the movie she wouldn't let me take her back to Harlem. When I put her in a taxi she asked me, "Why did we bother?"

For the steak, I wanted to say. Instead I said, "You're worth the bother."

"Thanks anyway."

Kiddo, I thought to myself after the taxi left, you just found out what's what, now the best thing is forget her.

It's easy to say. In August we went out the second time. That was the night she wore a purple dress and I thought to myself, my God, what colors. Who paints that picture paints a masterpiece. Everybody looked at us but I had pleasure. That night when she took off her dress it was in a furnished room I had the sense to rent a few days before. With my sick mother, I couldn't ask her to come to my apartment, and she didn't want me to go home with her where she lived with her brother's family on West 115th near Lenox Avenue. Under her purple dress she wore a black slip, and when she took that off she had white underwear. When she took off the white underwear she was black again. But I know where the next white was, if you want to call it white. And that was the night I think I fell in love with her, the first time in my life though I have liked one or two nice girls I used to go with when I was a boy. It was a serious proposition. I'm the kind of a man when I think of love I'm thinking of marriage. I guess that's why I am a bachelor.

That same week I had a holdup in my place, two big men— both black—with revolvers. One got excited when I rang open the cash register so he could take the money and he hit me over the ear with his gun. I stayed in the hospital a couple of weeks. Otherwise I was insured. Ornita came to see me. She sat on a chair without talking much. Finally I saw she was uncomfortable so I suggested she ought to go home.

"I'm sorry it happened," she said.

"Don't talk like it's your fault."

When I got out of the hospital my mother was dead. She was a wonderful person. My father died when I was thirteen and all by herself she kept the family alive and together. I sat shive for a week and remembered how she sold paper bags on her pushcart. I remembered her life and what she tried to teach me. Nathan, she said, if you ever forget you are a Jew a goy will remind you. Mama, I said, rest in peace on this subject. But if I do something you don't like, remember, on earth it's harder than where you are. Then when my week of mourning was finished, one night I said, "Ornita, let's get married. We're both honest people and if you love me like I love you it won't be such a bad time. If you don't like New York I'll sell out here and we'll move someplace else. Maybe to San Francisco where nobody knows us. I was there for a week in the Second War and I saw white and colored living together."

"Nat," she answered me, "I like you but I'd be afraid. My husband woulda killed me."

"Your husband is dead."

"Not in my memory."

"In that case I'll wait."

"Do you know what it'd be like—I mean the life we could expect?"

"Ornita," I said, "I'm the kind of a man, if he picks his own way of life he's satisfied."

"What about children? Were you looking forward to half-Jewish polka dots?"

"I was looking forward to children."

"I can't," she said.

Can't is can't. I saw she was afraid and the best thing was not to push. Sometimes when we met she was so nervous that whatever we did she couldn't enjoy it. At the same time I still thought

I had a chance. We were together more and more. I got rid of my furnished room and she came to my apartment—I gave away Mama's bed and bought a new one. She stayed with me all day on Sundays. When she wasn't so nervous she was affectionate, and if I know what love is, I had it. We went out a couple of times a week, the same way—usually I met her in Times Square and sent her home in a taxi, but I talked more about marriage and she talked less against it. One night she told me she was still trying to convince herself but she was almost convinced. I took an inventory of my liquor stock so I could put the store up for sale.

Ornita knew what I was doing. One day she quit her job, the next she took it back. She also went away a week to visit her sister in Philadelphia for a little rest. She came back tired but said maybe. Maybe is maybe so I'll wait. The way she said it it was closer to yes. That was the winter two years ago. When she was in Philadelphia I called up a friend of mine from the Army, now a CPA, and told him I would appreciate an invitation for an evening. He knew why. His wife said yes right away. When Ornita came back we went there. The wife made a fine dinner. It wasn't a bad time and they told us to come again. Ornita had a few drinks. She looked relaxed, wonderful. Later, because of a twenty-four hour taxi strike I had to take her home on the subway. When we go to the 116th Street station she told me to stay on the train, and she would walk the couple of blocks to her house. I didn't like a woman walking alone on the streets at that time of the night. She said she never had any trouble but I insisted nothing doing. I said I would walk to her stoop with her and when she went upstairs I would go back to the subway.

On the way there, on 115th in the middle of the block before Lenox, we were stopped by three men—maybe they were boys. One had a black hat with a half-inch brim, one a green cloth hat, and the third wore a black leather cap. The green hat was wearing a short coat and the other two had long ones. It was under a street light but the leather cap snapped a six-inch switchblade open in the light.

"What you doin' with this white son of a bitch?" he said to Ornita.

"I'm minding my own business," she answered him, "and I wish you would too."

"Boys," I said, "we're all brothers. I'm a reliable merchant in the neighborhood. This young lady is my dear friend. We don't want any trouble. Please let us pass."

"You talk like a Jew landlord," said the green hat. "Fifty a week for a single room."

"No charge fo' the rats," said the half-inch brim.

"Believe me, I'm no landlord. My store is 'Nathan's Liquors' between Hundred Tenth and Eleventh. I also have two colored clerks, Mason and Jimmy, and they will tell you I pay good wages as well as I give discounts to certain customers."

"Shut your mouth, Jewboy," said the leather cap, and he moved the knife back and forth in front of my coat button. "No more black pussy for you."

"Speak with respect about this lady, please."

I got slapped on my mouth.

"That ain't no lady," said the long face in the half-inch brim, "that's black pussy. She deserve to have evvy bit of her hair shave off. How you like to have evvy bit of your hair shave off, black pussy?"

"Please leave me and this gentleman alone or I'm gonna scream long and loud. That's my house three doors down."

They slapped her. I never heard such a scream. Like her husband was falling fifteen stories.

I hit the one that slapped her and the next I knew I was laying in the gutter with a pain in my head. I thought, goodbye, Nat, they'll stab me for sure, but all they did was take my wallet and run in three different directions.

Ornita walked back with me to the subway and she wouldn't let me go home with her again.

"Just get home safely."

She looked terrible. Her face was gray and I still remembered her scream. It was a terrible winter night, very cold February, and it took me an hour and ten minutes to get home. I felt bad for leaving her but what could I do?

We had a date downtown the next night but she didn't show up, the first time.

In the morning I called her in her place of business.

"For God's sake, Ornita, if we got married and moved away we wouldn't have that kind of trouble that we had. We wouldn't come in that neighborhood any more.

"Yes, we would. I have family there and don't want to move anyplace else. The truth of it is I can't marry you, Nat. I got troubles enough of my own."

"I coulda sworn you love me."

"Maybe I do but I can't marry you."

"For God's sake, why?"

"I got enough trouble of my own."

I went that night in a cab to her brother's house to see her. He was a quiet man with a thin mustache. "She gone," he said, "left for a long visit to some close relatives in the South. She said to tell you she appreciate your intentions but didn't think it will work out."

"Thank you kindly," I said.

Don't ask me how I got home.

Once on Eighth Avenue, a couple of blocks from my store, I saw a blind man with a white cane tapping on the sidewalk. I figured we were going in the same direction so I took his arm.

"I can tell you're white," he said.

A heavy colored woman with a full shopping bag rushed after us.

"Never mind," she said, "I know where he live."

She pushed me with her shoulder and I hurt my leg on the fire hydrant.

That's how it is. I give my heart and they kick me in my teeth.

"Charity Sweetness—you hear me?—come out of that god-damn toilet!"

The Jewbird

The window was open so the skinny bird flew in. Flappity-flap
with its frazzled black wings. That's how it goes. It's open, you're
in. Closed, you're out and that's your fate. The bird wearily
flapped through the open kitchen window of Harry Cohen's
top-floor apartment on First Avenue near the lower East River.
On a rod on the wall hung an escaped canary cage, its door wide
open, but this black-type longbeaked bird—its ruffled head and
small dull eyes, crossed a little, making it look like a dissipated
crow—landed if not smack on Cohen's thick lamb chop, at least
on the table, close by. The frozen foods salesman was sitting at
supper with his wife and young son on a hot August evening a
year ago. Cohen, a heavy man with hairy chest and beefy shorts;
Edie, in skinny yellow shorts and red halter; and their ten-year-
old Morris (after her father)—Maurie, they called him, a nice
kid though not overly bright—were all in the city after two
weeks out, because Cohen's mother was dying. They had been
enjoying Kingston, New York, but drove back when Mama got
sick in her flat in the Bronx.

"Right on the table," said Cohen, putting down his beer glass
and swatting at the bird. "Son of a bitch."

"Harry, take care with your language," Edie said, looking at
Maurie, who watched every move.

The bird cawed hoarsely and with a flap of its bedraggled
wings—feathers tufted this way and that—rose heavily to the
top of the open kitchen door, where it perched staring down.

"Gevalt, a pogrom!"

"It's a talking bird," said Edie in astonishment.

"In Jewish," said Maurie.

"Wise guy," muttered Cohen. He gnawed on his chop, then put down the bone. "So if you can talk, say what's your business. What do you want here?"

"If you can't spare a lamb chop," said the bird, "I'll settle for a piece of herring with a crust of bread. You can't live on your nerve forever."

"This ain't a restaurant," Cohen replied. "All I'm asking is what brings you to this address?"

"The window was open," the bird sighed; adding after a moment, "I'm running. I'm flying but I'm also running."

"From whom?" asked Edie with interest.

"Anti-Semeets."

"Anti-Semites?" they all said.

"That's from who."

"What kind of anti-Semites bother a bird?" Edie asked.

"Any kind," said the bird, "also including eagles, vultures, and hawks. And once in a while some crows will take your eyes out."

"But aren't you a crow?"

"Me? I'm a Jewbird."

Cohen laughed heartily. "What do you mean by that?"

The bird began dovening. He prayed without Book or tallith, but with passion. Edie bowed her head though not Cohen. And Maurie rocked back and forth with the prayer, looking up with one wide-open eye.

When the prayer was done Cohen remarked, "No hat, no phylacteries?"

"I'm an old radical."

"You're sure you're not some kind of a ghost or dybbuk?"

"Not a dybbukk," answered the bird, "though one of my relatives had such an experience once. It's all over now, thanks God. They freed her from a former lover, a crazy jealous man. She's now the mother of two wonderful children."

"Birds?" Cohen asked slyly.

"Why not?"

"What kind of birds?"

"Like me. Jewbirds."

Cohen tipped back in his chair and guffawed. "That's a big laugh. I've heard of a Jewfish but not a Jewbird."

"We're once removed." The bird rested on one skinny leg, then on the other. "Please, could you spare maybe a piece of herring with a small crust of bread?"

Edie got up from the table.

"What are you doing?" Cohen asked her.

"I'll clear the dishes."

Cohen turned to the bird. "So what's your name, if you don't mind saying?"

"Call me Schwartz."

"He might be an old Jew changed into a bird by somebody," said Edie, removing a plate.

"Are you?" asked Harry, lighting a cigar.

"Who knows?" answered Schwartz. "Does God tell us everything?"

Maurie got up on his chair. "What kind of herring?" he asked the bird in excitement.

"Get down, Maurie, or you'll fall," ordered Cohen.

"If you haven't got matjes, I'll take schmaltz," said Schwartz.

"All we have is marinated, with slices of onion—in a jar," said Edie.

"If you'll open for me the jar I'll eat marinated. Do you have also, if you don't mind, a piece of rye bread—the spitz?"

Edie thought she had.

"Feed him out on the balcony," Cohen said. He spoke to the bird. "After that take off."

Schwartz closed both bird eyes. "I'm tired and it's a long way."

"Which direction are you headed, north or south?"

Schwartz, barely lifting his wings, shrugged.

"You don't know where you're going?"

"Where there's charity I'll go."

"Let him stay, papa," said Maurie. "He's only a bird."

"So stay the night," Cohen said, "but no longer."

In the morning Cohen ordered the bird out of the house but Maurie cried, so Schwartz stayed for a while. Maurie was still on vacation from school and his friends were away. He was lonely and Edie enjoyed the fun he had, playing with the bird.

"He's no trouble at all," she told Cohen, "and besides his appetite is very small."

"What'll you do when he makes dirty?"

"He flies across the street in a tree when he makes dirty, and if nobody passes below, who notices?"

"So all right," said Cohen, "but I'm dead set against it. I warn you he ain't gonna stay here long."

"What have you got against the poor bird?"

"Poor bird, my ass. He's a foxy bastard. He thinks he's a Jew."

"What difference does it make what he thinks?"

"A Jewbird, what a chuzpah. One false move and he's out on his drumsticks."

At Cohen's insistence Schwartz lived out on the balcony in a new wooden birdhouse Edie had bought him.

"With many thanks," said Schwartz, "though I would rather have a human roof over my head. You know how it is at my age. I like the warm, the windows, the smell of cooking. I would also be glad to see once in a while the *Jewish Morning Journal* and have now and then a schnapps because it helps my breathing, thanks God. But whatever you give me, you won't hear complaints."

However, when Cohen brought home a bird feeder full of dried corn, Schwartz said, "Impossible."

Cohen was annoyed. "What's the matter, crosseyes, is your life getting too good for you? Are you forgetting what it means to be migratory? I'll bet a helluva lot of crows you happen to be acquainted with, Jews or otherwise, would give their eyeteeth to eat this corn."

Schwartz did not answer. What can you say to a grubber yung?

"Not for my digestion," he later explained to Edie. "Cramps.

Herring is better even if it makes you thirsty. At least rainwater
don't cost anything." He laughed sadly in breathy caws.

And herring, thanks to Edie, who knew where to shop, was
what Schwartz got, with an occasional piece of potato pancake,
and even a bit of soupmeat when Cohen wasn't looking.

When school began in September, before Cohen would once
again suggest giving the bird the boot, Edie prevailed on him to
wait a little while until Maurie adjusted.

"To deprive him right now might hurt his school work, and
you know what trouble we had last year."

"So okay, but sooner or later the bird goes. That I promise
you."

Schwartz, though nobody had asked him, took on full responsibility for Maurie's performance in school. In return for
favors granted, when he was let in for an hour or two at night,
he spent most of his time overseeing the boy's lessons. He sat
on top of the dresser near Maurie's desk as he laboriously wrote
out his homework. Maurie was a restless type and Schwartz gently
kept him to his studies. He also listened to him practice his
screechy violin, taking a few minutes off now and then to rest his
ears in the bathroom. And they afterwards played dominoes. The
boy was an indifferent checker player and it was impossible to
teach him chess. When he was sick, Schwartz read him comic
books though he personally disliked them. But Maurie's work improved in school and even his violin teacher admitted his playing
was better. Edie gave Schwartz credit for these improvements
though the bird pooh-poohed them.

Yet he was proud there was nothing lower then C minuses on
Maurie's report card, and on Edie's insistence celebrated with a
little schnapps.

"If he keeps up like this," Cohen said, "I'll get him in an Ivy
League college for sure."

"Oh I hope so," sighed Edie.

But Schwartz shook his head. "He's a good boy—you don't
have to worry. He won't be a shicker or a wifebeater, God for-

bid, but a scholar he'll never be, if you know what I mean, although maybe a good mechanic. It's no disgrace in these times."

"If I were you," Cohen said, angered, "I'd keep my big snoot out of other people's private business."

"Harry, please," said Edie.

"My goddamn patience is wearing out. That crosseyes butts into everything."

Though he wasn't exactly a welcome guest in the house, Schwartz gained a few ounces although he did not improve in appearance. He looked bedraggled as ever, his feathers unkempt, as though he had just flown out of a snowstorm. He spent, he admitted, little time taking care of himself. Too much to think about. "Also outside plumbing," he told Edie. Still there was more glow to his eyes so that though Cohen went on calling him crosseyes he said it less emphatically.

Liking his situation, Schwartz tried tactfully to stay out of Cohen's way, but one night when Edie was at the movies and Maurie was taking a hot shower, the frozen foods salesman began a quarrel with the bird.

"For Christ sake, why don't you wash yourself sometimes? Why must you always stink like a dead fish?"

"Mr. Cohen, if you'll pardon me, if somebody eats garlic he will smell from garlic. I eat herring three times a day. Feed me flowers and I will smell like flowers."

"Who's obligated to feed you anything at all? You're lucky to get herring."

"Excuse me, I'm not complaining," said the bird. "You're complaining."

"What's more," said Cohen, "even from out on the balcony I can hear you snoring away like a pig. It keeps me awake at night."

"Snoring," said Schwartz, "isn't a crime, thanks God."

"All in all you are a goddamn pest and free loader. Next thing you'll want to sleep in bed next to my wife."

"Mr. Cohen," said Schwartz, "on this rest assured. A bird is a bird."

"So you say, but how do I know you're a bird and not some kind of a goddamn devil?"

"If I was a devil you would know already. And I don't mean because your son's good marks."

"Shut up, you bastard bird," shouted Cohen.

"Grubber yung," cawed Schwartz, rising to the tips of his talons, his long wings outstretched.

Cohen was about to lunge for the bird's scrawny neck but Maurie came out of the bathroom, and for the rest of the evening until Schwartz's bedtime on the balcony, there was pretended peace.

But the quarrel had deeply disturbed Schwartz and he slept badly. His snoring woke him, and awake, he was fearful of what would become of him. Wanting to stay out of Cohen's way, he kept to the birdhouse as much as possible. Cramped by it, he paced back and forth on the balcony ledge, or sat on the birdhouse roof, staring into space. In the evenings, while overseeing Maurie's lessons, he often fell asleep. Awakening, he nervously hopped around exploring the four corners of the room. He spent much time in Maurie's closet, and carefully examined his bureau drawers when they were left open. And once when he found a large paper bag on the floor, Schwartz poked his way into it to investigate what possibilities were. The boy was amused to see the bird in the paper bag.

"He wants to build a nest," he said to his mother.

Edie, sensing Schwartz's unhappiness, spoke to him quietly.

"Maybe if you did some of the things my husband wants you, you would get along better with him."

"Give me a for instance," Schwartz said.

"Like take a bath, for instance."

"I'm too old for baths," said the bird. "My feathers fall out without baths."

"He says you have a bad smell."

"Everybody smells. Some people smell because of their thoughts or because who they are. My bad smell comes from the food I eat. What does his come from?"

"I better not ask him or it might make him mad," said Edie.

In late November Schwartz froze on the balcony in the fog and cold, and especially on rainy days he woke with stiff joints and could barely move his wings. Already he felt twinges of rheumatism. He would have liked to spend more time in the warm house, particularly when Maurie was in school and Cohen at work. But though Edie was good-hearted and might have sneaked him in in the morning, just to thaw out, he was afraid to ask her. In the meantime Cohen, who had been reading articles about the migration of birds, came out on the balcony one night after work when Edie was in the kitchen preparing pot roast, and peeking into the birdhouse, warned Schwartz to be on his way soon if he knew what was good for him. "Time to hit the flyways."

"Mr. Cohen, why do you hate me so much?" asked the bird. "What did I do to you?"

"Because you're an A-number-one trouble maker, that's why. What's more, whoever heard of a Jewbird? Now scat or it's open war."

But Schwartz stubbornly refused to depart so Cohen embarked on a campaign of harassing him, meanwhile hiding it from Edie and Maurie. Maurie hated violence and Cohen didn't want to leave a bad impression. He thought maybe if he played dirty tricks on the bird he would fly off without being physically kicked out. The vacation was over, let him make his easy living off the fat of somebody else's land. Cohen worried about the effect of the bird's departure on Maurie's schooling but decided to take the chance, first, because the boy now seemed to have the knack of studying—give the black bird-bastard credit—and second, because Schwartz was driving him bats by being there always, even in his dreams.

The frozen foods salesman began his campaign against the bird by mixing watery cat food with the herring slices in Schwartz's dish. He also blew up and popped numerous paper bags outside the birdhouse as the bird slept, and when he had got Schwartz good and nervous, though not enough to leave, he brought a full-grown cat into the house, supposedly a gift for little Maurie, who had always wanted a pussy. The cat never stopped springing up at Schwartz whenever he saw him, one day managing to claw out several of his tailfeathers. And even at lesson time, when the cat was usually excluded from Maurie's room, though somehow or other he quickly found his way in at the end of the lesson, Schwartz was desperately fearful of his life and flew from pinnacle to pinnacle—light fixture to clothestree to door-top—in order to elude the beast's wet jaws.

Once when the bird complained to Edie how hazardous his existence was, she said, "Be patient, Mr. Schwartz. When the cat gets to know you better he won't try to catch you any more."

"When he stops trying we will both be in Paradise," Schwartz answered. "Do me a favor and get rid of him. He makes my whole life worry. I'm losing feathers like a tree loses leaves."

"I'm awfully sorry but Maurie likes the pussy and sleeps with it."

What could Schwartz do? He worried but came to no decision, being afraid to leave. So he ate the herring garnished with cat food, tried hard not to hear the paper bags bursting like fire crackers outside the birdhouse at night, and lived terror-stricken closer to the ceiling than the floor, as the cat, his tail flicking, endlessly watched him.

Weeks went by. Then on the day after Cohen's mother had died in her flat in the Bronx, when Maurie came home with a zero on an arithmetic test, Cohen, enraged, waited until Edie had taken the boy to his violin lesson, then openly attacked the bird. He chased him with a broom on the balcony and Schwartz frantically flew back and forth, finally escaping into his birdhouse. Cohen triumphantly reached in, and grabbing both skinny legs, dragged the bird out, cawing loudly, his wings wildly beating.

He whirled the bird around and around his head. But Schwartz, as he moved in circles, managed to swoop down and catch Cohen's nose in his beak, and hung on for dear life. Cohen cried out in great pain, punched the bird with his fist, and tugging at its legs with all his might, pulled his nose free. Again he swung the yawking Schwartz around until the bird grew dizzy, then with a furious heave, flung him into the night. Schwartz sank like stone into the street. Cohen then tossed the birdhouse and feeder after him, listening at the ledge until they crashed on the sidewalk below. For a full hour, broom in hand, his heart palpitating and nose throbbing with pain, Cohen waited for Schwartz to return but the broken-hearted bird didn't.

That's the end of that dirty bastard, the salesman thought and went in. Edie and Maurie had come home.

"Look," said Cohen, pointing to his bloody nose swollen three times it normal size, "what that sonofabitchy bird did. It's a permanent scar."

"Where is he now?" Edie asked, frightened.

"I threw him out and he flew away. Good riddance."

Nobody said no, though Edie touched a handkerchief to her eyes and Maurie rapidly tried the nine times table and found he knew approximately half.

In the spring when the winter's snow had melted, the boy, moved by a memory, wandered in the neighborhood, looking for Schwartz. He found a dead black bird in a small lot near the river, his two wings broken, neck twisted, and both bird-eyes plucked clean.

"Who did it to you, Mr. Schwartz?" Maurie wept.

"Anti-Semeets," Edie said later.

The Magic Barrel

Not long ago there lived in uptown New York, in a small almost meager room, though crowded with books, Leo Finkle, a rabbinical student in the Yeshivah University. Finkle, after six years of study, was to be ordained in June and had been advised by an acquaintance that he might find it easier to win himself a congregation if he were married. Since he had no present prospects of marriage, after two tormented days of turning it over in his mind, he called in Pinye Salzman, a marriage broker whose two-line advertisement he had read in the *Forward*.

The matchmaker appeared one night out of the dark fourth-floor hallway of the graystone rooming house where Finkle lived, grasping a black, strapped portfolio that had been worn thin with use. Salzman, who had been long in the business, was of slight but dignified build, wearing an old hat, and an overcoat too short and tight for him. He smelled frankly of fish, which he loved to eat, and although he was missing a few teeth, his presence was not displeasing, because of an amiable manner curiously contrasted with mournful eyes. His voice, his lips, his wisp of beard, his bony fingers were animated, but give him a moment of repose and his mild blue eyes revealed a depth of sadness, a characteristic that put Leo a little at ease although the situation, for him, was inherently tense.

He at once informed Salzman why he had asked him to come, explaining that his home was in Cleveland, and that but for his parents, who had married comparatively late in life, he was alone in the world. He had for six years devoted himself almost entirely to his studies, as a result of which, understandably, he had found himself without time for a social life and the company of young women. Therefore he thought it the better part of trial and error —of embarrassing fumbling—to call in an experienced person to advise him on these matters. He remarked in passing that the function of the marriage broker was ancient and honorable, highly approved in the Jewish community, because it made practical the necessary without hindering joy. Moreover, his own parents had been brought together by a matchmaker. They had made, if not a financially profitable marriage—since neither had possessed any worldly goods to speak of—at least a successful one in the sense of their everlasting devotion to each other. Salzman listened in embarrassed surprise, sensing a sort of apology. Later, however, he experienced a glow of pride in his work, an emotion that had left him years ago, and he heartily approved of Finkle.

The two went to their business. Leo had led Salzman to the only clear place in the room, a table near a window that overlooked the lamp-lit city. He seated himself at the matchmaker's side but facing him, attempting by an act of will to suppress the unpleasant tickle in his throat. Salzman eagerly unstrapped his portfolio and removed a loose rubber band from a thin packet of much-handled cards. As he flipped through them, a gesture and sound that physically hurt Leo, the student pretended not to see and gazed steadfastly out the window. Although it was still February, winter was on its last legs, signs of which he had for the first time in years begun to notice. He now observed the round white moon, moving high in the sky through a cloud menagerie, and watched with half-open mouth as it penetrated a huge hen, and dropped out of her like an egg laying itself. Salzman, though pretending through eyeglasses he had just slipped on, to be engaged in scanning the writing on the cards, stole occasional glances at the young man's distinguished face, noting with pleasure the long, severe scholar's nose, brown eyes heavy with learning, sensitive yet ascetic lips, and a certain, almost hollow quality of the dark cheeks. He gazed around at shelves upon shelves of books and let out a soft, contented sigh.

When Leo's eyes fell upon the cards, he counted six spread out in Salzman's hand.

"So few?" he asked in disappointment.

"You wouldn't believe me how much cards I got in my office," Salzman replied. "The drawers are already filled to the top, so I keep them now in a barrel, but is every girl good for a new rabbi?"

Leo blushed at this, regretting all he had revealed of himself in a curriculum vitae he had sent to Salzman. He had thought it best to acquaint him wtih his strict standards and specifications, but in having done so, felt he had told the marriage broker more than was absolutely necessary.

He hesitantly inquired, "Do you keep photographs of your clients on file?"

"First comes family, amount of dowry, also what kind promises," Salzman replied, unbuttoning his tight coat and settling himself in the chair. "After comes pictures, rabbi."

"Call me Mr. Finkle. I'm not yet a rabbi."

Salzman said he would, but instead called him doctor, which he changed to rabbi when Leo was not listening too attentively.

Salzman adjusted his horn-rimmed spectacles, gently cleared his throat and read in an eager voice the contents of the top card:

"Sophie P. Twenty four years. Widow one year. No children. Educated high school and two years college. Father promises eight thousand dollars. Has wonderful wholesale business. Also real estate. On the mother's side comes teachers, also one actor. Well known on Second Avenue."

Leo gazed up in surprise. "Did you say a widow?"

"A widow don't mean spoiled, rabbi. She lived with her husband maybe four months. He was a sick boy she made a mistake to marry him."

"Marrying a widow has never entered my mind."

"This is because you have no experience. A widow, especially if she is young and healthy like this girl, is a wonderful person to marry. She will be thankful to you the rest of her life. Believe

me, if I was looking now for a bride, I would marry a widow."
Leo reflceted, then shook his head.

Salzman hunched his shoulders in an almost imperceptible gesture of disappointment. He placed the card down on the wooden
table and began to read another:

"Lily H. High school teacher. Regular. Not a substitute. Has
savings and new Dodge car. Lived in Paris one year. Father is
successful dentist thirty-five years. Interested in professional man.
Well Americanized family. Wonderful opportunity."

"I knew her personally," said Salzman. "I wish you could see
this girl. She is a doll. Also very intelligent. All day you could
talk to her about books and theyater and what not. She also
knows current events."

"I don't believe you mentioned her age?"

"Her age?" Salzman said, raising his brows. "Her age is thirty-
two years."

Leo said after a while, "I'm afraid that seems a little too old."

Salzman let out a laugh. "So how old are you, rabbi?"

"Twenty-seven."

"So what is the difference, tell me, between twenty-seven and
thirty-two? My own wife is seven years older than me. So what
did I suffer?—Nothing. If Rothschild's a daughter wants to marry
you, would you say on account her age, no?"

"Yes," Leo said dryly.

Salzman shook off the no in the yes. "Five years don't mean a
thing. I give you my word that when you will live with her for
one week you will forget her age. What does it mean five years—
that she lived more and knows more than somebody who is
younger? On this girl, God bless her, years are not wasted. Each
one that it comes makes better the bargain."

"What subject does she teach in high school?"

"Languages. If you heard the way she speaks French, you will
think it is music. I am in the business twenty-five years, and I
recommend her with my whole heart. Believe me, I know what
I'm talking, rabbi."

"What's on the next card?" Leo said abruptly.

Salzman reluctantly turned up the third card:

"Ruth K. Nineteen years. Honor student. Father offers thirteen thousand cash to the right bridegroom. He is a medical doctor. Stomach specialist with marvelous practice. Brother in law owns own garment business. Particular people."

Salzman looked as if he had read his trump card.

"Did you say nineteen?" Leo asked with interest.

"On the dot."

"Is she attractive?" He blushed. "Pretty?"

Salzman kissed his finger tips. "A little doll. On this I give you my word. Let me call the father tonight and you will see what means pretty."

But Leo was troubled. "You're sure she's that young?"

"This I am positive. The father will show you the birth certificate."

"Are you positive there isn't something wrong with her?" Leo insisted.

"Who says there is wrong?"

"I don't understand why an American girl her age should go to a marriage broker."

A smile spread over Salzman's face.

"So for the same reason you went, she comes."

Leo flushed. "I am pressed for time."

Salzman, realizing he had been tactless, quickly explained. "The father came, not her. He wants she should have the best, so he looks around himself. When we will locate the right boy he will introduce him and encourage. This makes a better marriage than if a young girl without experience takes for herself. I don't have to tell you this."

"But don't you think this young girl believes in love?" Leo spoke uneasily.

Salzman was about to guffaw but caught himself and said soberly, "Love comes with the right person, not before."

Leo parted dry lips but did not speak. Noticing that Salzman had snatched a glance at the next card, he cleverly asked, "How is her health?"

"Perfect," Salzman said, breathing with difficulty. "Of course, she is a little lame on her right foot from an auto accident that it happened to her when she was twelve years, but nobody notices on account she is so brilliant and also beautiful."

Leo got up heavily and went to the window. He felt curiously bitter and upbraided himself for having called in the marriage broker. Finally, he shook his head.

"Why not?" Salzman persisted, the pitch of his voice rising.

"Because I detest stomach specialists."

"So what do you care what is his business? After you marry her do you need him? Who says he must come every Friday night in your house?"

Ashamed of the way the talk was going, Leo dismissed Salzman, who went home with heavy, melancholy eyes.

Though he had felt only relief at the marriage broker's departure, Leo was in low spirits the next day. He explained it as arising from Salzman's failure to produce a suitable bride for him. He did not care for his type of clientele. But when Leo found himself hesitating whether to seek out another matchmaker, one more polished than Pinye, he wondered if it could be—his protestations to the contrary, and although he honored his father and mother—that he did not, in essence, care for the matchmaking institution? This thought he quickly put out of mind yet found himself still upset. All day he ran around in the woods—missed an important appointment, forgot to give out his laundry, walked out of a Broadway cafeteria without paying and had to run back with the ticket in his hand; had even not recognized his landlady in the street when she passed with a friend and courteously called out, "A good evening to you, Doctor Finkle." By nightfall, however, he had regained sufficient calm to sink his nose into a book and there found peace from his thoughts.

Almost at once there came a knock on the door. Before Leo could say enter, Salzman, commercial cupid, was standing in the room. His face was gray and meager, his expression hungry, and he looked as if he would expire on his feet. Yet the marriage broker managed, by some trick of the muscles, to display a broad smile.

"So good evening. I am invited?"

Leo nodded, disturbed to see him again, yet unwilling to ask the man to leave.

Beaming still, Salzman laid his portfolio on the table. "Rabbi, I got for you tonight good news."

"I've asked you not to call me rabbi. I'm still a student."

"Your worries are finished. I have for you a first-class bride."

"Leave me in peace concerning this subject." Leo pretended lack of interest.

"The world will dance at your wedding."

"Please, Mr. Salzman, no more."

"But first must come back my strength," Salzman said weakly. He fumbled with the portfolio straps and took out of the leather case an oily paper bag, from which he extracted a hard, seeded roll and a small, smoked white fish. With a quick motion of his hand he stripped the fish out of its skin and began ravenously to chew. "All day in a rush," he muttered.

Leo watched him eat.

"A sliced tomato you have maybe?" Salzman hesitantly inquired.

"No."

The marriage broker shut his eyes and ate. When he had finished he carefully cleaned up the crumbs and rolled up the remains of the fish, in the paper bag. His spectacled eyes roamed the room until he discovered, amid some piles of books, a one-burner gas stove. Lifting his hat he humbly asked, "A glass tea you got, rabbi?"

Conscience-stricken, Leo rose and brewed the tea. He served it with a chunk of lemon and two cubes of lump sugar, delighting Salzman.

After he had drunk his tea, Salzman's strength and good spirits were restored.

"So tell me, rabbi," he said amiably, "you considered some more the three clients I mentioned yesterday?"

"There was no need to consider."

"Why not?"

"None of them suits me."

"What then suits you?"

Leo let it pass because he could give only a confused answer.

Without waiting for a reply, Salzman asked, "You remember this girl I talked to you—the high school teacher?"

"Age thirty-two?"

But, surprisingly, Salzman's face lit in a smile. "Age twenty-nine."

Leo shot him a look. "Reduced from thirty-two?"

"A mistake," Salzman avowed. "I talked today with the dentist. He took me to his safety deposit box and showed me the birth certificate. She was twenty-nine years last August. They made her a party in the mountains where she went for her vacation. When her father spoke to me the first time I forgot to write the age and I told you thirty-two, but now I remember this was a different client, a widow."

"The same one you told me about? I thought she was twenty-four?"

"A different. Am I responsible that the world is filled with widows?"

"No, but I'm not interested in them, nor for that matter, in school teachers."

Salzman pulled his clasped hands to his breast. Looking at the ceiling he devoutly exclaimed, "Yiddishe kinder, what can I say to somebody that he is not interested in high school teachers? So what then you are interested?"

Leo flushed but controlled himself.

"In what else will you be interested," Salzman went on, "if you not interested in this fine girl that she speaks four languages and has personally in the bank ten thousand dollars? Also her father guarantees further twelve thousand. Also she has a new car, wonderful clothes, talks on all subjects, and she will give you a first-class home and children. How near do we come in our life to paradise?"

"If she's so wonderful, why wasn't she married ten years ago?"

"Why?" said Salzman with a heavy laugh. "—Why? Because she is *partikiler*. This is why. She wants the *best*."

Leo was silent, amused at how he had entangled himself. But Salzman had aroused his interest in Lily H., and he began seriously to consider calling on her. When the marriage broker observed how intently Leo's mind was at work on the facts he had supplied, he felt certain they would soon come to an agreement.

Late Saturday afternoon, conscious of Salzman, Leo Finkle walked with Lily Hirschorn along Riverside Drive. He walked briskly and erectly, wearing with distinction the black fedora he had that morning taken with trepidation out of the dusty hat box on his closet shelf, and the heavy black Saturday coat he had thoroughly whisked clean. Leo also owned a walking stick, a present from a distant relative, but quickly put temptation aside and did not use it. Lily, petite and not unpretty, had on something signifying the approach of spring. She was au courant, animatedly, with all sorts of subjects, and he weighed her words and found her surprisingly sound—score another for Salzman, whom he uneasily sensed to be somewhere around, hiding perhaps high in a tree along the street, flashing the lady signals with a pocket mirror; or perhaps a cloven-hoofed Pan, piping nuptial ditties as he danced his invisible way before them, strewing wild buds on the walk and purple grapes in their path, symbolizing fruit of a union, though there was of course still none.

Lily startled Leo by remarking, "I was thinking of Mr. Salzman, a curious figure, wouldn't you say?"

Not certain what to answer, he nodded.

She bravely went on, blushing, "I for one am grateful for his introducing us. Aren't you?"

He courteously replied, "I am."

"I mean," she said with a little laugh—and it was all in good taste, or at least gave the effect of being not in bad—"do you mind that we came together so?"

He was not displeased with her honesty, recognizing that she meant to set the relationship aright, and understanding that it took a certain amount of experience in life, and courage, to want to do it quite that way. One had to have some sort of past to make that kind of beginning.

He said that he did not mind. Salzman's function was traditional and honorable—valuable for what it might achieve, which, he pointed out, was frequently nothing.

Lily agreed with a sigh. They walked on for a while and she said after a long silence, again with a nervous laugh, "Would you mind if I asked you something a little bit personal? Frankly, I find the subject fascinating." Although Leo shrugged, she went on half embarrassedly, "How was it that you came to your calling? I mean was it a sudden passionate inspiration?"

Leo, after a time, slowly replied, "I was always interested in the Law."

"You saw revealed in it the presence of the Highest?"

He nodded and changed the subject. "I understand that you spent a little time in Paris, Miss Hirschorn?"

"Oh, did Mr. Salzman tell you, Rabbi Finkle?" Leo winced but she went on, "It was ages ago and almost forgotten. I remember I had to return for my sister's wedding."

And Lily would not be put off. "When," she asked in a trembly voice, "did you become enamored of God?"

He stared at her. Then it came to him that she was talking not about Leo Finkle, but of a total stranger, some mystical figure, perhaps even passionate prophet that Salzman had dreamed up for her—no relation to the living or dead. Leo trembled with rage and weakness. The trickster had obviously sold her a bill of goods, just as he had him, who'd expected to become acquainted with a young lady of twenty-nine, only to behold, the moment he laid eyes upon her strained and anxious face, a woman past thirty-five and aging rapidly. Only his self control had kept him this long in her presence.

"I am not," he said gravely, "a talented religious person," and in seeking words to go on, found himself possessed by shame and fear. "I think," he said in a strained manner, "that I came to God not because I loved Him, but because I did not."

This confession he spoke harshly because its unexpectedness shook him.

Lily wilted. Leo saw a profusion of loaves of bread go flying like ducks high over his head, not unlike the winged loaves by which he had counted himself to sleep last night. Mercifully, then, it snowed, which he would not put past Salzman's machinations.

He was infuriated with the marriage broker and swore he would throw him out of the room the minute he reappeared. But Salzman did not come that night, and when Leo's anger had subsided, an unaccountable despair grew in its place. At first he thought this was caused by his disappointment in Lily, but before long it became evident that he had involved himself with Salzman without a true knowledge of his own intent. He gradually realized—with an emptiness that seized him with six hands—that he had called in the broker to find him a bride because he was incapable of doing it himself. This terrifying insight he had derived as a result of his meeting and conversation with Lily Hirschorn. Her probing questions had somehow irritated him into revealing—to himself more than her—the true nature of his relationship to God, and from that it had come upon him, with shocking force, that apart from his parents, he had never loved anyone. Or perhaps it went the other way, that he did not love God so well as he might, because he had not loved man. It seemed to Leo that his whole life stood starkly revealed and he saw himself for the first time as he truly was—unloved and loveless. This bitter but some-how not fully unexpected revelation brought him to a point of panic, controlled only by extraordinary effort. He covered his face with his hands and cried.

The week that followed was the worst of his life. He did not eat and lost weight. His beard darkened and grew ragged. He stopped attending seminars and almost never opened a book. He seriously considered leaving the Yeshivah, although he was deeply troubled at the thought of the loss of all his years of study—saw them like pages torn from a book, strewn over the city—and at the devastating effect of this decision upon his parents. But he had lived without knowledge of himself, and never in the Five Books and all the Commentaries—mea culpa—had the truth been revealed to him. He did not know where to turn, and in all this desolating loneliness there was no *to whom*, although he often thought of Lily but not once could bring himself to go down-stairs and make the call. He became touchy and irritable, espe-cially with his landlady, who asked him all manner of personal questions; on the other hand, sensing his own disagreeableness, he waylaid her on the stairs and apologized abjectly, until mortified, she ran from him. Out of this, however, he drew the consolation that he was a Jew and that a Jew suffered. But gradually, as the long and terrible week drew to a close, he regained his composure and some idea of purpose in life: to go on as planned. Although he was imperfect, the ideal was not. As for his quest of a bride, the thought of continuing afflicted him with anxiety and heart-burn, yet perhaps with this new knowledge of himself he would be more successful than in the past. Perhaps love would now come to him and a bride to that love. And for this sanctified seeking who needed a Salzman?

The marriage broker, a skeleton with haunted eyes, returned that very night. He looked, withal, the picture of frustrated ex-pectancy—as if he had steadfastly waited the week at Miss Lily Hirschorn's side for a telephone call that never came.

Casually coughing, Salzman came immediately to the point: "So how did you like her?"

Leo's anger rose and he could not refrain from chiding the matchmaker: "Why did you lie to me, Salzman?"

Salzman's pale face went dead white, the world had snowed on him.

"Did you not state that she was twenty-nine?" Leo insisted.

"I give you my word—"

"She was thirty-five, if a day. *At least* thirty-five."

"Of this don't be too sure. Her father told me—"

"Never mind. The worst of it was that you lied to her."

"How did I lie to her, tell me?"

"You told her things about me that weren't true. You made me out to be more, consequently less than I am. She had in mind a totally different person, a sort of semimystical Wonder Rabbi."

"All I said, you was a religious man."

"I can imagine."

Salzman sighed. "This is my weakness that I have," he confessed. "My wife says to me I shouldn't be a salesman, but when I have two fine people that they would be wonderful to be married, I am so happy that I talk too much." He smiled wanly. "This is why Salzman is a poor man."

Leo's anger left him. "Well, Salzman, I'm afraid that's all."

The marriage broker fastened hungry eyes on him.

"You don't want any more a bride?"

"I do," said Leo, "but I have decided to seek her in a different way. I am no longer interested in an arranged marriage. To be frank, I now admit the necessity of premarital love. That is, I want to be in love with the one I marry."

"Love?" said Salzman, astounded. After a moment he remarked, "For us, our love is our life, not for the ladies. In the ghetto they—"

"I know, I know," said Leo. "I've thought of it often. Love, I have said to myself, should be a by-product of living and worship rather than its own end. Yet for myself I find it necessary to establish the level of my need and fulfill it."

Salzman shrugged but answered, "Listen, rabbi, if you want love, this I can find for you also. I have such beautiful clients that you will love them the minute your eyes will see them."

Leo smiled unhappily. "I'm afraid you don't understand."

But Salzman hastily unstrapped his portfolio and withdrew a manila packet from it.

"Pictures," he said, quickly laying the envelope on the table.

Leo called after him to take the pictures away, but as if on the wings of the wind, Salzman had disappeared.

March came. Leo had returned to his regular routine. Although he felt not quite himself yet—lacked energy—he was making plans for a more active social life. Of course it would cost something, but he was an expert in cutting corners; and when there were no corners left he would make circles rounder. All the while Salzman's pictures had lain on the table, gathering dust. Occasionally as Leo sat studying, or enjoying a cup of tea, his eyes fell on the manila envelope, but he never opened it.

The days went by and no social life to speak of developed with a member of the opposite sex—it was difficult, given the circumstances of his situation. One morning Leo toiled up the stairs to his room and stared out the window at the city. Although the day was bright his view of it was dark. For some time he watched the people in the street below hurrying along and then turned with a heavy heart to his little room. On the table was the packet. With a sudden relentless gesture he tore it open. For a half-hour he stood by the table in a state of excitement, examining the photographs of the ladies Salzman had included. Finally, with a deep sigh he put them down. There were six, of varying degrees of attractiveness, but look at them long enough and they all became Lily Hirschorn: all past their prime, all starved behind bright smiles, not a true personality in the lot. Life, despite their frantic yoohooings, had passed them by; they were pictures in a brief case that stank of fish. After a while, however, as Leo attempted to return the photographs into the envelope, he found in it another, a snapshot of the type taken by a machine for a quarter. He gazed at it a moment and let out a cry.

Her face deeply moved him. Why, he could at first not say. It gave him the impression of youth—spring flowers, yet age—a sense of having been used to the bone, wasted; this came from the eyes, which were hauntingly familiar, yet absolutely strange. He had a vivid impression that he had met her before, but try as he might he could not place her although he could almost recall her name, as if he had read it in her own handwriting. No, this couldn't be; he would have remembered her. It was not, he affirmed, that she had an extraordinary beauty—no, though her face was attractive enough; it was that *something* about her moved him. Feature for feature, even some of the ladies of the photographs could do better; but she leaped forth to his heart—had *lived*, or wanted to—more than just wanted, perhaps regretted how she had lived—had somehow deeply suffered: it could be seen in the depths of those reluctant eyes, and from the way the light enclosed and shone from her, and within her, opening realms of possibility: this was her own. Her he desired. His head ached and eyes narrowed with the intensity of his gazing, then as if an obscure fog had blown up in the mind, he experienced fear of her and was aware that he had received an impression, somehow, of evil. He shuddered, saying softly, it is thus with us all. Leo brewed some tea in a small pot and sat sipping it without sugar, to calm himself. But before he had finished drinking, again with excitement he examined the face and found it good: good for Leo Finkle. Only such a one could understand him and help him seek whatever he was seeking. She might, perhaps, love him. How she had happened to be among the discards in Salzman's barrel he could never guess, but he knew he must urgently go find her.

Leo rushed downstairs, grabbed up the Bronx telephone book, and searched for Salzman's home address. He was not listed, nor was his office. Neither was he in the Manhattan book. But Leo remembered having written down the address on a slip of paper after he had read Salzman's advertisement in the "personals" column of the *Forward*. He ran up to his room and tore through his papers, without luck. It was exasperating. Just when he needed the matchmaker he was nowhere to be found. Fortunately Leo remembered to look in his wallet. There on a card he found his name written and a Bronx address. No phone number was listed, the reason—Leo now recalled—he had originally communicated with Salzman by letter. He got on his coat, put a hat on over his skull cap and hurried to the subway station. All the way to the far end of the Bronx he sat on the edge of his seat. He was more than once tempted to take out the picture and see if the girl's face was as he remembered it, but he refrained, allowing the snapshot to remain in his inside coat pocket, content to have her so close. When the train pulled into the station he was waiting at the door and bolted out. He quickly located the street Salzman had advertised.

The building he sought was less than a block from the subway, but it was not an office building, nor even a loft, nor a store in which one could rent office space. It was a very old tenement house. Leo found Salzman's name in pencil on a soiled tag under the bell and climbed three dark flights to his apartment. When he knocked, the door was opened by a thin, asthmatic, gray-haired woman, in felt slippers.

"Yes?" she said, expecting nothing. She listened without listening. He could have sworn he had seen her, too, before but knew it was an illusion.

"Salzman—does he live here? Pinye Salzman," he said, "the matchtmaker?"

She stared at him a long minute. "Of course."

He felt embarrassed. "Is he in?"

"No." Her mouth, though left open, offered nothing more.

"The matter is urgent. Can you tell me where his office is?"

"In the air." She pointed upward.

"You mean he has no office?" Leo asked.

"In his socks."

He peered into the apartment. It was sunless and dingy, one large room divided by a half-open curtain, beyond which he could see a sagging metal bed. The near side of a room was crowded with rickety chairs, old bureaus, a three-legged table, racks of cooking utensils, and all the apparatus of a kitchen. But there was no sign of Salzman or his magic barrel, probably also a figment of the imagination. An odor of frying fish made Leo weak to the knees.

"Where is he?" he insisted. "I've got to see your husband."

At length she answered, "So who knows where he is? Every time he thinks a new thought he runs to a different place. Go home, he will find you."

"Tell him Leo Finkle."

She gave no sign she had heard.

He walked downstairs, depressed.

But Salzman, breathless, stood waiting at his door.

Leo was astounded and overjoyed. "How did you get here before me?"

"I rushed."

"Come inside."

They entered. Leo fixed tea, and a sardine sandwich for Salzman. As they were drinking he reached behind him for the packet of pictures and handed them to the marriage broker.

Salzman put down his glass and said expectantly, "You found somebody you like?"

"Not among these."

The marriage broker turned away.

"Here is the one I want." Leo held forth the snapshot.

Salzman slipped on his glasses and took the picture into his trembling hand. He turned ghastly and let out a groan.

"What's the matter?" cried Leo.

"Excuse me. Was an accident this picture. She isn't for you."

Salzman frantically shoved the manila packet into his portfolio. He thrust the snapshot into his pocket and fled down the stairs.

Leo, after momentary paralysis, gave chase and cornered the

marriage broker in the vestibule. The landlady made hysterical outcries but neither of them listened."

"Give me back the picture, Salzman."

"No." The pain in his eyes was terrible.

"Tell me who she is then."

"This I can't tell you. Excuse me."

He made to depart, but Leo, forgetting himself, seized the matchmaker by his tight coat and shook him frenziedly.

"Please," sighed Salzman. "*Please.*"

Leo ashamedly let him go. "Tell me who she is," he begged. "It's very important for me to know."

"She is not for you. She is a wild one—wild, without shame. This is not a bride for a rabbi."

"What do you mean wild?"

"Like an animal. Like a dog. For her to be poor was a sin. This is why to me she is dead now."

"In God's name, what do you mean?"

"Her I can't introduce to you," Salzman cried.

"Why are you so excited?"

"Why, he asks," Salzman said, bursting into tears. "This is my baby, my Stella, she should burn in hell."

Leo hurried up to bed and hid under the covers. Under the covers he thought his life through. Although he soon fell asleep he could not sleep her out of his mind. He woke, beating his breast. Though he prayed to be rid of her, his prayers went unanswered. Through days of torment he endlessly struggled not to love her; fearing success, he escaped it. He then concluded to convert her to goodness, himself to God. The idea alternately nauseated and exalted him.

He perhaps did not know that he had come to a final decision until he encountered Salzman in a Broadway cafeteria. He was sitting alone at a rear table, sucking the bony remains of a fish. The marriage broker appeared haggard, and transparent to the point of vanishing.

Salzman looked up at first without recognizing him. Leo had grown a pointed beard and his eyes were weighted with wisdom.

"Salzman," he said, "love has at last come to my heart."

"Who can love from a picture?" mocked the marriage broker.

"It is not impossible."

"If you can love her, then you can love anybody. Let me show you some new clients that they just sent me their photographs. One is a little doll."

"Just her I want," Leo murmured.

"Don't be a fool, doctor. Don't bother with her."

"Put me in touch with her, Salzman," Leo said humbly. "Perhaps I can be of service."

Salzman had stopped eating and Leo understood with emotion that it was now arranged.

Leaving the cafeteria, he was, however, afflicted by a tormenting suspicion that Salzman had planned it all to happen this way.

Leo was informed by letter that she would meet him on a certain corner, and she was there one spring night, waiting under a street lamp. He appeared, carrying a small bouquet of violets and rosebuds. Stella stood by the lamp post, smoking. She wore white with red shoes, which fitted his expectations, although in a troubled moment he had imagined the dress red, and only the shoes white. She waited uneasily and shyly. From afar he saw that her eyes—clearly her father's—were filled with desperate innocence. He pictured, in her, his own redemption. Violins and lit candles revolved in the sky. Leo ran forward with flowers outthrust.

Around the corner, Salzman, leaning against a wall, chanted prayers for the dead.

The German Refugee

Oskar Gassner sits in his cotton-mesh undershirt and summer bathrobe at the window of his stuffy, hot, dark hotel room on West Tenth Street while I cautiously knock. Outside, across the sky, a late-June green twilight fades in darkness. The refugee fumbles for the light and stares at me, hiding despair but not pain.

I was in those days a poor student and would brashly attempt to teach anybody anything for a buck an hour, although I have since learned better. Mostly I gave English lessons to recently-arrived refugees. The college sent me, I had acquired a little experience. Already a few of my students were trying their broken English, theirs and mine, in the American market place. I was then just twenty, on my way into my senior year in college, a skinny, life hungry kid, eating himself waiting for the next world war to start. It was a goddamn cheat. Here I was palpitating to get going, and across the ocean Adolph Hitler, in black boots and a square mustache, was tearing up and spitting out all the flowers. Will I ever forget what went on with Danzig that summer?

Times were still hard from the Depression but anyway I made a little living from the poor refugees. They were all over uptown Broadway in 1939. I had four I tutored—Karl Otto Alp, the former film star; Wolfgang Novak, once a brilliant economist; Friedrich Wilhelm Wolff, who had taught medieval history at Heidelberg; and after the night I met him in his disordered cheap hotel room, Oskar Gassner, the Berlin critic and journalist, at one time on the *Acht Uhr Abenblatt*. They were accomplished men. I had my nerve associating with them, but that's what a world crisis does for people, they get educated.

Oskar was maybe fifty, his thick hair turning gray. He had a big face and heavy hands. His shoulders sagged. His eyes, too, were heavy, a clouded blue; and as he stared at me after I had identified myself, doubt spread in them like underwater currents. It was as if, on seeing me, he had again been defeated. I had to wait until he came to. I stayed at the door in silence. In such cases I would rather be elsewhere but I had to make a living. Finally he opened the door and I entered. Rather, he released it and I was in. "Bitte," he offered me a seat and didn't know where to sit himself. He would attempt to say something and then stop, as though it could not possibly be said. The room was cluttered with clothing, boxes of books he had managed to get out of Germany, and some paintings. Oskar sat on a box and attempted to fan himself with his meaty hand. "Zis heat," he muttered, forcing his mind to the deed. "Impozzible. I do not know such heat." It was bad enough for me but terrible for him. He had difficulty breathing. He tried to speak, lifted a hand, and let it drop like a dead duck. He breathed as though he were fighting a battle; and maybe he won because after ten minutes we sat and slowly talked.

Like most educated Germans Oskar had at one time studied English. Although he was certain he couldn't say a word he managed to put together a fairly decent, if sometimes comical, English sentence. He misplaced consonants, mixed up nouns and verbs, and mangled idioms, yet we were able at once to communicate. We conversed in English, with an occasional assist by me in pidgin-German or Yiddish, what he called "Jiddish." He had been to America before, last year for a short visit. He had come a month before Kristallnacht, when the Nazis shattered the Jewish store windows and burnt all the synagogues, to see if he could find a job for himself; he had no relatives in America and getting a job would permit him quickly to enter the country. He had been promised something, not in journalism, but with the help of a foundation, as a lecturer. Then he returned to Berlin, and after a frightening delay of six months was permitted to emigrate. He had sold whatever he could, managed to get some paintings, gifts of Bauhaus friends, and some boxes of books out by bribing two Dutch border guards; he had said goodbye to his wife and left the accursed country. He gazed at me with cloudy eyes. "We parted amicably," he said in German, "my wife was gentile. Her mother was an appalling anti-Semite. They returned to live in Stettin." I asked no questions. Gentile is gentile, Germany is Germany.

His new job was in the Institute for Public Studies, in New York. He was to give a lecture a week in the fall term, and during next spring, a course, in English translation, in "The Literature of the Weimar Republic." He had never taught before and was afraid to. He was in that way to be introduced to the public, but the thought of giving the lecture in English just about paralyzed him. He didn't see how he could do it. "How is it pozzible? I cannot say two words. I cannot pronounziate. I will make a fool of myself." His melancholy deepened. Already in the two months since his arrival, and a round of diminishingly expensive hotel rooms, he had had two English tutors, and I was the third. The others had given him up, he said, because his progress was so poor, and he thought he also depressed them. He asked me whether I felt I could do something for him, or should he go to a speech specialist, someone, say, who charged five dollars an hour, and beg his assistance? "You could try him," I said, "and then come back to me." In those days I figured what I knew, I knew. At that he managed a smile. Still, I wanted him to make up his mind or it would be no confidence down the line. He said, after a while, he would stay with me. If he went to the five-dollar professor it might help his tongue but not his stomach. He would have no money left to eat with. The Institute had paid him in advance for the summer but it was only three hundred dollars and all he had.

He looked at me dully. "Ich weiss nicht wie ich weiter machen soll."

I figured it was time to move past the first step. Either we did that quickly or it would be like drilling rock for a long time.

"Let's stand at the mirror," I said.

He rose with a sigh and stood there beside me, I thin, elongated, red-headed, praying for success, his and mine; Oskar, uneasy, fearful, finding it hard to face either of us in the faded round glass above his dresser.

"Please," I said to him, "could you say 'right'?"

"Ghight," he gargled.

"No—right. You put your tongue here." I showed him where as he tensely watched the mirror. I tensely watched him. "The tip of it curls behind the ridge on top, like this."

He placed his tongue where I showed him.

"Please," I said, "now say right."

Oskar's tongue fluttered. "Rright."

"That's good. Now say 'treasure'—that's harder."

"Tgheasure."

"The tongue goes up in front, not in the back of the mouth. Look."

He tried, his brow wet, eyes straining, "Trreasure."

"That's it."

"A miracle," Oskar murmured.

I said if he had done that he could do the rest.

We went for a bus ride up Fifth Avenue and then walked for a while around Central Park Lake. He had put on his German hat, with its hatband bow at the back, a broad-lapeled wool suit, a necktie twice as wide as the one I was wearing, and walked with a small-footed waddle. The night wasn't bad, it had got a bit cooler. There were a few large stars in the sky and they made me sad.

"Do you sink I will succezz?"

"Why not?" I asked.

Later he bought me a bottle of beer.

2

To many of these people, articulate as they were, the great loss was the loss of language—that they could not say what was in them to say. You have some subtle thought and it comes out like a piece of broken bottle. They could, of course, manage to communicate but just to communicate was frustrating. As Karl Otto Alp, the ex-film star who became a buyer for Macy's, put it years later, "I felt like a child, or worse, often like a moron. I am left with myself unexpressed. What I know, indeed, what I am, becomes to me a burden. My tongue hangs useless." The same with Oskar it figures. There was a terrible sense of useless tongue, and I think the reason for his trouble with his other tutors was that to keep from drowning in things unsaid he wanted to swallow the ocean in a gulp: Today he would learn English and tomorrow wow them with an impeccable Fourth of July speech, followed by a successful lecture at the Institute for Public Studies.

We performed our lessons slowly, step by step, everything in its place. After Oskar moved to a two-room apartment in a house on West 85th Street, near the Drive, we met three times a week at four-thirty, worked an hour and a half, then, since it was too hot to cook, had supper at the 72nd Street Automat and conversed on my time. The lessons we divided into three parts: diction exercises and reading aloud; then grammar, because Oskar felt the necessity of it, and composition correction; with conversation, as I said, thrown in at supper. So far as I could see, he was coming along. None of these exercises was giving him as much trouble as they apparently had in the past. He seemed to be learning and his mood lightened. There were moments of elation as he heard his accent flying off. For instance when sink became think. He stopped calling himself "hopelezz," and I became his "bezt teacher," a little joke I liked.

Neither of us said much about the lecture he had to give early in October, and I kept my fingers crossed. It was somehow to come out of what we were doing daily, I think I felt, but exactly how, I had no idea; and to tell the truth, though I didn't say so to Oskar, the lecture frightened me. That and the ten more to follow during the fall term. Later, when I learned that he had been attempting with the help of the dictionary, to write in Eng-glish and had produced "a complete disahster," I suggested maybe he ought to stick to German and we could afterwards both try to put it into passable English. I was cheating when I said that because my German is meager, enough to read simple stuff but certainly not good enough for serious translation; anyway, the idea was to get Oskar into production and worry about translating later. He sweated with it, from enervating morning to exhausted night, but no matter what language he tried, though he had been a professional writer for a generation and knew his subject cold, the lecture refused to move past page one.

It was a sticky, hot July and the heat didn't help at all.

3

I had met Oskar at the end of June and by the seventeenth of July we were no longer doing lessons. They had foundered on the "impozzible" lecture. He had worked on it each day in frenzy and growing despair. After writing more than a hundred opening pages he furiously flung his pen against the wall, shouting he could no longer write in that filthy tongue. He cursed the German language. He hated the damned country and the damned people. After that what was bad became worse. When he gave up attempting to write the lecture, he stopped making progress in English. He seemed to forget what he already knew. His tongue thickened and the accent returned in all its fruitiness. The little he had to say was in handcuffed and tortured English. The only German I heard him speak was in a whisper to himself. I doubt he knew he was talking it. That ended our formal work together, though I did drop in every other day or so to sit with him. For hours he sat motionless in a large green velours armchair, hot enough to broil in, and through tall windows stared at the colorless sky above 85th Street, with a wet depressed eye.

Then once he said to me, "If I do not this legture prepare, I will take my life."

"Let's begin, Oskar," I said. "You dictate and I'll write. The ideas count, not the spelling."

He didn't answer so I stopped talking.

He had plunged into an involved melancholy. We sat for hours, often in profound silence. This was alarming to me, though I had already had some experience with such depression. Wolfgang Novak, the economist, though English came more easily to him, was another. His problems arose mainly, I think, from physical illness. And he felt a greater sense of the lost country than Oskar. Sometimes in the early evening I persuaded Oskar to come with me for a short walk on the Drive. The tail end of sunsets over the Palisades seemed to appeal to him. At least he looked. He would put on full regalia—hat, suit coat, tie, no matter how hot or what I suggested—and we went slowly down the stairs, I wondering whether he would ever make it to the bottom. He seemed to me always suspended between two floors.

We walked slowly uptown, stopping to sit on a bench and watch night rise above the Hudson. When we returned to his room, if I sensed he had loosened up a bit, we listened to music on the radio; but if I tried to sneak in a news broadcast, he said to me, "Please, I can not more stand of world misery." I shut off the radio. He was right, it was a time of no good news. I squeezed my brain. What could I sell him? Was it good news to be alive? Who could argue the point? Sometimes I read aloud to him—I remember he liked the first part of *Life on the Mississippi*. We still went to the Automat once or twice a week, he perhaps out of habit, because he didn't feel like going anywhere—I to get him out of his room. Oskar ate little, he toyed with a spoon. His dull eyes looked as though they had been squirted with a dark dye.

Once after a momentary cooling rainstorm we sat on newspapers on a wet bench overlooking the river and Oskar at last began to talk. In tormented English he conveyed his intense and everlasting hatred of the Nazis for destroying his career, uprooting his life after half a century, and flinging him like a piece of bleeding meat to the hawks. He cursed them thickly, the German nation, and inhuman, conscienceless, merciless people. "They are pigs mazquerading as peacogs," he said. "I feel certain that my wife, in her heart, was a Jew hater." It was a terrible bitterness, an eloquence almost without vocabulary. He became silent again. I hoped to hear more about his wife but decided not to ask.

Afterwards in the dark Oskar confessed that he had attempted suicide during his first week in America. He was living, at the end of May, in a small hotel, and had one night filled himself with barbiturates; but his phone had fallen off the table and the hotel operator had sent up the elevator boy who found him unconscious and called the police. He was revived in the hospital.

"I did not mean to do it," he said, "it was a mistage."

"Don't ever think of it again," I said, "it's total defeat."

"I don't," he said wearily, "because it is so arduouz to come back to life."

"Please, for any reason whatever."

Afterwards when we were walking, he surprised me by saying, "Maybe we ought to try now the legture onze more."

We trudged back to the house and he sat at his hot desk, I trying to read as he slowly began to reconstruct the first page of his lecture. He wrote, of course, in German.

4

He got nowhere. We were back to nothing, to sitting in silence in the heat. Sometimes, after a few minutes, I had to take off before his mood overcame mine. One afternoon I came unwillingly up the stairs—there were times I felt momentary surges of irritation with him—and was frightened to find Oskar's door ajar. When I knocked no one answered. As I stood there, chilled down the spine, I realized I was thinking about the possibility of his attempting suicide again. "Oskar?" I went into the apartment, looked into both rooms and the bathroom, but he wasn't there. I thought he might have drifted out to get something from a store and took the opportunity to look quickly around. There was nothing startling in the medicine chest, no pills but aspirin, no iodine. Thinking, for some reason, of a gun, I searched his desk drawer. In it I found a thin-paper airmail letter from Germany. Even if I had wanted to, I couldn't read the handwriting, but as I held it in my hand I did make out a sentence: "Ich bin dir siebenundzwanzig Jahre treu gewesen." There was no gun in the drawer. I shut it and stopped looking. It had occurred to me if you want to kill yourself all you need is a straight pin. When Oskar returned he said he had been sitting in the public library, unable to read.

Now we are once more enacting the changeless scene, curtain rising on two speechless characters in a furnished apartment, I, in a straightback chair, Oskar in the velous armchair that smothered rather than supported him, his flesh gray, the big gray face, unfocused, sagging. I reached over to switch on the radio but he barely looked at me in a way that begged no. I then got up to leave but Oskar, clearing his throat, thickly asked me to stay. I stayed, thinking, was there more to this than I could see into? His problems, God knows, were real enough, but could there be something more than a refugee's displacement, alienation, financial insecurity, being in a strange land without friends or a speakable tongue? My speculation was the old one; not all drown in this ocean, why does he? After a while I shaped the thought and asked him, was there something below the surface, invisible? I was full of this thing from college, and wondered if there mightn't be some unknown quantity in his depression that a psychiatrist maybe might help him with, enough to get him started on his lecture.

He meditated on this and after a few minutes haltingly said he had been psychoanalyzed in Vienna as a young man. "Just the jusual drek," he said, "fears and fantazies that afterwaards no longer bothered me."

"They don't now?"

"Not."

"You've written many articles and lectures before," I said. "What I can't understand, though I know how hard the situation is, is why you can never get past page one."

He half lifted his hand. "It is a paralyzis of my will. The whole legture is clear in my mind but the minute I write down a single word—or in English or in German—I have a terrible fear I will not be able to write the negst. As though someone has thrown a stone at a window and the whole house—the whole idea, zmashes. This repeats, until I am dezperate."

He said the fear grew as he worked that he would die before he completed the lecture, or if not that, he would write it so disgracefully he would wish for death. The fear immobilized him.

"I have lozt faith. I do not—not longer possezz my former value of myself. In my life there has been too much illusion."

I tried to believe what I was saying: "Have confidence, the feeling will pass."

"Confidenze I have not. For this and alzo whatever elze I have lozt I thank the Nazis."

5

It was by then mid-August and things were growing steadily worse wherever one looked. The Poles were mobilizing for war. Oskar hardly moved. I was full of worries though I pretended calm weather.

He sat in his massive armchair with sick eyes, breathing like a wounded animal.

"Who can write aboud Walt Whitman in such terrible times?"

"Why don't you change the subject?"

"It mages no differenze what is the subject. It is all uzelezz."

I came every day, as a friend, neglecting my other students and therefore my livelihood. I had a panicky feeling that if things went on as they were going they would end in Oskar's suicide; and I felt a frenzied desire to prevent that. What's more, I was sometimes afraid I was myself becoming melancholy, a new talent, call it, of taking less pleasure in my little pleasures. And the heat continued, oppressive, relentless. We thought of escape into the country but neither of us had the money. One day I bought Oskar a second-hand fan—wondering why we hadn't thought of that before—and he sat in the breeze for hours each day, until after a week, shortly after the Soviet-Nazi nonaggression pact was signed, the motor gave out. He could not sleep at night and sat at his desk with a wet towel on his head, still attempting to write his lecture. He wrote reams on a treadmill, it came out nothing. When he slept out of exhaustion he had fantastic frightening dreams of the Nazis inflicting tortures on him, sometimes forcing him to look upon the corpses of those they had slain. In one dream he told me about, he had gone back to Germany to visit his wife. She wasn't home and he had been directed to a cemetery. There, though the tombstone read another name, her blood seeped out of the earth above her shallow grave. He groaned aloud at the memory.

Afterwards he told me something about her. They had met as students, lived together, and were married at twenty-three. It wasn't a very happy marriage. She had turned into a sickly woman, physically unable to have children. "Something was wrong with her interior strugture."

Though I asked no questions, Oskar said, "I offered her to come with me here but she refused this."

"For what reason?"

"She did not think I wished her to come."

"Did you?" I asked.

"Not," he said.

He explained he had lived with her for almost twenty-seven years under difficult circumstances. She had been ambivalent about their Jewish friends and his relatives, though outwardly she seemed not a prejudiced person. But her mother was always a violent anti-Semite.

"I have nothing to blame myself," Oskar said.

He took to his bed. I took to the New York Public Library.

I read some of the German poets he was trying to write about, in English translation. Then I read *Leaves of Grass* and wrote down what I thought one or two of them had got from Whitman. One day, towards the end of August, I brought Oskar what I had written. It was in good part guessing but my idea wasn't to write the lecture for him. He lay on his back, motionless, and listened utterly sadly to what I had written. Then he said, no, it wasn't the love of death they had got from Whitman—that ran through German poetry—but it was most of all his feeling for Brudermensch, his humanity.

"But this does not grow long on German earth," he said, "and is soon deztroyed."

I said I was sorry I had got it wrong, but he thanked me anyway.

I left, defeated, and as I was going down the stairs, heard the sound of someone sobbing. I will quit this, I thought, it has gotten to be too much for me. I can't drown with him.

I stayed home the next day, tasting a new kind of private misery too old for somebody my age, but that same night Oskar called me on the phone, blessing me wildly for having read those notes to him. He had got up to write me a letter to say what I had missed, and it ended by his having written half the lecture. He had slept all day and tonight intended to finish it up.

"I thank you," he said, "for much, alzo including your faith in me."

"Thank God," I said, not telling him I had just about lost it.

6

Oskar completed his lecture—wrote and rewrote it—during the first week in September. The Nazi had invaded Poland, and though we were greatly troubled, there was some sense of release; maybe the brave Poles would beat them. It took another week to translate the lecture, but here we had the assistance of Friedrich Wilhelm Wolff, the historian, a gentle, erudite man, who liked translating and promised his help with future lectures. We then had about two weeks to work on Oskar's delivery. The weather had changed, and so, slowly, had he. He had awakened from defeat, battered, after a wearying battle. He had lost close to twenty pounds. His complexion was still gray; when I looked at his face I expected to see scars, but it had lost its flabby unfocused quality. His blue eyes had returned to life and he walked with quick steps, as though to pick up a few for all the steps he hadn't taken during those long hot days he had lain torpid in his room.

We went back to our former routine, meeting three late afternoons a week for diction, grammar, and the other exercises. I taught him the phonetic alphabet and transcribed long lists of words he was mispronouncing. He worked many hours trying to fit each sound into place, holding half a matchstick between his teeth to keep his jaws apart as he exercised his tongue. All this can be a dreadfully boring business unless you think you have a future. Looking at him I realized what's meant when somebody is called "another man."

The lecture, which I now knew by heart, went off well. The director of the Institute had invited a number of prominent people. Oskar was the first refugee they had employed and there was a move to make the public cognizant of what was then a new ingredient in American life. Two reporters had come with a lady photographer. The auditorium of the Institute was crowded. I sat in the last row, promising to put up my hand if he couldn't be heard, but it wasn't necessary. Oskar, in a blue suit, his hair cut, was of course nervous, but you couldn't see it unless you studied him. When he stepped up to the lectern, spread out his manuscript, and spoke his first English sentence in public, my heart hesitated; only he and I, of everybody there, had any idea of the anguish he had been through. His enunciation wasn't at all bad —a few s's for th's, and he once said bag for back, but otherwise he did all right. He read poetry well—in both languages—and though Walt Whitman, in his mouth, sounded a little as though he had come to the shores of Long Island as a German immigrant, still the poetry read as poetry:

> "And I know the spirit of God is the brother of my own,
> And that all the men ever born are also my brothers, and the women my sisters and lovers,
> And that the kelson of creation is love . . ."

Oskar read it as though he believed it. Warsaw had fallen but the verses were somehow protective. I sat back conscious of two things: how easy it is to hide the deepest wounds; and the pride I felt in the job I had done.

7

Two days later I came up the stairs into Oskar's apartment to find a crowd there. The refugee, his face beet-red, lips bluish, a trace of froth in the corners of his mouth, lay on the floor in his limp pajamas, two firemen on their knees, working over him with an inhalator. The windows were open and the air stank.

A policeman asked me who I was and I couldn't answer.

"No, oh no."

I said no but it was unchangeably yes. He had taken his life —gas—I hadn't even thought of the stove in the kitchen.

"Why?" I asked myself. "Why did he do it?" Maybe it was the fate of Poland on top of everything else, but the only answer anyone could come up with was Oskar's scribbled note that he wasn't well, and had left Martin Goldberg all his possessions. I am Martin Goldberg.

I was sick for a week, had no desire either to inherit or investigate, but I thought I ought to look through his things before the court impounded them, so I spent a morning sitting in the depths of Oskar's armchair, trying to read his correspondence. I had found in the top drawer a thin packet of letters from his wife and a airmail letter of recent date from his anti-Semitic mother-in-law.

She writes in a tight script it takes me hours to decipher, that her daughter, after Oskar abandons her, against her own mother's fervent pleas and anguish, is converted to Judaism by a vengeful rabbi. One night the Brown Shirts appear, and though the mother wildly waves her bronze crucifix in their faces, they drag Frau Gassner, together with the other Jews, out of the apartment house, and transport them in lorries to a small border town in conquered Poland. There, it is rumored, she is shot in the head and topples into an open tank ditch, with the naked Jewish men, their wives and children, some Polish soldiers, and a handful of gypsies.

The Last Mohican

Fidelman, a self-confessed failure as a painter, came to Italy to prepare a critical study of Giotto, the opening chapter of which he had carried across the ocean in a new pigskin leather brief case, now gripped in his perspiring hand. Also new were his gum-soled oxblood shoes, a tweed suit he had on despite the late-September sun slanting hot in the Roman sky, although there was a lighter one in his bag; and a dacron shirt and set of cotton-dacron underwear, good for quick and easy washing for the traveler. His suitcase, a bulky, two-strapped affair which embarrassed him slightly, he had borrowed from his sister Bessie. He planned, if he had any money left at the end of the year, to buy a new one in Florence. Although he had been in not much of a mood when he had left the U.S.A., Fidelman picked up in Naples, and at the moment, as he stood in front of the Rome railroad station, after twenty minutes still absorbed in his first sight of the Eternal City, he was conscious of a certain exaltation that devolved on him after he had discovered that directly across the many-vehicled piazza stood the remains of the Baths of Diocletian. Fidelman remembered having read that Michelangelo had had a hand in converting the baths into a church and convent, the latter ultimately changed into the museum that presently was there. "Imagine," he muttered. "Imagine all that history."

In the midst of his imagining, Fidelman experienced the sensation of suddenly seeing himself as he was, to the pinpoint, outside and in, not without bittersweet pleasure; and as the well-known image of his face rose before him he was taken by the depth of pure feeling in his eyes, slightly magnified by glasses, and the sensitivity of his elongated nostrils and often tremulous lips, nose divided from lips by a mustache of recent vintage that looked, Fidelman thought, as if it had been sculptured there, adding to his dignified appearance although he was a little on the short side. But almost at the same moment, this unexpectedly intense sense of his being—it was more than appearance—faded, exaltation having gone where exaltation goes, and Fidelman became aware that there was an exterior source to the strange, almost tri-dimensional reflection of himself he had felt as well as seen. Behind him, a short distance to the right, he had noticed a stranger—give a skeleton a couple of pounds—loitering near a bronze statue on a stone pedestal of the heavy-dugged Etruscan wolf suckling the infant Romulus and Remus, the man contemplating Fidelman already acquisitively so as to suggest to the traveler that he had been mirrored (lock, stock, barrel) in the other's gaze for some time, perhaps since he had stepped off the train. Casually studying him, though pretending no, Fidelman beheld a person of about his own height, oddly dressed in brown knickers and black, knee-length woolen socks drawn up over slightly bowed, broomstick legs, these grounded in small, porous, pointed shoes. His yellowed shirt was open at the gaunt throat, both sleeves rolled up over skinny, hairy arms. The stranger's high forehead was bronzed, his black hair thick behind small ears, the dark, close-shaven beard tight on the face; his experienced nose was weighted at the tip, and the soft brown eyes, above all, *wanted*. Though his expression suggested humility, he all but licked his lips as he approached the ex-painter.

"Shalom," he greeted Fidelman.

"Shalom," the other hesitantly replied, uttering the word—so far as he recalled—for the first time in his life. My God, he thought, a handout for sure. My first hello in Rome and it has to be a schnorrer.

The stranger extended a smiling hand. "Susskind," he said, "Shimon Susskind."

"Arthur Fidelman." Transferring his brief case to under his

left arm while standing astride the big suitcase, he shook hands with Susskind. A blue-smocked porter came by, glanced at Fidelman's bag, looked at him, then walked away.

Whether he knew it or not Susskind was rubbing his palms contemplatively together.

"Parla italiano?"

"Not with ease, although I read it fluently. You might say I need the practice."

"Yiddish?"

"I express myself best in English."

"Let it be English then." Susskind spoke with a slight British intonation. "I knew you were Jewish," he said, "the minute my eyes saw you."

Fidelman chose to ignore the remark. "Where did you pick up your knowledge of English?"

"In Israel."

Israel interested Fidelman. "You live there?"

"Once, not now," Susskind answered vaguely. He seemed suddenly bored.

"How so?"

Susskind twitched a shoulder. "Two much heavy labor for a man of my modest health. Also I couldn't stand the suspense."

Fidelman nodded.

"Furthermore, the desert air makes me constipated. In Rome I am light hearted."

"A Jewish refugee from Israel, no less," Fidelman said good humoredly.

"I'm always running," Susskind answered mirthlessly. If he was light hearted, he had yet to show it.

"Where else from, if I may ask?"

"Where else but Germany, Hungary, Poland? Where not?"

"Ah, that's so long ago." Fidelman then noticed the gray in the man's hair. "Well, I'd better be going," he said. He picked up his bag as two porters hovered uncertainly nearby.

But Susskind offered certain services. "You got a hotel?"

"All picked and reserved."

"How long are you staying?"

What business is it of his? However, Fidelman courteously replied, "Two weeks in Rome, the rest of the year in Florence, with a few side trips to Siena, Assissi, Padua and maybe also Venice."

"You wish a guide in Rome?"

"Are you a guide?"

"Why not?"

"No," said Fidelman. "I'll look as I go along to museums, libraries, et cetera."

This caught Susskind's attention. "What are you, a professor?"

Fidelman couldn't help blushing. "Not exactly, really just a student."

"From which institution?"

He coughed a little. "By that I mean a professional student, you might say. Call me Trofimov, from Chekov. If there's something to learn I want to learn it."

"You have some kind of a project?" the other persisted. "A grant?"

"No grant. My money is hard earned. I worked and saved a long time to take a year in Italy. I made certain sacrifices. As for a project, I'm writing on the painter Giotto. He was one of the most important—"

"You don't have to tell me about Giotto," Susskind interrupted with a little smile.

"You've studied his work?"

"Who doesn't know Giotto?"

"That's interesting to me," said Fidelman, secretly irritated. "How do you happen to know him?"

"How do you?"

"I've given a good deal of time and study to his work."

"So I know him too."

I'd better get this over with before it begins to amount up to something, Fidelman thought. He set down his bag and fished with a finger in his leather coin purse. The two porters watched with interest, one taking a sandwich out of his pocket, unwrapping the newspaper and beginning to eat.

"This is for yourself," Fidelman said.

Susskind hardly glanced at the coin as he let it drop into his pants pocket. The porters then left.

The refugee had an odd way of standing motionless, like a cigar store Indian about to burst into flight. "In your luggage," he said vaguely, "would you maybe have a suit you can't use? I could use a suit."

At last he comes to the point. Fidelman, though annoyed, controlled himself. "All I have is a change from the one you now see me wearing. Don't get the wrong idea about me, Mr. Susskind. I'm not rich. In fact, I'm poor. Don't let a few new clothes deceive you. I owe my sister money for them."

Susskind glanced down at his shabby, baggy knickers. "I haven't had a suit for years. The one I was wearing when I ran away from Germany, fell apart. One day I was walking around naked."

"Isn't there a welfare organization that could help you out—some group in the Jewish community, interested in refugees?"

"The Jewish organizations wish to give me what they wish, not what I wish," Susskind replied bitterly. "The only thing they offer me is a ticket back to Israel."

"Why don't you take it?"

"I told you already, here I feel free."

"Freedom is a relative term."

"Don't tell me about freedom."

He knows all about that, too, Fidelman thought. "So you feel free," he said, "but how do you live?"

Susskind coughed, a brutal cough.

Fidelman was about to say something more on the subject of freedom but left it unsaid. Jesus, I'll be saddled with him all day if I don't watch out.

"I'd better be getting off to the hotel." He bent again for his bag.

Susskind touched him on the shoulder and when Fidelman exasperatedly straightened up, the half dollar he had given the man was staring him in the eye.

"On this we both lose money."

"How do you mean?"

"Today the lira sells six twenty-three on the dollar, but for specie they only give you five hundred."

"In that case, give it here and I'll let you have a dollar." From his billfold Fidelman quickly extracted a crisp bill and handed it to the refugee.

"Not more?" Susskind sighed.

"Not more," the student answered emphatically.

"Maybe you would like to see Diocletian's bath? There are some enjoyable Roman coffins inside. I will guide you for another dollar."

"No, thanks." Fidelman said goodbye, and lifting the suitcase, lugged it to the curb. A porter appeared and the student, after some hesitation, let him carry it toward the line of small dark-green taxis in the piazza. The porter offered to carry the brief case too, but Fidelman wouldn't part with it. He gave the cab driver the address of the hotel, and the taxi took off with a lurch. Fidelman at last relaxed. Susskind, he noticed, had disappeared. Gone with his breeze, he thought. But on the way to the hotel he had an uneasy feeling that the refugee, crouched low, might be clinging to the little tire on the back of the cab; however, he didn't look out to see.

Fidelman had reserved a room in an inexpensive hotel not far from the station, with its very convenient bus terminal. Then, as was his habit, he got himself quickly and tightly organized. He was always concerned with not wasting time, as if it were his only wealth—not true, of course, though Fidelman admitted he was an ambitious person—and he soon arranged a schedule that made the most of his working hours. Mornings he usually visited the Italian libraries, searching their catalogues and archives, read in poor light, and made profuse notes. He napped for an hour after lunch, then at four, when the churches and museums were re-opening, hurried off to them with lists of frescoes and paintings he must see. He was anxious to get to Florence, at the same time a little unhappy at all he would not have time to take in in Rome. Fidelman promised himself to return again if he could afford it, perhaps in the spring, and look at anything he pleased.

After dark he managed to unwind himself and relax. He ate as the Romans did, late, enjoyed a half litre of white wine and smoked a cigarette. Afterward he liked to wander—especially in the old sections near the Tiber. He had read that here, under his feet, were the ruins of Ancient Rome. It was an inspiring business, he, Arthur Fidelman, after all, born a Bronx boy, walking around in all this history. History was mysterious, the remembrance of things unknown, in a way burdensome, in a way a sensuous experience. It uplifted and depressed, why he did not know, except that it excited his thoughts more than he thought good for him. This kind of excitement was all right up to a point, perfect maybe for a creative artist, but less so for a critic. A critic, he thought, should live on beans. He walked for miles along the winding river, gazing at the star-strewn skies. Once, after a couple of days in the Vatican Museum, he saw flights of angels—gold, blue, white—intermingled in the sky. "My God, I got to stop using my eyes so much," Fidelman said to himself. But back in his room he sometimes wrote till morning.

Late one night, about a week after his arrival in Rome, as Fidelman was writing notes on the Byzantine style mosaics he had seen during the day, there was a knock on the door, and though the student, immersed in his work, was not conscious he had said "Avanti," he must have, for the door opened, and instead of an angel, in came Susskind in his shirt and baggy knickers.

Fidelman, who had all but forgotten the refugee, certainly never thought of him, half rose in astonishment. "Susskind," he exclaimed, "how did you get in here?"

Susskind for a moment stood motionless, then answered with a weary smile, "I'll tell you the truth, I know the desk clerk."

"But how did you know where I live?"

"I saw you walking in the street so I followed you."

"You mean you saw me accidentally?"

"How else? Did you leave me your address?"

Fidelman resumed his seat. "What can I do for you, Susskind?" He spoke grimly.

The refugee cleared his throat. "Professor, the days are warm but the nights are cold. You see how I go around naked." He held forth bluish arms, goosefleshed. "I came to ask you to reconsider about giving away your old suit."

"And who says it's an old suit?" Despite himself, Fidelman's voice thickened.

"One suit is new, so the other is old."

"Not precisely. I am afraid I have no suit for you, Susskind. The one I presently have hanging in the closet is a little more than a year old and I can't afford to give it away. Besides, it's gabardine, more like a summer suit."

"On me it will be for all seasons."

After a moment's reflection, Fidelman drew out his billfold and counted four single dollars. These he handed to Susskind.

"Buy yourself a warm sweater."

Susskind also counted the money. "If four," he said, "then why not five?"

Fidelman flushed. The man's warped nerve. "Because I happen to have four available," he answered. "That's twenty-five hundred lire. You should be able to buy a warm sweater and have something left over besides."

"I need a suit," Susskind said. "The days are warm but the nights are cold." He rubbed his arms. "What else I need I won't say."

"At least roll down your sleeves if you're so cold."

"That won't help me."

"Listen, Susskind," Fidelman said gently, "I would gladly give you the suit if I could afford to, but I can't. I have barely enough money to squeeze out a year for myself here. I've already told you I am indebted to my sister. Why don't you try to get yourself a job somewhere, no matter how menial? I'm sure that in a short while you'll work yourself up into a decent position."

"A job, he says," Susskind muttered gloomily. "Do you know what it means to get a job in Italy? Who will give me a job?"

"Who gives anybody a job? They have to go out and look for it."

"You don't understand, professor. I am an Israeli citizen and this means I can only work for an Israeli company. How many Israeli companies are there here?—maybe two, El Al and Zim, and even if they had a job, they wouldn't give it to me because I have lost my passport. I would be better off now if I were stateless. A stateless person shows his laissez passer and sometimes he can find a small job."

"But if you lost your passport why didn't you put in for a duplicate?"

"I did, but did they give it to me?"

"Why not?"

"Why not? They say I sold it."

"Had they reason to think that?"

"I swear to you somebody stole it from me."

"Under such circumstances," Fidelman asked, "how do you live?"

"How do I live?" He chomped with his teeth. "I eat air."

"Seriously?"

"Seriously, on air. I also peddle," he confessed, "but to peddle you need a license, and that the Italians won't give me. When they caught me peddling I was interned for six months in a work camp."

"Didn't they attempt to deport you?"

"They did, but I sold my mother's old wedding ring that I kept in my pocket so many years. The Italians are a humane people. They took the money and let me go but they told me not to peddle anymore."

"So what do you do now?"

"I peddle. What should I do, beg?—I peddle. But last spring I got sick and gave my little money away to the doctors. I still have a bad cough." He coughed fruitily. "Now I have no capital to buy stock with. Listen, professor, maybe we can go in partnership together? Lend me twenty thousand lire and I will buy ladies' nylon stockings. After I sell them I will return you your money."

"I have no funds to invest, Susskind."

"You will get it back, with interest."

"I honestly am sorry for you," Fidelman said, "but why don't you at least do something practical? Why don't you go to the Joint Distribution Committee, for instance, and ask them to assist you? That's their business."

"I already told you why. They wish me to go back, but I wish to stay here."

"I still think going back would be the best thing for you."

"No," cried Susskind angrily.

"If that's your decision, freely made, then why pick on me? Am I responsible for you then, Susskind?"

"Who else?" Susskind loudly replied.

"Lower your voice, please, people are sleeping around here," said Fidelman, beginning to perspire. "Why should I be?"

"You know what responsibility means?"

"I think so."

"Then you are responsible. Because you are a man. Because you are a Jew, aren't you?"

"Yes, goddamn it, but I'm not the only one in the whole wide world. Without prejudice, I refuse the obligation. I am a single individual and can't take on everybody's personal burden. I have the weight of my own to contend with."

He reached for his billfold and plucked out another dollar.

"This makes five. It's more than I can afford, but take it and after this please leave me alone. I have made my contribution."

Susskind stood there, oddly motionless, an impassioned statue, and for a moment Fidelman wondered if he would stay all night, but at last the refugee thrust forth a stiff arm, took the fifth dollar and departed.

Early the next morning Fidelman moved out of the hotel into another, less convenient for him, but far away from Shimon Susskind and his endless demands.

This was Tuesday. On Wednesday, after a busy morning in the library, Fidelman entered a nearby trattoria and ordered a plate of spaghetti with tomato sauce. He was reading his *Messaggero,* anticipating the coming of the food, for he was unusually hungry, when he sensed a presence at the table. He looked up, expecting the waiter, but beheld instead Susskind standing there, alas, unchanged.

Is there no escape from him? thought Fidelman, severely vexed. Is this why I came to Rome?

"Shalom, professor," Susskind said, keeping his eyes off the table. "I was passing and saw you sitting here alone, so I came in to say shalom."

"Susskind," Fidelman said in anger, "have you been following me again?"

"How could I follow you?" asked the astonished Susskind. "Do I know where you live now?"

Though Fidelman blushed a little, he told himself he owed nobody an explanation. So he had found out he had moved—good.

"My feet are tired. Can I sit five minutes?"

"Sit."

Susskind drew out a chair. The spaghetti arrived, steaming hot. Fidelman sprinkled it with cheese and wound his fork into several tender strands. One of the strings of spaghetti seemed to stretch for miles, so he stopped at a certain point and swallowed the forkful. Having foolishly neglected to cut the long spaghetti string he was left sucking it, seemingly endlessly. This embarrassed him.

Susskind watched with rapt attention.

Fidelman at last reached the end of the long spaghetti, patted his mouth with a napkin, and paused in his eating.

"Would you care for a plateful?"

Susskind, eyes hungry, hesitated. "Thanks," he said.

"Thanks yes or thanks no?"

"Thanks no." The eyes looked away.

Fidelman resumed eating, carefully winding his fork; he had had not too much practice with this sort of thing and was soon involved in the same dilemma with the spaghetti. Seeing Susskind still watching him, he soon became tense.

"We are not Italians, professor," the refugee said. "Cut it in small pieces with your knife. Then you will swallow it easier."

"I'll handle it as I please," Fidelman responded testily. "This is my business. You attend to yours."

"My business," Susskind sighed, "don't exist. This morning I had to let a wonderful chance get away from me. I had a chance to buy ladies' stockings at three hundred lire if I had money to buy half a gross. I could easily sell them for five hundred a pair. We would have made a nice profit."

"The news doesn't interest me."

"So if not ladies' stockings, I can also get sweaters, scarves, men's socks, also cheap leather goods, ceramics—whatever would interest you."

"What interests me is what you did with the money I gave you for a sweater."

"It's getting cold, professor," Susskind said worriedly. "Soon comes the November rains, and in winter the tramontana. I thought I ought to save your money to buy a couple of kilos of chestnuts and a bag of charcoal for my burner. If you sit all day on a busy street corner you can sometimes make a thousand lire. Italians like hot chestnuts. But if I do this I will need some warm clothes, maybe a suit."

"A suit," Fidelman remarked sarcastically, "why not an overcoat?"

"I have a coat, poor that it is, but now I need a suit. How can anybody come in company without a suit?"

Fidelman's hand trembled as he laid down his fork. "To my mind you are utterly irresponsible and I won't be saddled with you. I have the right to choose my own problems and the right to my privacy."

"Don't get excited, professor, it's bad for your digestion. Eat in peace." Susskind got up and left the trattoria.

Fidelman hadn't the appetite to finish his spaghetti. He paid the bill, waited ten minutes, then departed, glancing around from time to time to see if he were being followed. He headed down the sloping street to a small piazza where he saw a couple of cabs. Not that he could afford one, but he wanted to make sure Susskind didn't tail him back to his new hotel. He would warn the clerk at the desk never to allow anybody of the refugee's name or description even to make inquiries about him.

Susskind, however, stepped out from behind a plashing fountain at the center of the little piazza. Modestly addressing the speechless Fidelman, he said, "I don't wish to take only, professor. If I had something to give you, I would gladly give it to you."

"Thanks," snapped Fidelman, "just give me some peace of mind."

"That you have to find yourself," Susskind answered.

In the taxi Fidelman decided to leave for Florence the next day, rather than at the end of the week, and once and for all be done with the pest.

That night, after returning to his room from an unpleasurable walk in the Trastevere—he had a headache from too much wine at supper—Fidelman found his door ajar and at once recalled that he had forgotten to lock it, although he had as usual left the key with the desk clerk. He was at first frightened, but when he tried the armadio in which he kept his clothes and suitcase, it was shut tight. Hastily unlocking it, he was relieved to see his blue gabardine suit—a one-button jacket affair, the trousers a little frayed on the cuffs, but all in good shape and usable for years to come—hanging amid some shirts the maid had pressed for him;

and when he examined the contents of the suitcase he found nothing missing, including, thank God, his passport and travelers' checks. Gazing around the room, Fidelman saw all in place. Satisfied, he picked up a book and read ten pages before he thought of his brief case. He jumped to his feet and began to search everywhere, remembering distinctly that it had been on the night table as he had lain on the bed that afternoon, re-reading his chapter. He searched under the bed and behind the night table, then again throughout the room, even on top of and behind the armadio. Fidelman hopelessly opened every drawer, no matter how small, but found neither brief case, nor, what was worse, the chapter in it.

With a groan he sank down on the bed, insulting himself for not having made a copy of the manuscript, for he had more than once warned himself that something like this might happen to it. But he hadn't because there were some revisions he had contemplated making, and he had planned to retype the entire chapter before beginning the next. He thought now of complaining to the owner of the hotel, who lived on the floor below, but it was already past midnight and he realized nothing could be done until morning. Who could have taken it? The maid or hall porter? It seemed unlikely they would risk their jobs to steal a piece of leather goods that would bring them only a few thousand lire in a pawn shop. Possibly a sneak thief? He would ask tomorrow if other persons on the floor were missing something. He somehow doubted it. If a thief, he would then and there have ditched the chapter and stuffed the brief case with Fidelman's oxblood shoes, left by the bed, and the fifteen-dollar R. H. Macy sweater that lay in full view of the desk. But if not the maid or porter or a sneak thief, than who? Though Fidelman had not the slightest shred of evidence to support his suspicions he could think of only one person—Susskind. This thought stung him. But if Susskind, why? Out of pique, perhaps, that he had not been given the suit he had coveted, nor was able to pry it out of the armadio? Try as he would, Fidelman could think of no one else and no other reason. Somehow the peddler had followed him home (he suspected their meeting at the fountain) and had got into his room while he was out to supper.

Fidelman's sleep that night was wretched. He dreamed of pursuing the refugee in the Jewish catacombs under the ancient Appian Way, threatening him a blow on the presumptuous head with a seven-flamed candalabrum he clutched in his hand; while Susskind, clever ghost, who knew the ins and outs of all the crypts and alleys, eluded him at every turn. Then Fidelman's candles all blew out, leaving him sightless and alone in the cemeterial dark; but when the student arose in the morning and wearily drew up the blinds, the yellow Italian sun winked him cheerfully in both bleary eyes.

Fidelman postponed going to Florence. He reported his loss to the Questura, and though the police were polite and eager to help, they could do nothing for him. On the form on which the inspector noted the complaint, he listed the brief case as worth ten thousand lire, and for "valore del manuscritto" he drew a line. Fidelman, after giving the matter a good deal of thought, did not report Susskind, first, because he had absolutely no proof, for the desk clerk swore he had seen no stranger around in knickers; second, because he was afraid of the consequences for the refugee if he were written down "suspected thief" as well as "unlicensed peddler" and inveterate refugee. He tried instead to rewrite the chapter, which he felt sure he knew by heart, but when he sat down at the desk, there were important thoughts, whole paragraphs, even pages, that went blank in the mind. He considered sending to America for his notes for the chapter but they were in a barrel in his sister's attic in Levittown, among many notes for other projects. The thought of Bessie, a mother of five, poking around in his things, and the work entailed in sorting the cards, then getting them packaged and mailed to him across the ocean, wearied Fidelman unspeakably; he was certain she would send the wrong ones. He laid down his pen and went into the street, seeking Susskind. He searched for him in neighborhoods where he had seen him before, and though Fidelman spent hours looking, literally days, Susskind never appeared; or if he perhaps did, the sight of Fidelman caused him to vanish. And when the student inquired about him at the Israeli consulate, the clerk, a new man on the job, said he had no record fo such a person or his lost passport; on the other hand, he was known at the Joint Distribution Committee, but by name and address only, an impossibility, Fidelman thought. They gave him a number to go to but the place had long since been torn down to make way for an apartment house.

Time went without work, without accomplishment. To put an end to this appalling waste Fidelman tried to force himself back into his routine of research and picture viewing. He moved out of the hotel, which he now could not stand for the harm it had done him (leaving a telephone number and urging he be called if the slightest clue turned up), and he took a room in a small pensione near the Stazione and here had breakfast and supper rather than go out. He was much concerned with expenditures and carefully recorded them in a notebook he had acquired for the purpose. Nights, instead of wandering in the city, feasting himself upon its beauty and mystery, he kept his eyes glued to paper, sitting steadfastly at his desk in an attempt to re-create his initial chapter, because he was lost without a beginning. He had tried writing the second chapter from notes in his possession but it had come to nothing. Always Fidelman needed something solid behind him before he could advance, some worthwhile accomplishment upon which to build another. He worked late, but his mood, or inspiration, or whatever it was, had deserted him, leaving him with growing anxiety, almost disorientation; of not knowing—it seemed to him for the first time in months—what he must do next, a feeling that was torture. Therefore he again took up his search for the refugee. He thought now that once he had settled it, knew that the man had or hadn't stolen his chapter— whether he recovered it or not seemed at the moment immaterial

—just the knowing of it would ease his mind and again he would *feel* like working, the crucial element.

Daily he combed the crowded streets, searching for Susskind wherever people peddled. On successive Sunday mornings he took the long ride to the Porta Portese market and hunted for hours among the piles of second-hand goods and junk lining the back streets, hoping his brief case would magically appear, though it never did. He visited the open market at Piazza Fontanella Borghese, and observed the ambulant vendors at Piazza Dante. He looked among fruit and vegetable stalls set up in the streets, whenever he chanced upon them, and dawdled on busy street corners after dark, among beggars and fly-by-night peddlers. After the first cold snap at the end of October, when the chestnut sellers appeared throughout the city, huddled over pails of glowing coals, he sought in their faces the missing Susskind. Where in all of modern and ancient Rome was he? The man lived in the open air—he had to appear somewhere. Sometimes when riding in a bus or tram, Fidelman thought he had glimpsed somebody in a crowd, dressed in the refugee's clothes, and he invariably got off to run after whoever it was—once a man standing in front of the Banco di Santo Spirito, gone when Fidelman breathlessly arrived; and another time he overtook a person in knickers, but this one wore a monocle. Sir Ian Susskind?

In November it rained. Fidelman wore a blue beret with his trench coat and a pair of black Italian shoes, smaller, despite their pointed toes, than his burly oxbloods which overheated his feet and whose color he detested. But instead of visiting museums he frequented movie houses sitting in the cheapest seats and regretting the cost. He was, at odd hours in certain streets, several times accosted by prostitutes, some heartbreakingly pretty, one a slender, unhappy-looking girl with bags under her eyes whom he desired mightily, but Fidelman feared for his health. He had got to know the face of Rome and spoke Italian fairly fluently, but his heart was burdened, and in his blood raged a murderous hatred of the bandy-legged refugee—although there were times when he bethought himself he might be wrong—so Fidelman more than once cursed him to perdition.

One Friday night, as the first star glowed over the Tiber, Fidelman, walking aimlessly, along the left riverbank, came upon a synagogue and wandered in among a crowd of Sephardim with Italianate faces. One by one they paused before a sink in an antechamber to dip their hands under a flowing faucet, then in the house of worship touched with loose fingers their brows, mouths, and breasts as they bowed to the Arc, Fidelman doing likewise. Where in the world am I? Three rabbis rose from a bench and the service began, a long prayer, sometimes chanted, sometimes accompanied by invisible organ music, but no Susskind anywhere. Fidelman sat at a desk-like pew in the last row, where he could inspect the congregants yet keep an eye on the door. The synagogue was unheated and the cold rose like an exudation from the marble floor. The student's freezing nose burned like a lit candle. He got up to go, but the beadle, a stout man in a high hat and short caftan, wearing a long thick silver chain around his neck, fixed the student with his powerful left eye.

"From New York?" he inquired, slowly approaching.

Half the congregation turned to see who.

"State, not city," answered Fidelman, nursing an active guilt for the attention he was attracting. Then, taking advantage of a pause, he whispered, "Do you happen to know a man named Susskind? He wears knickers."

"A relative?" The beadle gazed at him sadly.

"Not exactly."

"My own son—killed in the Ardeatine Caves." Tears stood forth in his eyes.

"Ah, for that I'm sorry."

But the beadle had exhausted the subject. He wiped his wet lids with pudgy fingers and the curious Sephardim turned back to their prayer books.

"Which Susskind?" the beadle wanted to know.

"Shimon."

He scratched his ear. "Look in the ghetto."

"I looked."

"Look again."

The beadle walked slowly away and Fidelman sneaked out.

The ghetto lay behind the synagogue for several crooked, well-packed blocks, encompassing aristocratic palazzi ruined by age and unbearable numbers, their discolored façades strung with lines of withered wet wash, the fountains in the piazzas, dirt-laden, dry. And dark stone tenements, built partly on centuries-old ghetto walls, inclined towards one another across narrow, cobblestoned streets. In and among the impoverished houses were the wholesale establishments of wealthy Jews, dark holes ending in jeweled interiors, silks and silver of all colors. In the mazed streets wandered the present-day poor, Fidelman among them, oppressed by history, although, he joked to himself, it added years to his life.

A white moon shone upon the ghetto, lighting it like dark day. Once he thought he saw a ghost he knew by sight, and hastily followed him through a thick stone passage to a blank wall where shone in white letters under a tiny electric bulb: VIETATO URINARE. Here was a smell but no Susskind.

For thirty lire the student bought a dwarfed, blackened banana from a street vendor (not S) on a bicycle, and stopped to eat. A crowd of ragazzi gathered to watch.

"Anybody here know Susskind, a refugee wearing knickers?" Fidelman announced, stooping to point with the banana where the pants went beneath the knees. He also made his legs a trifle bowed but nobody noticed.

There was no response until he had finished his fruit, then a thin-faced boy with brown liquescent eyes out of Murillo, piped: "He sometimes works in the Cimitero Verano, the Jewish section."

There too? thought Fidelman. "Works in the cemetery?" he inquired. "With a shovel?"

"He prays for the dead," the boy answered, "for a small fee."

Fidelman bought him a quick banana and the others dispersed. In the cemetery, deserted on the Sabbath—he should have come Sunday—Fidelman went among the graves, reading legends carved on tombstones, many topped with small brass candelabra, whilst withered yellow chrysanthemums lay on the stone tablets of other graves, dropped stealthily, Fidelman imagined, on All Souls Day—a festival in another part of the cemetery—by renegade sons and daughters unable to bear the sight of their dead bereft of flowers, while the crypts of the goyim were lit and in bloom. Many were burial places, he read on the stained stones, of those who, for one reason or another, had died in the late large war, including an empty place, it said under a six-pointed star engraved upon a marble slab that lay on the ground, for "My beloved father/ Betrayed by the damned Fascists/ Murdered at Auschwitz by the barbarous Nazis/ *O Crime Orribile*." But no Susskind.

Three months had gone by since Fidelman's arrival in Rome. Should he, he many times asked himself, leave the city and this foolish search? Why not off to Florence, and there, amid the art splendors of the world, be inspired to resume his work? But the loss of his first chapter was like a spell cast over him. There were times he scorned it as a man-made thing, like all such, replaceable; other times he feared it was not the chapter per se, but that his volatile curiosity had become somehow entangled with Susskind's strange personality— Had he repaid generosity by stealing a man's life work? Was he so distorted? To satisfy himself, to know man, Fidelman had to know, though at what a cost in precious time and effort. Sometimes he smiled wryly at all this; ridiculous, the chapter grieved him for itself only—the precious thing he had created then lost—especially when he got to thinking of the long diligent labor, how painstakingly he had built each idea, how cleverly mastered problems of order, form, how impressive the finished product, Giotto reborn! It broke the heart. What else, if after months he was here, still seeking?

And Fidelman was unchangingly convinced that Susskind had taken it, or why would he still be hiding? He sighed much and gained weight. Mulling over his frustrated career, on the backs of envelopes containing unanswered letters from his sister Bessie he aimlessly sketched little angels flying. Once, studying his minuscule drawings, it occurred to him that he might someday return to painting, but the thought was more painful than Fidelman could bear.

One bright morning in mid-December, after a good night's sleep, his first in weeks, he vowed he would have another look at the Navicella and then be off to Florence. Shortly before noon he visited the porch of St. Peter's, trying, from his remembrance of Giotto's sketch, to see the mosaic as it had been before its many restorations. He hazarded a note or two in shaky handwriting, then left the church and was walking down the sweeping flight of stairs, when he beheld at the bottom—his heart misgave him, was he still seeing pictures, a sneaky apostle added to the overloaded boatful?—ecco, Susskind! The refugee, in beret and long green G.I. raincoat, from under whose skirts showed his black-stockinged, rooster's ankles—indicating knickers going on above though hidden—was selling black and white rosaries to all who would buy. He held several strands of beads in one hand, while in the palm of the other a few gilded medallions glinted in the winter sun. Despite his outer clothing, Susskind looked, it must be said, unchanged, not a pound more of meat or muscle, the face though aged, ageless. Gazing at him, the student ground his teeth in remembrance. He was tempted quickly to hide, and unobserved observe the thief; but his impatience, after the long unhappy search, was too much for him. With controlled trepidation he approached Susskind on his left as the refugee was busily engaged on the right, urging a sale of beads upon a woman drenched in black.

"Beads, rosaries, say your prayers with holy beads."

"Greetings, Susskind," Fidelman said, coming shakily down the stairs, dissembling the Unified Man, all peace and contentment.

"One looks for you everywhere and finds you here. Wie gehts?"

Susskind, though his eyes flickered, showed no surprise to speak of. For a moment his expression seemed to say he had no idea who was this, had forgotten Fidelman's existence, but then at last remembered—somebody long ago from another country, whom you smiled on, then forgot.

"Still here?" he perhaps ironically joked.

"Still," Fidelman was embarrassed at his voice slipping.

"Rome holds you?"

"Rome," faltered Fidelman, "—the air." He breathed deep and exhaled with emotion.

Noticing the refugee was not truly attentive, his eyes roving upon potential customers, Fidelman, girding himself, remarked, "By the way, Susskind, you didn't happen to notice—did you?— the brief case I was carrying with me around the time we met in September?"

"Brief case—what kind?" This he said absently, his eyes on the church doors.

"Pigskin. I had in it—" Here Fidelman's voice could be heard cracking, "—a chapter of a critical work on Giotto I was writing. You know, I'm sure, the Trecento painter?"

"Who doesn't know Giotto?"

"Do you happen to recall whether you saw, if, that is—" He stopped, at a loss for words other than accusatory.

"Excuse me—business." Susskind broke away and bounced up the steps two at a time. A man he approached shied away. He had beads, didn't need others.

Fidelman had followed the refugee. "Reward," he muttered up close to his ear. "Fifteen thousand for the chapter, and who has it can keep the brand new brief case. That's his business, no questions asked. Fair enough?"

Susskind spied a lady tourist, including camera and guide book. "Beads—holy beads." He held up both hands, but she was just a Lutheran, passing through.

"Slow today," Susskind complained as they walked down the

stairs, "but maybe it's the items. Everybody has the same. If I had some big ceramics of the Holy Mother, they go like hot cakes —a good investment for somebody with a little cash."

"Use the reward for that," Fidelman cagily whispered, "buy Holy Mothers."

If he heard, Susskind gave no sign. At the sight of a family of nine emerging from the main portal above, the refugee, calling addio over his shoulder, fairly flew up the steps. But Fidelman uttered no response. I'll get the rat yet. He went off to hide behind a high fountain in the square. But the flying spume raised by the wind wet him, so he retreated behind a massive column and peeked out at short intervals to keep the peddler in sight.

At two o'clock, when St. Peter's closed to visitors, Susskind dumped his goods into his raincoat pockets and locked up shop. Fidelman followed him all the way home, indeed the ghetto, although along a street he had not consciously been on before, which led into an alley where the refugee pulled open a left-handed door, and without transition, was "home." Fidelman, sneaking up close, caught a dim glimpse of an overgrown closet containing bed and table. He found no address on wall or door, nor, to his surprise, any door lock. This for a moment depressed him. It meant Susskind had nothing worth stealing. Of his own, that is. The student promised himself to return tomorrow, when the occupant was elsewhere.

Return he did, in the morning, while the entrepreneur was out selling religious articles, glanced around once and was quickly inside. He shivered—a pitch black freezing cave. Fidelman scratched up a thick match and confirmed bed and table, also a rickety chair, but no heat or light except a drippy candle stub in a saucer on the table. He lit the yellow candle and searched all over the place. In the table drawer a few eating implements plus safety razor, though where he shaved was a mystery, probably a public toilet. On a shelf above the thin-blanketed bed stood half a flask of red wine, part of a package of spaghetti, and a hard panino. Also an unexpected little fish bowl with a bony gold fish swimming around in Arctic seas. The fish, reflecting the candle flame, gulped repeatedly, threshing its frigid tail as Fidelman watched. He loves pets, thought the student. Under the bed he found a chamber pot, but nowhere a brief case with a fine critical chapter in it. The place was not more than an ice-box someone probably had lent the refugee to come in out of the rain. Alas, Fidelman sighed. Back in the pensione, it took a hot water bottle two hours to thaw him out; but from the visit he never fully recovered.

In this latest dream of Fidelman's he was spending the day in a cemetery all crowded with tombstones, when up out of an empty grave rose this long-nosed brown shade, Virgilio Susskind, beckoning.

Fidelman hurried over.

"Have you read Tolstoy?"

"Sparingly."

"Why is art?" asked the shade, drifting off.

Fidelman, willy nilly, followed, and the ghost, as it vanished, led him up steps going through the ghetto and into a marble synagogue.

The student, left alone, for no reason he could think of lay down upon the stone floor, his shoulders keeping strangely warm as he stared at the sunlit vault above. The fresco therein revealed this saint in fading blue, the sky flowing from his head, handing an old knight in a thin red robe his gold cloak. Nearby stood a humble horse and two stone hills.

Giotto. San Francesco dona le vesti al cavaliere povero.

Fidelman awoke running. He stuffed his blue gabardine into a paper bag, caught a bus, and knocked early on Susskind's heavy portal.

"Avanti." The refugee, already garbed in beret and raincoat (probably his pajamas), was standing at the table, lighting the candle with a flaming sheet of paper. To Fidelman the paper looked the underside of a typewritten page. Despite himself, the student recalled in letters of fire his entire chapter.

"Here, Susskind," he said in a trembling voice, offering the bundle, "I bring you my suit. Wear it in good health."

The refugee glanced at it without expression. "What do you wish for it?"

"Nothing at all." Fidelman laid the bag on the table, called goodbye and left.

He soon heard footsteps clattering after him across the cobblestones.

"Excuse me, I kept this under my mattress for you." Susskind thrust at him the pigskin brief case.

Fidelman savagely opened it, searching frenziedly in each compartment, but the bag was empty. The refugee was already in flight. With a bellow the student started after him. "You bastard, you burned my chapter!"

"Have mercy," cried Susskind, "I did you a favor."

"I'll do you one and cut your throat."

"The words were there but the spirit was missing."

In a towering rage, Fidelman forced a burst of speed, but the refugee, light as the wind in his marvelous knickers, his green coattails flying, rapidly gained ground.

The ghetto Jews, framed in amazement in their medieval windows, stared at the wild pursuit. But in the middle of it, Fidelman, stout and short of breath, moved by all he had lately learned, had a triumphant insight.

"Susskind, come back," he shouted, half sobbing. "The suit is yours. All is forgiven."

He came to a dead halt but the refugee ran out. When last seen he was still running.